Praise for Shane Gericke

"A high-rev, page-turning thriller that offers a searing look at the very thin blue line separating good and evil. Set in a sharply observed Midwest, *Torn Apart* features one of the best heroines to come along in years, Detective Emily Thompson, whose dedication to her job throws her into a deadly cat-and-mouse game against complex, fleshed-out villains, some driven by good, some by evil, but all intent on leaving plenty of carnage in their wake."

—Jeffery Deaver

"*Torn Apart* will keep you turning the pages so fast, you won't even notice that half the night's already gone. Shane Gericke knows how to tighten the screws and keep the fear and tension building."

—Tess Gerritsen

"A no-nonsense thriller, action-packed and explosive. A real page-turner!"

—Erica Spindler

"Beautifully drawn characters, sharply observed detail, and exceptional writing. Has the impact of a large-caliber handgun fired at point-blank range."

—Douglas Preston

"One of those scary rides through criminality that can melt away a fifteen-hour flight. The scenarios (trust me on this) will haunt you for weeks."

—John J. Nance

TORN APART

SHANE GERICKE

PINNACLE BOOKS
KENSINGTON PUBLISHING CORP.
www.kensingtonbooks.com

PINNACLE BOOKS are published by

Kensington Publishing Corp.
119 West 40th Street
New York, NY 10018

All Kensington titles, imprints, and distributed lines are available at special quantity discounts for bulk purchases for sales promotions, premiums, fund-raising, educational, or institutional use. Special book excerpts or customized printings can also be created to fit specific needs. For details, write or phone the office of the Kensington special sales manager: Kensington Publishing Corp., 119 West 40th Street, New York, NY 10018, attn: Special Sales Department; phone 1-800-221-2647.

This book is a work of fiction. Names, characters, businesses, organizations, places, events, and incidents either are the product of the author's imagination or are used fictitiously. Any resemblance to actual persons, living or dead, events, or locales is entirely coincidental.

PINNACLE BOOKS and the Pinnacle logo are Reg. U.S. Pat. & TM Off.

ISBN-13: 978-0-7860-2039-3
ISBN-10: 0-7860-2039-3

First printing: July 2010

10 9 8 7 6 5 4 3 2 1

Printed in the United States of America

To Jerrle,
whose smile makes the sun seethe with jealousy.

And to Mark Becker,
who left us much too soon.

Sometimes you eat the bear.
Sometimes the bear eats you.
                    —*Old saying*

1

Thunderbolts attacked from the rioting sky.

Most zigged. Some zagged. One ripped a spectacular *Z*-for-Zorro that stained the storm clouds mildew green. Homes ignited on each side of Interstate 94. Cyclonic wind punched the worn cargo van dangerously close to the flooded-out median.

"Could be worse!" Cancer shouted from the back.

"How's that?" Gemini said from the wheel.

"Could be snow."

A gasoline tanker roared by in the fast lane, throwing a hurricane of water. The van's wipers sputtered across the windshield like a failing heart, trying to keep up. A wolf pack of semis pursued the gas man, throwing their own hurricanes. The van jittered and jigged, then skittered and slid.

The teenager screamed from the back.

"Shut up," Gemini snapped, feeling his nuts tighten as he white-knuckled the van through the exploding water.

"Please," she whimpered. "Let me out. I won't tell, I swear, just don't hurt me any more—"

Vicious slaps from Aquarius, Cancer, and Virgo. Yips and cries from the girl. A rat-a-tat of thunder, followed by rain so intense it felt like the inside of a fire hose.

"Could be snow," Gemini muttered.

An earsplitting *ka-blam* jerked the van sideways, banging Gemini's triangular head off the window. He blinked away stars as he wrestled the Ford Econoline straight, muttering every curse he'd learned collecting debts on the shrimp docks in the Easy. He'd give anything to wait out this monster at an off-ramp honky-tonk, with a bartender asking no questions except, "Nuther, brother?"

Wasn't gonna happen. They were hours behind schedule, thanks to the dickhead narcotics supplier in Minneapolis who'd rope-a-doped them on the handoff, whining that he needed more money because Katrina was so hot it smoked. Six bloody rips with a can opener convinced the screaming maggot that money really wasn't the most important thing in his life, was it? But the convincing slowed them, and Gemini was acutely aware that Maxximus would be, um, *displeased* if they were late—

Ah, Christ. Now she's blubbering. Gemini snapped his eyes at the rearview.

The crew beat her to mumbles, went back to splitting her logs.

The booty call started east of Minneapolis, where they'd spotted the teenager thumbing a ride on eastbound I-94. She'd hopped in, putting extra wiggle in her hips because there's no such thing as a free lunch. The crew kidded with her awhile, sharing their Pepsi and Fritos, asking her what was up with the midnight run. She said she was hitching to Chicago, gonna find a fancy job to pay for her big dreams. They blew her some smoke about being a Hustler video crew and did she want to make ten Ben Franklins then and there.

"A video crew?" she'd said, eyeing the paint cans, brushes, plastic, and drop cloths littering the cargo area of the extended-length van. "You're, like, kidding, right?"

Gemini, like, wasn't, and held up the cash to prove it. Virgo worked the videocam as she expressed her appreciation. Gemini loaded the first three minutes into his cell phone.

Video-texted it to Freddie-Boy.

"Are you a moron?" Freddie-Boy yelled. "I said *young*. This one looks fifteen for chrissakes. Throw her back and grab up baby sister." Since Freddie-Boy paid five figures per child delivered, Gemini said he'd find what he wanted.

"You damn well better," Freddie-Boy warned. "By close of business today. See what happens if you don't."

Gemini protested the ridiculous deadline, but heard only dead air—the child trafficker had already disconnected. Scowling, he told the boys to have some real fun.

Sometimes you eat the bear, he thought as the teeny shrieked from the frenzied rape and mauling. *Sometimes the bear eats you.*

Something dear old dad liked to pound into Gemini growing up, that bit about the bear, not realizing his firstborn would someday grow mean enough for grizzly-sized payback. After ruining Gemini's fourteenth birthday with a foul, drunken rant—the old man hated anyone but him getting attention—he chased Gemini into the basement then stomped down himself, swinging the orange electrical cord he used to whip his kid's back into streamers.

The moment the fat bastard hit the last step, he was scrabbling the cold concrete floor like a stepped-on roach. When the pain of the broken legs finally broke through the shock of Gemini's blitz attack with the galvanized pipe, he shrieked.

Just like the drug maggot had during his can-opener scrap-ing—girly high, a wheeze almost, hairball strangling a cat, not understanding what just happened, yet there it was, all over the floor. The can opener in Gemini's hand, with its rusty steel head and *Drink Blatz Beer* on the handle, flayed twenty-seven strips off dear old dad, ending only when mom said, "Don't kill him, boy, he'll haunt us like them Dracula vampires. . . ."

Good times.

He checked the rearview, saw nothing but rain and bouncing asses. He pinched out a smile. The runaway, who'd introduced herself as "Kandy, with a K," was a pleasant way to kill the eight-hour drive from Minneapolis to Naperville, the Chicago suburb where they'd drop their load of drugs and collect their suitcase of dead presidents. Gemini checked his watch. Not bad. Even with the storm they were moving all right: Naperville by six, rich by seven—

Another wail erupted from the back.

Gemini sighed. What the hell should he do with her? The teenager was more appealing than he'd expected from a hitchhiker. Polo-shirted, blue-jeaned, and knob-kneed. Loose swingy hair, legs up to her armpits, narrow hips, grapefruit boobs. Creamy face with a smile to make a corpse stiff. Exactly the kind of girl Freddie-Boy should wet him-self to own, the picky goddamn pervert . . .

"Enough," Gemini said.

A moment later he heard the distinctive clack of a fore-arm breaking a windpipe. It wasn't loud like in the movies. More like a dry stick across a knee.

"Women," Cancer said, wagging his finger in mock dis-may as she thrashed like a gaffed marlin, trying to suck air.

"Can't live with 'em," Gemini said.

She turned blue.

Virgo spread her dancer legs. "One for the road?" he asked.

She gurgled.

"Thanks, baby, you're great too."

Five minutes later he was done.

So was Kandy, with a K.

"Onward and upward," Gemini said, tapping the GPS map suctioned to the dash.

Cancer crawled up to the shotgun seat to find a place to dump the body. Aquarius and Virgo bundled her into a paint-spattered drop cloth, tied it neat with clothesline.

The van roared sideways through the rain.

2

The wasp crawled into Emily's ear.

She couldn't swat the beast—one of the psychos might notice the jerky movement. It took a blood bite, crawled into her hair for dessert. She gasped at the searing pain.

Then brought her eyeballs to the window, peeking through the gap between Budweiser's neon bowtie and the flashing green bikini of Coors Light.

Two bulky shadows raced up the aisle, waving flashlights. They stopped every few seconds to look toward the back, then shoved liquor into bags.

The cold bite of adrenaline scoured her arteries.

She inched to the entry door. Squatted till her rump smacked her heels, examined the quarter-inch gap between door and frame.

No lock.

She tugged the door's handle.

It moved.

Too freely for midnight, when the store closed at ten.

Armed robbery in progress, she decided. *Time to call in the cavalry.*

Vibrating with excitement, she crept backwards, brushing the yellow brick wall with one hand and pulling her pistol with the other. She glanced around every few seconds, made sure she wasn't a target herself. The walking crouch blowtorched her thighs. She ignored it. She had to stay below the windows while moving. She couldn't chance alerting the heavily armed bandits inside.

She settled in twenty yards west, pulled her iPhone from her Wranglers. Her hands were dewy with August humidity. She pushed nine. Her thumb slipped sideways, mashed the pound sign instead. Scowling, she dried her fingers on her jeans, pushed more carefully. Connected. She clamped the phone between shoulder and ear, bashed the wasp with her free hand. Looked at her palm. Grinned. *Suck* my *blood, will you . . .*

One ring.

Two rings.

Anybody home? she fumed, impatient to get the attack rolling. *Let's go, c'mon, let's—*

"Naperville nine-one-one," said a nasally voice. "What's your—"

"This is Detective Emily Thompson," she interrupted. "Officer needs immediate backup at Premium Wine and Spirits, One Hundred Eleventh Street and Route Fifty-nine."

"For?"

"Armed robbery in progress. Two robbers, maybe more." The adrenaline made her voice squeak. She elbowed it out by clearing her throat.

"Any chance it's our bad boys?" the dispatcher said.

"I hope so," Emily said.

A three-man stickup crew—two goons and a wheel man—had terrorized bars and liquor stores throughout the Chicago area since Memorial Day. Sometimes they burgled.

Mostly they robbed, brutally and efficiently, whipping out steel guns and beating employees toothless if the cash register was even a penny short of expectation. One such victim was in a coma. Another had undergone complete facial reconstruction.

She hoped the bastards chose to shoot their way out, rather than surrender.

"Describe the suspects," the dispatcher said.

Emily shook her head as if he could see. "I saw only silhouettes from their flashlights," she said. "They're still inside. What's the status of backups?"

"Ten units inbound, running silent," he said. "I've mobilized SWAT. What else you need?"

"An armored car," Emily said, feeling naked without her bulletproof vest. She'd been heading home from the gym, so exhausted from cardio kickboxing she could sleep for a week. But Chief Kendall Cross had asked everyone to eyeball liquor establishments during their drives around town, on duty and off. She took that job seriously—the first coma victim had been behind the register because his Social Security didn't stretch far enough. The bandits bounced his head off a refrigerated case, cracking his skull in three places. "Just kidding. I'm fine. I've moved west of the store's front entrance."

The dispatcher repeated her new location. She confirmed.

"Tell me how you're dressed," he said.

"Blue jeans, mango top, running shoes. Black leather jacket. I'm carrying a Glock and a SureFire." Pistol and flashlight. "My badge is on my belt."

"Got it. I'll describe you to all units," he said.

So they don't shoot me by mistake, Emily translated. His heads-up play impressed her. Friendly fire was a serious risk for plainclothes cops, as adrenalized responders sometimes mistook them for bad guys and bombs away. She owed him a margarita.

"No imminent danger," she said. "I'll stay put and observe till backup arrives."

"Understood. Let me know when—"

She didn't hear the rest because her face began to pulse heat. Her arms trembled, and her thighs went numb. Disemboweled bodies spun and danced in her brain.

No, no, no! she screamed at herself. *Not now, dammit. Not now.*

The feeling disappeared.

"Uh . . . sorry . . . repeat that, dispatch?" she said, trying to catch her breath.

"Let me know when backup arrives," the dispatcher said.

From the corner of her eye, she saw a black-and-white bump into the sprawling asphalt lot of the strip mall. Per the drill on silent runs, its sirens, flashers, and headlights were off. She straightened herself, fanned November air under her jacket. The Crown Victoria Police Interceptor aimed her way. Twenty seconds later it was angled into the curb, out of the line of vision of the liquor store's windows.

Another on-the-ball colleague, she thought.

The door opened without sound or interior light. The driver unsnapped a hip holster and hustled her way. The orange anti-crime lights turned his navy-blue Naperville Police uniform mildew green.

She smiled at the driver's gelled, spiky hair.

"Hey, Hawk," she whispered, glad for such fearsome backup.

"Back at ya, Em," said Sergeant Robert Hawkins. He was five-nine and rangy, with wide eyes and a smile that displayed a gap between his top front teeth. The gap made the smile charming, not hillbilly-ish. He had ginger-colored hair, spatters of reddish freckles on his face and neck, and ropy veins along his muscled arms. He was a computer crimes cop, cracking felonies committed via Internet. He kicked down doors for SWAT. Occasionally, he filled in as a night-shift patrol sergeant, to keep his street skills fresh. "Situation?"

She explained.

"We're eyes and ears only?"

"Till the rest of the circus arrives," she said.

"Cool. I'll go around back," he said. "In case they—"

A long, wet shriek erupted from the store.

Hawk moved forward a quarter step. Emily's heart kicked as fresh adrenaline scoured her body. Her vision sharpened; her muscles tightened. She hardened her grip on her custom-made 9-millimeter Glock.

"So much for waiting," she said.

"Screams in the building," Hawk spat into his radio. "We're going inside."

"First three backups are one minute out," the dispatcher objected.

"She doesn't have that long," Hawk said, holding out the mike to the rolling wail.

"Jesus," the dispatcher said. "Uh, go."

Hawk hustled to the cruiser, pulled a Heckler & Koch MP-5 machine gun from the trunk.

They sprinted to the unlocked front door.

Emily crouched next to it, breathing fast and shallow. Hawk jammed up behind her, so close she could smell his cologne. They peered through the door, saw no one. She gripped the door handle. "Three, two, one . . ." he counted.

She yanked the door and exploded into the gap, staying low as she swung her pistol into the left side of the store.

Hawk followed high, sweeping his machine gun right.

Their SureFires lit the aisles like miniature lightning strikes.

No bandits.

No victims.

Just Chivas and Ketel and Bud.

"They moved," Emily stage-whispered. "Let's try—"

Another curdling female scream.

"Shut up, or I'll kill you now," a male voice warned. A dozen slaps followed. The scream tailed to a whimper.

Emily pointed to a vertical hole in the darkness at the rear of the store.

Hawk nodded to show he understood.

They raced down the tiled hallway, her in front, him trailing, muzzles up and hunting, staying as quiet as possible. The only light was a doorway next to the back exit. It was triple the brightness of the usual office fluorescent. Music poured out with the whiteness.

They crept the final ten feet.

Hard-core rap thumped their spines. "Bitches" and "whores" and "pig-ass Five-O" blended with "slaughter, maim, destroy." The woman's howl became so toxic Emily strained to not shoot her tormenters through the wall.

"All right, scream all you want," male voices taunted. "It'll hurt that much more when we drink your blood."

Hawk stiffened, and put the machine gun's red laser dot on the wall next to Emily. She snapped her Glock to eye level.

Three, two, one . . .

3

Cancer tapped the GPS with a fingernail loosened by blood blisters. "Found our dumping ground," he said.

"Where?" Gemini said, wiping the fogged windshield with the sleeve of his hoodie.

"Millston," Cancer said. "It's right off the interstate, so small it won't have a separate police department. Only the sheriff's patrol. And those guys are so busy with this storm they don't know whether to shit or go blind. They'll never know we were there."

"How far is it?"

"Thirteen miles," Cancer said.

"That could take forever in this rain. Anything closer?"

"Nope. It's the next exit."

Gemini nodded approval.

"All right, boys," he said. "We're dumping the chick at the next exit."

"Can't hear ya," Aquarius said over the thunder crash.

"We're dumping Kandy in Millston," Gemini repeated. "Next exit, small town, no cops, easy in and out."

"Cool," Aquarius said.

"Think they got a mill?" Virgo said.

"Uh . . . what?" Gemini said as the van plunged into a deep road pond. The engine sputtered. He cranked the wheel this way and that, looking for high ground—if it died, they were done for. A moment later the tires bit into solid pavement. The engine recovered. His shoulders joined his head pounding with pain.

"A mill," Virgo repeated. "Millston. I wonder if they got a mill?"

"Who cares?" Gemini said, digging a knuckle between his eyes.

"I do," Virgo said. "I like history. Lots of these towns have mills from the old days. Just wondering if this one does, that's all."

"They do or they don't," Gemini said, "or they did and it burned to the ground and the smoke killed all the fuckin' cows. It makes no difference to me."

"Grain," Virgo said.

"What?"

"You said cows. Mills are for grain. Not cows."

Gemini glared in the rearview. "What part of 'I don't care' don't you understand?"

Virgo shrugged. "I'm just sayin'."

"Say it to yourself," Gemini said. He whipped his head to the shotgun seat. "Cancer, you give a damn about some stupid mill?"

"Nope," Cancer said cheerfully.

"Aquarius?"

"Not me, boss."

"See?" Gemini said. "So shut up about it already."

"Jesus Christ, what a grouch," Virgo grumbled. "Go get yourself laid when we cash in this load, willya?"

"Why you being so nice to him?" Cancer said. "I found your little mill town."

"You mean they *got* a mill?" Virgo said, hopeful.

Gemini groaned. Everyone laughed.

Tension broken.

Gemini honked at the SUV drifting into his lane. Damn things thought they owned the road. He'd love to pull his heater, turn the driver's face to tomato soup. But rolling down the window would let in the monsoon, and this was a brand-new shirt.

"What are we looking for in Millston?" Gemini said instead. "A swamp? Junkyard?"

"River. A mile from the off-ramp," Cancer said. The neon colors from the GPS reflected off his rectangular glasses. "It'll be running heavy with all this rain. We toss her in the drink, get back to the interstate. No way cops will see us in this slop." He patted the Uzi machine gun in the nylon gym bag between his feet. "If they do . . ."

"Leave the gun, take the cannoli," Aquarius quipped.

Gemini peered at the interstate signs. Couldn't make out the words through the sheets of rain. He rubbed his eyes, which were sandpapery from road stare. "Where exactly are we now?"

"Wisconsin."

His thin lips pressed flat. "Lotta fuckin' comedians in this clown car."

Cancer looked at him, concerned. "You all right, boss? I can drive if you wanna take a break."

"Nah," Gemini said, forcing himself to lighten up. Wasn't their fault the weather stunk. "I'm good." He bumped fists with each of his crewmen.

"How far?" Virgo said.

"Just passed Black River Falls," Cancer said. "Another thirteen miles to the Millston exit."

"That's forever in this slop," Aquarius complained, climbing into the rear seat from the cargo area and kicking off his shoes. "Girl's gonna stink by then."

"No worse than your feet," Virgo said, waving the air in front of his flattish nose.

Aquarius punched him.

Virgo smacked him back. "That's the best you got?" he gibed. "My grandma hits harder'n that, and she's dead ten years. . . ."

Cancer punched the radio buttons for weather updates.

Gemini stared south toward payday, the taillights ahead of him blurring pink from eyestrain and rain.

Kandy chilled in her canvas coffin.

4

"Police!" Hawk and Emily shouted as they charged through the doorway, eyes darting for weapons. A woman sprawled languidly on a table. The four beefcakes attacking her jumped like they'd been Tasered. "Get on the ground, get on the ground, do it now!"

The rear door blasted off its hinges as uniformed backups flooded inside.

Everyone screamed and dove for the floor.

Everyone but the naked guy with the video cam.

"Yeah, baby," he was yowling, swinging the camera with a slavering grin. "Bring it on, crime dawgs. *That's* my Weeping Jesus."

Emily flew across the sardine-can space, smacked the camera from his bony hands. It bounced under a chair, spitting parts like broken teeth.

The cameraman squealed in disbelief. "That's a two-thousand-dollar camera, you stupid—"

Emily pile-drove him into the tiles. "Quit fighting, or I'll break your arm," she snapped, ducking his cursing round-houses. A cop flung handcuffs her way. She snatched them midair, muscled the man's arms behind his back, snapped the cuffs on his pencil wrists.

The woman bounced off the banquet table, screeching like a train derailment.

"Don't you dare hurt Garry!" she shouted to Hawk, double-D's dancing as she hopped around in anger. "He didn't do anything wrong. We're making a reality—"

"Quiet," Hawk ordered. "Everyone, just shut up."

It didn't help.

"Naperville Police," Emily tried, the higher timbre of her voice chopping through the thunder of noise. "Shut up till we sort this out. Now." She hopped on a chair and stamped her foot. A strap broke. "Everybody. Pipe down. Hush."

The room fell silent but for the sound of ratcheting hand-cuffs.

Emily blew out her breath, and surveyed their catch.

One woman, five men. A sixteen-by-twenty work room. A mechanical time clock, with slots for putty-colored punch cards. Liquor bottles, some opened. A coffee maker holding two scorched pots. A browned-out Boston ivy plant, tendrils draping limp over a steel file cabinet. Two eight-foot banquet tables smothered in heart-shaped pillows, lace doilies, and fluffy red blankets edged in white satin.

Emily shook her head. This was the strangest robbery she'd ever seen.

A row of chairs on the short wall. Tape dispensers, ring binders, paper, click pens, and rumpled jeans and tops, scattered across the seats. Shoes tucked underneath, between the spindle legs. A video cam, twin to the one she'd punched. Next to it, a still camera and a pile of memory cards. Movie lights in various wattages, with white umbrella reflectors. Their intensity painted her skin with heat. The usual job postings—overtime, drug testing, wash your hands after peeing—and a poster with a flock of seagulls and the caption *Teamwork: The lifting power of many wings can achieve twice the distance of any bird flying alone.*

Oh, gag me, Emily thought.

She turned her attention to her grounded birds, none of whom seemed concerned they were naked and cops were staring.

The woman was a curvy, five-nine blonde whose carpet didn't match her drapes. She was mid to late twenties, and attractive under her blue-dominated makeup. The cameraman was older, skinnier, hirsute, and adorned with a ponytail and goatee that recalled Kurt Cobain on a heroin jag. His knees were hair-covered knobs, and his butt slacked like wet cement. The four men who'd attacked the woman were young, hunky, blond, earringed, and shaved clean as apples.

Everywhere.

"All right," Emily said, pointing to the woman. "What's your name?"

"Denise," she said. "You got a cigarette?"

"No," Emily said.

Denise shrugged.

"How did you get in here?" Emily said.

"It's my daddy's store," Denise said, more cheerfully than Emily anticipated, given how thoroughly she'd been, uh, searched during the felony takedown. "I'm the executive assistant manager, so I have a key. You can check."

"We will," Hawk said, pointing to the owner contact sheet thumbtacked next to the shift schedule. A potbellied cop waddled off to make the call.

Emily stifled a yawn. With the excitement all but vanished, her weariness was returning. "So what are you doing here?" she asked, trying to recall what Denise said before hitting the floor. "Something about a reality?"

"Video," Denise said. "We're making a reality video."

"Why?" Hawk said.

"For a movie blog," Denise said, her heretofore guarded eyes now gleaming with excitement. "A tequila company is offering fifty grand for best amateur video of the year. So, we're making a vampire cop movie. *Dracula* meets *Law and Order*, that sort of thing. But with bunches of sex and glam."

"I'm guessing that's where you come in," Emily said.

"Naturally," Denise said, shaking the girls.

Appreciative murmurs from the uniforms.

"Out, boys," Emily said, not unkindly, to the ones who didn't need to be there. They trundled out of the room, snickering.

"So what do you call this opus, Denise?" Hawk asked. "*Dying Sucks*?"

Denise brightened. "I like that," she said. "We were thinking *Born to Die*, but your idea totally brings in the humorous element. That's important to our core audience demographic of white males ages eighteen to thirty-five, meaning it's important to the judges." She looked at the cameraman. "What do you think?"

"I don't know. I guess it's okay," he said, grudgingly.

Denise flipped her hair, swung her attention back to Emily and Hawk.

"It's settled, then," she declared. "Thanks to this quick-thinking officer—"

"Sergeant," Hawk corrected.

"Sergeant," Denise said, "we're calling our movie *Dying Sucks*."

"Gee, Hawk, can I have your autograph?" a cop said.

"Autograph this," Hawk said.

Denise laughed. "I'm not surprised you guys thought up such a great name," she said. "After me, you guys are the real stars."

"'You guys'?" Emily asked.

"You police. The way you busted in waving your guns? Two words: awe, some." Denise wriggled upright. Her bare cheeks squeaked on the waxed tiles. "We originally shot this scene with friends dressed as police. That didn't work. They weren't commanding enough. Not enough pizzazz. They didn't have the Weeping Jesus, know what I mean?"

Emily didn't. She nodded anyway. Keep the story moving.

"We weren't sure what to do," Denise continued, her silver handcuffs jangling as she talked with her hands. "We couldn't hire actors because the rules say amateurs only. So Garry"—she pointed at the cameraman—"had the most certifiable idea."

"It's certifiable, all right," Hawk said.

"For real," Denise said, not getting the sarcasm. "Garry said, 'Screw using make-believe cops. We'll film in your daddy's store and start screaming bloody murder. Someone will call the police.'" She beamed at the bespectacled cameraman. "Those were my practice screams, but you guys showed up anyway. Like knights on white horses or something. Garry is a genius."

Garry dipped his head modestly. Peeked to make sure everyone saw.

"A genius," Denise repeated, looking at Emily. "Just like you, officer."

"Detective," Emily said.

"Jesus. Don't you cops make officers anymore?" Denise complained, brushing hair from her eyes. The cuffs clinked. "Anyway, Detective, the way you punched out Garry's camera? So real. So strong and emotional. So authentic and . . . well . . . you know . . ." She pursed her lips, trying to think of the word. "It's like that judge said about porn—he couldn't describe it, but he knew it when he saw it."

"Ask the judge to pay for my camera," Garry grumbled.

"Don't pout, darling," Denise said. "It gives you wrinkles. I'll get Daddy to pay for it." She turned back to Emily, flashed a tooth-filled beamer. "It's like I tell everyone in film class—when your movie needs the right touch of real, call nine-one-one."

"I got some more real for you," Hawk said.

"Wow, really?" Denise said. "What is it?"

"We call it jail."

Her black eyebrows shot up. "You're arresting us?"

"Think of it as being voted off the island," Emily said.

She called off the rest of the police tsunami, then headed to the parking lot with Hawk to let the uniforms process the catch. Emily noticed the intense sparkle in the asphalt. *Like somebody dropped a glitter ball.* She knew it was mica, the shiny mineral mixed in with the gravel and tar to make blacktop, and the sparkle was a reflection of the anti-crime lights. But it was more fun to think of it as fairy dust. . . .

"Thought I'd seen everything," Hawk said, pulling cigarettes from his shirt pocket. "Then Little Miss Ditsy Tits came into my life."

"And, you named a Hollywood movie," she said.

Hawk slapped the pack on his palm. A single white tube popped up. He lipped it free. "Don't tell Cross," he said, pulling out a Zippo adorned with a golf ball, "but nights like this I'd do this job for free."

Emily snickered, imagining how their straight-arrow chief of police was going to explain this bit of boom-chicka-wah-wah to the press. She high-fived Hawk, then called Marty to explain why she'd be late getting home. He asked if she wanted him to swing by. She said no, she'd be leaving soon. He said he'd wait up as the story sounded too good to miss. "Two words: awe, some," she assured. Hawk smoked in comfortable silence. Uniforms escorted the now-dressed movie moguls to prisoner transport, which would haul them to police headquarters on Aurora Avenue, where they'd be checked for warrants and have their statements taken. If

Denise was telling the truth, Emily doubted charges would be preferred. They were in the store legally, it being Daddy's and her being a manager. They weren't disturbing the peace—Emily had called the police. Their nudity wasn't public. They were adults, with no weapons, on private property, with no drugs, and blah-de-blah-ho-hum.

Fun while it lasted.

A raindrop bounced off the asphalt. Another joined it. *Pat. Pit-pat. Pit-pat-pit.* Cops ran to close the windows in their cruisers. She saw lightning dance between clouds. She stepped under the store's long overhang. Hawk joined her.

"Mind if I ask you something?" he said, cranking the Zippo's wheel.

"Sure, go ahead," she said.

"You didn't look so hot when I pulled up. You feeling all right?"

The question startled her. How could he possibly have noticed?

"What do you mean?" she parried.

Hawk sucked a lungful. "You were out of breath," he said, smoke leaking from his nose and lips. "Sweating. Trembling a little. Catching swine flu or something?"

Or something. "Nothing so dramatic," Emily lied. "Kickboxing went two hours tonight instead of one. Between that and the reconnaissance of the liquor store"—she described her thigh-burning duck walk—"I got a little rubbery, that's all."

"What you get doing healthy things," he kidded. "If you smoked, you'd be fine."

"I thought you'd quit."

"I did," he said. "But fun times like this deserve a salute, don't you think?"

She thought about that, held up two fingers in a V. He slapped up another cigarette. She took it, fired the end, sucked deep. Coughed her lungs out.

"Gotta work on your form," Hawk said, laughing. "Rest of you feels all right, though?"

"Never better," she said. "Nothing like a takedown to clear the mind."

"Ten-four," Hawk said.

He craned his head at the trooping actors. "Hey Denise," he hollered.

The woman looked their way.

"What's a Weeping Jesus?"

She swept her hair back, as if it were Oscar night. "A scene shot so perfectly it'd make Jesus weep," she said. "It's Garry's personal anthem as a filmmaker."

"I'm shocked, shocked," Hawk said.

"Huh?" Denise said.

"Never mind," Hawk said. "Thanks."

She disappeared into the transport. He and Emily watched it pull away.

"No wonder Jesus wept," he muttered.

"Not to mention Bogie," Emily said. "How's your daughter doing?"

Hawk took a drag, blew it out in a thin stream. Emily breathed in the warm blue smoke. Smiled to herself. It reminded her of the friendly neighborhood VFW hall of her youth, where Dad took her Saturday mornings for doughnuts and card games with his steelworker pals. It was a nice feeling.

"Funny you should ask," he said, allowing a small smile to peek out. "I got the money. Every last dime."

"Hawk!" she said, pumping her fist. "That's wonderful. I'm so happy for you."

The smoke from the tip twisted like calligraphy, betraying the emotion under his cool-cop exterior. "The bank says we'll hit three million today," he said. "Every damn cent the hospital needs for Sammy's treatment. As soon as they confirm transfer of payment—"

"You fly to Los Angeles and get your little girl well."

Hawk beamed. "There were times I thought we wouldn't make it. You know how sick she gets. But now?"

"The end is in sight."

"And it isn't a train coming at me," he said.

Emily gave him a quick hug, then started for her car. "Baby's gonna get the cure," she heard Hawk murmur. "And then maybe Bonnie will—"

His pager warbled.

Hers joined a moment later.

They stared at the messages, astonished.

"What are the odds?" Hawk said.

"A million to one," Emily said.

"A gazillion," Hawk said.

"You're a sergeant," Emily said. "You ought to know."

They ran for their cars, whooping, as the sky opened up.

"SWATs," one cop said as they skidded onto Route 59, sirens blaring.

"Crazy as bedbugs, every one," the other agreed.

5

"Launch gas," Annie Bates ordered.

Cops raised launchers. Igniters roared, followed by the soft *sputs* of tear gas leaving the gas guns. The black canisters spiraled like footballs through the driving rain. The warheads smashed through the plateglass and exploded inside the house. Thick clouds of noxiousness puffed out window frames, doorjambs, vents, outlet covers, sill cocks, and siding.

"Tell me what's happening, Audio," Annie told the tech who'd wired the house for sound.

"Yelling, hacking, coughing," the tech reported, his tiny head enveloped by boxing-glove-sized earphones. "Three distinct voices, like before."

"Understood. Talk to me, Video."

"Three human images in the living room," Emily reported, working the laptop linked to SWAT's thermal imager. "They dropped to the floor as soon as the gas exploded, haven't left the room. Nothing in the rest of the house."

"Very well," Annie said. "Grab the remote imager and come with me."

"On it," Emily said, donning mask and helmet. Another cop took her place at the laptop.

Annie tightened her chin strap. "Alpha, Bravo, and Charlie teams, you have a green light for assault," the Naperville SWAT commander said. "Repeat, green light."

"Alpha ready," Hawk replied. Bravo and Charlie reported likewise.

Annie glanced at Chief of Police Kendall Cross and Deputy Chief Hercules Branch.

Both nodded.

Annie stalked to her forward command position, toggled the radio to attack-live. "You will launch on my three-count. Three . . . two . . . one . . ."

Ribbons of plastic explosives blew front, back, and mudroom doors off their hinges. Armored and masked SWAT cops tornadoed into the white gas clouds, machine guns up and hunting the three hardened robbers they'd kill or capture in the next thirty seconds.

Annie drew her long-barreled .45, a Springfield Armory XDm, and pounded up the stairs. Emily stayed tight on her flank. A sniper covered them from his perch on the other side of Saranell Avenue. They dashed across the white wooden porch—surprisingly large for new construction, Annie noted—and knelt on either side of the shattered door. Twisted shards of building material crunched under their industrial-strength boots. Emily poked the nose of the camera through the doorway. Interior images appeared on the monitor clamped to her helmet, and at the A/V table next to the charcoal gray SWAT truck.

"All clear," Branch told her. "Nobody's inside the doorway."

Emily repeated the confirmation.

"Got it," Annie said.

They listened to the play-by-play of Hawk and other assaulters rushing the room where the three armed bandits hid. Sideways rain mixed with hail pellets swept them like machine gun nests. Continuous rolls of thunder created chop in the deepening rain-swamp in the yard. The wind rose and fell like tornado sirens.

Then abruptly shifted direction.

"Whoa," Emily said, instantly unable to see her hands.

"We're blind from gas," Annie reported as the thick white clouds swept out the front door and across the porch. Not a problem, she was wearing a biothreat-level gas mask. "Should be clear in three or four—*ahhgh*."

"What's wrong? Are you hit?" Emily asked.

Annie couldn't answer. Her lungs had seized so badly she thought the house had fallen on her. Ice picks punctured her eyeballs, poured in acid. Her skin burned as if welded. Tears, saliva, and mucus poured out of eyes, ears, nose, and throat. Nausea rumbled in her belly.

"Gassed," she managed as the caustic mixture of pepper spray and tear gas penetrated deep. "Mask bad. Can't . . . breathe."

Emily lunged across the opening, grabbed Annie's arm and waist, and hustled her down the steps. Annie's boots skidded on a rain-slickened plank. She torpedoed between the railings and into a snarl of yews.

"Hold on, I'm coming," Emily yelled, leaping the rail.

The tough wood of the yew branches stuck her like swords. She ignored the pain and hauled the whoop-coughing SWAT commander to her feet. She dragged Annie out of the thicket and threw her at the barricades. Paramedics ran out to catch the pass.

Annie started retching into her mask. A paramedic ripped it off. She vomited three times in the open air, then snatched back the mask and flung it like a baseball. The paramedic ducked. The mask banged off the cab of a fire truck, disappeared in a puddle. Emily raced to retrieve it so they could find the defect. The scrum of cops half carried Annie to the SWAT truck, where Branch was issuing commands to the assault teams. Annie's cough was tubercular.

"Hose her," Cross ordered.

A firefighter opened a nozzle and power-washed Annie's face and head. The water was so cold she felt like she'd dropped into a glacier.

"Ah . . . Christ . . ." she choked, the waterboarding even worse than the gas.

She slapped the nozzle aside, then dropped to her knees to vomit water, snot, and gas. A second firefighter added her hose. Annie cupped her hands around her nose and mouth, creating a pocket so she could breathe. *In. Out. In. Out. In. Out.* Paramedics broke out syringes in case Annie experienced an allergic reaction to the gas, which could swell her throat and cut off her air.

"Are you all right?" she heard Cross say. She knew he was yelling because she felt the breath blast in her ear. But he was muffled, as if talking through a bale of hay. She assumed her ears were clogged with snot.

"I'm fine, Chief," she gargled.

"Uh, right," Cross said. "What happened?"

She vomited till empty, then cupped her hands in the spray for a drink. She tasted hose and dirt, spit it out like bad chicken. *Ptou.* Last thing she needed was dysentery from a holding tank of rancid water. The kidding from the firefighters would be merciless, and she wouldn't give them the satisfaction. . . .

"Bad mask, Chief," she managed. "I ate some gas. We get 'em?"

Cross handed her a damp towel. She scrubbed her face best she could, then turned to where he was pointing. She saw several indistinct images. They moved like they were underwater. Were those her ninjas, leading three flailing men toward the prisoner transport truck? She wasn't sure. Her eyes still bled gas.

"Yep, that's them," Cross confirmed, wiping rain from her helmet. "The liquor store bandits we've hunted since May."

"How much fight did they put up?" she said.

Cross made a zero with thumb and finger.

She stared. *"None?"*

"Moment they saw Hawk's machine gun, their hands went up."

"Knuckleheads," she muttered, profoundly annoyed. "If they were gonna give up so fast, why didn't they do it before I ate all that gas?"

Cross patted her back. "The important thing, Commander, is nobody got hurt."

She glared.

"Nobody who can sue me, anyway," he said.

She tried not to laugh.

Failed.

Humor marks tightened around Cross's gray eyes. "Outstanding job, Annie," he said, punching her shoulder. "The FBI couldn't nail these freaks, but you did."

Annie looked around for her best friend. "Thanks. How's Emily?"

"She's good," Cross said. "Did a nice job hauling your butt out of those bushes. She was coated with gas, so I sent her home to scrub up. Rest of the team is fine. Not a scratch among them. You can go home with a clear conscience."

"Home?" she said, bristling. "I can't. I still need to debrief them—"

"I'll take care of that. You're out of here," Cross said in a voice that brooked no quarrel.

Normally, she'd still argue. The care of her ninja turtles was her responsibility. Their baths and feeding came before hers, each and every time.

Instead, she lay back in the puddle. Cold, watery mud

flowed into her shirt and down her pants, swamping every nook of her over-amped body. She didn't care—it was literally impossible to get more dirty. She closed her eyes, pretending this was a day spa and she'd forked over a mortgage payment to be swaddled in this fragrant crapola. The cramp in her lower back began to ease. The gabble of cops and media fell away as she concentrated on nothingness. The boiling in her eyes fell to simmer, and her breath came more easily as the wheezing eased in her lungs—

"Fabuloso work, Annie, just terrific," a familiar voice chirped.

She felt her back tighten. It was the state's attorney, Terrence Beck. Maybe if she played dead he'd go away.

"Commander," he persisted. "Annie. Yo, girlfriend, you awake?"

"No," she said.

"Hey. Pretty funny. I like a good sense of humor."

Beck clearly wasn't leaving. She opened her eyes, glared at the thousand-dollar suit.

"So how about it?" he said, either not noticing or not caring. "Cracking this robbery ring is a big deal. I want you at my side at the press conference."

"When is it?"

"Noon. I need your report by eight, though, so my guys can salt details into my speech. You'll be there, right?"

"No, thanks."

"Aw, c'mon, Annie, please?" Beck wheedled. "TV will be there. Even CNN and Fox. Be a great opportunity to shine. Cameras love you."

"I hate them. Besides, the chief won't approve—"

"I already asked Ken. He said it's fine with him if you're willing, but if you say no, then that's that." He blew on his fingers to warm them. "He says the heroics you performed would exhaust someone half your age, and you'll probably need to sleep late."

Her eyes popped open, and she squinted around. Saw Cross leaning against a fire truck, looking at her with a trace of a smile. She made a face that said, "I'll get you for this."

His smile became a smirk, and he added a little finger-wave.

Then disappeared into the media horde yelling for his comment on the drama.

"Sure," Annie sighed, resigning herself to her fate. "Why not?"

"That's my girl," he said, bouncing on the muddy balls of his Ferragamo'd feet. "That's why you're the leader of the pack. My go-to girl. The girl I depend on when the going gets tough—"

"Terrence?" she interrupted.

"Yes?"

"Call me a girl one more time and you'll eat this mud."

Silence.

Then, a cackling laugh.

"Yessir, that's my Annie," he said, walking away. "Helluva sense of humor—"

6

Wham.

Bam.

"Uh, sorry, ma'am," Marty murmured as he drew back.

"Honey, it's okay," Emily said, interlocking her long, slender fingers with what Marty called his "knockwursts with nails." She paused to let the thunder echo out. "It happens."

"Not to me."

Emily studied Marty's cupped hand. What it held looked so sad. So drained of possibilities. She reached up, gently pushed the tip to the side.

No response.

"That bad boy emptied faster than we thought," she said.

"Yeh," he said.

A string of thunder claps walked her mother's tortoiseshell comb and brush set across her triple dresser. Wet wind howled through the open windows. Her hair blew across her face. She finger-combed it in place, opened the emerald sheets.

"*You're* still full though, right?" she said with an arch of the thin white scar that bisected her left eyebrow.

Marty grinned.

Slapped the empty can of whipped cream onto the lamp table.

Dove into bed.

Sheets tangled. Pillows flew. Squeals erupted.

Phone warbled.

"Go away," Emily groaned.

"Can't," Marty said. "You asked her to call." He checked the number, picked up.

"Nice technique on those stairs," he said. "You learn that in ninja school?"

"Shut up."

"I would, but I'm too busy laughing," Marty said. "How are your eyes?"

"Terrible," Annie Bates said, rubbing madly. "They won't stop itching."

He sympathized, having swallowed his own share of gas over the years. "They reformulated that brand. Sticks to your eyeballs something fierce now. But I know a cure."

"I'll pay anything. . . ."

"Go wash your head in grape juice."

"Say, uh, what?"

"Grape juice," he repeated. "Sounds weird, but it works. Use a gallon or so, and work it in real good. As cold as you can stand it. Get the girls to help you scrub. Don't rinse, just go to sleep with your hair wet."

"Huh. That really works?"

"Well, no," Marty said. "But thinking about you doing it makes me all smiley inside."

Annie's reply was pointed.

"Guinness record for cuss words in one breath," he said, laughing. "Seriously, get a good night's sleep. That'll take care of it."

Annie slowed for the turn into her subdivision. "I'm glad we nailed those creeps, Marty," she said. "Reminds me why I got into this business."

Marty recalled his undercover infiltration of a violent biker gang. It was a soul-sucking job in which he'd been forced to beat a young man to death or be killed himself. But it ended with twelve whack jobs in maximum security and thirty million dollars of cocaine seized. Ten years later, he still got death threats. He pinned them on the bulletin board outside his office so the deputies could vote for most deranged.

"I know Em was unhappy to be sent home early," Annie continued. "But Ken was right to get that gas off her skin."

Marty looked at Emily, whose taut body, backlit by the lamp, slid softly against her emerald silk nightgown. "Couldn't agree more," he said. "And with that I'll sign off."

"Wait, wait. I need her one more time."

Marty gurgled like he was drowning.

"Only a minute, I promise," Annie said, grinning at the phone. "Oh, and not that you care, but don't eat too much fat and sugar while you're gone."

"You're right," Marty said. "I don't care."

He heard her laughing as he handed the phone back to Emily.

"Nice work with that thermal imager," Annie said. "You handled it like a pro. Keep it up I'll put you on SWAT permanently."

"Cool," Emily said, knowing her best friend was really saying, *Thank you for pulling me out of those bushes.*

"See you in a few hours," Annie said.

They groaned simultaneously, then hung up.

"So, my little commando. Need to get some sleep?" Marty said.

Emily pulled the gown over her head and held out her arms.

"I couldn't have said it better myself," Marty said.

7

"I can't sleep," Samantha Hawkins whispered from her father's doorway.

"How come, Ladybug?" Robert Hawkins said. "The thunder?"

The girl shrugged. The Little Mermaids on her hot-pink nightgown shrugged with her.

"I know. I miss her too," Hawk said, moving his cell phone and laptop to the empty side of the king-sized bed. "Hugs?"

His daughter bobbed her head.

"Well, come on in, then," he said, opening his arms.

Sammy jumped for the middle of the bed. Couldn't quite make it—the pillow-top mattress came nearly to her neck. She regrouped, gripped the sewn edge with both hands, and threw her left foot up and over, like she was mounting a pony, which she'd done last summer at the Yellowstone Park, her and Daddy and Mommy and her little rented pony, Mr.

Ed, on their last family vacation, back when everyone used to smile.

She skittered off, hit the carpet with a thud.

"Want some help?" Hawk asked, suppressing a grin because he knew the answer.

"No. I can do it myself," Sammy said, biting her bottom lip as she backed all the way to the closet. She planted her feet, bent her pipe-cleaner legs, wrinkled her nose, wiggled her behind, ran, and leaped, thin arms pointed like she was bodysurfing.

"Atta girl," Hawk said as all the Little Mermaids crash-landed in the blankets.

Whooping triumphantly, Sammy crawled to her father. He raised his arm. She snuggled underneath, resting her ear on his T-shirted chest.

He wrapped his freckled arm around her shoulders, fingers lightly brushing her hip. Its emerging boniness alarmed him, but he made sure not to show that in his hug.

"I love you, Ladybug," he said.

She whispered, "I love you more."

"You more," he said, tickling her belly.

"No fair, Daddy," she shrieked through high-pitched giggles. "I can't breathe through the tickles to talk."

He stopped.

"*You* more," she said. "That means I win. Yay me."

He kissed her scalp, breathing in her soapy scent. She sang the Alphabet Song backwards, to show she knew how. It was only a little out of key. He told her a bedtime story, which started with the Brothers Grimm but tumbled into wizards, soccer, joke-telling vampires, and Barbie going to prom. She squealed when Barbie put orange lipstick on Ken.

Thunder shook the house. Sammy clapped her hands over her ears, cringing. Hawk shook a knotted fist, warned the storm that this very special seven-year-old was under his protection so scram, and furthermore he'd spank any monsters that came in from the rain. Relieved, Sammy settled back into his chest. Her breathing slowed. Her eyelids fluttered, then closed.

Hawk felt his tension leak away.

This was the time he loved most. Just father and daughter. No doctors. No disease. No runaway mom. Just a long black ponytail that smelled of peaches. Not the canned kind with stale metallic perfume. Fresh peaches, sodden with juice, snapped off the drooping tree in Grandpa's backyard and broken into clumps by a delighted little girl as Grandma spooned maple ice cream from the hand churn . . .

"Daddy?" she murmured from somewhere near dreamland.

"Yes, baby?" he said.

"Will I be dead by Christmas?"

8

Dr. Amanda Barrett tossed.

Turned.

Sighed.

Rolled out of bed and padded to the computer. Clicked on Samantha Hawkins's website. Stared at the TEST YOUR STRENGTH graphic with the old-fashioned muscleman swinging the hammer. "One more swing and we hit three million!" a cartoon barker said. "Will you be the one who rings the bell? Will you be the one who Saves Our Samantha?"

She slammed the keyboard in frustration.

The letters P and U flew off.

"No kidding," she muttered.

Left them on the floor, went back to bed.

9

Red dripped from Cancer's fingers.

"She's bleeding through the drop cloth," he announced from the cargo area.

Gemini's jaw vibrated with irritation. Highway patrols pulled random DUI inspections when they got bored. If a trooper spotted the leaking red . . .

"Wait a minute," he said, suspicious. "Blood doesn't leak through plastic."

Aquarius stared out his window. Virgo looked sheepish.

"Chrissakes, you guys," Gemini said. "That's why we have plastic in the first place, to keep this from happening. You wrap her in plastic, *then* the drop cloth."

Virgo cleared his throat. "Sorry, Karl. Guess we forgot."

Gemini's face hardened. "Yeah, you did. And you used my real name. Don't fucking do it again."

Virgo looked out the window, embarrassed.

Gemini sighed, recalling how maniacally the boys had

put it to Kandy while she gasped for air. He chided himself for not paying attention to the wrap job afterwards.

"Thing is, Five-O sees blood and we're all staring down the barrel of a shotgun," he said, less harshly. "Unless you two knuckleheads enjoy maximum-security prisons for some reason I don't want to know about, use your head next time."

"My bad, Gemini, my fault," Virgo said, holding up his hands as Aquarius nodded contrition. "I guess we should unwrap that girl and put on the plastic, huh?"

"Ain't no 'we' about it," Gemini said. "You made the mess, you clean it up."

10

"Bacon and eggs?" Annie said, sniffing the air theatrically as she padded into the kitchen from the garage. "At two in the morning? We'll never get back to sleep."

"Not much chance of that anyway," Joshua Bates said, nodding at the window over the stove. Raindrops the size of Buicks smeared the glass.

"I think it'll stop soon," Annie said.

Tristen picked up the remote, clicked on The Weather Channel. The map was sunburned from Des Moines to Cincinnati. But the dry-air line was shoving the monster east.

"Good thing, Mom," Alexa said, pouring milk for her and her big sister. White swirled mocha from the chocolate she'd squirted into the glass. "Aunt Emily leaves at four."

"She's not going, remember?" Annie said, dropping four sugar cubes into her coffee. Each made a tiny *ploop*. "Only Marty and Branch. It's their week in Wisconsin, hunting deer."

"That is *so* gross," Tristen said, dangling a bacon strip over her mouth. "Why would anyone want to murder a poor living creature?" Joshua shared a look of amusement with Annie at the irony. Alexa nudged everything to the edges of the plate, hating her food to touch. Joshua one-handed eggs into the skillet. The scent of caramelized butter filled the air.

"How hungry are you?" he asked, adding thick-cut Oscar Mayer. The hard sizzle gave the thunder a rhythm section.

Annie's stomach growled. The last time she'd eaten a real meal was . . . well, she couldn't exactly remember. Last night? Not even then. She'd joined her husband for a late bite at Quincy's on Ogden Avenue, greeted Tomas, their favorite waiter, and ordered red snapper. As the plate touched down, Emily's alert came in. Annie abandoned the meal, got SWATs rolling. Emily called in the false alarm. Annie headed for home. Halfway there, an informant of decent credibility called to say the liquor-store bandits she was hunting were holed up in a house near Fox Valley Mall, on the city's far west side. She went lights and sirens, negotiated for hours, wolfing down Power Bars instead of snapper, then decided enough was enough.

"Three eggs, six bacons," Annie decided. "I'll sleep when I'm dead."

"Mo-om!" Alexa said, laughing.

Tristen slapped her fork on the plate. Yolk bits splashed.

Annie's eyes narrowed. "What's that about?" she said.

"Nothing," Tristen mumbled, not looking up.

Annie sighed. Till a few months ago, her oldest was happy, enthused, engaged. Then she'd turned sullen, erupting at the most innocent questions and spitting out the answers with a pinched, hard face. Some of the venom spattered her father and sister, but most was reserved for Mom. Annie and Joshua checked for drugs, depression, Internet, grades, and bullying. Nothing. The moodiness of turning thirteen, they decided.

"You're not acting like nothing's wrong," Annie pressed.

"Mom, I said I'm all right. Let's drop this, okay?"

"Fine," Annie snapped, the long standoff making her suddenly too tired to continue.

Joshua caressed Annie's neck as he delivered her plate. A triangle of seeded rye toast teetered over the edge, hit the table butter-side-down. Tristen was closest. She didn't move to help. Joshua cleared his throat. She grudgingly placed the toast on Annie's plate, but cleaned her fingers by licking them, pointedly not using her napkin. Annie refused the bait.

"All right, you two," Annie said when their plates were empty. "Time for bed."

Tristen was off like a shot, her door slamming so hard it rattled the dirty fry pans. Alexa's door closed gently, as if in apology. Joshua held up the Mr. Coffee. Annie nodded. They wandered hand-in-hand to the maple-paneled family room.

"Little shit," Annie mumbled as she flopped onto their leather couch. Not one drop of coffee spilled, a skill honed by years of hard cornering in fast-moving vehicles. "You shouldn't say that about your own kid, but God she works my last nerve. . . ." She took a deep breath, blew it out. "Thanks for making breakfast, hon. It was fun, eating together."

"Mostly," Joshua agreed, rubbing her slender, muscled legs. "How'd it go out there?"

Annie snorted. "Great, except for my stepping on my weenie on that porch."

"You don't have one of those," Joshua said, waving his hand dismissively. "I checked." He took a deep drink. "Morning soon. We should get to bed already."

"I wish I could," she said, explaining about the report she owed the state's attorney.

"Pity." Joshua said. "I was going to serve you breakfast in bed."

She cocked her head. "Didn't we just eat?"

"That was bacon. Thought maybe you'd like some sausage."

Annie smiled at the possibilities.

11

"There's the exit," Cancer said as he rubbed fresh peep-holes. It took so long to get here from Black River that Kandy was rancid. So they'd cracked the windows. It diluted her stink well enough, but the saturated air fogged the wind-shield. "Just like the GPS promised."

"Sure wish I'd invented that thing," Gemini said, power-ing into the curve of the exit ramp. "When you got billions of dollars, you don't gotta drive through any—"

He mashed the brakes, sliding the van sideways. The crew banged off the cabin walls like corn in a popper. "Lookit," he said, pointing to the side of the road.

The deer was magnificent. He was a buck. He stood in front of a curtain of pine trees crusted with snow lumps, which steamed in the cold rain. His fur was a mottled brown, turning gray near the rump. White tufts spackled his ears, throat, and snout. Hooves and nose were the blue-black of engine oil. His antlers were large and airy. Each branched into a chandelier of tips that twinkled in the vapor lamp standing lonely sentry over the exit.

"Beautiful," Virgo admired.

"Target practice," Gemini said.

Cancer grinned as he handed over the Uzi from the gym bag. "You always gotta be killing something, don't you?"

"You say that like it's a bad thing," Gemini said.

Everyone cackled.

Gemini worked the bolt. Cancer leaned forward till he hugged the dashboard. Virgo and Aquarius, in the backseat, scooted to the driver's side. Gemini leaned across to the passenger door, rested the long snout of the silencer on the half-unrolled window, keeping the rest of the gun inside the van. He aimed for the closest brisket. Fondled the trigger.

Copper-jacketed bullets squirted from the silencer.

Measles popped from the fur.

Rabbits and squirrels bolted into the forest.

The deer staggered as if drunk. His long ears twitched from the nerves exploding under the fur. His eyes rolled up in the sockets, showing white under the spasming lids. His mouth flapped, but no sound emerged. He pitched left, then yawed right, struggling for some semblance of forward motion. He scraped against a pine trunk, leaving fur and blood, and managed to get his nose into the underbrush.

Gemini fired the rest of the magazine.

The deer collapsed with a mighty splash.

"So where's that river?" Gemini said, handing the machine gun to Aquarius. Cancer and Virgo picked up the ejected brass shells and shoved them into an empty paint can. Aquarius slapped in another stick of 9-millimeter howlers, returned the gun to the gym bag.

"Straight south of here," Cancer said, zooming the GPS to street detail. "Lee River Bridge, that's what we dump her from."

The van accelerated.

12

"You're not going to die, Ladybug," Hawk repeated, touching Sammy's hair. The strands were as smooth as cashmere. *Like mother, like daughter. Bonnie's hair felt that way too. . . .*

He closed his eyes, trying to wish away the hurt and exhaustion that welled when he thought about his wife. No good. Like the aftermath of too much whiskey, thinking about Bonnie made the room spin faster. "Why do you think you are?"

"Callie said so."

"Callie's a classmate?"

"Uh-huh. Her mom told her everyone dies from rabbo-dabbo." Sammy's nickname for the rhabdomyosarcomal cancer eating her insides. "And that I won't make it till Christmas."

Anger lit Hawk like a road fuse. He'd find this woman and pull her lungs out, talking that way about his child. . . .

Get your head back in the game. Now.

"Callie's mom is wrong," Hawk said. "You aren't going to die, you're going to be fine."

"Really?"

"Really. Do you remember Miss Amanda? From that hospital we visited in Los Angeles?"

"No."

Hawk bit his lip. He'd told her a hundred times, but the illness had whacked her memory like a piñata. All he could do was tell her again. "Well, this hospital has a program that helps sick little girls with rabbo-dabbo. And Miss Amanda's in charge of it."

"Will she cure me, Daddy?" she said, sitting up straighter.

"Yes," he said, praying for the billionth time Dr. Barrett hadn't overhyped the miracles of the treatment, which involved such exotica as stem cells, nano delivery, and molecular engineering. "We'll fly there as soon as the hospital says okay."

He didn't tell her "okay" meant, "As soon as you give us three million dollars because your insurance doesn't cover this, Mr. Hawkins."

When Denton Schoolsby, the squishy-chinned man from patient financial services, told him and Bonnie the price of the experimental treatment, they felt dropkicked. Three million dollars was so staggering they couldn't get their heads around it.

But Lord, they tried. A second mortgage on their home. Loans from parents and friends. Draining their retirement accounts. Donations from strangers through the "S.O.S.— Save Our Samantha"—website, which they'd built with her formal name instead of Sammy because a consultant said sick little girls make more money than sick little boys. Begging via Facebook and Twitter. Telethons on cable access. Once, Hawk dug a nickel out of slimy brown bird crap on a sidewalk. He was so revolted he scrubbed his fingers for weeks.

They raised two million.

It wasn't enough. The hospital was adamant about having every penny in hand before starting treatment. "Stem cells don't grow on trees, Mr. Hawkins," Schoolsby had said when Hawk objected. "I'm sorry, but if you don't pay, we'll move to the next on the list."

Bonnie picked up side jobs. Hawk grabbed all the overtime the department could offer. They had no life other than Sammy, work, and fundraising. Hawk practically sleepwalked through his day, scraping by on caffeine, catnaps, and a self-flagellation that boiled down to, *Suck it up*. Bonnie coped for almost a year. Then, she couldn't. . . .

"It's going to work out great," Hawk said, aching so badly for a cigarette that his lips formed the familiar *O*. But except for the rare "victory cig," he'd quit smoking the day Sammy was diagnosed, hoping the sacrifice would please whatever gods looked out for little girls. It also added a few grand to the S.O.S. fund. "I'll get you to Los Angeles, and the rabbodabbo will disappear. Your mother and I will dance at your wedding."

"I'm getting married? Really, Daddy?" she said, eyes widening to full moons.

"When you're older."

"I'm going to get older?"

"Yes, baby, you are."

"Do you promise?"

"Cross my heart," Hawk said.

He wouldn't say the last part.

13

His ears twitched.

His nose wiggled.

He tried to open his eyes.

The glue-like blood crust made that impossible.

He listened awhile, heard no predators. Made a bleating sound, to see what might answer.

Nothing but wind.

He moved one limb, then another. The pain burned like fire, but movement didn't make it worse.

He flexed his legs. Turned his head left, right, up. Scraped the crust onto a fallen log, then peered over the mound of branches and needles that cloaked him from the giants.

No more deafening thunder-stick.

He worked himself upright, one leg, then the next. Felt his muscles shake violently. Saw breath-smoke pour from his mouth.

Became faint.

He unlocked his legs and settled back to the squishy ground.

After a while, he stood again, joints clicking, blood oozing from several of the holes.

Less shake.

Better.

He sniffed and licked the icy breeze. No more giants. Good. Their thunder-sticks stole the heartbeats of hundreds of his clan. Every time one toppled from the thunder, a giant pulled a shiny object from its fur. "Knife," he heard one call it, in the giants' strange language of clicks, grunts, and whistles. The giant split the fallen deer into many pieces, wrapped each piece in clear fur, and hauled them away in a box strapped to the giant's back. Very strange.

He whinnied.

Wondered where that came from. He'd never made that noise before.

He heard ice crackle as the pine needles broke into little pieces. He sank till the needles covered his hooves.

It didn't matter. He was upright.

He turned in a circle, searching again for predators. He fought the urge to lay down and close his eyes. He hoped his dizzy head would clear soon.

Because he needed to get to the river.

The river was home.

He'd be safe at the river.

He started out, one foot then the next, dragging along his unwilling body, shaking the wet from his antlers.

Dreaming of the river.

14

Emily propped herself up against the headboard as Marty stepped out of the shower.

He glistened in the bathroom lights, each bead of water a diamond against his tan. *Fairy dust,* she thought, recalling the glitter of the liquor store asphalt. His face was all angles and planes, loose now because he was content. They hardened into tectonic plates when he wasn't.

She watched him towel his head with the navy terrycloth, wipe his ears with a twisted corner. It took time to dry his body, she noted with not a little pride—Marty was six-six and two-forty, most of it hard from weightlifting, amateur auto racing, and his demanding job as the county sheriff's chief of detectives. His prowess at the latter had earned him the nickname "Little Dick Tracy" from his best friend, Hercules Branch, who also took great pleasure in adding a hyphen between Little and Dick.

Smiling at the guy-ness of it all, she scooted to Marty's side till their wall mirror captured them together. She traced her full lips with her pinkie, breathed the musky scent from his goose-down pillows.

Such a contrast we are.

She was a foot shorter and a hundred pounds lighter. Her eyes were emerald to his molten chocolate. His nose was long, and triple-humped from bikers. Hers was pert, and surprisingly straight for having smashed it flat during the first serial killer attack. His skin was leathery from his love of the outdoors, with fine wrinkles that reminded her of antique silk. Her skin was fine-pored and unblemished, just tawny enough to avoid makeup other than lipstick—

Knife swinging . . .

Heat billowed from her face.

Flesh ripping . . .

Her muscles trembled like mice in a bag.

Bones breaking . . .

She began curling in on herself.

Not now, not again, not twice in one day . . .

She bit her tongue till she tasted blood, hoping pain would abort the flashbacks. No good. Pinched her inner thigh till tears brightened her eyes. Wrapped hair around her finger, yanked till the roots ripped. *Oh yes, sweet pain, the panic is fading, lighter, lighter . . .*

"Still awake in there?" Marty called.

She struggled to speak.

"Em? You hear me?"

"Bright-eyed and bushy-tailed," she managed. Something her mother said before she and Dad were murdered—

Stop it. Focus on you and Marty.

They had wide, easy smiles, his crooked, hers straight. Her teeth were large and gleaming; his were Chiclets with a slight yellow cast but perfectly spaced. Both bodies were bounce-a-nickel tight, hers from a lifetime of morning runs, his from pumping iron. His hair was salt and pepper. Hers was chestnut, jungle-thick, short shag, and leavened with ruby highlights that weren't from a bottle—she'd had the glow-patches ever since she could remember.

Should I tell him the flashbacks are escalating?

Her hand went unconsciously to her neck.

No. He'll cancel 'cause he's worried. Tell him when he gets home.

"I'm so glad you understand me," she murmured to her silver lining in the mirror.

"Sorry, didn't catch that," Marty said, poking his head through the doorway.

"Nothing," she said, vaguely embarrassed he'd heard. "Just clearing my throat."

He studied her tip to toe, returned to toweling. She wondered not for the first time what it was about her that got him so hot. All she saw were the marks of the beast. They dotted her body, those glossy scars from bullets, knives, glass, flames, and noose. She wore them with pride, having earned them fighting for her life against the two serial killers who'd come to Naperville to destroy her. But they were ugly, the scars. . . .

"Why are you sitting with the light off?" he asked into the blackness of their bedroom.

"I'm resting my eyes," she said. "Till you're ready."

He folded the damp towel over the chrome bar, squaring the corners as she did. He'd started doing that after they moved in together. It said something about two lives becoming one. What, she didn't know. Something nice, though.

"Ready for what?" he asked.

Emily smiled.

"For whatever you like, Mr. Tracy."

15

"Hurry the hell up," Gemini said, head on swivels for unwanted visitors. Virgo did the same next to the left rear tire, where he'd attached a wrench to a lug nut. If anyone did chance by, it'd look like they were changing a flat. "I hate being this exposed."

"Going as fast as we can," Cancer said as Aquarius lowered Kandy to the churning river.

Gemini looked at the hoodoo clouds, thankful the rain had ceased. The respite wouldn't last—he heard more throat-clearing rumbles to the west—but he'd take what he could get. After shooting the deer, they'd agreed it was best to toss Kandy and hightail it back to the interstate. But when they got to the bridge, they saw gravel bars popping from the water like angry gray boils. They needed to aim her precisely. Otherwise, she could wind up on a gravel bar, attracting attention like an airport beacon. They broke out the clothesline, hitched it around her middle, started the slow descent—

"Headlights," Virgo warned. "Just popped the ridge."

"Cut the clothesline," Gemini ordered.

Aquarius swung a knife. The line parted with a *thwup*.

No splash. Cancer thrust his long upper body over the railing. "The rope snagged," he said, his tone saying he could hardly believe it either. "Hooked on some rebar sticking out of the concrete. Get me a roller extension I'll knock it loose—"

"Cherries," Virgo said, urgency in his voice.

Gemini's forehead leaked sweat as police lights started spinning atop the approaching vehicle. The van was swimming with narcotics, cash, and weapons. It was parked atop a young, beautiful teeny who'd drowned in her own blood. Problems didn't get much worse. He ran his hands over his mushroom haircut, wiped them on his cargo pants.

"We're commercial painters," he said. "Driving to St. Louis to start a new job." That part was true enough—after abandoning New Orleans after the hurricane, Gemini started the painting company in Chicago to cover his crew's more lucrative opportunities. "We pulled off the interstate for coffee. Nothing open, so we headed back. The tire blew, we stopped on this bridge to fix it. Everyone clear?"

Everyone nodded.

"Get on it."

Aquarius and Cancer leaned into the side door to retrieve their weapons. Virgo cranked the jack like his hair was on fire. The lug wrench slipped. His hand slammed the bridge, slashing his knuckle. "Son of a bitch," he said, sucking and spitting blood to make it stop. Drops ran down his chin. He resumed cranking with the other hand. The van inched upward.

Gemini climbed into the driver's seat as the cop turned on a door-mounted flood light. It lit them like the Fourth of July. The .45 in his waistband dug into his hip. He cranked the ignition till the engine caught, then fussed with the radio.

Locked in a station playing smooth jazz. He hated that sissy crap with its whiny-white-guy singers—"Entwine my soul with your honesty, my love"—but turned it loud anyway. Like the paint gear in back, it was camouflage, to show they were harmless.

He hung his elbow out the window, waiting for the storm.

Kandy jerked an inch closer to the mist cooking off the river, as the rebar, greasy with raindrops, loosened one finger of its grip on the clothesline.

16

"I'm sleeping, Dad," Tristen Bates said from under the blanket, which she'd hurriedly yanked over her head when her bedroom door creaked.

"Then wake up," Joshua said. "We need to talk."

He strode across the purple carpet, which still had the new-car smell from installation. He pulled a chair from his daughter's desk, dragged it over to the bed. Static arced between finger and chair. It sounded like a rubber band snapping. He eased into the chair, wincing as the arms crowded his hips. He turned her bedside lamp to the first click. The bulb glowed pale orange, casting spidery shadows across the small, basketball-postered room.

"Look at me when I'm speaking to you," he said.

Tristen sighed, but poked her head from the top of the plaid blanket.

"What?"

"Your mother loves you."

Silence.

"I know," she muttered.

"And you love her. So why do you treat her like a piece of shit?"

Tristen's eyes widened. Her father rarely swore. She tugged the blanket lower to see him more clearly. His face was hard, his eyes narrowed. He was breathing fast.

He was very angry. Something else she didn't see much.

She sat against the headboard. Listened to it squeak. Licked her dry lips. Wondered what to say.

"I don't," she tried.

"Yeah, you do," Joshua said. "Every time you talk to your mother, it's all over your face. You resent her. You don't like her. She pisses you off."

Tristen shrugged.

"That's not an answer."

She made an exasperated sound. "I guess."

"Also not an answer."

She squirmed uncomfortably. She didn't know what to say. Her professor father demanded logic. She had none to give. "Dad, I don't know what to tell you—"

"The truth, Tristen. I need to understand why you're acting this way."

"I wish I could," she said, her heart starting to race.

"Meaning you know and won't say?" he pressed. "Or meaning you don't know?"

"I . . . don't know."

He bent closer. "You're a good kid, Tris. Until a few months ago, a loving kid. Something changed. Are you taking drugs?"

Her face stung. "No."

"You can tell me, you know." His voice turned soft, reassuring. "We'll get you all the help you need, and we'll beat it together. There's great rehab places these days—"

"I swear, I'm not taking drugs."

Joshua nodded. "I didn't think so; you're smarter than that. Is someone bullying you?"

"No."

"Something at church? Basketball? Anywhere else?"

She shook her head. "Nobody's bothering me, Dad."

"Then what? Tell me what's going on with you. I need to know, so we can fix it. Your behavior is breaking your mother's heart. I won't have that."

Tears welled in Tristen's eyes. She plain didn't know where her intense anger with her mother came from. It was with her constantly, and sometimes got so heavy she could barely hack it. But she didn't understand it.

"Dad, I feel . . . I don't know. It's hard to explain. I just get, like, mad. Whenever I see Mom. Annoyed. Angry."

"Frustrated," he said.

"Yes. If I knew why, I'd tell you. But I don't. I can't. Something about her sets me off." Tristen touched her chest with her long, trembling fingers. "In here. Way deep inside. I can't figure it out. I don't know how." A tear dripped. Then another. She sniffed, trying to hold back the tide. She was thirteen. Practically an adult. Practically adults don't cry. They figure things out. They plan the work, then work the plan. Make the basket to win the game. They don't say, "I don't know," like some stupid little crybaby.

Her father leaned even closer. The bacon smell became overpowering, like he'd bathed in pork fat. She smiled, in spite of herself.

"You think this is funny, young lady?" Joshua roared, standing up so hard the chair flew backwards. "Some kind of joke?"

Tristen's smile collapsed. She shook her head hard. "It's just that you smell, like, uh, breakfast," she said.

He cocked his head. Picked up his shirttail. Buried his face in it.

"Well, damn," he said. "I guess I do."

They both laughed, cracking the ice.

"Look, Tris—"

"Look, Dad—"

"You first," he said, retrieving the chair and tucking it back on his hips.

Tears meandered down her porcelain skin.

"I don't know why I feel this way. About Mom. I just don't," she said, sobs bursting like hiccups. She tried to catch her breath. Couldn't. Forced herself to breathe. That worked, at least enough to keep talking. "I hate it. I do. You know that, right?"

Joshua nodded. "That's why it's painful for everyone, Tris. Especially your little sister."

Tristen sucked in her breath. "That's not true."

"Unfortunately, it is. It hurts her terribly to see you and Mom fight so much."

"I'd never hurt Alexa. Not in a million years."

"Not deliberately. But you are."

She hung her head, flushing.

"I don't mean to. I'd never hurt her. Or you. Or . . . Mom." Her eyes shone wet. "I know she loves me."

"She does," Joshua said. He took Tristen's hand, squeezed gently. "Your mother loves you so much she'd take a bullet for you. Without thinking twice."

Tristen's face folded so hard it looked like she was throwing up.

"I don't want her to take a bullet," she whispered.

Joshua cradled his daughter as the dam burst.

17

Jackson County Sheriff's Sergeant Spencer Abbott stifled a yawn as he squinted through the grime on his windshield. Man, was he beat. Fourteen hours humping this storm, another twenty likely. *Oh, well. That's why Folgers grows those beans.*

His blackwall tires splashed through a dozen puddles on the steep hill. He went airborne a few seconds as the cruiser flew over the crest, grinned at the belly flop on the other side. As the springs quit bouncing, the Lee River, its belly swollen with flood water, popped into view.

As did the rusted steel bridge, the unmoving van near the edge, and the four people milling around both.

Hmm, Abbott thought.

He stopped the cruiser and retrieved a pair of Zeiss binoculars from his patrol case. He fiddled with the focus knob, then scouted what was happening.

The van was a white Ford Econoline. It wore Illinois commercial tags. It was set up for cargo, with its plated-over side windows. It was old, late nineties, judging from the small, square headlights and the grille that resembled a gaping mouth. The sliding door was open, and kissing-close to the riveted railings. Abbott wrote the tags on his incident log, in case he needed to file a report.

It was parked at an angle on the northbound shoulder. The windshield was pocked with mud and mashed insects. The front bumper was dented. The antenna was bent. The oval Ford medallion was missing from the hood. A tree branch stuck out from the grille like an unlit cigar. The van looked rode hard and put away wet, most likely making it a company vehicle. Even a peasant would take better care of his personal ride, Abbott figured.

He turned on his roof flashers to keep from being rear-ended, and shifted the binoculars to the four individuals.

Two leaned against the upper bridge support. They were male, Caucasian, late twenties. They smoked what Abbott hoped were cigarettes. He wasn't in the mood for a penny-ante reefer bust. Too much paperwork on a night like this.

The first was five-eight and skinny. The other, standing a few feet to his buddy's right, was the same height, and twice as wide. "Portly," they used to call it. Each had his hands in his pockets, and a foot hooked over the lower bridge railing. They wore black jeans, green sweatshirts with the hoods down, and white gym shoes. Their breathing shot contrails into the cold, damp air. Their glum expressions said they'd rather be anywhere but on a rusty bridge in the middle of the nowhere. Abbott knew how they felt.

He shifted the binoculars to the third.

This one was pushing up the rear chassis with a tire jack. His jeans were blue. His shoes were dull black leather with thick soles. His hoodie was the faded red of an American Legion poppy. He looked up from the jack, mouthed something to the others.

Abbott repositioned the spotlight, flooded the van's interior with bright 'n' white.

The person slumped in the driver's seat was—*quelle surprise!*—male, Caucasian, late twenties. His hair was the glowing yellow of a harvest moon, cropped nearly bald at the sides, left long on top. What they called a mushroom cut. His ears were undersized, and tight to his skull. His head was wide at the top and angled sharply to a narrow chin. It reminded Abbott of a snake he'd seen in an old *Geographic* in his dentist's waiting room. The man's left arm dangled casually from the rolled-down window.

It bent into a friendly-looking wave.

"Six to County," Abbott said as he stowed the binoculars.

"Go ahead, Six," the lead dispatcher replied.

Kaye Barley's voice was shot with weariness, Abbott noted. Not surprising. It had been a long, crazy night pulling citizens out of flooded basements, burned houses, felled trees, snapped power lines, and stranded vehicles, along with arresting the morons who were taking advantage by looting. Abbott caught one walking out of a grocery store with an armful of Hostess Fruit Pies. It was unbelievable— the guy stole *apple pies* when the cash register was just ten feet away, sprung open for the world to see. Abbott could only shake his head at the slipping quality of the American criminal.

"I'm at the Lee River Bridge in Millston," he said, loud over the radio's static. "Four male subjects are parked in the middle, changing a flat. I'm going to lend 'em a hand."

"Do you need backup?"

Abbott considered it, shook his head. Deputies were spread across hundreds of square miles of west central Wisconsin, handling a phone book's worth of calls. Even the sheriff's older children were taking reports, that's how stretched they'd become from this bitch of a storm. Pulling someone for backup meant something else didn't get fixed. Besides, didn't the Texas Rangers say, *One riot, one Ranger*?

"Nah," Abbott said. "I'll check they know what they're doing, then head to Red and Joanne's, write up their lightning strike. Red'll need the report for the insurance man."

"Poor Red," Kaye said. "His homeowner's is going to double."

"Triple," Abbott said. "Insurance loves to poke your eyes out then charge you for being blind." He read out the tag numbers, described the Econoline.

"Wait one," Kaye said.

He tuned in the fire frequencies as she searched. Man, those guys were hopping. More than the deputies, even. He admired how hard firemen worked. Not that he'd ever tell them, of course. It was more fun to mock them about sleeping with their teddy bears in the firehouse while the poor sheriffs ground out midnight to eights.

"Tag's registered to a painting company in Chicago," Kaye said.

"As in Illinois?"

"And they say college is wasted on cops," Kaye said.

Abbott snorted. "Makes these boys painters, I guess. Heading to a job."

"Why on their way, as opposed to going home?"

"Who else would drive in this mess except someone who doesn't get paid unless he shows up?"

"You," the dispatcher said.

"Yeah, but I'm too dumb to get out of the rain," Abbott said, laughing. "Anything important I need to do before talking to them?"

"Bring me a box of doughnuts."

"Custard-filled? Or jelly?" Abbott said.

"You find either, I'll name that bridge after you," Kaye said.

18

Alexa Bates wrung her hands. Her big sister was her idol. She was the toughest jock at Kennedy Junior High. One of the smartest, earning straight A's. The most popular with classmates. She even got respect from the boys Mom said were a half step from juvenile detention. Nobody and nothing bothered Tristen.

So why was she crying so hard?

It began when Dad said something about Mom taking a bullet for her. But that was only a guess—Alexa hadn't woken till Dad shouted, "You think this is funny?" She kicked off her blankets and hurried to the wall separating their rooms. Sticking her ear against the Sheetrock, she'd expected laughter—that's what funny meant, right? But there was only Tris bawling and Dad lecturing. Whatever "it" was, it was serious.

She had to make Tris feel better.

Alexa had just turned nine. She was chubby. Clumsy. Not pretty or outgoing, and stinky at sports. Yes, her IQ was off the charts, the school told Mom and Dad, who'd bragged to the family at supper that night. Tris gave her hugs and high fives, genuinely proud. But to Alexa, the "honor" made her even more of a nerd, not a somebody like her adored sister.

Made her a target.

A half-dozen older girls caught up with Alexa one day. They slapped her cheeks scarlet, then "put out the fire" by dousing her with Cokes. They called her "fattie" and "puke" and "toad." Alexa tried to kick and chop them like Mom did in karate tournaments. They laughed, then knocked her to the ground, spitting all over her.

Tris saw the bruises and dried hockers as soon as Alexa got home, and demanded the truth. Alexa told her, unable to stop shaking, so miserable she wished she would die. Tris hugged her, ruffled her hair, told her everything would be fine. Then she went crazy, racing her mountain bike to the playground where the girls hung out. She hit them till they cried then shoved them in the mud. The girls tried to fight back. Tris made them eat worms and leaves. Nobody touched Alexa after that.

Alexa was desperate to return the favor.

Her round face clouded as she thought about what to do.

A couple of minutes later, she brightened. She knew.

It would be awesome.

19

Marty pulled a small, square box from his armoire.

"This was in the mailbox," he said, tossing it on the bed. "Must have come after you brought in the mail."

"Uh-oh," Emily said.

"Yeah."

She began to tremble.

Marty sat next to her. "Yeah," he said quietly. "Hacksaw's back." They'd nicknamed him that because that's what he used to cut apart his victims. "Want me to open it?"

She shook her head.

He repeated the offer.

She blew out her breath. Studied the box, picked at the tape. Broke a nail. Sucked her finger, cursing. Marty handed her a knife. She cut away the tape, pulled off the lid.

An obscenity stared back.

"It's someone's middle finger," Emily said, swallowing hard.

"Yeah," Marty said, looking at the ragged stub. "And there's the paperwork."

She donned latex gloves and unfolded the too-familiar card.

Third time's the charm, it said in ten-point Times New Roman.

Marty sighed. "How many parts does this make?" he asked. "Twelve?"

"Thirteen," Emily said. "Lucky me."

He nodded sourly.

She put the finger, note, and packaging into an evidence bag and locked it in the collection box on the front stoop. Marty called CSI. "Hacksaw again," he said. "Come get it."

He disconnected, looked at her.

"No, I don't want you to cancel," she said.

"I would," he said.

"I know," she said.

The first shipment arrived a year ago. The box was small and square, with a made-up return address. It bore a Chicago postmark, and contained a human neck bone sawn from the victim by a hacksaw. The FBI couldn't match it to anyone, as Hacksaw had boiled it in sodium hypochlorite—bleach—to destroy the DNA.

Same with the thumb, leg, elbow, shin, back, hip, collar, and spinal bones he sent, and the nose, nipple, and eyeball: the DNA was boiled away. According to crime lab analyses of the tool marks, the same saw blade was used to harvest the twelve body parts from the twelve separate victims, and presumably would match this thirteenth. The cartons they arrived in were anonymous—prepaid, postmarked from Chicago, Omaha, St. Louis, Minneapolis, Kansas City, and Detroit, and dropped into equally anonymous sidewalk mailboxes. No fingerprints. No security videos. No clothing fibers. No nothing.

Each part was accompanied by the folded card. Not all had been laser-printed like this one. One was scrawled in orange Crayola. Another was scissored, one letter at a time, from newspaper headlines. Another was pecked out on a manual typewriter, which the lab identified as a 1957 Underwood. Yet another was written in silver paint. It infuriated Emily, and sometimes she wished he'd attack her already, get it over with. But there'd been no contact from this third serial killer. Just the parts and *Third time's the charm*.

She shuddered, and changed topics.

"Do you have everything?" she said.

"I've got jerky and bullets," Marty said, folding his camouflage pants. "What more could I possibly need?"

"Shavon make the jerky?"

"Yep. It's a fresh batch, he says, smoky and sweet. Comes from that elk he bagged."

"Taste like chicken?"

He smiled. "Beef, actually. Want some?"

She nodded.

He fished a piece from the Ziploc. She bit and chewed. Her face brightened.

"This is scrumptious," she said.

"Yep," he said. "So to answer your question, I have everything. All I need is the deer to cooperate."

"I wouldn't," Emily said, putting Under Armour in his duffel bag. "Were I they."

"That's why Shavon gave me the jerky," Marty said. "To quote, 'If Bambi kicks your ass again, you won't starve.'"

Emily smiled. The last time Branch and Marty went hunting, Branch hauled home eighty pounds of venison and a nice rack of antlers. Marty didn't see a single deer worth shooting, not even a doe. He hadn't been shut out in all the years they'd gone, and he'd plotted a million strategies to avenge his honor.

"All right, let's check it," he said.

She clicked the lamp to reading strength, looked at his packing list. "Pants."

"Check."

"Shirts."

"Check."

"Rain gear."

"Check."

"First-aid kit."

"Check."

"Maps."

"State of Wisconsin. County of Jackson. Black River Falls, Millston, and the Black River State Forest. Topographic of area hunting zones. Check, check, check . . ."

Ten minutes later, Marty zipped his waterproof pack and duffel and placed them outside the bedroom door. "Only thing missing is the deer," he said.

"And your rifle," she said, miming the throw of the hand loop that jacked bullets into the firing chamber of a lever-action rifle. "Taking the Winchester?"

"Oh, yah, sure, you betcha," he said.

She clapped her hands to her face, like that kid in *Home Alone*. "That's either the worst Sarah Palin I've ever heard . . ."

Marty made a sour face.

"Or it's Marge Gunderson in *Fargo*."

"Very good, grasshopper," he said. " 'Do ya feel lucky, punk? Well, do ya?'"

"Harry Callahan, *Dirty Harry*," she said.

"Gotta love Clint," he agreed. " 'I want vipers, snipers, mugs, thugs, nitwits, halfwits, bank robbers, train robbers, ass-kickers, shit-kickers, and Methodists. . . .'"

"Uhhhh . . ."

He mimed riding a horse, shooting a six-gun.

"Hedley Lamarr," she said, snapping her fingers. "*Blazing Saddles*. But that doesn't count. It's not a cop movie."

"Sure it is," Marty argued. "Cleavon Little was the sheriff of Rock Ridge. . . ."

They continued quoting dialogue as Marty pulled two handguns from his nightstand. The larger was the .44 magnum he carried on his belt in case of bear attacks. The smaller was the 9-millimeter "baby Glock" he hid in his front pants pocket. "Bad guys find the first gun, they think they've disarmed you," he'd replied when she'd asked why two. "I prefer they're wrong."

She scanned the checklist one more time. "That's everything," she confirmed, folding it into an airplane. Marty grabbed it near the ceiling, returned the toss. It sailed under the bed.

"Hope that's not an omen," he said.

"Since when are you superstitious?"

"Since Bambi dissed me and I became the butt of Branch's cruel jokes."

"Yeah, like you've never insulted him," she said.

Marty tried to look offended.

"Not buying it, darling, I know how you two get," she said, cat-curling against the headboard. "Is he picking you up at four?"

"Yep," Marty said. "We'll head straight out, stop in the Dells for breakfast." He rubbed his hands and smacked his lips.

"By that you mean heart healthy, right?" she said. "No unnecessary sugar, fat, or caffeine?"

He looked at her.

Puffed out his cheeks and belly.

"Nothing unnecessary, I promise," he said.

Emily laughed, loving Marty's little-boy excitement. The Wisconsin deer hunt came but once a year, and he and Branch had tramped the woods, fields, bogs, and lakes of the Dairy State for two decades. As always, they sought that mystical buck with an antler rack so heavy and grand it seemed a crown on a Caesar.

This year, they'd asked her along. Emily had hunted the Wisconsin northwoods with her father when she was a teenager, and after three years of tactical rifle training, she was almost as good a shot as Annie. Which said something. Emily's best friend, in addition to commanding Naperville SWAT, was a U.S. Army sniper instructor who'd been blooded in Iraq and Afghanistan. Emily was pleased to be asked.

But she'd turned them down. This was the boys' time to do whatever they saw fit. Besides, they liked to rough it—tent, cook fire, open-air latrine. Getting away from civilization was so essential to their perfect hunt that the moment they pulled out of the driveway, they turned off their cell phones, BlackBerrys, and pagers. They wore the electronic slave collars the other fifty-one weeks. The fifty-second was not negotiable. None of that was for her. She was happy to sweat her buns off in mud, blood, dirt, and weeds, but at the end of the day she wanted a hot shower, soft mattress, and a glass of chilled pinot grigio.

"I'm really going to miss you," she said.

Marty leaned down and kissed her. "It's not too late to join us."

She drummed her chin like she was actually considering it. "You think there's a motel that smells like curry and has dried lumpy stuff on the pillow?"

He laughed. "Several. Want me to make a reservation?"

"Mm. You know how much I'd love that," she said. "But I just remembered Chief Cross asked me to stay in Naperville this week."

"Just remembered," Marty said.

"Uh-huh. He says someone has to protect the innocent while you two heroes are gone."

"Selfless is your middle name," he said, patting her cheek.

"Actually, it's Flush Toilet. . . ."

They talked a while longer; then the fog in her head became insistent. "If I don't get some sleep," she said, yawning so hard her jaw clicked, "I'll be a zombie in the morning."

"It is morning," Marty pointed out.

"Don't remind me," Emily said, looking at her alarm clock. "Nap with me till he arrives?"

"You already wore me out, little lady."

"A *nap*-nap," she said, pinching his arm. "I'll set the alarm so you don't oversleep."

"Nah. If I lay down, I won't want to get up." Thunder shook the apartment, and he glared at the ceiling. "Hasn't rained *once* since Halloween, and now this," he complained. "The Big Fella clearly has it in for me."

"Wouldn't you, if you were Him?"

"Hell, yeah." Long, rolling waves rattled the apartment like old bones. When he was a kid, Uncle Al and Aunt Marlyne told him thunder was God bowling strikes in Heaven. He still liked to think that. "Want some earplugs?"

"No, thanks. An air horn couldn't keep me awake." She snuggled into the emerald sheets, shivering delightedly as cold whistled in from the storm. Marty draped the cranberry-stripe comforter over her, tucked it around her neck.

"Wake me up when you leave," she murmured. "Wanna say good-bye."

"You got it." He wouldn't, of course. She desperately needed the sleep. He'd leave a mushy note instead. "Sweet dreams."

No response but soft breathing.

A wind gust knocked over the whipped-cream can. He picked it up, nozzled it at sleeping beauty. Not even a hiss of propellant. They'd thoroughly exhausted it. Which was nice.

"Hehe," he said.

She replied with sleep-mumbles.

He trundled down the hall to lubricate the Winchester. After that, he'd check the weather radars, then shave nice and close, sparing, per usual, his moustache. He hadn't shaved the luxuriant handlebar since the first black hair sprouted in high school. With one exception.

The day his wife died.

Because they'd met in grad school, she'd never seen the skin under his moustache. She'd teased him about it for years. He stood firm. Giving up his moustache would be like cutting off an ear, and he was no Van Gogh.

Then they found bone cancer.

Widespread.

Incurable.

Four months after the shocking diagnosis, Marty woke before dawn. He turned over to hold his wife. His hand touched bare sheets. He blinked confusion, then remembered she'd moved into hospice and he still wasn't used to her side being empty.

He sat up, drummed his feet on the carpet. Walked into their bathroom, grabbed eyebrow scissors from the medicine cabinet. He had no idea what was driving him to do this. He just knew it needed to be done, and now.

He dumped the hairy clumps in the waste can. Lathered himself with Barbasol, shaved to a glass finish, then dabbed Old Spice on his freshly shorn lip. The skin tingled, unused to the cold bite of aftershave. He shrugged into the clothes his wife liked best—button-fly blue jeans, red T-shirt, black leather jacket—picked up coffee at Dunkin' Donuts, drove to the hospice, and walked into her room.

His wife stared.

Opened her mouth without speaking. Stared some more.

Then giggled, eyes bright.

"As I live and breathe, Martin Benedetti," she said in a voice pounded gravelly by the disease. "I finally know everything about you." He crawled into bed with her and told all the cop stories he could remember, the funny ones with the stupid crooks that cracked her up. They reminisced about their first date. Their first kiss. The first time they Did It. The day they bought their house . . .

Then she died. He knew the precise moment because he was holding her with both arms and legs and felt the essence of her just . . . leave.

They stayed that way till her scent turned waxy. Then he closed her eyelids with his fingers, and called for the nurses.

That night, after the funeral arrangements were made and the relatives called, he retrieved the moustache clippings from the trash can. Spread them on the kitchen table, mixed them with drippings from a Christmas candle. He pinched and molded the waxed hair into the shape of a handlebar, complete with upturned tips.

His eyes filled. He blinked it away, smoothed the work till it was perfect.

At the funeral, he pressed the moustache into her hand, folded her fingers around it. Branch saw it, nodded microscopically, then turned away, pretending he hadn't noticed.

Marty appreciated his best friend's thoughtfulness.

He also was deeply happy this most intimate part of him would be with her forever, because there'd never be another woman he'd love as fiercely, as loyally, and as thoroughly.

He thought of Emily, wrapped in emerald and cranberry.

Until you.

20

"Think she's awake?" Alexa whispered.

"Only one way to find out," Tristen said. "Mom. Hey, Mom."

No reply but a fluttering whistle.

Tristen grabbed a magazine from the pile. Held it arm's-length and tore out a page. The slick paper made a loud ripping noise.

Mom didn't stir.

Tris wadded the paper, sky-hooked it off Mom's chest.

Nothing but the flutter-whistle.

"Let's do it," Alexa said.

Brushes, bottles, and Magic Markers poking from between their fingers, the girls crept across the lamp-lit family room. Annie's head drifted. The girls froze, tensing their legs to flee if her eyelids started moving.

The flutter-whistling became louder.

They reached the leather couch.

Annie's head was a meadow of springy blond curls. They

wedged into the gap where the back cushions met. Her torso and legs were upright, her arms crossed over her tidy breasts. Her laptop computer was slumped to one side, her paperwork slumped to the other. Some of the paper remained on the slippery leather seat. The rest were scattered across the floor. Her bare feet sat in the middle of the mess, square-up on the carpet.

Tristen put her lips to Alexa's ear.

"You're pretty smart," she whispered. "For a Mo."

Alexa felt a surge of pride. Tristen called only her best friends morons.

They uncapped the bottles and began.

Deep in the shadows, Joshua watched the girls work. He didn't know what they were up to. Didn't matter, really. They were together, and they were happy. That's what counted.

Tristen surveyed the room, hand over her eyes like a pirate captain. If they spotted him, it would ruin the moment. He tiptoed away.

Went into the master bedroom and closed the door. Retrieved his cell phone from his armoire. Padded into the bathroom, switched to text messaging, thumbed:

HAVEN'T HEARD FROM YOU. EVERYTHING ALL RIGHT?
LET ME KNOW.

No signature necessary.
The recipient knew.
He pushed *send*, returned the cell, and went to bed.

21

"Howdy, boys," Spencer Abbott said as he walked toward the van. He'd ditched his bulky slicker because the rain had stopped, but left his Smokey the Bear hat swaddled in the waterproof yellow nylon. "Fine night you picked to visit Jackson County."

"You can say that again," Gemini said from the driver's seat. "We water-skied the entire way, and that was in the middle of I-94. I've never driven in a storm this big."

Abbott picked up a faint accent. It was southern, but not deep-fried. Atlanta? Louisville? No. A shovel of grits in the musical twang. Like that political guy on TV, the baldy who pimped for the Democrats. What was it, Cajun? *Yep, Cajun. This guy's from New Orleans.* Abbott smiled. He had an ear for languages. He'd learned a half dozen over the years, letting him pick up good money moonlighting as a court translator.

"More on the way, if that thunder's any indication," Abbott said. Then again, the wind was hitting him in the face now, instead of sideways. Maybe the next round would blow straight into Canada. *Let the Mounties take the next bath, eh?* "Where you in from?"

"Minneapolis," Gemini said, turning off the music so he could better judge the cop's tone and inflection. He reminded himself to be careful—the man's prudence showed in the way his hand stayed near the butt of his gun. "We just finished a job there. Due in Kansas City tonight to start another one."

Abbott raised an eyebrow. "And you're driving I-94? That'd odd. From Minneapolis, I-35 is a straight shot to Kansas City."

The cop wasn't poking holes in his story, Gemini sensed. He was being helpful. Rural policemen were good that way, when they weren't blizzarding tickets because the county needed the money and you weren't local. "I have to go to Chicago first. Change my clothes, make sure the lights are on in the office. My company's based there."

"I-94 makes sense, then," Abbott conceded. "What kind of work you do?"

"We're commercial painters."

"Tough racket," Abbott said, meaning it. He'd recently scraped his tri-level bare and coated it with Sherwin-Williams's finest. His calluses sprouted calluses over the six weeks that nasty chore took—thinking about it even now made his hands hurt. "You do houses?"

Gemini shook his head. "Warehouses, stores, like that. Nothing as big as an auto plant or refinery, but I'll get there one of these days."

"So you're the owner, then."

"I am," Gemini said. "The boys and I supervise the crews. We work right alongside them to make sure the jobs get done on time."

"Painting 'R' Us," chorused the two at the bridge railings as they paintbrushed the air.

Abbott nodded. "Glad to know there's still a few hard-working young men in these United States," he said. "Most'd rather sit on their butts, watching videos." He glanced at the tire, which looked properly round and firm. "Need a hand with that?"

"No, thanks. I already changed it," the man in the black shoes said from the jack. "Soon as I stow this, we're outta here."

Something tingled in Abbott's head. He didn't know what. Maybe he needed more coffee. "Don't forget those," he said, chinning at the lug nuts on the pavement. "Losing a wheel at highway speed would screw up your whole day."

"Good Lord," Gemini said, horrified. "Thanks for catching that, Sergeant." He swung his long legs out of the van, put out his hand. They shook, exchanged small talk, watched Black Shoes retrieve the lug wrench and spin on the nuts.

"No problem," Abbott said.

"Could you do me one last favor?" Gemini said.

"What's that?" Abbott said.

"Tell me how to get back to I-94. I'm all turned around. . . ."

Bridge metal sang like coyotes. Kandy twisted in the rising wind. Each revolution pulled at the clothesline, which tugged at the jam, which yanked on the rebar.

Weakening the rusty spur's hold with each pass of her swaddled head.

Weakening . . .

Weakening . . .

The jam popped.

The rope went slack.

Kandy plunged.

* * *

Aquarius, stretching on the bridge railing, saw Kandy bounce off the gravel bar and tumble down the slope. She stopped two feet short of the churning water. He grimaced, then turned and caught Gemini's eye. Shook his head minutely.

"Ah, thanks again, Sergeant," Gemini said, stepping toward the cruiser to give the cop the hint. "I'm sure you have more important things to do than babysit a bunch of painters. . . ."

Abbott walked toward his pearl-gray cruiser, nodding at the men he thought of as Cajun, Fat, Skinny, and Black Shoes. He wondered why Cajun seemed so eager for him to leave. Solicitous of Abbott's time on a storm-drenched night? Or something less altruistic?

He felt another funny tingle.

It wasn't coffee, he knew.

It was Cajun's hand.

They'd shaken enough for Abbott to realize it was soft, not the callused leather of someone who painted factories for a living. The man had flat-out lied to his face, without a breath of hesitation. *And how'd you know I was a sergeant?* Abbott's chevrons were on his shirt sleeves, which were covered by his bomber jacket. The only chevrons visible were the small, flat-black ones pinned to his shirt collars. Most people wouldn't notice them in the single-bulb bridge lighting. The few who did called him, erroneously, "Officer." Only cops and crooks knew the difference. And a cop would have flashed his tin and laid on the yada about fellow warriors on the thin blue line.

Then there's the tire.

When Abbott watched them through the binoculars, Black Shoes was pumping the van up to remove the allegedly flat tire. Moments later, when Abbott offered to help, the man claimed he'd already changed it.

Abbott's brain clicked with analysis. . . .

Question: When did the flat magically reinflate?

Answer: There wasn't any flat.

Conclusion: They're lying to hide something worse.

Problem: Four of them, one of me, and they're probably armed.

Solution: I need a bigger boat.

Abbott started hacking like he'd swallowed pepper flakes.

"Whoa, dude, you all right?" Cajun said, looking concerned.

Abbott bent double at the waist, blocking Cajun's view of the microphone Velcro'd to his shirt. He felt around for the red button recessed into the bottom. The mayday signal would bring every cop within fifty miles. He found it, pushed.

It didn't depress.

Abbott tried again. No good. It was stuck.

Stay calm. Stay calm. Stay calm.

"Swallowed . . . wrong," Abbott coughed. "Fine . . . in a . . . minute."

"Want a drink?" Cajun said. "We got Pepsi in the truck. I'll bring you a can and get you on your way—"

"Thanks, no . . . I'm better now," Abbott said. The radio on his belt contained another red button, and they couldn't both be frozen. But Cajun's eyes had narrowed with suspicion. Abbott decided to get to the cruiser, drive to cover, call for reinforcements. Then break out his assault rifle and keep the four pinned like flies on sticky paper, till the cavalry arrived.

Walk away slow and easy . . .

He hacked a few more times to stay in cover, then started for the cruiser, praying he'd get there before a bullet hit his back.

* * *

Frothy waves rushed under Kandy's heels, hips, and head, eroding the gravel, which let in more water, which floated her head, then legs, then butt and back.

She slid into the water like a smelly canoe.

My hands are hidden, they'll never see, Abbott thought as he neared the cruiser. *Reach for the red button on my belt. Play it cool, they won't know what hit them.*

The cop's shoulder was moving up and back, Gemini saw. He'd smelled the con, and was going for the pistol on his belt. "Waste him!" he shouted, pulling his .45 from his waistband, bloodlust squirting out his ears.

Abbott was simultaneously whirling, pulling his gun, searching for cover, and locking his eyes on Cajun, whom he'd shoot first as leader of the pack. He watched three pistols and a machine gun free themselves from hiding. His breath caught in his throat, but he wasn't afraid. That surprised him. All the sweat-ass training he'd endured to prepare for a multiple-subject gun battle, all the scenarios, the mental what-ifs, he always figured he'd be afraid.

Instead, he heard himself order them to give up, and them refuse to obey.

Fair enough.

He pulled the trigger of his .40-caliber SIG Sauer, sending flame-geysers at the gunmen. They wheeled and ducked, and the hollowpoint Hydra-Shok bullets thocked into the grille of the van. Abbott sprinted for the rifle in his trunk. The Uzi acquired him, belched fire and smoke. He barely heard the gun go off. *Silencer*, his lizard brain screamed.

He jinked like a Green Bay receiver. Most of the slugs flew wide. But one smashed into his belt, sending his key ring down a bridge hole. Another whacked into his bulletproof vest. The shock wave sucked out his momentum. He lurched now rather than ran.

The Uzi fired. . . .

Three bullets stitched his vest, breaking ribs underneath. The crushing pain made his brain clicky.

The Uzi fired. . . .

Two bullets plowed his unarmored left arm, chewing muscle and nerves. He screamed at the unholy burn.

The Uzi fired. . . .

He tripped on a raggedy pothole, smashed face-first into the bridge deck. Bullets buzzed just over his head. He rolled like a dervish, blood sputtering from his broken nose. Bullets pinged off the pavement the moment he left it. He reached the back of the cruiser, where he was relatively protected. He fumbled for his keys. Looked down when he couldn't find them. *Shot away*, he realized. He couldn't unlock the trunk.

Bullets closed in on him.

He returned fire with the SIG, fumbling for the panic button on the radio. His numbed index finger dropped it like a one-putt. He bared his teeth. No matter what happened to him, his brothers would blow so many holes in these bastards they'd look like a Swiss cheese—

He heard a clatter. Looked down again. Went cold. The button had fallen off, followed by the faceplate and battery. One of the bullets had shattered the two-way.

Did the signal get off in time?

"Cop's behind the squad car. Get him," he heard Cajun bark.

Abbott peered around the trunk. Black Shoes, Fat, and Skinny were fanning out from the van, wolves on a crippled deer. He fired fast, forcing them to back off. Then he broke

for the cruiser's front passenger door, which he'd left unlocked. Bullets bit into his legs. He returned fire, stumbling
backwards to the trunk. His last shot locked the slide back,
silencing the SIG.

Silencing.

Silencing.

Silencing.

"Hey! He's out of ammo," Skinny shouted.

"You got that right, pal," Abbott muttered. He figured he
had ten seconds before they swarmed—six to decide he
wasn't playing possum, four to swarm him.

Working one-handed because the other was Silly String,
he punched the magazine release. The empty mag popped
from the handle with a *cling*. He laid the gun on the pavement and ripped a fully charged mag from his belt. *Two seconds. Three seconds. Four seconds.* He clamped the full mag
between his knees, fresh bullets peeking from the top.

He saw the killers creep from behind the van.

He picked up the SIG, put the mag in the handle. His vision blurred. His lightheadedness became profound. He ignored it. He ignored everything but the reload. Hand shaking
like a drug overdose, he slid the mag into the SIG till it
clicked in place.

Triumphant, he lifted the gun.

The mag popped out.

Cursing, he slammed the gun butt on his knee, reseating
the mag. He mashed the slide release, ramming the first bullet into the firing chamber.

Seven seconds.

Best he'd ever done one-handed.

I'll brag about it if I live.

He lined up the glowing green night sights and fired.
"Ahhhgh!" Black Shoes screamed, pitching to the ground as
the others scrambled. "I'm hit, Dettmer, I'm hit!"

"No names, goddammit!" Cajun screamed back.

"He's bleeding, Gemini," Skinny said. "Want me to go get him?"

"Get the cop first," Cajun ordered. Louder, to his downed crewman, "Can you hold on?"

"Yeah, Dettmer—uh, Gemini, yeah," Black Shoes grunted. His anguish was profound. "Just kill . . . that cop . . . uhhhnnn . . ."

Gemini. Dettmer. Gemini is Dettmer. Gemini is Cajun is Snakehead is Dettmer, Abbott thought, grinding his teeth against the pain. *Remember that.* He peeked around the bumper, saw Black Shoes rocking side to side, clutching his midsection. Abbott laid his sights on the man's flat head. Take out the brain stem and he'd fight no more.

The others spotted the movement and sprayed Abbott's position.

Abbott drew into a ball, letting Detroit steel absorb the lead. He peered under the cruiser, looking for shoes. There—tennies. He bounced bullets off the pavement, trying to connect a ricochet. No screams. The tennies scrambled backwards, though. That was something.

Another slide lock, another fumbling reload. His final magazine.

He peeked around the tire, chin on the road to minimize his profile. Cajun, Fat, and Skinny were headed his way again, hate pouring from skeleton faces. Abbott knew now he wouldn't get inside the cruiser. He was inches from the door, but it was too far because they were too close. He was down to a few bullets. He was bleeding. He was outmanned and outgunned.

But not out-thought.

He worked his legs under him, tried to stand. Branding irons hissed in ribs, legs, and arms. His head swirled so violently he felt seasick. He made it to half crouch. He pushed the gun around the trunk, pulled the trigger as fast as he could.

"Here I come, you soulless bastards!" he bellowed over the wall of sound. "Die, die, die, die, die!" He watched them scurry back like the rats they were.

He staggered to the side of the bridge. Leaned against the railing, pushed the SIG over his head. Sighted carefully, praying the wobbles to stop for that one brief instant.

The bridge lamp exploded.

"Yessss," he hissed. Now everything was black but his roof lights. That was fine. The pulsating colors would distract them more than they'd illuminate him.

Spencer Abbott fired his remaining rounds, then crawled between the railings and jumped off the bridge.

"Who in tarnation would play with firecrackers in this weather?" Walter Meesely said.

"Hmph?" Doris Meesely answered, groggy from being shaken from a sound sleep.

"Don't you hear it?" Walter said, cupping his ears. His expression changed from grumpy to concerned. "Hey, that's not fireworks. Someone's shooting out there."

Doris pulled the electric blanket over her head. "You're dreaming about the war again," she said. "It's nothing, just thunder. Go back to sleep."

"I know what gunfire sounds like, woman," Walter grumped. "I was in the war, you know. The big one. Dubya dubya two."

"You showed Patton how to win, I know," she said. "Now go back to sleep."

Walter looked at her under the blanket. She was eighty-two, and lumpy. Then again, he was eighty-three and lumpier. He squeezed her in his favorite place.

"Dang it, Walter, I'm trying to sleep."

He chortled, patted her wide behind. "Guess I'll check the windows, then," he said. "Long as you ain't interested."

"I am interested, you old coot," she said. "But not till these curlers are out of my hair, and that's not till nine in the a.m. You're going to phone the sheriff, aren't you?"

Walter sighed.

"I darn well better know you after sixty-three years of marriage," Doris said, squeezing his bird leg. "Tell Kaye hi for me, and remind her I'm dropping off her cake plate tomorrow."

Abbott felt his left knee shatter as bullets struck his body. He hit the water like the nose cone of a missile.

"I got the sumbitch," Gemini bragged, scanning the water. "Blood squirted from that knee like a sump pump."

"I got him too," Aquarius said, nodding rapidly. "We all did. Bastard's dead."

Did one of them come with me? Abbott wondered as frigid water shot up his nose. *Are his hands around my neck?* He'd stepped outside himself to observe a man looking just like him doing everything the real Abbott would find impossible. . . .

It's my hat, he realized as he slammed into the boulders at the bottom of the river. The deep crown of his Smokey the Bear sheriff's hat had filled with water, tightening the narrow leather neck strap into a garrote. *My hat is choking me, get it off, get it off!*

Unable to see in the murk, he tried using his fingers. No good. Too swollen to wedge into the choke collar. Abbott saw blackness at the edges of his eyes. He had only seconds before he drowned. He felt around for something, anything, to pry off the strap. A stick. A flat stone . . .

Remembered he had a knife.

He reached across himself, unclipped the Strider folding knife from his trouser pocket. It slipped from his near useless fingers. He paddled frantically at the water. Slapped the knife. Took the handle in a choke hold. The exertion forced bubbles from his lips. His chest burned. The black edges were nearly to the center of his eyes.

He flicked open the stainless steel blade, shoved the tip under the strap. The edge sliced into his throat. *Don't cut worse,* he prayed. *Don't cut deep.*

Darkness closed.

Strap parted.

The Smokey rushed up and away.

He could breathe.

But all was water.

Air or die, his lungs screamed.

He pushed off the rocks one-legged and swam for the top. His head broke the waterline as his elbow thumped into something soft. He sucked in fresh air, gasping and coughing and retching, praying the river would cover the noise. He drank cold air till he was dizzy, clutching the something-soft like a life preserver. He heard guns pop. He ducked under the something-soft, held it like a shield, felt the bullets thwock it.

"Idiots, you're shooting the girl," he heard Cajun yell from somewhere over his head. "The cop's over there. Thirty yards downstream to your left—yeah, that way. Empty your guns."

The Smokey, Abbott realized as World War III erupted. *They're shooting at my hat. It's wrapped in the yellow slicker, so it's easy to see in the water. They think I'm still wearing it.*

He let the current take him, hiding under the something-soft, his good hand jammed into it below the water line so they wouldn't see.

The gunshots faded.

* * *

"How we getting out of here?" Aquarius said, scowling at the pools of green and red spreading from under the van. "That's coolant and transmission fluid. Cop shot us up good."

"He didn't shoot the cruiser," Gemini said.

Aquarius considered that. Grinned.

"What'll we do with Virgo?" Cancer said.

"You two grab the car," Gemini said. "I'll take care of Virgo."

"Heyyyy, Aaaabbottttttt," Kaye crooned into a tactical radio channel she knew the sergeant monitored. She ran her hands through her short white bob, fingered the silver dangly in her right ear. "Where're those doughnuts you owe me, huh?"

No reply.

Maybe he's taking a leak. The dispatcher waited a minute, tried again.

Still no reply.

She switched to the main channel. "County to Sheriff's Six, report your status."

More silence.

Kaye frowned. This was very unlike Abbott. He never forgot to clear an assignment, and responded immediately to dispatch requests. She messaged his pager, dialed his cell. The page went unanswered. The cell went to voicemail.

Worried, she called Red and Joanne.

"Spencer hasn't shown up yet," Red said, in the soft lilt he'd picked up wintering in Arizona. "Think he'd like a cup of coffee when he does?"

Kaye assured Red he would, hung up, and activated an area-wide alert.

Radio chatter fell silent.

"All units, be advised," she said. "Jackson County Sheriff's Six has not cleared his last assignment and is not responding to inquiries. He's assist-motorist at the Lee River Bridge in Millston. I can't raise him." She read the tag, described the van. "Who's close?"

A flurry of adrenalized voices reported. Nearest was twenty minutes. Next was forty.

"Responding units, Code Three," she said, clearing them for lights, sirens, and speed, which would be modest at best with the flooding and washouts. She dashed off an emergency request to Madison for air assets, but getting a chopper up in this soup was pure wishful thinking. "Report the minute you find him—"

The nine-one-one line rang.

"Jackson County Emergency," she said.

"Good morning, Kaye, it's Walt Meesely."

"Hi, Walter," she said. She liked the garrulous senior a lot, but didn't have time to chat. "We're busy right now with the storm. Can I call you back?"

"Not a social call," he said. "I got business."

"Really? What is it?"

"Gunshots. I just heard a bunch."

Fear dripped down Kaye's spine. Walter and Doris lived right down the street from the bridge. "You're sure?" she said, gripping the arms of her chair.

"I am," he said. "A few dozen, at least. It got quiet for a minute, then started up again."

"And you're sure it wasn't thunder?"

"I know the difference, missy," he said, annoyed. "When I fought the Nazis in—"

"Walter, listen to me," Kaye interrupted. "Are the shots coming from the bridge?"

He thought about it. "Yes. The wind's pretty fierce, but I accounted for that. Why?"

"Sergeant Abbott's there, helping a motorist. I can't raise him."

"Oh, my," Walter said. "You go on and find him, girl. Spencer's a good boy, and we don't want him harmed—"

Kaye cut him off midsentence, hit the alert tone again.

"Officer needs help; repeat, officer needs help," she said into her microphone, struggling to keep her voice neutral. "Shots fired, Lee River Bridge in Millston. Sheriff's Six is on scene by himself, still not responding to inquiries. Officer needs help. . . ."

She routed everyone within an hour, updated her boss, the sheriff, asked Monroe County if anyone was closer, learned nobody was, put out a statewide flash alert, pinched her eyes, and said a prayer he'd be all right. Then grabbed the phone and dialed Madison. She'd get a chopper up if she had to fly the damn thing herself.

"Christ, it hurts," Virgo groaned.

"'Course it does, m'man," Gemini said, probing the wound with a paintbrush handle. The flesh was mangled from the police hollowpoint, but there was no break in the abdominal wall. "Good news, it didn't go through. You don't have any internal damage, just a big divot. You'll be fine with antiseptic and bandages."

"Think I could take me a hit of that Katrina?" Virgo said, tears leaking from the ferocity of the pain. "Just a little, so Maxx won't know?"

Gemini laughed. "Not know? Cash Maxximus notices when a fly shits on his drugs. But the hell with him, you deserve a taste." Virgo would be instantly addicted, but better that than the screaming. "Soon as we're on the road, you'll be higher than the Big Dipper."

"G-g-g-good," Virgo said.

Gemini gently wiped the man's sweaty-shiny face. Virgo

had been with him since New Orleans, and he loved him like a brother. "Think you can walk to the cop car? Or should I carry your sissy ass?"

"Kiss my ass, Karl Dettmer, I can walk fine, you don't gotta help me none," Virgo snapped, gritting his teeth. His entire body vibrated as he tried to sit up.

Karl Dettmer.

Ah, hell.

Gemini pulled his .45.

Cranked three into Virgo's head.

Blood and bone sprayed the bridge deck.

Virgo's expression said, *What the fuck?*

He died without learning the answer.

"Just where do you think you're going?" Doris Meesely demanded as she turned on the kitchen light.

Walter Meesely tightened the collar of his slicker. His hawk face glowed from the deep of his rain hood. "Kaye Barley confirmed gunshots at the bridge," he said. "And Spence Abbott's there by himself. I'm gonna go help him."

"With what?" Doris said, eyes flaring, hands on her hips. "You can hardly walk 'cause your knees go out when you look at 'em cross-eyed. How are you going to fight even if Spencer does need the help?"

Walter lifted the bottom of his slicker. The oil-soaked grips of his World War II combat pistol gleamed dully in the kitchen light.

"Mr. Colt does my talking," he said.

"Dagnabbit, Walter, that's crazy. You can't go—"

"I can and I will, woman. Spence is out there alone, and I'm the closest."

She huffed.

Then kicked out of her slippers.

"What do you think you're doing?" Walter asked.

"Well, someone's got to drive you," Doris said, ramming her feet into rubber galoshes. "Seeing as how you're also half blind from the cataracts."

His grin said, *I darn well know you too, woman.*

"You old coot," she said, opening the door to the garage.

"Damn, that's cold," Aquarius muttered as Virgo's skull collapsed.

"Had it coming," Cancer said. "Man used Gemini's name twice, probably did it just again. He called attention to himself with those stupid lug nuts. And back in Minneapolis, he held that dealer so loose Gemini cut himself with that church key."

"Still."

"Yeah. I know."

They watched quietly as Gemini threw him over the railing.

Cancer backed toward their boss. A woman on the radio demanded that "Sheriff's Six" respond immediately. Probably the cop they'd just aced in the river.

"You two got something to say," Gemini said as he slid in, "now's the time."

Silence.

"He call you Dettmer again?" Aquarius said.

Gemini nodded.

"That gets us all sent to prison," Aquarius said.

He's on board, Gemini decided.

Looked at Cancer.

"We oughta burn the van," Cancer said. "Slow the police evidence teams."

Two for two.

"Real good idea," Gemini said. "But remove the Katrina first, okay? Don't wanna singe our pretty asses rescuing it."

They all laughed. Then soaked the Ford Econoline in gasoline and paint thinner.

It blew with a satisfying *whump* in the cruiser's rearview mirror.

Sheriff's Deputy Kharise Lenell hunched over the wheel of her pearl-gray cruiser, dodging one puddle then the next. She was the best pursuit driver in Jackson County, and she was going to save her Sarge. He'd been a rock when she was a rookie, not dinging her for small infractions, even though he was supposed to, because he thought she'd make a good cop. Damned if she wouldn't prove him right by kicking a bunch of killer van guys in the—

The pavement, weakened by storm wash, gave way.

Her cruiser skidded into the mammoth pothole.

Spun.

Bounced.

Crashed into the ditch.

Ramming the steel culvert.

Which ripped through the gas tank with a stream of sparks.

Exploding the gas.

Melting the deputy.

"Sheriff's Nine?" the radio squawked. "Kharise, can you hear me?"

22

Clatter.

Bam.

Crash.

Hawk rolled out of bed, raced for the sound of shattering glass. "What's wrong? Sammy, are you all right?" he said, wheeling into her pink-and-yellow room.

She flailed in her bed, face blue.

Oh, Jesus, a rabbo attack.

"I've got you, I've got you," he said, grabbing the emergency kit. He threw back her covers and jammed the hypodermic through the nose of a Little Mermaid.

"Help . . . Daddy," she gurgled.

"I'm here, baby, I'm here. Don't you worry; you'll be fine real soon," Hawk said, tightening a vise around his ballooning panic. He wrapped his arms around her, pulled his fists into her belly. Ooze pulped from her airway. He cleared her mouth with his fingers.

Her blue face tinged purple.

Willing his hands to steady, Hawk sat her against the headboard and shoved the emergency inhaler down her throat, blasted her spasming lungs once, twice, thrice.

Her breathing began to saw, as if cutting wood.

He pumped till the can was empty. It was fifty times the maximum dosage. But her agony eased. He knew it wouldn't hold. Not when the attack was this bad.

He held her in one arm, pulled the phone from his shorts.

"This is Hawk," he told the Naperville dispatcher. "My daughter can't breathe."

"I'm rolling paramedics," the dispatcher assured. "Code Three."

"Help me, Mommy," Sammy whispered, voice stringy, as muscles across her body popped and twitched. "Whatever I did I'm sorry, please come home and save me—"

She passed out.

Hawkins put his ear to her lips. Still breathing, but barely. No time for ambulances.

"I'm taking her to Edward!" he shouted, Sammy's mermaids bending into a *U* as he shouldered her like a sack of flour. "Call the emergency room. Tell them she's injected and inhaled but turning purple." He snatched up his keys without slowing. "Tell them she needs immediate intubation. Tell them, goddammit, make sure they understand."

"They'll be ready, Hawk," the dispatcher said, routing cruisers to clear the intersections between Hawk's house and the hospital.

Hawk stuck a Kojak cop flasher on the roof of his truck and screamed out of the garage, his daughter drooling unconscious in his lap.

Eleven minutes to Edward.

Six if he drove like a maniac.

He prayed he was maniac enough.

23

Emily floated through the doorway, into the room.

She looked around, not quite sure where she was or what had brought her here. The ceiling, floor, and walls were the unrelenting black of shark eyes. A bed with corner posts of stacked body parts sat squarely in the center. An incandescent bulb dangled from wires stripped to bare copper. Its meager glow died when it reached the dark corners of the room.

She watched herself float to the center of the bed. She hovered a moment, then descended, halting six inches from the mattress. Her arms raised, lowered, raised, as if salaaming. Her clothes fell off her body and floated off into the bathroom. They arranged themselves neatly on a claw-foot tub, their corners perfectly squared.

None of this made sense. She tried to stop it.

Couldn't.

She began to turn slowly, as if on a spit. Six revolutions

and she was screwed tight to the mattress, facing the doorway through which she'd been entered.

A puff of smoke wandered around the frame and into the room. She smelled its cellar dankness. Felt its heat on breasts and belly. She didn't flinch. She was stronger than the heat.

Another puff floated through a closed window. She couldn't see the puff or window; she was faced the wrong way. But something was whispering it was there. Something evil.

Shards of anxiety broke off her body and into the shadows, where they shimmied like the mercury from a broken thermometer.

She tried to decipher the smoke puffs. They weren't the speckled gray of a house fire. They were red and yellow, blue and white. They doubled in size every sixty seconds, folding in on themselves, milk condensing to cheese curds.

Marty floated through the entry door. He wore deer antlers and camouflage pants. Otherwise, he was naked, and shorn of all hair but his moustache. His lips and jaw moved. No words emerged. She urged him closer, so she could hear. He joined her on the bed.

The puff-colors grew richer, as if infused with gold and platinum.

They tried talking with their eyes, but couldn't decipher. The colors swirled in the superheated air. Sweat gushed off their slickened bodies. Her stomach morphed into a nest of squealing rats. They gnawed at her belly lining, trying to escape.

Head pulsing with fear, she tried grabbing Marty and running for the door. She couldn't. She looked down to find out why. To her shock, she had no legs. They'd been hacksawn at the knees, leaving a pair of ragged stumps that somehow didn't bleed.

The dense smoke fractured into a kaleidoscope, melting and mending, shifting and collapsing. Color shards flew down Emily's throat, slicing her open from the inside. Rats boiled out, flaying her with titanium claws. Her body bloated with blood, tinged red and yellow, blue and white. She daren't breathe for fear she'd drown. Her anxiety smoldered to flash point, the colors becoming a fire hose, blasting so hard that color slammed up her nose and down her throat. She vomited. What came out were smoke tendrils, red and yellow, blue and white. The expelled colors danced briefly at their freedom, then twisted themselves into the snorting beast she hoped she'd never see again.

The panic dragon.

The last time she saw this monster, it was burning her and Marty to death inside their exploding house. They managed to escape, and she thought it was gone forever.

She was wrong.

The dragon roared its happiness at reuniting with its favorite victim, then wrapped its tail around her scarred neck. Emily coughed and drooled, fighting the choke. The dragon slapped her with its razor tail. Her cheeks separated from their anchoring bones. Multicolored pus flooded her eyes and face. She blinked it away only to see her leg stumps melt into the same hues as the dragon's tail. Fire roared through the room. High-pitched steam bounced off the walls, multiplying the noise thousands-fold. Color, smoke, flames, keen, and panic became a compressed ball of Crayola, ready to blow with the tiniest of reagent—

The window by the tree cracked from the heat. Cold, wet air roared inside.

The explosion lopped off Emily's head.

She watched herself bounce across the floor, settle upright on her shorn neck.

Watched Marty fly backwards through the storm, and the dragon turn his way.

She tried to scream, distract the dragon from raining its fire. But her tongue had liquefied into a bubbling milk, spilling down her chest in red and yellow, blue and white. Marty mewled as his body crackled from the dragon's hell breath, and Emily wept steam tears. He was doomed because she didn't know how to beat the dragon. The best thing that ever happened to her was burning alive because she was so weak and pathetic and useless. . . .

The panic screamed with laughter.

Emily screamed fire.

24

Pad-pad.

Pad-pad.

Pad-pad.

Steps through the snow.

The deer's eyes widened. He knew that sound well.

It was a timber wolf.

The deer shivered violently. A wolf could open him with one swipe, and rip out his organs before he drew his dying breath. He fell completely quiet. If he didn't breathe, didn't make a sound, perhaps the wolf would ignore him. . . .

He heard a tiny *plip*.

Looked down.

The snow pack was a-dot with blood. His blood. From the holes of the thunder-sticks. There wasn't much, not even a tongue lap. But the wolf would smell it. Even now he sensed a shift in the wolf's pad. Toward this hiding place, not away.

The deer pushed out of the pine hideaway. Puffed out his

chest, looking fierce. He heard the low rumble. Spotted two eyes in the forest shadows. They were yellow as full moons, glinted dangerously. Behind the glint were snout and teeth and silvery fur.

Death on four legs.

The deer bellowed like he was diseased, hoping the wolf would think twice. It didn't. It padded closer, bent into the attack position. The deer stared with unblinking eyes. Shook his antler rack. It was a strong thing, the rack, made of long, dense bone that ended with tips sharp enough to impale the killer if it made the smallest mistake.

The wolf licked its lips with a darting pink tongue. Judged the risk.

Hunkered on its muscled haunches and began the run.

The deer tracked every jink and juke, jabbing the rack at the killer. The wolf charged, yowling, probing for weaknesses. The deer shoved the rack at its face.

The wolf bounced sideways. Rabbits and squirrels scattered, fearing the thundering hooves. The deer turned with the wolf. The wolf attacked.

The deer feinted.

The wolf changed its attack angle on the fly, to beat the feint.

Which the deer already anticipated. The longest of the tips plunged into the wolf's left eye. Pulp and juice burst like an overripe boil. The wolf screamed, clawed madly at the deer. The deer scuttled backwards, lashing out with horned front feet. One connected with the wolf's face. More blood splashed.

The wolf disengaged, circled the deer. Spotted a hole in the defense. Darted in, swiped the ribs, took out a section of meat. The deer bellowed. Dug his front legs into the snow. Kicked hard with his rears. Caught the wolf double-barrel.

The wolf yowled as broken teeth fell to the snow. It retreated twenty yards, panting. Didn't like what it saw in the bucking, feverish deer with the crushing feet and swordlike antlers. Backed awkwardly into the woods, reassessing at every step, then ran off with a soft bark.

Plenty of lesser prey with meat just as tasty.

Trembling from fresh pain, the deer moved on.

25

"How could you miss the bridge, woman?" Walter Meesely grumped. "We live practically next door."

"I went past the turnoff, that's all," Doris Meesely said. "You're so damn smart, why didn't you say something when it could have helped?"

"I'm straining my eyes for Sergeant Abbott," Walter said.

"Oh, that's right. You can't walk and chew gum at the same time."

Walter chuckled. Even at this ungodly hour, the wife could bite like a tick. He snuck his hand over to her plump chest, gave a squeeze. She shrieked.

"Chew gum and that too," he said.

"I swear," Doris said, shaking her head. "You're randy as a goat, you are, even with curlers in my hair."

"Baaaah," Walter said.

"Well, now, that's good," she said, not unpleased, running her hand across her rain hood. "Now glue your eyes on those ditches while I turn around. Last thing we need is to fall in and give poor Kaye more to do."

She executed a snap-wheel reverse without hitting either ditch.

"Dang," Walter admired.

"Gotta dump this cop car," Gemini said as he flew toward I-94. "Every swinging dick with a badge is looking for it by now. Keep your eyes peeled for—"

"There's one," Aquarius said, pointing from the shotgun seat.

A well-kept Cadillac flashed by.

"Is that Spence?" Walter said, cranking his head around to the passing county cruiser.

"I'll bet it is," Doris said, laying on the horn while pumping the brakes. Walter rolled down his window, waved his arms.

"Hey, Spencer!" they both hollered. "Come back. Everyone's looking for you."

"They're waving at us," Aquarius said, dumbfounded.

Gemini reversed the cruiser in a bootlegger turn, and slipped neatly into the Cadillac's wake. He flipped on the roof lights and belched the siren.

"Shoot them?" Cancer said.

"Yeah, but don't hit the car," Gemini said. "Bullet holes attract cops."

* * *

Doris put on her turn signal.

"You don't gotta do that," Walter said. "He knows we're pulling over."

"Why would I break a law in front of a policeman?" she said, pulling to the edge of the pavement. The pearl-gray cruiser tucked in behind. Three men hopped out.

"That doesn't look like Spence," Walter said, eyes narrowing. "Who are those guys? Why are their hoods over their heads?"

The three broke into a run.

"Something's wrong," Walter said, pulling the war gun from his waistband. "Quick, drive us out of here."

Doris stomped the gas pedal.

Flooded the engine.

"Oh no," she gasped.

"Bail out," Walter ordered. "Run straight into those woods, fast as you can. I'll cover you."

"No, Walter, I won't leave you here—"

"Move, woman," he said, cocking the steel hammer of the Nazi-killer.

She did, galoshes flopping.

"Just like hunting rabbits," Gemini said, swinging his .45 onto the old gal's whale ass as she scampered for the thick stand of trees. Then caught, from the corner of his eye, an old guy stretching low across the fender and aiming a pistol even bigger than his own.

They fired at the same time.

The old guy's bullet skidded across Gemini's forearm, making him yelp.

Gemini's bullet hit solid.

Blood spurted from the old man's chest.

Didn't seem to matter. The guy didn't even flinch.

"That's my woman, ya bastards!" the guy bellowed. "Leave her the hell out of this. It's fighting you want, I got plenty to give ya."

The big Colt barked again.

Road chips blasted Gemini's legs.

All three killers scrambled back to the cruiser.

The old guy gimped away from the Caddy as fast as his bowed legs would manage.

Aquarius put the Uzi's muzzle on his back.

The old guy seemed to sense it.

Wheeled and fired.

Aquarius ducked away swearing. The Uzi burst went wide. The old guy kept running.

"Geezer got game," Gemini said.

"Can't run worth shit, though," Cancer said, aiming. "I'll finish him off, then find the broad."

"Don't waste ammo," Gemini said, pushing the barrel aside. "Grandpa'll bleed out soon enough, and neither of them saw our faces."

"Speaking of bleed," Cancer said, "you're hit."

Gemini looked, surprised. The wound was lengthy but shallow.

"Better'n Gramps," he said, accepting the paint rag from Aquarius and wrapping it around the oozing wound. "Take the cruiser and dump it in the woods. Shut off the two-way so nobody hears the squawks. We'll follow, pick you up."

They took off, tires squealing.

"Walter," Doris wailed, bounding out of the woods. "Where are you? Please tell me you're all right."

She heard a groan. Spotted him near the ditch, water lapping at his splayed feet.

She hurried over and dragged him to the high spot of the pavement. Flopped him over.

Blood poured from the bullet hole in his chest.

"Oh, my God," Doris whispered. She dropped to her knees, smooshed her hands over the wound.

Blood sprayed out both sides.

She stuck her hand in her husband's pants pocket. Found his pocketknife. The handle was jigged bone, worn smooth from a lifetime of handling. The blade was dark silver, and wicked sharp from Walter's endless babying. She opened it and cut pieces from the flannel shirt under his slicker. Twisted the pieces tight, stuffed them in the hole.

The blood slowed momentarily.

Then spit out the rags like bad meat.

"Nazis," Walter moaned over chatter-teeth. "They're here. . . . Run, Dorrie. . . . I won't let them catch you. . . . Krauts do terrible things they get you alive. . . . Saw . . . I saw what they do to pretty gals like you. . . . Run. . . . Run. . . . I'll cover you, Dorrie. I'll save you. . . . " His right hand formed a loose pistol, index finger pointing, thumb lifting and dropping.

The blood flow worsened.

In seconds he'd be drained.

In seconds she'd be alone.

Not going to happen. Not after all these years.

She made a little noise.

Threaded her fingers through his.

Snuggled up close to his blood-saturated breath. Ran her fingers over his bone-white face. Kissed his lips. Cold, they were. Unresponsive.

She picked up his knife. Walter carried it in the war, all four years, same as the Colt. He'd used it more than once to get his buddies safely home.

So would she.

Her blood hesitated at abandoning its home of eighty-two years.

Then jumped out headfirst.

"Nazis," Walter murmured. "I can't save you . . . from . . . Nazis. . . ."

"But you did, honey, you did," Doris said, blubbering and inhaling and coughing all at the same time, scared out of her mind, yet not, watching her blood join his on the road and drain toward the lapping ditch. "They only win if they take me alive. They didn't. You stopped them with your bravery, Walter. You did it; you beat the Nazis. You saved me."

He didn't reply.

She began crying.

"I love you so much, Walter. And now we're going home." Her head swirled. "We'll dry ourselves off from this terrible rain and take to our bed and . . . you'll touch me like you did in the car. Like you always do. You make me feel so pretty when I know I'm not and . . . I'll touch you the same way, and you'll tell me how General Patton shook . . . shook your hand because you were brave against those . . . those Nazis and . . . and . . ."

Her head fell onto his.

Their breath commingled.

Then it didn't.

26

Marty hurled his razor and grabbed the gun under the bathroom sink. Two were hidden in every room in case one of his threat letters turned real—too many undercover officers had found out too late just how massive a grudge a psychotic biker gang could carry. He charged into the bedroom, muzzle up and hunting.

Nothing.

Nobody.

Just Emily.

And her screams.

Nightmare?

He laid the gun on his armoire, rushed to the bed. She thrashed like a deer in a jaw trap, tangled in emerald and cranberry.

"Emily, wake up," he said, shaking the mattress. "Come on, wake up."

The thrashing got worse. He'd have to do it the hard way.

He moved in to untangle her. Elbows slammed his chest.

A knee sank into his belly. He stripped off the comforter, then the sheets, exposing her to the cold, which would help.

"C'mon, honey," he said. "You're having a bad dream. Open your eyes."

She swung. He ducked. Her fist bashed the headboard. Her head followed suit, slamming against the hard wood. He grabbed her flailing legs, dragged her clear. Then leapt on top, using all two hundred forty pounds to pin her arms.

She fought with knees and legs, bluing the air with curses. That told him how bad this nightmare was, because she never swore, ever. A promise she'd made her father when she was a kid, and then he was murdered, so she honored it still.

He turned on the lamp. Her face twitched. Her eyes, under the lids, jumped like bags of mice. Heavy REM. She was deep in whatever swamp she'd fallen into.

Marty slapped and shouted. Neighbors banged on floor and walls. He ignored them, kept slapping till his hand buzzed. "Open your eyes, let's go, wake up, wake up."

"Wha . . . wha . . . wha," she sputtered, steam heat pouring off her. Sweat pooled between her breasts, ran down her body. She shook uncontrollably, lashed out again.

"Quit fighting me, Emily Marie Thompson. Stop it right now," Marty said, directly into her ear, slow so she understood. "You're having a nightmare."

"A . . . what?"

"Nightmare," he repeated. "You have to wake up now."

She groaned.

He released her arms and stroked her hair. It was greasy with sweat.

"What was it?" he said. "What were you dreaming about?"

The explanation burned on her tongue. The dragon, the kaleidoscope, the dragon, the fear, the melting psychos, the dragon—

"Shower," she croaked instead.

27

"When did Cadillacs get so small?" Gemini complained as he idled Walter Meesely's through the rest-stop parking lot. "I got cramps."

Cancer rubbed his own aching legs. "Used to be, you stole a Caddy and rode in comfort," he said. "Now they're sardine cans."

"Like everything else Detroit makes," Aquarius said, reloading the Uzi's magazines.

"It's those damn sheiks, you know," Gemini said, steering clear of a pothole. "If we'd kicked 'em in the nuts to start with, we'd never had to shrink our rides." He hawked up, spit it out the window. "I say nuke the bastards and hand 'em over to Texaco. Then we get our big cars back. And pick up some of those ninety-nine virgins."

"Seventy-two," Cancer said.

"Seventy-two what?"

"Virgins. I think there's only seventy-two."

"I knew them boys were slackers," Gemini said.

They all cackled.

"Old cars," Aquarius said, eyes crinkling in fondness. "They were football fields inside. You could pork two girls in the backseat and one won't know the other's there."

"Those seats were so roomy even your fat ass would fit," Cancer said.

Aquarius showed him both middle fingers. "And that ain't fat, dawg," he said. "It's Johnson. Got so much I gotta wrap it around back—"

"There's a van," Cancer interrupted, pointing to one pulling into a slot. L.M. GRAY, EXPERT PLUMBING was painted on the side. "Looks comfy enough. Take it?"

"Too many kids around," Gemini said as the van spilled a half-dozen children and a harried-looking dad with juice boxes. "Don't want to hit 'em if we shoot."

Cancer snorted. "Since when do you care?"

"I don't," Gemini said. "It's practical, that's all. Kids go nuts when they're scared, and they all got cell phones. Next thing you know the cops have our tags and description again. Whatever we grab now, we need to keep. Barely gonna get to Naperville on time as it is." He sighed. "And I *still* need a kid for Chester the Molester."

"Helluva thing to call Freddie-Boy," Aquarius teased. "Being he's your best friend."

"Should hear what I say about you."

They finished scouting the lot, looped around for a second pass.

28

Neither said a word.

Just soaked in the thrumming heat of the shower.

After a while, Marty picked up Emily's shampoo, squeezed a quarter cup on her hair. It smelled like strawberries and oranges. That's what the bottle said, anyway. He couldn't smell anything since he breathed that battery acid a decade ago.

He hooked his hands in deep, worked her scalp with his finger pads, then his nails. Pads, nails, gentle, hard, wiping soufflé-shaped foam clots off her face and shoulders, keeping the warmed muscles of his arms tight to her ears and neck. He felt himself pulse from the intimacy. He warned himself to cut it out. This wasn't about that.

She knelt.

Hmm. Maybe it was . . .

After a while she rose, and squeezed him tight.

"Better?" he asked.

He felt the nod against his breastbone.

"Me, uh, too," he said.

He felt her smile.

They stayed that way till the water turned to ice.

29

"There's our new ride, gentlemen," Gemini said, pointing to the raspberry-colored van pulling into the farthest slot from the building. "Don't forget the Uzi."

Aquarius checked the silencer. The bulbous tube was screwed tight to the barrel.

They parked the well-kept Cadillac, bailed out.

"Excuse me, sir," Gemini said, waving his GPS at the approaching driver. "This darn thing quit working, so we pulled off the highway to figure out where we are. Do you know?"

"Tomah," the man said. "Gateway to the Dells."

Gemini glanced at Cancer, who'd peeked inside the van. His nod said the man was alone.

"How far are we from Chicago?" Gemini asked.

"Couple hours," the man said, holding out red, chapped hands. "Mind if I look? I repair vending machines, maybe I can fix your—"

The combat knife slid noiselessly into the man's neck,

then snapped out the front. The move severed windpipe, jugular, carotid, and nerve stems.

The man's eyes glazed.

They carried him into the woods behind the parking lot, dumped him in a bramble of branches and vegetation. Took his keys, headed back.

"Park the Caddy next to the restrooms," Gemini told Aquarius. "Be sure to lock up, like we're inside taking a dump. We'll pick you up in front." His smile showed pointy teeth. "Nice job with that toad-stabber. I thought you'd use the machine gun."

"I needed the practice," Aquarius said, polishing the blade on his jeans.

Gemini clapped him on the back.

Eight minutes later they were on the interstate, heading south.

30

"Yes, I'm sure," Emily said to Marty's questioning look. The dragon's taunts still echoed in her head. But if she breathed a word, he'd tell his best friend to go without him. She adored Marty's protective instinct, the one that put her above all other needs. But damned if she'd ruin his adventure. "Now go. Bambi's waiting."

Marty kissed her and picked up his gear. She pinched his bottom, then followed him to the front door, waving at Deputy Chief Hercules Branch, a good friend even before she joined the Naperville Police because her late husband, Jack, had been workmates with Branch's wife, Lydia, a fellow telecommunications engineer, and they'd all become close.

"Good morning, sunshine," Branch said.

"You're awfully cheerful for four o'dark," she said.

"The rain is done. The road awaits. Life doesn't get any better."

"Breakfast?" Marty said.

"I stand corrected," Branch said. "It *does* get better."

31

Charred van.

Hundreds of spent shells.

No sign of Abbott or his cruiser.

The Black River Falls patrolman grabbed his radio. "I'm at the Lee River Bridge," he reported. "Helluva firefight, but all that's left is a burned-up cargo van." He sniffed, shook his head. Gasoline for sure. Maybe something else, given the completeness of the destruction. Fire boys would know. "I'll look around and—wait one."

His flashlight glinted off something familiar sixty yards downstream.

"Ah," the cop said.

"What did you find?" Jackson County Sheriff Vaughn Buehler said.

The patrolman didn't want this on the air. "Meet me on county tactical."

"Switching," Buehler said.

A moment later.

"Looks like a body, Vaughn," the patrolman said. "On a gravel bar, sixty yards downstream.

"Ah, crap," Buehler said. "Is it Spencer?"

"Too far away to know," the patrolman said. "I'll get a boat in the water, but that's going to take a while. I'll try my binoculars first."

"Thanks," Buehler said. "I'll call your chief, tell him what's happening. Try not to touch anything, okay? It's a crime scene, and it's important to keep it pristine."

Well that's a big hunk of duh, the patrolman thought, looking at the burned carcass of the van. Then again, maybe he'd say the same thing if he was Buehler and making that point would keep a cop-killer from going free.

The patrolman turned his cruiser so the door spot was close to the railing. Several million candlepower shot downstream. Three more cruisers pulled up, mixed jurisdictions.

"Put up the yellow tape," the patrolman hollered. "We got a crime scene here. It's important to keep it pristine."

He picked up his binoculars, and started the sweep.

32

The pervert slicked back his waxed hair. Adjusted his small, round glasses. Ran his delicate hands down the girl's nude body. The girl shuddered, shrank back.

The pervert smiled.

"I won't hurt you, Precious," Freddie-Boy cooed, gentle as a dove. "You're my friend. I never hurt my friends."

The five-year-old looked up from the well-lighted bed.

"I want to go home," she whined, kicking her coltish legs. "You said I could."

"And you shall, darling," Freddie-Boy said. "As soon as you do what you promised."

"I'm too tired," Precious said, crossing her arms over her flat chest.

The scar-faced man moved toward the bed. Freddie-Boy waved him off with a flick of his bowling-ball head.

"I'm tired, too, pretty lady," he said. "But you said you'd help me make this movie. As soon as you do, I'll let you go home." He held out the candy, rubbed the cellophane wrapper.

Precious smiled.

Laid back on the crisp white sheets.

Spread her legs, let her smoothness show.

"So that's what you really wanted," Freddie-Boy said. "More candy."

"I love candy," Precious said, giggling.

"Getting that?" Freddie-Boy asked his director.

"Every freckle," Lindy Archer said, moving the camera close. "This kid is gold."

"I certainly hope so," Freddie-Boy said. "Gemini charged me enough."

"Don't be cheap," Lindy said, moving for a side shot. "She's worth every penny."

"Easy for you to say, Sis," Freddie-Boy said. "It's not your money."

He walked to the bed.

"Well, aren't you just wonderful," he cooed. "Spreading your legs like a big girl."

"I *am* a big girl," she said.

"Yes, you are," he said. "So, do you like being in the movies?"

Precious's head bobbed. "I'm the star," she said.

"You're the star," Freddie-Boy confirmed, handing her a peppermint patty laced with Katrina. "And stars get the best candy."

She gobbled it like a starving wolf.

He'd hooked Precious the morning Gemini delivered her. It wasn't difficult—the designer drug was instantly addicting. It worked by magnifying thousands-fold the pleasure centers of the brain. The downside was withdrawal. It was as devastating as its hurricane namesake. A single day without candy delivered a pain so shattering that death was begged for and welcome. Freddie-Boy fed his little girls a full week of Katrina . . . then gave them the day. That tiny walk through Hell ensured compliance with his every wish and direction. *For the most part, anyway,* he thought with a smile. *Girls are sugar and spice and everything nice. Even with Katrina, one made allowances for the spice.*

"Yum-yum," Precious said, cleaning off the cellophane with her little pink tongue.

"Indeed," Freddie-Boy said.

They were in an industrial park on Naperville's southwest side. He'd rented the space on both sides, to ensure no snoopy neighbors. The facility was soundproofed, double-walled, then soundproofed again. It was registered with the state as an industrial video and media business.

Precious wasn't industrial or media.

But she certainly was the business.

So were the other underage children Freddie-Boy acquired, videoed in HD, then shipped to his international circle of live-child fans.

"Ready for your leading man?" Freddie-Boy said.

Precious cocked her head. "What's that?"

"The handsome prince I told you about," he said. "To star in the movie with my beautiful princess."

Precious clapped her hands.

"I'm so happy to hear that, darling," Freddie-Boy said, doing a little shuffle-dance for her. He liked working with kids. Loved their moods and unpredictability every bit as much as their violin-string bodies and unblemished innocence. Capturing those complexities on video was, at times, a challenge. But that was his sister's job, and her Swiss bank balance showed she was particularly good at it. "Let's bring on the handsome prince."

"Yay, prince," Precious said.

Scarface opened the door to the dressing room. A man lumbered out. He was tall. Hairy. Muscled. Masked in leather, and erect as a beanpole.

"Love is a little blue pill," Scarface said to Freddie-Boy.

The leading man smiled at Precious.

She smiled back, coyly tucking her legs under herself.

"All right, little lady," director Lindy cooed. "Do you remember what you promised? That you'd sit on his lap and play?"

Precious ran her hand down her heavily made-up face.

"Yes," she said, chewing the tip of a finger.

As the action progressed from kissing to petting to no-holes-barred, Scarface sidled over to Freddie-Boy. "Her passport and papers are excellent," Scarface said. "Your forgers do fine work."

"I hire only the best."

Scarface dipped his head, accepting the compliment. "Also, the plane is ready. The pilot predicts a smooth arrival in Belarus."

"Excellent," Freddie-Boy. Smuggling out of the United States was far less complicated than smuggling into, as border officials in developing countries were so much more . . . understanding of the proper bribe. "Who bought her, and for how much?" He knew, of course, but constantly tested his contractors. This business was full of scumbags.

"A minor Saudi prince," Scarface said. "For seven hundred thousand Euros."

Freddie-Boy calculated the exchange rate. Precious was more than living up to the name he'd given her. He couldn't remember her real name. Soon, Precious wouldn't either.

"Take fifty thousand for yourself," Freddie-Boy said. He paid even the scumbags well so they wouldn't turn on him. If they did anyway, there were Gemini and his zodiac butchers.

Scarface showed steel teeth.

"How long till the girl's ready to transport?" he asked.

"An hour," Freddie-Boy said.

The leading man gasped and shuddered.

"Thirty minutes," Freddie-Boy said.

33

Black leather shoes on his feet.

Bullet holes in his crankcase.

"It's a body all right," the patrolman radioed as he stared through his binoculars. "But not Abbott's. Repeat, not Abbott."

Cheers erupted from cops on each side of the bridge.

"That's great," Buehler replied, vastly relieved. "But if that's not Spencer in the river . . ."

"Then where the hell is he?" the patrolman said.

34

"Where the hell am I?" Spencer Abbott mumbled. Even with the full moon, he could only make out shapes. Squat triangles were pines. Poles with crowns, broadleaves. Uneven dark bumps, branches, rocks, and leaf litter.

Some kind of forest.

He lay in a tangle of mud and rocks. His boots were submerged in water rushing so hard it sounded like Niagara. *Forest with a river.* But where? How did he get here in the first place?"

"Best get up and find out," he said.

He pulled his head from the crook of a fallen limb, and lifted his legs. They didn't respond.

Frowning, he tapped one.

No feeling but a deep, radiating cold.

He slapped the other.

Same.

His stomach lurched.

He wasn't prone to panic, he knew. He'd seen bikers

blown to bits in meth-lab explosions. Infants mangled in car crashes. Husbands crushed by snow machines, wives beaten to festered goo, farmers splashed into dells by wood chippers and combines.

But having no legs? That was pinching hard.

He took a deep breath, blew it out. Tried the legs again. No dice.

Same with his left arm, which flopped uselessly.

"Another fine mess you've gotten yourself into, Ollie," Abbott muttered.

He ran his good hand over the sleeve of his cop jacket. Found holes in the thick leather. Poked a finger through, felt the matching holes in his arm. Took a look. They were small, round, whitish, and puckered, and definitely not there when he put on his uniform.

Jesus! Was I shot?

He found more holes in the front of his shirt. He unbuttoned, checked his body armor. Felt the matching dimples. Dug with his fingernail. Flattened copper slugs fell out.

"Guess I was," he said.

He wrapped his hand around the back of his left knee, pulled hard. His foot released from the river mud with a sucking sound. He did the same with the other foot, then rolled onto his belly, trying to ease the fire in his ribs. He started crawling up the long, steep riverbank, figuring he might spot something familiar from the top of the ridge. Sweat began to pour a few seconds into it. The effort was brutal. He kept at it.

His face ran into something soft.

Oh, yeah, he remembered. *The something-soft from the river. Thanks for taking the bullets meant for me.*

The something-soft didn't acknowledge.

Abbott laughed at himself for talking to a bundle of canvas and clothesline.

Bits and pieces of memory floated back. He'd pulled over

a car—no, wait, it was a van, and they were already stopped. Some kind of car trouble. Kaye asked if he wanted backup. Like a dummy, he refused. They traded gunfire. He was hit several times. Then he was out of ammo, unable to use his radio, unable to reach his rifle. He shot out the bridge light and jumped into the river, leaving the four bastards—*three, I shot one of them*—free to escape.

And here he was.

Wherever "here" was.

He shivered. If he didn't get dry soon, he'd croak from hypothermia. Helluva thing, dying of a little cold water after he'd survived a machine gun, a bridge jump, and almost drowning. He couldn't let that happen. The firemen would make fun.

And, he'd spent all that money on house paint.

"Dettmer," he whispered, the killer's triangular face popping into his brain. "Cajun is Gemini is Snakehead is Dettmer. Remember that."

He patted around for his radio and gun.

Both gone.

"Yeah, that would be too easy," he said to the man in the moon.

The man smiled back. Then again, he always did. Pleasant fellow, he.

Abbott rummaged in his shirt. Notebook. Pen. Throat lozenges. All waterlogged to uselessness. He checked his pants. Wallet, handkerchief, spare handcuff key, flashlight . . .

Flashlight?

He clicked it on and off. Still worked. God bless SureFire engineers. He kept looking. Maybe there was something even better. . . .

Knife.

He stared. He'd used the Strider folder underwater to free himself of the Smokey-choke. That he'd had the presence of mind to clip it back on his pocket was a miracle. Or the end result of years of training. He decided it was training. He might need the miracle later, and didn't want to use it up now.

He shivered violently. Time to find shelter. Before he couldn't.

"Terribly sorry, old chap," he said, addressing the something-soft. "But I need to borrow your wrap." Didn't know why he was imitating a British dandy. "I'm catching my death and all that rot, pip-pip."

The something-soft had no sense of humor.

Abbott clamped the knife between his teeth, elbowed himself into position. The effort made his head spin. He flicked the blade, cut the clothesline wrapping the lump's midsection, then slit the cloth to see what was inside.

Another layer of cloth.

He slit that, shaking his head.

A layer of heavy plastic.

Holding an attic's worth of crap, no doubt. Despite the conservation department's best efforts, citizens dumped all kinds of refuse in area rivers because garbage crews charged by the can. He hoped this was clothes. Blankets. Something warm. He could dry off, then figure out which direction to start crawling. Once his blood got flowing and his legs warmed, maybe he could even walk. He slit the heavy plastic, powered the flashlight . . .

Recoiled at the eyes staring back.

35

"I won't lie, Hawk, it was close," Dr. Barbara Winslow said, dropping her stethoscope into her white coat. "But Sammy's going to pull through."

"Thank God," the sergeant said. He paced the cubicle where emergency room doctors delivered the news to loved ones. "How long till she can travel?"

Winslow shook her head. "Tomorrow at the earliest. Most probably the day after."

"Two days?" he said, eyebrows rocketing. "It's never taken her that long to recover."

Edward Hospital's chief of emergency medicine rubbed her tired eyes. "I know. But this was her worst attack yet. It really ate into her reserves. She needs extra time to bounce back." She sighed. "All we're doing is treading water, Hawk. I don't know how much longer it will work. She needs that cure, and she needs it—"

"I *know* that, goddammit," he roared, slamming the wall

with his fist. The framed landscapes rattled. "What do you think I've been doing this past year, picking my nose?"

Winslow jumped, startled. Hawk was the most even-tempered policeman she knew, and one of the kindliest. Then again, his daughter had very nearly died tonight. Maybe she'd have a hair trigger, too, if one of her kids had this monstrous disease.

"Sorry, Doc," Hawk muttered, folding his arms around himself and collapsing into a chair. "I'm pretty jacked up from this."

"Don't give it a second thought," Winslow said, taking the chair next to him. She touched his trembling arm. His eyes were downcast. He had more gray hair than just a few months ago. Robert Hawkins was worn down. Wrung out. A scrub rag.

"You look like hell, you know," she said.

"I'll bet that sounds better in Latin."

She smiled. "Are you working today?"

"Usual shift. Why?"

"I want you to call in sick," Winslow said. "I'll prescribe a sedative."

"I'm fine," he said, waving it off. "Couple slugs of coffee and I'm as good as new."

Winslow shook her head. "You need sleep, and now's the time to get it." She waved in the direction of ICU. "Sammy's so drained she won't wake up till tonight. We'll go down and see her, you'll kiss her good night, and you'll go home and sleep."

Hawk flattened his lips. "I'm going to sit with my daughter, then head to work. My turnout gear's a mess. We had a SWAT callout a few hours ago."

"So I heard," Winslow said. Ken Cross had called her with the news, because she'd doctored one of the robbers' early victims. The young woman had been stomped so brutally she'd be confined to a wheelchair the rest of her life. Winslow hoped they'd be raped in prison.

She considered Hawk's refusal to shirk his responsibilities. The man was a bull when it came to right and wrong. "Right" was doing what you needed to do, each and every time. "Wrong" was handing off that burden to someone else. So this wasn't surprising.

It also wasn't acceptable.

"I'll personally look after Sammy," Winslow said. "As for work, you have two choices."

"Which are?"

"Sleep today, I'll let you go to work tomorrow," she said. "Don't, I'll recommend Chief Cross place you on medical disability."

"You wouldn't."

"Try me. I got his daughter into medical school, and now I'm his living goddess."

He glared. She glared back, jaw quivering.

He finally laughed.

"I knew you'd be reasonable," Winslow said.

"Did I have a choice?"

"No." She opened the door. "Let's go see angel. Then it's beddie-bye for you."

Their heels clacked down the hallway to ICU. Everyone said hello.

"You know every one of these five thousand employees?" Hawk said.

"Maybe not all," Winslow said. "But most. I've been here long enough."

Hawk nodded. Fell back a step. Let his gaze linger on the forty-something doctor. She wasn't beautiful as much as pretty, with her wide, caring eyes, sprays of freckles across her nose and forearms, and gently swaying hips that worked him like a fever dream. . . .

"What did you mean by travel?" he heard Winslow say.

"Huh?" he said, pulling back into the moment.

"You asked how long till Sammy can travel," she said. "Not how long till she can go home, which is what you usually say."

Did I mention she's sharp as a tack? He looked at her. "I got the money, Barbara."

Winslow skidded to a halt. "All three million?"

"Every dime."

She put out her hand. He shook it solemnly.

"Oh, that just won't do," she said, pulling him in for a hug.

They embraced for a dozen heartbeats. Her warmth made his blood rush—he'd been so lonely since Bonnie ran away. She felt him shudder, held him tighter. He admired the extra mile she always went for Sammy. She worried about him getting home all right because he was so exhausted. He drank in her scent. She liked how he'd checked her out. Hawk was smart, good-looking, and utterly devoted to saving his baby when others cut and run. Acting on it wasn't going to happen—she liked her husband too much—but still, for a moment, in the middle of entwined emotion, she took deep pleasure in the intimacy. . . .

They released.

"Hawk, that's terrific news," she said, brushing her hair back. "When are you leaving?"

"My bank transfers the funds when we hit three million, which should be around noon. Soon as Amanda confirms receipt, we're leaving." His face fell a little. "Well, we were."

"You'll get there, just not quite yet," Winslow said. "A day or two, like I said, but she'll have no problem handling the trip. Can I book an air ambulance for you?"

"If you would," he said, nodding. "If she seizes, I want something more than a flight attendant with pretzels."

They took the corner into ICU, then into Samantha's machine-choked room. Hawk made a sound between a croak and a sob.

"She's better than she looks, I promise," Winslow said, touching his arm.

"I know," Hawk said, eyes filling. "But damn, it's hard to see."

She rummaged through a drawer, came up with a comb. "I'll bet she'd like it if you'd fix her hair," she said. "Maybe tell her a story, too."

Hawk looked so pleased a lump formed in her throat.

"Will she know?" he said.

"I like to think so," she said.

Hawk dragged over his chair.

"Once upon a time there was this robot named Atchy McClatchy," he began as he drew the narrow tines through her damp locks. "Atchy lives on the planet Zirconium, where everything glitters like diamonds. He flew his rocket ship to New York and saw Barbie on Fifth Avenue. She was shopping for shoes and eating a pretzel."

"With mustard?" Winslow said.

"No other kind," Hawk said.

To Sammy: "Atchy fell in love with Barbie on the spot, and asked her on a date to Coney Island. They'd walk along the sand, eat a Nathan's hot dog, ride a pony named Mr. Ed. But Barbie was already in love with Santa's no-good brother Earl, so she decided to find a girlfriend she could introduce to Atchy McClatchy. She called Midge and said—"

"Mommy," Sammy murmured in an otherworldly voice. "Mommy, where are you? Did I do something wrong, is that why you're gone . . . ?"

Hawk's face darkened.

"I'm scared. Come hold me. Please, Mommy, stay till I fall asleep. . . ."

"There's nothing wrong with her," Winslow assured, misinterpreting his expression. "She's talking in her sleep, that's all."

"She should be here," Hawk said.

"Who?"

"Bonnie. Her mother. She should be here, goddammit."

He flung the comb and stalked out.

Winslow started after him, but stopped outside Sammy's door. Hawk was crawling into his cave trying to cope, and she needed to respect that.

So she retrieved the comb, rinsed it, and picked up where Hawk left off, making the split ends lay neat on the faded hospital gown.

"Yes, Bonnie, you should," she murmured.

Then, louder: "And Barbie's friend Midge said, 'Girlfriend, I'm busy right now, mashing potatoes for my pet skunks. But I'll send my friend Honey McBunny. I know she'll go out with Atchy McClatchy. Honey will date anyone, anytime.'"

"Maybe she knows my ex," the nurse said.

36

Pedal.

Metal.

Emily roared.

Flashed by a trooper at one forty-five.

Was a half-mile away when he put on his reds.

Two miles when he got up to speed.

Emily laughed.

Felt the numbing tornado from the open windows, the bass hammer from the stereo. Icy. Vibrant. Electrifying.

Peeling away the dragon.

She powered into the next exit, headed north.

Moved to the shoulder at the railroad tracks.

Waited patiently.

The trooper finally showed. Bumped over the tracks and back, pulled up so their windows almost touched.

"That the best you got, Nancy Drew?" the trooper said.

"Waxed *your* Flintmobile," Emily said.

They high-fived.

Illinois State Police Trooper Shavon Little worked this stretch of I-88, a concrete slash in the cornfields way far west of Naperville. At this hour, it was devoid of traffic. Making it the perfect place to test souped-up cars.

The adoration of which Emily, Marty, and Shavon shared.

Shavon and Marty were longtime fishing and hunting buddies, and competed in the same amateur racing circuit. Emily joined the act when she and Marty started dating. Shavon sold her the Dodge Charger she was driving now, in fact. They'd tricked it out at Shavon's hunting cabin-slash-garage in Gardner, and she could break one eighty if she put her mind to it.

But she'd leave that to test tracks. One forty-five was as high as she'd get on an imperfectly surfaced interstate, and even that was short stretches—at that speed, one Michelin dropping into one unexpected pothole made for one crispy-fried detective.

"So what's the occasion?" Shavon asked.

"Can't sleep," Emily said.

"Keyed up from nabbing those robbers?"

She nodded.

"But if there wasn't that?"

"I'd think of some other excuse."

Shavon passed her a doughnut.

Emily had tried going back to sleep after Marty and Branch left. She lay wide-eyed and buzzing. So she grabbed her keys and got on the ramp a mile from the apartment. Cranked up the heavy metal music that always cleared her cobwebs. Realized which Static-X song was playing—"Wisconsin Death Trip"—and hurriedly switched. No need to court disaster.

She passed Aurora, DeKalb, and some farm towns.

Lit her afterburners.

It felt so good to fly.

"Boys get off to Wisconsin all right?" Shavon said.

"They and your jerky left at four o'clock," she said, smacking her lips.

"He let you try that?" Shavon said.

"Yep."

"Good man. What'd you think?"

"Delicious. Seriously."

"Glad you liked it."

"I did. Elk, right?"

Shavon smiled faintly. "The real other white meat. He said he asked you to go."

He was referring to the deer hunt, she knew. "He did."

"How come you're here, then?"

"Guys need guys too."

He considered that.

"Marty's right," he said.

"How's that?"

"You *are* smarter than you look."

She batted her eyelashes. "Wah, you make a lady swoon, suh."

Shavon smiled. "Heading back to Naperville?"

She nodded.

"Stay alive, do fifty-five."

Emily cracked up.

He burped the siren, took off.

She fired the Hemi and headed whence, face glowing blue in the dashboard lights.

37

Dead,
Dead,
Dead,
the girl was,
Spencer Abbott knew.
Lifeless eyes.
Mottled flesh.
No breath.
No soul.
Someone stole it.
He knew who.
Cajun is Gemini is Snakehead is Dettmer.
Cajun is Gemini is Snakehead is Dettmer.
Cajun is Gemini is Snakehead is Dettmer.
Same ones tried to kill him.
Same ones wouldn't succeed.
"If I can get us out of here," Abbott muttered, hauling his

throbbing body over stumps and rocks and branches and potholes and fox dens, one elbow-stab at a time.

If, he noted.

Not certain like before,

breathing hard

shivering harder

knuckles bleeding

thoughts distorting

appearing in fractures not sentences

hauling a girl with milky eyes

that he should abandon

too heavy

too draining

too overwhelming

but could not.

Collapse.

Again.

Blood spurting from heathen shoulder.

Mumbling blue, aiming at soul-thieves.

Lifting knife

sawing a twist of bandage

shrinking the drop cloth yet another inch

wrapping his wound to save his life

so hers would have dignity.

Wrapping his bullet wounds, over and over,

like some kind of mummy.

I'm a mummiologist, he thought.

Is there such a thing?

I want my mummy.

He bark-laughed in tiny hiccups.

The rabbits and squirrels fled.

Fearing the beast with two heads.

Abbott dug in with his elbow and his knife.

Moved another eight inches.

Saving himself,
or digging his grave,
he wasn't sure which.
Move.

38

Emily flew.

Not as fast as in the Charger.

Just as much fun, though.

Left, right, left, right, left, right, left, right.

Feeling the burn.

She leaned into the curve of the forested running path, heart rat-a-tatting. Slipped on a clump of limestone slurry, tumbled into the dense trailside brush.

"C'mon, clumsy, move it," she shouted, bolting from the sopping vegetation.

She missed the mossy smell of the DuPage River and the Naperville Riverwalk, where she ran for so many years. But in many ways, this new routine was better. She lived literally across the street from Herrick Lake, a forest preserve laced with intersecting paths that allowed her to run one mile, six, or twenty without feeling like she was on a treadmill. The crushed limestone was easier on her knees than the unyielding brick pavers of the Riverwalk. The smell of the forest was primeval. The lake held hundreds of ducks and geese that loved to splash around. She occasionally saw deer and foxes. And running under a starlit sky rather than Riverwalk, security lights plucked at her romantic side.

She'd been running since grade school, when she first discovered that her thighs resembled the cannons guarding her friendly neighborhood VFW post on Chicago's Southwest Side. So early one morning, she rolled out of the sleigh bed Dad built for her and ran around the block. Liking how the panting burn made her feel—proud, confident, slim— she went farther the next day. The day after that, she asked Mom if they could go downtown for new sneakers. Mom agreed, and Sunday after church they rode the clackety L train into the Loop. They bought the sneakers on State Street, then walked to Marshall Field's, which Emily considered the most elegant department store in the world. They stopped to chat with the white-haired lady who sold Mom cookware, then had tea in the Walnut Room. The waiter even cut the crusts off their sandwiches! Emily loved those hightone times with Mom every bit as much as she did doughnut Saturdays with Dad. Gerald and Alexandra Thompson were gone now, but their memories would live forever— ·

A puddle splashed her back to reality. She shook off the milky water, flew past the stone picnic shelter, and decelerated into the parking lot. Skidded abruptly when she spotted a dark form leaning against her Charger.

She gripped the Glock under her shirt. The form moved into the light. It was short and muscular, with a blond flattop, piercing gray eyes, and loose-fitting running clothes.

"Hey, Chief," she said, suspicions disappearing. "What are you doing here?"

Kendall Cross limped her way. Several decades ago, he'd been shot by an FBI agent who mistook the then–Las Vegas Police undercover for the killer they were all chasing. The shotgun blast tore a buttock clean off the bone. The surgeons saved Cross's life, but no amount of rehab could erase the limp. When his cop buddies knew he'd be all right, he was awarded the nickname "Half-Ass." Like all bad nicknames, it stuck.

"Looking for you," he said. "You finished, or just starting?"

"Finished," she said. "But I could go another mile."

"That's all I need."

They loped toward the lake, which shimmered in the waning moonlight.

"Want to be my next sergeant?" he said.

She stumbled. Cross caught her arm.

"Easy, Detective," he said. "It's not like I'd give you my parking space or anything."

"You want to promote me?" Emily said.

"Yes. Any reason I shouldn't?" he said.

"I've only been a cop five years. That's not a lot of time."

Cross made the turn at the far end of the lake. "Your five are fifteen of anyone else's," he said. "You tracked and defeated two major serial killers. You've made a ton of good arrests. Your informant network is impressive. People pay attention when you have something to say. I care about those things far more than time on the job."

Her pulse quickened. She hadn't given a thought to promotion, figuring she'd need another five years on the street. How could she possibly be good enough?

"I wouldn't lean on your Charger if I didn't think you'd succeed," Cross said, correctly reading her expression. "Which I understand was gathering no moss a short while ago?"

Emily was stunned. How'd he hear about I-88? Shavon wouldn't have said anything. . . .

"Your informants are good, but mine are legendary," he said. "See you at the station."

Emily stared in wonder till his taillights disappeared.

Then hopped in the car and headed for the shower.

39

"Garlic or jalapeno?" Marty asked, holding up the cheese curds.

"Both," Branch said. "Make sure they're fresh. They gotta squeak when we eat 'em."

"Wouldn't be hunting without the squeak," Marty said.

Branch grabbed a four-pack of Sprecher, a local root beer, and piled it on the checkout desk with the cheese curds. Marty added a sharp cheddar shaped like a beer mug.

"Breakfast?" said the apple-cheeked checkout gal.

"Nah. But it'll tide us over," Branch said.

"Good for you," she said. Rang it up, threw a handful of meat sticks into their brown paper bag. Grease spots formed immediately.

"No charge," she said.

"Marry me," Branch said.

She winked, waved up the next customer.

* * *

"I don't hit a crapper soon," Aquarius warned as the van rumbled over pavement strips, "you're gonna bitch about the smell."

"Say no more," Gemini said, turning into the exit.

He pulled into the parking lot of a long, squat building with a King Arthur turret on each end. The roof held a neon sign so big the man in the moon could see it.

"The hell is this place?" Cancer said, groggy from just waking up.

"Mars Cheese Castle," Gemini said. "You've never been?"

"Nope," Cancer said, stretching.

"You gotta get out more," Aquarius said.

They started walking.

"'Marry me'?" Marty said, pushing through the doors.

"Happy guys say stuff like that," Branch said.

"You're not happy," Marty said. "You're a miserable pud-knocker." He pulled a root beer from the bag. The label glistened with meat-stick grease. "If I asked whether this glass was half full or half empty, you'd shoot it and say, 'What glass.'"

"Of course I would," Branch said. "'Cause it's a bottle."

"You know what I mean."

"Nope," Branch said. "I'm too busy spreading joy to think such negative thoughts."

"Bullshit. You're miserable and you know it."

"Am not."

"Are too."

"Am not."

"Since when?"

Branch did a soft shoe.

Smiled like dawn breaking.

"Since I can walk again," he said.

* * *

"Now *there's* a Cadillac," Aquarius said, spying the black Escalade SUV. "Those seats are so plush you could sit a year and not get ass sores. And, Tony Soprano drives one."

"He does?" Gemini said.

"Yeah. In *The Sopranos*. Tony's the head of this crime family in—"

"I know who Tony Soprano is, dumbass," Gemini said. He *was* tempted; be fun to ride like the king of New fucking Jersey. "Cancer? What do you think?"

"Our van ain't all that," Cancer said.

They headed for the Escalade.

"I have to admit," Marty said, shifting the bag from right arm to left, "that you have been less of a pain in the ass lately. And you walk good without that cane. Just a tiny little hitch in your stride, nothing you'd even notice unless you knew about it."

"No," Branch said.

"No what?"

"I won't marry you."

Marty snorted. "As DeNiro said to Grodin in *Midnight Run*, here come two words for you: shut the fuck up—"

Caught the hardening in Branch's expression. Followed the stare.

Three men hovered near the Escalade's driver's door. Young. Muscled. Stone-faced. Tense. Sending a vibe more greasy than the sausage.

Without breaking stride, Marty cut to his left and Branch to his right. Each shook his neck loose, flexed his hands.

Getting ready.

For whatever these three wanted.

* * *

"Let's go," Gemini said.

"Thought we were stealing the truck," Aquarius objected.

"Changed my mind," Gemini said. He'd watched these two since they'd exited the store. They talked and smiled like tourists, but their eyes were constantly moving, evaluating. They were relaxed, but not oblivious. Big enough not to scare easily, which was reinforced by the long, white scar curving down the face of the one who walked with just the slightest of hitches. He couldn't read them exactly, but he knew one thing.

These two would bite back.

Gemini felt their eyes on his back as they passed.

"Perhaps our manliness scared them," Branch said, placing the food in the cab.

"Good thing," Marty said. "Be a shame to get blood on our cheese."

"Their blood?" Branch said. "Or ours?"

Marty laughed.

Wasn't a predator alive the two of them couldn't handle.

Then again, they hadn't met them all.

"What say," Branch said, sliding behind the steering wheel, "we wait on breakfast till they're back on the road."

"Think they're robbing the place?"

"Crossed my mind."

"Aw, man, they're waiting," Cancer said, his voice straining as they exited the store.

Gemini glanced at the idling Escalade, which had moved to a strategic position near the back of the lot. "No problem," he said, slowing his stride. "Act like nothing's wrong and you'll be fine. Don't give them a reason to call their brothers in blue."

He put the vending machine repairman's raspberry-colored van into gear, and bumped onto the service road that fed southbound I-94.

"Think they're cops?" Aquarius said, fiddling with the GPS so he wouldn't stare.

"Anyone else would have left," Gemini said, accelerating.

"False alarm," Marty said as the van disappeared.

"Yeah," Branch said. "But I'd still bet they didn't get any free beef sticks."

They walked next door for breakfast.

Gemini shivered.

"What?" Aquarius said.

"Don't know why exactly, but we saved our own asses not tangling with those two," he said, biting into a chunk of caraway Swiss. "And we're not stopping again till we hit Naperville. You gotta pee, do it in your goddamn pants."

"To the hunt," Marty said, settling into the table.

"The first since we were hunted," Branch said.

They clacked cups and slugged down the thick coffee. Watched four young men swagger in, talking loudly. An older Asian man showed them to a table. The tallest said they were white enough to rate a booth, goddammit, so get on it. Marty frowned. The Asian reseated them.

Marty turned away, shrugging.

"No pain at all?" he said, admiring the abstract whorls the cream made in his coffee. Art in every cup.

"None," Branch said. "Honest to God, this titanium hip is a miracle." He'd been shot by one of Emily's serial killers, pulverizing his hip and forcing a replacement. The first one didn't fuse with the bone. This was the second. This trip was the final test in getting his life back completely. "Walking, running, lifting weights? No problem."

"Excellent . . ."

More noise. They turned. The guy who'd proclaimed his whiteness was pointing to the Asian man while bucking out his teeth and pulling his eyes into a slant. Belly laughs from his mates. He accepted the tribute with a head bow, fingering the long, fuzzy soul patch under his chapped lip. A young woman walked past the booth. She was pretty, with medium brown hair carefully combed and blue jeans neatly pressed. Soul Patch grabbed her butt. She pirouetted to break the grab, kept walking.

"Welcome to the Mars Cheese Castle Restaurant, now open for breakfast," she said, handing them menus shaped like muskies. "My name is Emily—"

Marty brightened.

"—Clark, but please call me Clark, cause we Martians are terribly formal." Her brows danced mischievously at the gag. "I'll be your server today."

Branch opened to the specials. "Those guys back there," he said casually, nodding at the booth. "Are they friends of yours?"

Clark's eyes rolled so high the irises disappeared. "Local football heroes," she said, disdain dripping from each syllable. "Think they own this town."

"Seem to think they own you too," Marty said.

Her wry smile said, *Goes with the territory of waitressing.* "Just passing through?" she said. "Or are you staying at one of our fine water-park resorts that provide a wonderful weekend getaway for you and the entire family?"

"I'm impressed," Branch said.

"At?"

"You said that with a straight face."

She showed perfect white teeth. "Mr. Teng is a proud member of the Dells chamber."

"Mr. Teng? Is that who seated us?"

"Yes. He's the manager."

"We're heading up to Black River Forest," Marty said. "Deer hunting."

"Well, the season opens at seven," Clark said, checking her watch. "So you're going to be late."

"We let the wannabes go first," Branch said. "Saves us getting shot by mistake."

"Smartest thing I've heard all day," Clark said. She pulled out a narrow green pad, standard waitress issue, and clicked her pen. "Do you know what you want?"

Another raucous burst from the booth.

"A cork for their big mouths," Marty said.

"Fine by me," Clark said. "They give Mr. Teng a really hard time, and he doesn't deserve it."

Branch looked at the middle-aged manager. He wore a white, long-sleeved shirt tucked neatly into pleated tan Dockers. His shoes gleamed, his socks matched his belt, and not a hair was out of place. He was answering the phone, writing lunch specials on a menu board, signing for a food delivery, and passing takeout orders to the cook. His restaurant was a beanery named after a planet, but he treated it like the hottest joint in Las Vegas.

"Why the hard time?" Marty said. "Because he's Asian?"

"Hmong," Clark said.

Branch and Marty looked at each other. In November 2004, Chai Vang, an immigrant from the Hmong tribe in Laos, shot eight white deer hunters in Meteor, a hamlet not far from Black River Falls. Several of the eight had accused Vang of trespassing on their deer stand. Vang denied it, but agreed to walk away. Racial slurs were hurled. Vang wheeled and opened fire with his rifle. Six hunters died. Two were crippled. Vang was sentenced to multiple life terms, but the racial radioactivity that followed had a half-life of forever.

"Just because one's a murderer doesn't means they all are," Branch said.

"I know," Clark said. She nodded at the booth. "They do, too. But they give him crap anyway because they think it's fun." She flourished the pad. "Enough of that. Let's get you fed and on your way to deer camp."

"Biscuits and gravy," Branch said. "With strawberry pancakes."

"I dunno, pal," Marty said. "Fruit might interfere with the grease."

"Good point," Branch said. "Make them chocolate chip."

Clark snickered. "And you, sir?"

Marty folded the menu. "Any chance of walleye this early in the morning?"

She looked doubtful.

"Well, if you can, that'd be cool," he said. "Otherwise, cheddar omelette with a side of bacon, side of biscuits and gravy."

She wrote it up and left. Skirted the booth on the way to the kitchen.

"So," Branch said, settling in. "When are you going to marry her?"

Marty stopped mid-sip. "Marry who? Clark?"

"No, wiseass. Our Emily."

"What makes you ask?"

"When the waitress said her first name was Emily, your face lit so bright it burned my retinas," Branch said. "You've got it bad."

Marty sighed. "Yeah, I guess I do."

"So marry her already. Before she realizes she could do a whole lot better."

"Ha," Marty said. "Who could be better than me?"

"Serial killers are less annoying than you."

Marty tried to look miffed, couldn't hold it. "The moment I think of a devastating comeback," he said, "I'll slap it on you like a dead muskie—"

Another racist burst from the booth. Several diners glared. The men glared back. The diners looked away fast.

"Those guys are annoying me," Marty said.

"Easy, tiger," Branch said. "Not our fight."

"Yeah, yeah," Marty muttered. "What were we talking about?"

"You."

"That's boring," Marty said. "Let's talk about something good, like Samantha Hawkins."

"Good?" Branch said, sipping more coffee. "How does that poor girl's problems translate to good?"

Marty waved his hands. "Not the disease. That's terrible. What's good is the fact Hawk's gonna have the three million he needs by noon."

"Really?" Branch said, perking up. "Damn. Where'd you hear that?"

"He told Em at the liquor store thing. He'll hit three million at noon today."

Branch looked exceptionally pleased.

"Lining up that trophy buck in your daydreams?" Clark said as she put down a steaming plate of pancakes.

"A little girl with a rare disease," Branch said.

"And that makes you smile?" she said warily.

Branch wagged his finger. "The cure does. Her dad is Robert Hawkins, a friend of ours. He's been raising money for a year to pay for it. This afternoon, he'll have the three million dollars he needs to put her in a Los Angeles specialty hospital and save her life."

"That's worth smiling about," Clark said. "What does the poor girl have?"

"Rhabdomyosarcomal carcinoma," Marty said. "Radical-ized."

"Wow," Clark said. "What's it mean?"

Marty fingered a chocolate chip from Branch's stack. "It's a new variant of a cancer that makes tumors sprout like dandelions. The clusters grow to the size of baseballs, and they go all over the place. If they're in the lungs, it's like an asthma attack. In the brain, you go into spasms. In the eyes, you're blind. The diaphragm, you quit breathing. The spine or heart . . ."

"We try not to think about that," Branch said.

"How dreadful," Clark said. "What's this girl's name?"

"Samantha. Goes by Sammy. She's seven."

The ache in Clark's expression could cut glass. "This rabbo-whatever goes where it wants?"

"Without warning," Branch said. "That's what makes it so maddening—you can't anticipate where it'll go next, or how long it'll stay." He broke off a chunk of biscuit, dipped it in sausage gravy. The yellow cream glowed in the overhead lights. "The drugs she's on slow the process, but can't stop it. Sammy gets weaker with each attack. She needs this experimental cure. It's her only chance to see eight."

Clark nodded. "What is this magic treatment?"

Marty explained. "It's cured dozens of kids in Europe and Asia. Sammy's specialist in L.A. says she's the ideal candidate. But since it's considered experimental in the United States—"

"—insurance refuses to pay," Clark interrupted. "I know all about that. My boyfriend in high school needed a bone marrow transplant. Insurance wouldn't approve it. The family couldn't raise the money. He died." Her mouth curled like she tasted something foul. "Insurance companies *are* the cancer."

"No argument here," Marty said. "Oh, and feel free to leave that."

Clark looked at her hands, which were filled with his breakfast. She served it with apologies. "We can make the walleye, no problem," she said, refilling their cups. "But that'll take a while cause it's frozen—the fresh shipment isn't in yet. I told chef to make your omelette, seeing as you want to get up north. If you still want the walleye, I can—"

"You made the right call," Marty assured. "I'll take a rain check, though. Nothing better than pan-fried walleye with—"

"Yo, Em-tard," Soul Patch shouted, waving his cup. "Out of coffee. Sashay over here and fill me up." He patted his crotch, then his cup. "I already put in the cream."

Marty turned full in his log chair. "Give it a rest, dick-weed," he said. "Your hot air's making my ears sweat."

Soul Patch tried to look tough. "Stick those ears up your ass, Gramps."

Marty rose from the chair. Branch put his hand on Marty's arm.

"Oooh, look," one of the others minced. "His boyfriend's sweet on him. Look at how they're touching. Get a room, you fruits."

They all howled.

Mr. Teng hurried to the booth.

"I do not want trouble," he told the four. "What if you fellows finish your breakfast, and I will pay for it. How would that be?"

Soul Patch snorted. "Why don't you just shoot us in the back, slant-eyes? Then you could steal our wallets and live large on white man money."

"Uh, Gramps?" Branch said.

"Yes, Sweetie?"

"I think it's our fight now."

"Mmm. I do believe you're right."

Marty took the coffeepot from Clark's hand, folded a napkin over his arm like a waiter, and headed for the booth.

"What's he going to do?" Clark whispered.

"I don't know," Branch said. "But it's sure to be entertaining."

"Boys," Marty said when he reached the booth. "I came to apologize. I should have minded my own business."

"Damn right you shoulda," Soul Patch snapped. "I got a constitutional right to say whatever the hell I want, and if Mr. Chinky here doesn't like it, he can go back where he came from."

"You're absolutely right," Marty said. "Like I said, I apologize. To show you my good faith, I'll fill you up myself."

"Well, now," Soul Patch said, grinning. "That's all right with me. Guess you know who's boss around this—ow! You son of a bitch!"

"I didn't say anything about a cup," Marty said, emptying the pot in Soul Patch's lap. "I said I'll fill you up myself."

The man screamed as the pain tsunami hit. He balled his fists, started getting up.

Marty grabbed the soul patch and twisted brutally.

Another scream.

"As for the rest of you," Branch said, grabbing a canoe paddle off the wall and reaching the booth in eight long strides. "Trying getting up and see what happens."

Mr. Teng dashed to the phone. Clark pulled pepper spray. Marty twisted again.

"Stop it, stop it, Jesus that hurts," Soul Patch sobbed.

"Listen up, you hemorrhoid," Marty hissed. "I like Miss Clark and I don't like you. I like Mr. Teng and I don't like you. I like Mars and I don't like you. Treat any of them like dirt again and I'll come back and find you. You don't want that. Do you understand me?"

"Y-y-yes . . ."

"Then say it."

"I understand, I understand, I won't disrespect them again."

Marty glared at the others. They raised their hands. "Good. Now get the hell out of here," he said, releasing the soul patch and stepping back. They fled so fast one tripped over his own feet, smacking his head on the exit door. The diners applauded.

Branch and Marty went back to their log chairs.

"A *paddle*?" Marty said.

Mr. Teng came over.

"Thank you very much," he said. "It was most kind of you to step in."

Marty nodded. "We hate to see that kind of nonsense, that's all."

"So do I," Mr. Teng said. "There was a time I would have kicked their pretty butts and swept them into my garbage cans. Now . . ."

"I thought you were hobbling," Branch said. "Accident?"

"Vietnam," Mr. Teng said. "A million years ago. I stepped on a land mine. Kept my right leg, but the left was not as lucky. I lost it below the knee. I came to this country after the war. Worked for the paper mills, but those jobs are gone now. So I started this restaurant."

"The Hmong were some of the most valiant fighters in the war," Branch said.

Mr. Teng smiled. "I appreciate your saying so," he said. "All we were doing was protecting our home from invaders. We were grateful to you Americans for helping repel them, and for letting so many of us settle here after the war ended. The communists would have thrown me into a death camp, if they didn't shoot me first."

A Wisconsin Dells cruiser pulled up to the entrance.

"I called the police," Mr. Teng said. "When I wrongly assumed the young men had the upper hand. I will explain what happened so there is no trouble for you."

"Appreciate that," Branch said.

The cop walked through the door. Mr. Teng walked his way.

Clark brought new food.

"Here you go," she said, putting the plates on the table. "I hope you're still hungry."

"That's never a problem," Marty said, raising his fork. Branch did likewise, and they picked up their conversation. A few minutes later, the cop joined them. He was medium-tall and beefy, with the nose of an outclassed welterweight.

"I'm Dell," he said.

"Ironic," Marty said. "Want some coffee?"

"Don't mind if I do," Dell said. "Been untangling highways since midnight, everyone heading to deer camp."

Clark brought him a mushroom omelette. They introduced themselves, fell into the food.

"So," Dell said after a while. "Which one of you works for Ken Cross?"

"That'd be me," Branch said. "You know him?"

"Some," Dell said. "Feds held a homeland security workshop in Black River Falls last year. Ken was a guest instructor. Smart guy."

"That he is," Branch said.

"Drank beer with us nights," Dell said. "Us local flatfoots, I mean. That meant something. The feds looked at us like the stuff they scraped off their shoes." He scratched his Spam-colored face. "Or is it flatfeet? I can never remember."

They laughed.

"Speaking of locals," Branch said. "We gonna catch any heat from this dustup with your homies?"

"Not from me," Dell said, spearing one of Marty's bacons. "Look up butt wipe in the dictionary, you'll see their picture. But their parents are muckety-mucks, so there's not much us poor ole coppers can do about them."

"But since we don't work for mommy and daddy . . ."

"To quote my esteemed chief, 'Gee, what a shame their little asses got kicked, but hey, you're from out of town, you didn't know how important they are.'"

"Works for me," Marty said.

"Welcome to Mars," Dell said.

40

"I'm still not comfortable with this," Cancer muttered.

"With what?" Gemini said.

"Having arranged this delivery through text messages. What if it wasn't Maxximus on the other end? What if it's a police sting? Or one of Maxx's competitors?"

"It isn't," Gemini said, steering the raspberry van into the empty garage.

"You don't know that. Could be a dozen zombies in there, waiting to cut our throats."

"You worry too much."

"And even if it is Maxx, maybe he's gonna rip us off," Cancer said, undeterred. "Katrina's hotter than Obama's dick—everybody wants a piece. What's to keep him from shooting us and keeping the drugs *and* money?"

Gemini was getting annoyed. Cancer's pessimism at end game had saved their bacon more than once, he had to admit. But now, just inches from pay dirt . . .

"We've run Maxx's drugs for years," Gemini said. "Has

he ever stiffed us? By even a dollar? When that supplier in Denver shorted us a kilo, did he take it out of our cut?"

"No," Cancer admitted.

"That's right, he didn't," Gemini said. "We were paid in full. He'll come through this time, just like always. He needs us to make his transfers and keep his suppliers in line. He also knows what'll happen if plays us."

"There is that," Aquarius said, remembering how many pieces they'd chopped the Denver supplier into when they'd discovered the holdback. Cops found body parts for months, with each fresh discovery making the news. It was an object lesson to Maxximus as much as to anyone else thinking of screwing with them.

"As for this," Gemini said, tapping his cell phone, "it's bulletproof. Nobody has the access codes but me and Maxx. Not cops, not zombies, not Davey Dipshit playing computer games in his mommy's basement. Maxx was on the other end, and our pay is waiting."

He flipped the house key around his finger.

"We handled eight long hours of storms. We slit a girl's throat, machine-gunned a cop, and torched his cruiser. We lost Virgo, shot the geezer, knifed the repairman, and *still* got here on time. I'm due, and I want it now. If you're too afraid to go inside, then stay out here and, I don't know, scrape the bugs off the windshield or something."

Cancer huffed.

Snatched up the box of Katrina.

Gemini smiled to himself.

They opened the door, guns drawn on the slim chance Cancer wasn't just being pissy.

"Gas company. There's a leak," Gemini hollered.

Nothing but hollowness.

"Maybe the zombies are in the basement," Aquarius said. "Or in the attic. No, wait, they're on the roof, ready to eat our livers with fava beans and a fine—"

"Oh, shut up," Cancer muttered, lowering the Uzi.

Gemini slapped his back. "Come on, m'man, it's payday. Time to par-tay."

They brought the Katrina to the master bedroom. Maxximus owned this house and dozens like it, scattered in suburbs throughout the Midwest. To the outside world, they were property investments, waiting for the sour market to turn. Gemini knew better. They were drop houses, created and maintained to get narcotics and money where they needed to be.

They entered the master bath, opened the vanity. Inside were two canvas bags. They removed twenty thousand dollars in cash—their payment for this run—refilled the bags with Katrina, and put them back in the vanity. Then they counted the money.

Three times.

"What now, boss?" said an enormously relieved Cancer.

"Beer," Gemini said, revving the van. "Then pussy, beer, and more pussy."

"And did I mention beer?" Aquarius said.

They rolled out of the garage and around Sylvan Circle. Waited at the corner of White Oak Drive for a school bus to fold its stop wings. The driver waved thanks. Gemini waved back, amused.

"If they only knew," Aquarius said.

"If they knew," Gemini said, "they'd run away screaming."

41

Abbott's fingers were wrinkled blue. His good arm was spasming, and almost as numb as his legs. The clothesline attaching the dead girl to his waist sawed him raw. His head throbbed, and he was so cold he was ready to close his eyes, drift painlessly into death.

He planted his knife, then his elbow, pulled till his shoulder screamed.

Inching closer to life.

He'd spotted the cave an hour ago. It took him this long to get here. But he'd done it.

Ten more feet.

Now eight.

"C'mon . . . lazy . . . get lead out," he urged himself. "Inside . . . warm and dry."

Now three.

Now two.

He crawled into the mouth of the cave.

Fell into the river.

"What?" he sputtered. "What?"

The shock of the water made him see it. The cave was a hallucination. His agony had been for naught. He'd crawled a big circle, and was back where he started. Back in the river.

He began to cry.

42

"Sammy was this close to dying!" Hawk shouted as he drove along Seventy-fifth Street. "But the only thing she asked for was you. She wanted you to hold her hand. Comb her hair. Tell her everything would be all right. Doesn't that mean anything to you anymore?"

Silence.

"Come on, Bonnie, say something," he said, trying to control his fury. He heard the beep of an incoming call. Ignored it. "Talk to me. I know you're there."

"Of course it means something," his wife said. "I love her more than anything in the world."

"Then come home and tell her."

"I want to be there. Take care of her. But I . . . I can't."

Hawk's temples pounded. "Sure you can," he said. "Just hop in the car and drive. Easy as pie. I've kept your side of the bed warm."

"That's nice," she said.

"Oh, fuck you," he snapped.

"I wasn't being sarcastic," Bonnie said. "I mean it, Hawk. You're a genuinely nice man, and you've treated me so . . . well. I don't deserve it."

"You did what you had to do," Hawk said, softening.

"A mother shouldn't abandon her sick child," she said, her voice thinning to translucency. "It's unforgiveable. If one of our friends walked away like I did . . ."

Hawk let her ramble. This is how their conversations went. Since the diagnosis last fall, Bonnie had watched their daughter go blind, lose teeth, bleed brown from Third World–level diarrhea, fall because her legs were too weak to keep her upright, and screech from the press of tumors on nerve junctions. She spent hours tracing the lumps of the various tumors pushing up Sammy's skin like tent poles. She blamed herself. She didn't nurse Sammy long enough, or choose the right brand of strained peas, or sterilize the sandbox. She hardly slept, wondering if this little cough or that skinned knee would turn fatal. She worked as many side jobs as Hawk, flogged the fundraising horse just as mercilessly. Then one day, she packed a suitcase and drove to her sister in Memphis. Hawk flew down, but Bonnie was too ashamed to face him. They talked almost every day, but the result was the same—Bonnie couldn't come home because she couldn't watch Sammy die.

But now, she wouldn't have to.

"I got the three million," he said.

Sammy's little hands crawled up her ribs, and onto her chest.

Felt the high, lumpy ridge of the tumors.

"Mommy," she whimpered.

No answer.

She remembered Daddy's promise. They'd fly to L.A. and make her well. They'd fly to L.A. and make the tumors go away. They'd fly to L.A. . . .

Make me pretty again.

She touched her little finger. Daddy had taken a Magic Marker and drawn a ring with a heart in the center, then drawn the same ring on himself. It was a magic ring, he said, to let any monsters in her dreams know Daddy was on the job and they shouldn't stay.

Her lips drifted upwards.

Barbara Winslow slowed her walk and stuck her head in the ICU room.

Saw Sammy smiling in her sleep.

"Pleasant dreams, baby," Winslow murmured. "Whatever they are."

"Omigod," Bonnie said, tears in her voice. "Omigod. Omigod."

"The air ambulance is on standby," Hawk said. "The minute Sammy can travel, we'll take off for L.A. You know what that means?"

"She'll . . . she'll . . . she'll . . . she'll . . ."

Bonnie couldn't say it. He barely believed it himself.

"She'll be cured," he said for them both.

"Cured," she mumbled, as if a child.

"We did it, Bonnie," Hawk said. "We're there."

She began to hiccup. Something she did when enormously excited.

"We got the money. All of it. Sammy isn't going to die anymore," he said, his words a tumble and rush. "So please, baby, come home. We'll go as a family and come back like nothing ever happened. Start over." He was so worked up he was crying himself.

"Are you all right, Hawk?" Bonnie said, her excitement

tempered with a deeply abiding concern for her husband. "With all this good news, you should be joyous. But you sound so, I don't know, depressed."

He ground his teeth. Bonnie could always read him. Every tone, every inflection, she *knew*.

How could he explain that what he'd had to do to make the numbers work ate at him so thoroughly he might not come back whole?

He couldn't. He needed her back in his life. He needed to watch her watching their daughter do jumping jacks in the middle of their bed, chatterboxing like Sammy of old, excited about Mr. Ed, the little pony they'd rented last summer at Yellowstone so she could ride. She'd wound up falling in horse-love, as little girls do before they grow up, and please Lord Jesus, he wanted his little girl to grow up.

"I'm fine," Hawk said, rubbing his eyes. "Please, Bonnie, just come home."

43

The ground tilted down.

Almost at the river, the deer realized.

He'd collapsed many times since leaving the wolf. He was weak from the thunder-sticks and the burning swipe in his ribs. But he'd managed to keep moving, and now, the river's mossy scent overwhelmed.

I'm there.

He tested the rushing water with one foot.

Shook his head.

Jumped in.

The shock of the cold made his teeth clack. But it numbed his pain.

After a while he climbed back on the bank, shook himself loose. Looked for the moon to get his bearings. Pointed himself upriver.

This way home.

44

Emily clicked her heels as she shot off a perfect hand salute.

"Shut up," Annie said.

"But I only live to serve you, O eminent and holy chiefness."

"Then pull up a chair and serve me coffee. You have breakfast yet?"

Emily nodded. "Stopped at Grandma Sally's."

"Denver with egg whites?"

"Yep."

"Still hungry?"

"Of course."

Annie pointed to the blue china plate filled with pumpkin bread. "Made that the other day," she said. "Tell me what you think. . . ."

A few minutes ago, Emily drove past Annie's house on White Oak Drive. She spied her best friend on the front porch of the brick-and-cedar ranch and tootled her horn.

Annie motioned, *come and join me.* Emily parked the Charger at the curb and hopscotched up the sidewalk to avoid the earthworms that had slithered out from the rain.

"So your reign of terror begins," Emily said, picking up the pot.

"Nobody's died in the past three hours," Annie said. "I'm a rousing success."

She noticed the pistol on Emily's hip.

"Is that the custom you've been waiting for?" she said, wiggling her hand.

"I love this thing," Emily said, handing it over.

Annie cooed over the crisp trigger, high-visibility sights, and grip reduction that made the Glock's blocky handle slim and trim. "Union Arms do this?" she asked.

"Mike and Matthew," Emily confirmed.

"Couple of magicians, they are," Annie said, patting the pistol. "Use it in good health."

Emily reholstered, then picked up the half-and-half. Land O'Lakes, she noted. The good stuff. Off-tone clangs began filling the air. She made a face. She despised the Naperville Millennium Carillon. The "music" was harsh and discordant, and the multistory bell tower thrusting skyward from the banks of the Riverwalk reminded her of an erection.

"I know, I hate it too," Annie said. "There're enough dicks in this town already." She raised an eyebrow. "Speaking of which, how'd your fond farewell go with Marty?"

Emily poured half-and-half till her cup crested over.

"Yeah, baby," Annie said, swinging her bare feet onto an empty chair.

Emily stared.

"*I* didn't do this," Annie said, wiggling her toes. "Critters attacked me."

"Critters . . ."

"Otherwise known as my daughters."

"Hi, Aunt Emily," Tristen chirped as she bounded out the front door. She smooched Emily's cheek. "Do you like Mom's makeover?"

"It's . . . amazing," Emily said. Each nail was painted orange, pink, or yellow. C-H-I-E-F was Magic Markered on the left nails. G-R-I-E-F was on the right. O-F was on the arch of her right foot. CHIEF OF GRIEF. "And they're upside-down so Mom can see. Nice touch."

"Whoever figured that out is smart," Tristen said, blowing a kiss, then running back inside.

"'Whoever'?" Annie said to her wake.

Alexa's round face smooshed against the window.

"Mom was on her computer last night, Aunt Emily," she explained. "But she fell asleep. Someone must have sneaked in and taken advantage."

"Someone and Whoever," Emily said, "are two of my favorite people."

Alexa giggled. "Mine too."

"Take a left," Cancer said, tapping the GPS. "Quickest way out of this subdivision."

Gemini turned onto White Oak Drive.

"Howdy, Detective," Joshua said, wandering onto the porch in a dove gray suit with a collar-less shirt. Emily reached up to squeeze his hand.

"You're looking mighty *GQ* today, Mr. English Professor," she said.

"Exactly what I need to be or not to be." He smiled. "Walk me to the car, Mrs. Bates?"

"Don't go away," Annie told Emily with a wink. "I want all the juicy details."

"About what?" Joshua asked.

"Guns," Emily and Annie chorused.

"Thelma and Louise," Joshua said.

Emily glanced at her watch. If traffic was cooperative, Marty and Branch were in the Dells.

She grabbed more pumpkin bread. Kind of wished it were fatty and greasy.

"My *job*?" Annie said, stunned.

"Yeah," Joshua said, describing Tristen's sobbing breakdown. "I'm pretty sure that's why she's so moody these days."

"She grew up with me in uniform," Annie argued. "Brags that Mommy's a SWAT. Still likes riding in a cruiser, blowing the siren. How could that threaten her now?"

"It doesn't threaten her," Joshua said, putting his briefcase in his car. "It scares her. She sees the news. She knows how much danger cops and soldiers are in these days."

Annie paced, snowblower to lawn mower.

"She's afraid I'll die next time," she muttered, recalling her family's horror at the first serial killer having broken her pelvis and stabbed her with a bayonet.

"Leaving her alone in the world," Joshua said.

Annie's pace quickened. "That's crazy. She'd have you. Alexa. Grandmas and grandpas and Aunt Emily and the relatives and our friends and—"

"A girl needs her mother," Joshua said.

"Jesus," Annie sighed, running her hands through her ringlets. "What'll we do?"

Joshua glanced at his watch. "Nothing, for now. I have to go."

She hugged him.

"I can't quit being who I am," she said. "Does that make me a bad mother?"

"Probably," Joshua said.

Annie stiffened. "I'm serious, Joshua."

"Fortunately, I'm not," he said. "You are who you are, Annabelle. That's why we love you, so that's who you need to be. Tris will understand when she gets older."

"But now?" Annie said, shaking her head. "What'll I do about it now?"

Joshua hit the opener, climbed into the car.

"Wear socks," he said.

"She loves those toenails," Tristen said.

"You really think?"

"'Course I do. I'm your older sister, and I know everything."

Alexa beamed. Her plan to cheer up Tris had been a roaring success. And the toes were pretty awesome. She'd upload them to Facebook if she had an account, but she didn't, because Mom and Dad said she was too young.

"Come on, Rembrandt," Tristen said, pinching Alexa's arm. "Bus'll be here in a minute."

They said good-bye to Aunt Emily and waved to Mom, who was walking out of the garage with a frown. Dad honked from the street.

They headed for the bus stop at the top of the hill.

"Everything all right?" Emily said, noticing Annie's distracted look.

Annie watched a raspberry-colored van fishtail up the hill. It was a sharp, tight corner, even a mile over the limit you lost control.

"Tristen's afraid I'm going to die," she said.

"What?" Emily said, sitting up.

Annie explained.

Emily shook her head. Like Annie and Joshua, she'd

thought it was the rebellion of being a teen. Or a mother-daughter thing. "I never sensed that in her. Not once."

"Me neither," Annie said. "Mother of the freakin' year, right?"

"You're a terrific mom," Emily protested. "If those girls didn't think so, they'd never have painted your toes."

"Well, there's that," Annie said, brightening. "How was it for you? Losing your mother, I mean. I know you were in college and that's a little older, but . . ."

"It was the worst day of my life," Emily said quietly.

The cheerful chatter of kids heading for the school bus wafted across the porch.

"You think your folks will live forever," she continued. "Then they don't, and you're stuck with a lifetime of what-ifs."

Annie winced.

"No, no," Emily hastened. "I'm sure that's not the case with Tristen."

"But what if it is?" Annie said, playing with her wedding ring, a thin band of yellow gold. "What if she's really afraid of me dying? Afraid of losing herself if I do?"

Emily didn't know how to respond. She didn't have kids. She didn't even have a goldfish. Her life seemed more about death. "They don't teach this stuff in sniper school, do they?"

Annie wiped her eyes. "I know a hundred ways to kill someone," she said. "But I can't make my daughter unafraid. What kind of insanity is that?"

The conversation unearthed the rawness of Emily's battle with the panic dragon. That was the real reason she'd come. She'd refused to spoil Marty's trip, but still needed to unburden herself, and that's what best friends were for.

"Your family is terrific. You'll come out on top," Emily said. "I wish I could say the same."

Annie blinked. "Here I am whining and you've got troubles. Are you all right? Is Marty?"

Emily waved her hands. "It's me. I've had some . . . problems."

Annie scooted closer, looked at her full face. "Tell me."

"I've been having flashbacks," she said, feeling the hot breath of the dragon on her neck.

"To what? The serial killings?"

"Yeah. They began a year ago."

"When you started getting the body parts."

Emily nodded. "The flashbacks were no big deal at first. Just fragments, now and again, easily ignored. But they got worse. More complete. More . . . violent."

"I'm not surprised, with what you went through," Annie said. "What triggers them?"

"Nothing. They come out of nowhere. But they hit me like a ton of bricks." She felt herself breathing harder. "I had one at the liquor store, before we went in. One later. They only lasted a few seconds, but . . . wow." She shook her head. "Everyone told me I'd have flashbacks, Annie. Bad dreams, nightmares, the whole enchilada. But I never believed it. I honestly thought I'd skate free." She despised the tremble in her voice. "I really did."

Annie squeezed Emily's hands. "We think we can forget, but trauma's always up there, rattling around. Most of the time it doesn't mess with us. But sometimes."

"You too?" Emily said, catching the undertone.

Annie nodded. "My first confirmed kill. To this day, I can count the hairs in the man's beard. See the hole I punched in his forehead."

"I didn't know," Emily said.

"It was a righteous takedown," Annie said, nodding for emphasis. "He was a Taliban commander. He planted a bomb in a fruit market. I saw the CIA videos of his massacre. A SEAL team tracked him, and I sniped him. I was happy to do it." She recalled her glee at watching the Taliban commander deflate like a torn balloon. "But it still wakes me up sometimes."

They fidgeted with their cups.

"Then, there was the nightmare," Emily said.

She explained.

"The dragon," Annie mused. "That's what you called the vision you had when you were trapped in your burning house. The fire-breathing dragon. I thought it was gone."

"It's baaaaaack," Emily said, bitterness spilling with the words.

"Did you tell Marty?"

"He'd cancel the trip if he knew."

"Wouldn't you?"

"Yes. So I lied, said I couldn't remember what the nightmare was about," Emily said. "So, is that a sin of commission, or omission?"

"It's compassion," Annie said. "Not all truth needs telling. At least not right away. When Marty gets home, tell him you finally remembered. Problem solved."

"I wish," Emily grumped.

"If wishes were horses, we'd all ride," Annie said.

"What the heck does that mean?"

Annie shrugged. "It's home-spun, so it must be good, right? As for those pesky flashbacks."

Emily leaned expectantly.

"We'll just have to talk about them till we figure it out. Like my problem with Tris. The two of us are smart enough, right?"

Emily turned her hand back and forth.

"All right, we're not that smart," Annie conceded. "But we're cute."

"That we are," Emily said.

* * *

"Damn," Cancer breathed. "She's perfect. Ever better than Kandy."

"Look at those legs," Aquarius said, admiring Tristen's rangy stride. "That little ass swishing back and forth. Freddie-Boy will cream himself."

"If he doesn't," Gemini said, "I'll walk down Michigan Avenue in panties and a top hat."

"Let's snatch her right now," Cancer said.

Gemini looked around. No threats he could see, only a couple of women gabbing on a front porch. But it paid to tread lightly in upper-class suburbs filled with anxious parents. If they screwed up, the police response would be brutal. "We'll drive past the bus," he said. "If everything looks all right, we'll come around again and take her."

Cancer worked the GPS for escape routes.

"What about the little one?" Aquarius said, videotaping the pair as they passed.

"We'll take her too," Gemini said, checking her in the rearview. "Foreign pervs love their baby fat." He pulled his cell phone, dialed Freddie-Boy.

"Got a two-fer," he said.

"Better than before?" Freddie-Boy said. "I was quite disappointed—"

"You were in some bad fuckin' mood and taking it out on me," Gemini said. "But never mind that. I got two. Might be sisters."

"Sisters? Those are exceedingly hard to find."

"Tell me about it," Gemini said. "One's thirteenish; the other's younger." He sent the video. Heard the sharp intake of breath, knew he had Freddie-Boy by the balls.

"One hundred K," Gemini said.

"Are you insane?" Freddie-Boy said.

"You'll get two million for this package, those freaks you deal with."

Freddie-Boy laughed. Gemini had always been smarter than he looked.

"All right," he said. "But if they don't measure up, you'll be sucking my—"

"That ain't *ever* gonna happen," Gemini said. "See you in an hour."

"Second time that van's turned up your street," Emily said with a frown. "A man's driving."

"You sure it's a man?" Annie said. "They're usually off to work by now."

"Triangular head, bright yellow hair, mushroom cut."

They looked at the bus stop. Tristen and Alexa were closing fast, waving at friends.

"It's probably nothing," Emily said, slipping into her shoes. "He's probably trying to find an address, drop off his kid for play date."

"Probably," Annie said.

They started for the street.

"Fifteen yards," Cancer muttered as Gemini steered corrections. "You can get closer. Perfect. Six yards. Four. Ready . . . set . . ."

The van darted to the curb, culling Tristen and Alexa from the herd. Two men thundered out the doors, hands grabbing.

"Run," Emily screamed, adrenaline crackling. She pulled the Glock from under her blazer.

"Go for the car, get the car," Annie said, charging up the hill. "I got the van."

Emily changed directions for the Charger. A root grabbed

her foot, sent her into the silver maple with a heavy *whump*. Bark rained. She spent several frantic seconds searching for the flown-away keys. Spotted them in a patch of dead grass. Snatched them up, raced for the car.

"Let go of me," Alexa screamed.

"Shut up, fatso," Aquarius said, dragging her to the van.

"Leave her alone," Tristen said, slamming her foot into something brittle.

"Bitch!" Cancer howled as his shin erupted in pain. He fell into Aquarius, who bounced off the back of the van. Alexa wriggled free, ran toward the house.

"Good girl, get away, run as fast as you—wait, where are you going?" Annie said as Alexa reversed course. "This way, run this way."

"Mommy, help!" Tristen screamed, legs flailing as Cancer and Aquarius dragged her to the open door.

"Hang on, Tris, I'm almost there," Annie said, reaching for her gun but grabbing air because she was still in sweats.

"I'll save her, Mom," Alexa said, squaring up like a snow plow and ramming herself into the kidnappers' legs. The shock loosed their grips. Tristen wrestled free and took off, grabbing up Alexa on the way. Cancer lunged, his face a mask of hate. He grabbed Tristen's ponytail just before it winked out of reach. She yelped, jerked backwards.

"Let's go, let's go," Gemini shouted, revving the engine.

Cancer pinned Tristen's arms. She fought back with head butts. He kept his face away. Aquarius grabbed her legs to prevent kicking. They wrestled her to the van.

"You're not taking her anywhere," Alexa yelled, wrapping herself around Cancer's leg and sinking her teeth. He screamed. Tristen rolled away, started running.

"Get off, get off, get off," Cancer yelled, dancing around. Alexa hung on like a pit bull.

"I'm free, Alexa, run!" Tristen shouted, turning back to help her.

"No way," Annie said, shoving her daughter sideways.

"But Mom, they've got Alexa—"

"I know who they have. Get out of here *now*," Annie ordered, resuming the chase.

Cancer hammered Alexa with a fist, knocking her cold. He threw her in the van and hopped inside. Aquarius followed.

"Get the other girl," Gemini shouted back. "She's the most important—"

"Cavalry," Aquarius warned, throwing himself on the floor.

Gemini checked the rearview, saw a tiny crazed blonde lunge for the back of the van.

Smoke poured from his tires.

A neighbor pumped a shotgun, swung it onto the van.

"My daughter's in there," Annie said, pushing the barrel skyward as he pulled the trigger. The shotgun roared. A dozen people dove to the ground screaming. "Put that away, you're gonna kill somebody."

The Charger roared to the curb. "Come on, Annie," Emily hollered.

"I've been terrible to you, Mommy, but now I'll be good, I'll be so good, just like I used to be, I promise, I swear," Tristen shrieked as her eyes darted with raw panic. "You're a SWAT, so find my sister and kill those awful—"

"I'll find Alexa, I promise," Annie said, smothering Tris in a fierce hug. "Go with Mrs. Karen now and call nine-one-one, the way we practiced. Tell them Emily and I are chasing the van and that your sister's inside."

"I will, I will, I will . . ."

"I'll save your sister, honey," Annie said, pushing her at

the neighbor. Tristen collapsed sobbing into Mrs. Karen's arms.

"Go, go, go," Annie said, yanking the door shut as Emily lit the afterburners.

"Kidnapping in progress, Chief," Watch Commander Dan Reynolds barked.

"Where?" Cross said, bounding into the dispatch center.

"White Oak Drive," Reynolds said. "Calls are pouring in."

"Roadblocks?" Cross said.

"On it."

"Dan," the dispatcher said, looking stricken. "Annie's children. They're the kidnap."

Cross's face hardened. "ISPERN and Amber Alert. Now."

The dispatcher turned to her console and sent the bulletin. The piercing tones of the Illinois State Police Emergency Radio Network filled the radio room. "Child kidnap in progress, repeat, child kidnap in progress," the robotic voice said. "Police officer's daughter is in a raspberry-colored van heading . . ."

"Tristen Bates on the line," another dispatcher said.

"I got her," Cross said.

The dispatcher pointed at a nearby phone.

"Tris, honey," Cross said. "It's Ken Cross. Are you all right?"

"They kidnapped my sister," Tristen wailed. "Mom and Aunt Emily are chasing them."

"You mom's the best," Cross said. "So is Emily. What car are they driving?"

"You have to save her," Tristen interrupted, sobbing so hard Cross could barely understand her. "We painted Mom's toes so she'd be happy and we were walking to the bus and the van cut us off us and Alexa bit the kidnappers and shoved me away and saved my life. Chief Ken, you have to save her, I'll die if you don't save her."

"I will, Tristen. I swear she'll come home safe," Cross said, throat tightening. He'd known these kids since they were born. He would not allow anyone to hurt them. "Where's your father? Is he at work?"

"Y-y-y-yes," she said. "He's teaching a Shakespeare seminar at the college."

"I'll go get him," Cross said. "I'm putting you on with Dan Reynolds. He's in charge of the day shift. Remember him from the Christmas party?"

"Uh-huh," she said.

"You tell Dan everything," Cross said. "I'll bring your father to you. Are you home?"

"Mrs. Karen next door."

"I'll be there soon, Tristen. Don't go anywhere till I arrive, all right?"

"Find my sister, Chief. Please find my sister."

"We'll get these bad guys, I promise." "Get" was a little benign, he knew. Annie would kill them given half an excuse. Emily too, for that matter. The prospect didn't overly trouble him. "Hold on, here's Dan."

He handed over the phone.

"Call out SWAT, this might wind up a hostage situation," he told the dispatcher. "Notify FBI and Homeland, in case it's ransom or terrorist."

"Where'll you be?" the dispatcher said.

"North Central College, picking up Joshua. I'm on radio and cell."

"Got it," he said, and started typing the SWAT paging codes.

"There they are, eleven o'clock!" Annie shouted over the siren as she struggled into her seat belt. If they hit something, she needed to roll out undamaged.

"Got 'em," Emily said, goosing the accelerator. They'd lost sight when the van turned on Parkside, but picked it up when it squealed onto Charles. The Kojak light on her dashboard strobed her eyeballs. She saw red dots when she blinked. "Spare gun in the glove."

Annie pulled out a .357 magnum. "Any artillery in the trunk?" she said. "Shotgun, rifle, flash-bangs?"

"No, just that."

"It'll do," Annie said. She opened the five-shot revolver, examined the load.

"Hydra-Shoks," Emily said. "Hundred and twenty-five grain."

"Moose load," Annie said, nodding approvingly. She shoved it in her front pocket. She pulled her phone, dialed nine-one-one. The connection broke after, "This is—"

"Dammit," Annie said, trying again. Same result.

"Try mine," Emily said, handing over the iPhone.

Three more disconnects.

They raced south on Charles, passing Gartner, Dark Star, Whirlaway, and Cavalcade, then leaned into Charles's sharp eastward turn. "Keeps going straight he'll dead-end on Omaha Court and we've got him—whoa, watch out!" Annie said.

Emily yanked the wheel, barely avoiding the PT Cruiser that roared out of a stub street. The driver was on a cell, oblivious. The Charger crashed over the curb and deep into a lawn.

"We're losing them," Annie groaned, trying to keep the van in sight.

Emily dropped into reverse and chopped her way across the putting-green lawn. The street-racer Michelins grabbed the pavement. She stomped the brake and slapped the wheel, shoved it into drive, hit the gas. The Charger jumped like it was shot. They flew by a dozen homes, spotted the van in the distance, turning east on Hobson Mill.

"Nice job," Annie said, trying both phones again. Tossed them into the back, disgusted. "If anyone knows where we are," she said, "it's by pure dumb luck."

"Charger's on our ass," Gemini muttered. "Do something about it."

Cancer and Aquarius climbed into the back, smashed out the rear windows with the lug wrench. Poked their guns out the ragged holes.

"Annie and Emily in hot pursuit," the dispatcher radioed. "Anyone see them?"

The Uzi winked lead. The windshield shattered. Emily jerked the wheel so hard the car went into a barely controlled spin. The next burst went harmlessly wide.

"What now?" she said as she reacquired at a much greater distance, hardly able to hear over her hammering heart. "Stay back and hope someone spots us?"

"Remember how to PIT?" Annie said.

"Please excuse me a minute," Dr. Joshua Bates told the audience.

He walked toward the president of North Central College, keeping the bewilderment off his face as the chair of the English department took over the podium.

"What's going on?" he asked. The president pointed at Cross.

Blood drained from Joshua's face. He reached Cross in eight seconds.

"Alexa's been taken," Cross said, steering him toward the exit.

"They didn't get the message," Aquarius said as the Charger roared back.

"Send it again," Gemini said, cursing the curved streets for not letting him go faster.

"Now," Annie said as the machine gun started winking.

Emily jerked from behind the van and red-lined the speedometer. Bullets flew safely to their right. Her front bumper drew even with the back of the van.

"PIT," Annie said.

Emily yanked her the wheel to her right. Her bumper hooked the van. Thousands of pounds of horsepower transferred from straight ahead to ninety degrees right.

Hitting the van like a wrecking ball.

Gemini, Cancer, and Aquarius screamed as the van spun four three-sixties and slammed headfirst into a tree, blowing tires, radiator, and windows.

"They're down, they're down," Annie shouted as the Charger skidded all over the place decelerating. The PIT maneuver was as dangerous for cops as it was for robbers.

"Us . . . too . . . *now*," Emily said, bailing the moment forward momentum stopped.

They ran for the van.

*   *   *

Gemini grabbed the unconscious girl and ran for the next cross street.

Aquarius opened up with the Uzi, Cancer with a pistol.

Emily dove behind a gnarled crab apple as bullets shattered the windows of the Cape Cod behind her. "Annie, where are you? Are you hit?" she yelled.

"Over here, I'm good!" Annie yelled back.

Emily saw her behind a station wagon. Annie was pointing at Emily, then the kidnappers, then making a gun with her finger and thumb.

Fire at will.

Emily sprang from behind the tree, flung lead, ducked back.

The one with the Uzi howled, clutching his ribs as he spun to the pavement. The pistol man took off running.

"Clear," Annie shouted.

They ran for the wounded gunman, who'd managed to get his hand on the butt of the Uzi.

"Go after Alexa," Annie said, emptying the .357.

Emily rounded the corner. Spotted Alexa in the crook of the lead man's arm.

Ran faster.

The kidnapper was still moving.

Annie slapped up the Uzi, put two bursts in his head. Brains flew like watermelon rind.

She kept moving.

Gemini ran up to a man stowing a suitcase in a Lexus.

"Damn, mister," the man said, spotting Alexa. "Is your girl all right—"

Gemini shot him three times. The man collapsed like his strings were cut.

Gemini threw Alexa in the passenger seat and backed down the driveway. Spotted Cancer hightailing it around the corner. Saw a dark-haired woman with a gun closing fast.

Took off the opposite way.

"Police!" Emily screamed.

Cancer whirled. Emily fired. Cancer staggered, but stayed on his feet.

She shot him till he collapsed.

"Call nine-one-one!" she yelled at startled neighbors. "Tell them officers need help."

She saw the Lexus roar away with the kidnapper and Alexis. She ran faster.

Annie caught up.

"Circle road," she panted, swerving off the pavement. "We'll catch him on the backside."

They charged through the yards, drenched in sweat, lungs on fire, churning along a fence, plowing through a flower garden, emerging on the back half of the street.

"Naperville nine-one-one—"

"People are running through my yard," the woman complained. "They made a mess of my chrysanthemums. I want you to arrest them."

"What do they look like, ma'am?" the dispatcher said.

"Well, they're purple and yellow and in very full bloom—"

"The runners," the dispatcher interrupted. "Describe the runners."

"Oh," the woman said. "There's two. One's a little blonde, the other's brunette—"

"I found 'em," the dispatcher shouted.

"Why do you keep interrupting me?" the woman said. "Don't you know I pay your salary?"

Gemini howled in disbelief as Annie and Emily shot out his tires. He spotted a Toyota Camry in the oncoming lane. Bailed from the Lexus, dragging Alexa. Pointed the gun at the driver, who panic-braked. The Camry shivered to a halt.

"Cease fire, Alexa's in his arms," Annie said.

"Get out," Gemini ordered. The driver froze, eyes big as dinner plates. He shot her through the glass. Opened the door, pulled out the bloody body, threw it on the pavement. Tossed Alexa into the passenger seat.

Which woke her from the cold-cock.

Gemini started into the car. The driver groaned from the pavement. Grabbed his leg.

Keeping him from entering.

"Alexa's clear," Annie said, decelerating as she raised the Uzi. "I'm taking him out—"

Her feet skidded out from under her. She slammed to the pavement on her once-broken pelvis. Her nervous system twanged. The Uzi flew away.

"I can't move," she gasped. "Take the shot, take the shot."

Emily thrust out her pistol as the killer raised his. *Too late, pal, I beat you by a second.* She locked the front sight on his heart. Her finger stroked the trigger—

"Mommy?" Alexa moaned, staggering to her knees behind the gunman. "What're all those loud noises?"

* * *

Emily spotted the familiar round face as her shot was leaving the barrel. She jerked the muzzle, praying she wasn't too late.

The bullet crashed through the back window.

"What are you doing?" Annie screamed. "Kill him—"

The gunman opened fire.

Emily threw herself on Annie.

Gemini knew an opening when he saw one.

He broke off the attack and jumped into the Camry. Knocked out the babbling kid with a sharp slam of his elbow. Freddie-Boy would have to disguise the bruises. The money he made from these kids, he could afford a little grease paint.

He punched the accelerator and roared away.

Emily got to her feet, started to run. But the Camry was gone.

She heard more gunfire and screaming.

Another carjack.

Another death.

She sank to the grass, exhausted.

"Why did you pull the shot?" Annie whispered. "Why did you pull the shot?"

Robert "Hawk" Hawkins walked through the house on Sylvan Circle, looking for disturbances in the dust. Found several. If he hadn't, that would have been worrisome.

He entered the bedroom, sat on the bed. The mattress sagged like it was terminal. He put his face in his hands, rubbed his tired eyes, took a mental stroll through what came next.

No problems he could see.

He walked into the bathroom and bent to the vanity. Pulled out the pair of canvas bags and slid back the metal zippers.

His smile faltered.

He should be turning cartwheels, he knew. This is what was getting Sammy to L.A. Not the triple mortgages. Not the telethons. Not the nickel in the bird crap.

This.

The Katrina.

More precisely, stealing it from Cash Maxximus, then selling it back to him. For the final half million he needed to get Sammy cured. He should be delirious with joy.

But I'm not. I'm a cop.

Not a fucking robber.

He shrugged.

Happiness is a warm little girl.

He left the way he came in, climbed back into his truck.

Got the K. Good doing business with you, he text-typed into his phone.

Hit SEND.

Backed onto Sylvan Circle.

The phone trilled in Gemini's pocket.

He didn't hear it over the thunder of acceleration.

Realized with a shock that no one was chasing him anymore.

Braked to the speed limit as a cop car screamed by, heading the way he'd just come.

Don't look around, he told himself. *Don't attract attention.*

Deliver the girl, and everything will be fine.

He stripped off his hooded sweatshirt and blanketed it over the paycheck.

Like she was napping, and he was doting daddy.

Hawk heard invasion-level acceleration.

Thought his heart would stop.

He cranked his head around.

Naperville Police cruisers, making the circle. Lights and sirens, attack formation.

What the hell?

He pulled out his pager.

It blinked rapidly.

He checked the stored message.

SWAT deployment.

Damn. He'd forgotten to restore the alert volume after he left the hospital.

He punched speed dial eight, heart ka-thumping.

"Hey, Sarge," the dispatcher said.

"I was at the hospital with Sammy," Hawk said. "She had an attack."

"Aw, man. Is she all right?"

"Touch and go, but she'll be fine," Hawk said. "I had to turn off my pager, it interferes with their electronics. We have a callout?"

"Three perverts just kidnapped Alexa Bates," the dispatcher said.

Hawk almost drove off the road. "*Annie's* daughter?"

"Uh-huh. In front of Annie's house. She and Emily were having coffee when a pervert van pulled up and grabbed Alexa. They chased down the van, killed two of the viruses. Third got away with Alexa." He sounded a little choked up. "Hunt's on."

Hawk couldn't imagine Annie and Joshua's pain. He knew how he'd feel if anyone touched Sammy. "What about Tristen?"

"She's at the house with her father," the dispatcher said. "Cross is talking with her."

Hawk saw the mob of cruisers on White Oak Drive.

"She hurt?" he asked.

"Bumps and scrapes. Apparently Alexa pushed her away from the kidnappers. Kept her out of the van."

"Gotta find her," Hawk said.

"We will," the dispatcher said. "She's family."

"Damn right."

"SWAT's hanging loose till we find the van," the dispatcher said. "You want to beg off because of Sammy? Dan's got plenty of door-kickers."

"Yeah, I think I will," Hawk said. "She's sleeping now, but that could change. Thanks."

"No prob," the dispatcher said. "Hey, when you see Emily, tell her great job for me."

Hawk caught the undertone. "You still want in her pants, don't you?"

"Wouldn't mind. 'Cept that Marty'd mash my potatoes."

Hawk recalled how Emily had charged into that liquor store when they thought it was rape and murder. "Forget Marty. She'd cut 'em off herself and make you a necklace. So, where are these dead perverts, anyway?"

"Some fun," the barrier cop greeted.

"Saves taxpayers the cost of a trial," Hawk said. "Any news on Alexa?"

The cop shook his head.

Hawk ducked under the crime tape, surveyed Hobson Mill Drive. Annie was stretched out under a parkway tree as paramedics prodded her lower body. Emily was leaning on a cruiser, scowling. The pervert in the intersection was dead. The pervert he'd passed on the way was equally dead. He couldn't see either for the crush of cops, CSIs, and coroners. He hoped their faces caught some bullets. If you looked like hell when you reached the pearly gates, he believed, St. Peter put you at a table nearest the kitchen.

He ducked under the inner ring of crime tape, shaded his eyes from the fast-rising sun. Reminded himself to keep a poker face, as laughing made TV reporters whiny—

Cancer.

He stumbled back three steps. *Have you lost your mind?* his head screamed at the cooling corpse. *You deliver the drugs, period. You don't stop to kidnap children.*

"Everything all right?" a familiar voice said.

Hawk turned to see Chief Cross.

"Tired from staying up late," he managed.

"I heard," Cross said. "Is Sammy all right?"

Bad news travels fast. "Serious attack, got into her lungs," Hawk said. "But she's out of the woods, according to Dr. Winslow."

"If Doc says so, you can take it to the bank," Cross said.

The knot in Hawk's stomach tightened. If Cancer was dead, that made the other perverts Gemini, Aquarius, and Virgo. The last four people on the planet he wanted to see right now.

"I just left the hospital," he said, suppressing an urge to throw up. "Heard about this and headed over. What can I do?"

"We're covered," Cross said. "Stay with Sammy till she's back on her feet."

Hawk had been counting on the chief's compassion to provide the window he needed to deliver the Katrina and pick up the money. "You sure?"

"Yes. I've got more than enough help."

"Then, thanks," Hawk said. "I really appreciate this." He

meant it. Cross transferred Hawk from night patrol to computer crimes when Sammy got sick. Monday through Friday work made caring for her a whole lot easier. "How's Tristen holding up?"

"As well as can be expected," Cross said. "I'll send Annie home as soon as the paramedics clear her. Tris needs her." He blew out his breath. "Christ, I wish I knew where Alexa was."

Hawk's heart pounded so hard he wondered if Cross could hear it. "Any ID on the perverts?"

Cross shook his head. "We'll run their fingerprints and DNA, but that'll take a while. The van has Wisconsin plates, so Madison's tracking—"

Shouting made them whirl.

"What the fuck were you thinking?" Annie snarled as she came off the ground and shoved Emily hard. "Why did you pull your shot?"

"Hey!" Emily said, stumbling backwards. "Hands off, Annie."

"That's deputy chief to you," Annie said, lunging again. Emily moved sideways and stuck out her foot. Annie fell with a thud. Sprang back up, turned her hands karate-edge.

Emily backed away, raising her fists.

"You're not thinking straight," she said. "Let me explain."

"You could have shot him. You didn't. Explain that," Annie said, stalking her. "You had him in your sights. He got away. Explain that. My daughter is gone thanks to you."

She unleashed a leg snap. Emily darted back but not fast enough to keep it from smashing her nose. Blood spurted.

"Stop it," Cross and Hawk shouted.

"Back off, I'm warning you," Emily said, putting her hand on her Glock.

"You going to shoot me? *Now* you're a tough guy?"

Annie said. "You could have shot a monster, but you let him go. What happened? Did you have a *flashback*?"

"Shut up," Emily hissed.

"Yeah, that's it, you had a flashback," Annie taunted. "With your little dragon friend." She spit. Emily took it in her face. "And to think I wanted you on SWAT. To think we were friends. You're nothing but a frightened little girl—"

"Deputy Chief Bates!" Cross roared as Hawk wrapped Annie in a bear hug. "Stand down. That's a direct order."

Annie tried wrestling away.

"Knock it off, boss," Hawk hissed in Annie's ear. "Don't want this on the news."

Emily looked around. The crowd was raising camera phones.

Annie snorted like a bull, but quit fighting. "Fine, Chief, I'm finished," she huffed. "But I'm done working with this trash. She's a disgrace to the uniform, freezing up like that."

"You have no idea what you're talking about," Emily said, pinching her nostrils to stop the bleeding. "I saved Alexa's life."

Annie's face hardened. "Don't you dare say my daughter's name," she hissed. "She's going to die because you didn't have the balls to—"

"Nobody's going to die, Annie," Cross said. "A million cops are looking for her, and it's only a matter of time." He pushed himself into her face. "Go home. Your family needs you. Or have you forgotten that Tristen went through this too?"

Annie glared like she wanted to punch him.

"Walk away," Cross said. "Or I'll cuff you myself."

She stomped off.

Cross turned to Emily, blew out his breath. "First, Detective, good work," he said. "I'm pleased these two are out of commission."

"Thank you," Emily said, heart thumping at the beat

down she'd just taken from her former best friend. She looked at the blood and saliva on her jacket. No use trying to wash it out. It was torn anyway from Annie's claw hands.

"Second, what in the hell was that about?"

Emily's legs were so wobbly she couldn't keep standing without assistance. She moved backwards till she felt a cruiser. "I had the third kidnapper in my sights. I intended to kill him. But I had to pull my shot."

"Why?"

"Alexa stood up."

Cross stroked his chin.

"From the top," he said.

She walked the chief through the entire sequence. "Just as I fired, I spotted Alexa. She was standing on the passenger seat, directly behind him. If I hadn't jerked my gun, the bullet would have struck the kidnapper square in the heart."

"And punched through to Alexa," Hawk said. "Yeah, I would have pulled the shot too."

Emily threw him a grateful glance. "He started returning fire," she said. "Annie was exposed with no body armor. I threw myself on her."

"You aren't wearing armor, either," Hawk said.

Emily shrugged.

Cross examined her face with unblinking eyes. "How's that feel?"

"Lousy," Emily said. "But it's not broken. Do you believe me, Chief?"

"Every word," Cross said.

"So . . ."

"I'll talk to Annie. Are you pressing charges?"

The question surprised her. "Charges? For what?"

"She attacked you." He nodded at Emily's nose. "Felony assault and battery, conduct unbecoming an officer. It's your right to file if you want."

Emily considered it, she was so boiling mad at the false

accusation. But she said, "Deputy Chief Bates slipped and fell."

"Oh?"

Hawk smiled, very faintly. "On maybe this, uh, loose gravel?" he said, kicking a piece.

Emily nodded. "We both went after the kidnapper. Her feet went out from under, undoubtedly on that gravel. She threw out her arms to catch herself and punched me by accident. My nose bled. Then we discussed how the kidnapper managed to elude us."

"Boisterously," Cross said.

"Adrenaline," Emily said firmly. "From our mutual eagerness to apprehend the suspect."

Cross's mouth twitched. "So Annie didn't assault you. It just looked that way."

"She slipped and fell, Chief. I was too tired from running to move out of the way." Emily looked at the murdered Camry driver. Her eyes were closed. Her skin was pale. Her black pumps were scuffed. Her fingers still curled from clutching the kidnapper's leg.

Was it just an hour ago life was good?

"All right, I'll consider this matter settled," Cross said. "I will talk to Annie, though. To make sure she understands . . . whatever."

"Good word," Hawk said, "whatever."

Cross's cell rang. He picked up.

"How are you, Sheriff?" he said, turning away. "Of course I remember you. What's up?"

Emily looked at Hawk.

"Only said what I would have done given the same circumstances," he said.

"And I appreciate it." She noticed he looked seasick. "You feel all right? You look . . . ill."

He shrugged. "Got no sleep last night. Sammy had another attack."

She cringed, but before she could ask details, Cross reappeared.

"That was Vaughn Buehler, the sheriff of Jackson County, Wisconsin," he said. "I know him from a Homeland Security conference last year. Sharp guy. Says our dead perverts might be the gunmen they're looking for up there."

"Up there being?" Hawk said.

"Black River Falls," Cross said.

Emily felt an electric tingle. "That's where Marty and Branch hunt," she said.

Cross nodded, then related what Buehler said.

"So these four assholes," Hawk said, incredulous, "shoot Abbott, steal his cruiser, jack the old folks because the cruiser's too hot, drive their Caddy to the rest stop in Tomah, jack the raspberry van, drive here, and kidnap Alexa. Oh, and shoot one of their own in the head and dump him in the river. Am I understanding this correctly?"

"We'll know for sure when they find the van driver," Cross said.

"Hundred-dollar boots and my feet still get wet," the young Wisconsin trooper grumbled, tugging a densely twigged oak branch off a pile. He and six local cops were searching the Tomah rest stop after a game warden stopping for a vend-all Danish spotted the Caddy stolen out of Millston. So here he was, wading bogs and sweating his ass off—

"Oh Jesus," he said as a nearly decapitated man with raw, red hands grinned back at him. The gappy slice was filled with ants, big black mothers marching away pieces of neck. The sight was so revolting he doubled over to heave. Managed to hold it. Didn't want to contaminate the crime scene. Especially in front of the feeb who'd just joined the hunt. He backed slowly out of the muck, boots making slurping sounds. The other cops came running.

He vomited bacon and eggs.

The FBI agent smirked.

Then peered into the limb tangle, stumbled backwards, heaved till he gasped.

The trooper felt better.

"He kidnapped a nine-year-old girl," Buehler said, pacing the radio room. "Evaded an entire police force and disappeared, taking her God knows where."

"Sounds like a movie," lead dispatcher Kaye Barley said, updating the database for the swelling ranks searching for Abbott.

"Wish to hell it was," Buehler said. "Movies, bad guys get theirs. Kidnapping the girl puzzles me, though. Why stir up that kind of heat when you're being hunted as a cop killer?"

"I have a theory," Kaye said.

"Hoping you might," Buehler said.

"The four men are narcotics drivers," she said. "They picked up their drugs in the cities and drove them to Naperville for distribution. Supply and demand—Naperville has money, needs drugs. These four were contracted to deliver them."

"Contracted by . . ."

"One of the Mexican cartels," she said. "My guess, Juarez. Naperville is their base in the Midwest; I-94 is one of their main pipelines. Plus they're crazy."

Buehler nodded. He'd been elected sheriff because his predecessor couldn't keep the various narco cartels from using the county as a transfer station. Buehler called in favors from Homeland and the DEA. A few headline-making busts, most of the traffickers got the message: Don't get caught here after sundown. Juarez was the only cartel crazy enough to thumb its nose at the DEA, keep making the runs.

"They weren't shipping marijuana, then," he said. "Not enough profit for Juarez."

"Higher-grade," she agreed. "Cocaine. Meth. Heroin."

"Designer drug," Buehler suggested. "DEA says there's a new one called Katrina. *Lot* of money in that, supposedly."

Kaye ran her hands through her pixie. "They get to Naperville, drop their load at a safe house, and drive away with their pay. Then, um . . ."

Buehler grinned at her hesitation. "This where your theory gets, um, interesting?"

"I still think I'm right."

"So go ahead."

"Narcotics drivers also transport sex slaves," she said. "They're on the road constantly and see a ton of girls. Far more money in sex than drugs, particularly sex with innocent young suburban white girls. So they grab Alexa and Tristen to sell to a pervert. Except Tristen escapes. Leaving Alexa to their tender mercies."

Buehler mulled it over, nodded. The theory fit the facts of his and Ken's cases. That must be what poor Abbott stumbled across during that "routine" traffic stop: heavily armed narcos who doubled as child traffickers.

"Remind me again why I haven't made you an investigator," Buehler said.

"You look like hell," Cross said. "Go see your daughter."

"Better get some sleep, too," Hawk said, nodding. "I pass out in front of the troops, they'll call me chicken hawk."

"Tough to the end," Emily said as he drove away.

"Has to be," Cross said. "To deal with the cards life dealt him."

"I couldn't do it," she said.

"I'd rather get shot again," Cross said. "And let you call me Flat-Ass."

Emily felt her face burn.

Cross laughed. "Relax, Detective. As hard on you as I was five years ago, I'd have called me names too."

Tristen burst onto the front porch.

"Did you find her, Mom?" she cried. "Is Alexa coming home?"

Annie caught her midair. The door slammed again, and Joshua's arms were around them.

"She's coming home," Annie said. "But not just yet. We're still searching. There're hundreds of cops out hunting. The National Guard is helping." The news that every armory in the Midwest volunteered a search team had made her weep. "We have a lot of friends, honey."

She saw cameras pointing from beyond the yellow tape.

"Let's get inside," she said with disgust. "Let those vultures find somebody else to pity."

"Is Aunt Emily helping?" Tristen said, arms tight around her mother's tiny waist as they walked inside. "Is she out there?"

"She's out there, all right," Annie said.

The flatness of her voice made Joshua raise a questioning eyebrow.

"Later," Annie mouthed as she pulled the door shut.

45

"Something you don't see every day," Marty said as the farmer spray-painted COW on the side of his herd.

"I don't blame him," Branch said. "The wannabes shoot a few every year, thinking they're deer." He looked in the rearview.

"Third time in five minutes," Marty said.

"What?"

"That you've checked the road behind us."

"I'm a safe and courteous driver," Branch said. "And, we're being followed."

"No kidding? How far back?" Marty said.

"Mile or so. Black Mercedes. Been with us since the Dells."

"Huh. Think it's our friends from Mars?"

"I do."

Marty thought about it.

"Well," he said. "I suppose we could shoot them."

Branch punched the iPod to Tom Petty.

"Homicide would delay the hunt."

"Good point," Marty said. "Plus, prison food."

Branch kicked the Escalade to ninety. The Mercedes passed a string of cars, kept pace.

"Not gonna outrun 'em, I see," Marty said.

Branch nodded at the exit sign. "Might as well deal with them now." He powered into the ramp, took the curve, swooped into a valley. At the stop sign, he pulled onto the shoulder. They got out and waited expectantly, flexing arms and legs.

The Mercedes climbed out of the valley. They put the Escalade between them and any ram job. The Mercedes closed, headlights flashing. Soul Patch clearly wanted blood.

From their left, an engine's whine overwhelmed their ears. A huge ATV with fat rubber tires crested the ridge and sailed down the slope, hard on the heels of a sprinting deer.

"Yahoo!" they heard its camouflaged passengers holler. "Ride 'em, cowboy!"

The deer bolted across the ramp. The ATV pursued. The Mercedes swerved, trying to avoid the collision. Spun three-sixty and belly-flopped into the ditch.

Ploom, the airbags chorused.

Marty laughed so hard he could barely breathe.

"Ya made me miss my deer, ya son of a bitch!" the ATV driver screamed.

"Where'd you learn to drive, asshole?" Soul Patch screamed back as he crawled out the open window. "Clown school?"

They fell on each other, trading punches, knees, and elbows; then everyone piled on, cursing, head-butting, a baseball fight in camouflage jackets. A cop car came out of the valley, roof lights blazing. Marty and Branch climbed into the Escalade, leaving the four losers to wonder how their lives went so tragically wrong.

"I love it," Branch said as he powered back onto I-94, "when a problem solves itself."

46

Horns blared.

Tires squealed.

Hawk jerked back to reality. Nearly sprained his wrists swerving back into his lane, waving "sorry" at the parade of middle fingers. Pounded the steering wheel in frustration, his horn blipping and blatting like Tourette's.

Am I protected?

Yes, he decided.

Cancer, Aquarius, Virgo, and Gemini—his unwitting partners in ripping off their boss Cash Maxximus—were dead or radioactive. The twenty-thousand-dollar payment they left in the van was untraceable, washed through the Save Our Samantha fund. Nobody knew he'd penetrated the "unbreakable" telephone link between Gemini and Maxximus—not for nothing was he a computer crimes cop—and tricked Gemini into delivering the Katrina to the dusty house on Sylvan Circle. Nobody knew he was going to resell those drugs to The Maxx for the half million he needed to get Sammy to L.A.

Steal from the rich and give to the poor.

The poor in this case: me.

He smiled. The kidnapping wouldn't splash back on him. In fact, he might even be able to find Alexa. Wouldn't that be something? He could use the GPS generator he'd slipped into Gemini's software to snatch the girl from the mouth of the tiger. Cross would call off the bloodhounds, ensuring no one stumbled onto his scheme and imperiled Sammy's trip. All he had to do was text-message Gemini's phone and tell him—

"Gemini's phone!" he shouted, swerving again.

47

The maggot woke.

Tried to roll out of bed.

The blood scabs on his arms made that impossible, sticking as they were to his sheets.

The maggot gritted his teeth, yanked hard.

"Ahhhuhnn," he gasped.

Now he leaked like a cheap faucet.

He padded into his bathroom, toweled the worst of the mess. All that terror, all this pain, just because he wanted a few more cents on the dollar.

Fuck Gemini.

And fuck Cash Maxximus, for making him work with a man who should have been drowned at birth.

He pulled a Schlitz from his fridge, sucked it down. Bubbles gassed from his nose. He sucked another, another, another. Poured a bowl of Sugar Smacks, used the fifth and sixth bottles for milk. Felt the buzz between crunches. It didn't make the can-opener slashes hurt less, but he didn't care quite as much.

I oughta kick Maxx's ass is what I oughta do. The bastard wasn't better than him. Sure, he lived in a ten-million-dollar house. Sure, he had international recording contracts. Sure, he owned furs, limos, women, and islands. Sure, he ran the Midwest region for the Juarez drug cartel. But underneath he was Elvern Dribble, hillbilly trash from the west side of Chicago, gobbling sausages for sawbucks till his pimp saw the potential in how beautifully the boy sang between tricks, and turned him into Cash Maxximus, rap artiste. Who the hell was a boy-ho named Dribble to slap him around?

He burped a cloud of beer.

Smelled assent.

Dragged over the phone.

"What?" a gruff voice answered.

"Condition red," the maggot said.

No reply. As the maggot expected. This was a special line, used only to contact Maxximus, and only in the direst of circumstances. The guy was paid to recognize the maggot's voice. When he did, he transferred the call to Maxx.

"Talk to me," said the familiar silken voice.

The maggot trembled with rage.

"Why'd you do me like that, Dribble?" he snapped.

"Do you? What are you talking about?" Maxximus said, hearing the slurring in his Katrina supplier's voice. "How much have you been drinking?"

"A lot, but that don't change the facts," the maggot said.

"Which are?"

"That your Nazi pals carved me up last night. Why'd you tell them to do that? I gave them your Katrina just like you asked, and this is how you pay me? You are one twisted son of—"

"Whoa, dawg," Maxximus said, his voice picking up

steel. "What you talking about, 'gave them your Katrina'? Who'd you give my fucking Katrina?"

"That faggot Gemini, or whatever the hell constellation he calls himself these days." The beer steam was reaching fever pitch. "He called last night, said pack up a bunch cause you needed it ASAP. He shows up, I ask for my money. Gemini laughs—*laughs*—and says you'd pay me next time. I said that ain't how it works. It's cash on delivery—no tickee, no laundry." He skipped the part about extorting an extra ten percent for himself. "That's when the can opener come out. Bastard ripped me so bad I'm shittin' blood."

"You gave away my Katrina?" Maxximus bellowed so loud the maggot yanked the phone from his ear. "I never authorized that. What the hell is wrong with you?"

"Wrong with *me*?" the maggot shouted back. "Fuck you, Dribble, ya stinkin' sausage gobbler. This was your deal from the beginnin'. I got your text message, same as always. Gemini followed up with the phone call, same as always. I grabbed everything the chemists had and gave it to Gemini, same as always. You got some nerve, sitting in your fancy Naper-ass mansion and lying straight to my face. . . ."

Either Gemini's gone cowboy, Maxximus realized, *or somebody broke the phone code and ripped me out of a big honking piece of drugs and money.*

"Shut up," he told the maggot. "And tell me how many ounces you gave him."

"Ounces?" the maggot said. "It was pounds, man. Five pounds—"

"Five pounds?" Maxximus choked. "That's five hundred thousand dollars."

"And you didn't pay me a dime," the maggot said. "Not one thin dime, all the loyalty I show you, all the risks I take . . ."

No way he could tell the maggot they'd both been ripped

off. That got out, it'd be open season on The Maxx from every predator in town. "I'm sorry for what they did to you," he said. "Don't know why it happened, but I'll make sure it doesn't again. I'll pay you right away. Fact, I'll throw in an extra ten grand, for your troubles. That gonna square us?"

The maggot beamed. "'Course it will, Maxx. I knew it had to be some kinda mix-up, 'cause the Maxx I know would never do a man without cause."

"Damn right I wouldn't," Maxximus said. "Especially the best man in my organization."

"I am? Really?" the maggot said, absurdly pleased.

"Course you are," Maxximus lied. "My man's leaving Naperville now. It's an eight-hour drive, so he'll get to your place late afternoon." He looked up the address in his Black-Berry. "You're still on Hennepin, right?"

"Thass right," the maggot said, swaying to music only he heard.

"Good. My man will deliver your money and bonus. You count it, make sure everything's there. Then hit the town on me. Lobster, pussy, the works."

"Damn," the maggot said, tearing up. "That's awful nice of you, Maxx. An' listen, I'm sorry I called you Dribble. I know you don't like it." His eyes blinked rapidly. "It's jess I was pissed cause my scabs stuck to my bed sheets an' I hadda rip them off an' it hurt like someone blowtorched me an' Dribble just slipped out." He hiccupped. "An' I had a coupla beers. . . ."

"No problem, my friend. But it's time to sleep it off. That way you're ready to par-tay when your money shows up."

"I dunno, boss," the maggot said slowly. "I need to visit the chemists, make sure they get production back to peak—"

"Don't worry about Lady K," Maxximus soothed. "You earned yourself a nice long nap. I'll give you a call tomorrow, work out the new production schedules."

"Thass so nice," the maggot said, burping and sniffling. "Thanks, Maxx. You're like the father I never had, you know?"

"Anything for my number-one son," Maxximus said.

He broke the connection.

Looked at his chief of staff, who'd listened in.

"We wuz robbed," Arthur Tatum said, gold incisor gleaming.

"No question. Think it's Gemini?" Maxximus said.

Tatum shook his head.

"Me neither," Maxximus said. "Man's a psycho, but he's our psycho. Someone hacked into my phone system. Someone who's planning to make a fortune off of my hard work."

"Hope he prepaid his funeral," Tatum said. "How do you think he'll play it?"

"Sell," Maxximus said. "No point taking the risk to skip payday."

"Yeah," the chief of staff said. "So the question becomes . . ."

"Who he'll approach," Maxximus said. "Me? Or my competitors?"

"Man be insane to try and sell it back to you."

Maxximus smiled. "He's proved he's insane, dawg. We just don't know how much."

Tatum nodded. "So what do we do?"

"You take the jet to Minneapolis and give Mr. Drunk and Disorderly his reward."

Tatum raised an eyebrow.

"Not that I mind the disrespect," Maxx said. "I got cut up like a chicken, I'd be pissed at me too. But drunk on his ass at eight in the morning?"

"And, he called you Dribble."

"That too."

Tatum stopped at the door.

Turned.

"Before I go, I need to tell you something, boss," he said.

"Tell me what?" Maxximus said.

"You're like the mother I never had."

He fled out the front door cackling, as Maxximus threw the BlackBerry at him.

48

Spencer Abbott opened his eyes.

Saw water.

Turned his head.

Saw more.

Lapsed into unconsciousness, came out a few minutes later.

A gray squirrel studied him from a bump on a log.

"Gotta . . . get out . . . of water . . ." Abbott mumbled.

The squirrel chattered.

"You . . . said . . . it."

He was so cold he didn't know if he could move.

One way to find out.

He tried his right arm.

It worked.

Tried his left.

It didn't.

Tried his legs.

Score.

He was surprised at how freely they moved, when they didn't before. The shock of the water? The hours spent healing? Adrenaline reasserting itself as he shifted into do or die?

Who cares?

He heaved up out of the mud, panting from exertion. Crawled an inch. Another inch. Another. Another. Soon, he was out of the water, and on dry land.

Shivering in the bitter wind.

Abbott looked around for shelter. He was lucky to not have died from exposure, and Mother Nature didn't screw up twice. He needed a warm, dry place to park his frosty behind.

He planted the knife, then his elbow, and moved, knife, elbow, moved. Got ten feet up the hill. Fifteen. Twenty. He felt so light he could fly—

Where's the girl?

He looked around. Ran his hand over his waist.

The rope that held them together had fallen apart.

Still in the water?

He squinted through half-frozen lashes. Saw her floating serenely near the bank he'd just climbed away from.

"You'll be all right," he called. "Soon as I find help, I'll come back for you. I promise."

She didn't answer.

Just bobbed her disappointment.

He sighed.

Turned uphill, dug in.

Thirty feet. Forty. Fifty.

"Nuts," Abbott said.

He couldn't leave her.

Not that she cared. She was dead. Bloating. Slippery from the shedding of waterlogged skin. Breathless lungs, leaking brains, bones dissolving to beaver chow.

It didn't matter. She hadn't abandoned him at the bridge.

How could he abandon her now?

He looked to the moon for affirmation.

But the man was gone. He was on his own.

He looked at the girl.

On our *own.*

Abbott started downhill. After a while, he was close enough to fish her from the drink.

He one-handed a branch, hooked it around her left wrist.

Her hand dissolved like wet toilet paper.

Abbott closed his eyes. Breathed in icy air. Tried again, hooking the dense bones in her armpit. "Come to Papa," he said, reeling her in.

She bobbed close. He grabbed her arm. The ground under him shifted. Sprang a thousand geysers.

"No, no, no, no, no," Abbott screeched, clawing madly for solid ground.

That gave way too.

He plunged into the water with a mighty splash.

The collapse made waves, which crashed against the logs.

Which sent them back to Abbott.

Along with the girl.

Who came to rest on Abbott's hip, sharing her blanket of cold.

49

Hawk dripped sweat. The acknowledgement he'd texted after departing the safe house with the Katrina—GOT THE K. GOOD DOING BUSINESS WITH YOU—was sitting on Gemini's phone. If the cops got hold of it and traced the message back to its sender . . .

That can't happen, Hawk tried to convince himself. *I tested that program a thousand times. It's bulletproof.*

Then again, Maxximus had been just as sure.

Time to find Gemini.

Rescue Alexa.

Put an end to this mess.

Horns sounded. With his mind everywhere but on driving, he was weaving like a drunk. He pulled into the Caribou Coffee on Ninety-fifth Street, opened his phone, thumbed a message:

C U ON TV W/GIRL. WTF ? M

Send.

* * *

Gemini drove into the industrial park. Everything looked quiet. Good. He'd taken the long way around, through Bolingbrook and Aurora and Plainfield, checking for cops, finding none.

The cell beeped in his pocket.

He ignored it.

He finger-combed the girl's hair, moving it away from her face. A cherub, she was, with wide eyes, chubby cheeks, and schoolgirl clothing. Not Catholic school with plaid skirts and starched blouses. Public school. Jeans, T-shirt, sneakers, and socks with purple dots. He tried to imagine the attraction. Couldn't. Little girls weren't his thing—he preferred to ride their mamas, whips and spurs—and for the life of him, he couldn't imagine doing someone whose voice still squeaked. But someone did, and it paid the bills.

He thought about Cancer, Aquarius, and Virgo. He'd miss them. Then again, if they had to die, now was a good time. Freddie's money was a lot more impressive without them.

He scratched his neck.

The girl snored quietly under his hoodie. The bruises were starting to show, but hey, slap on a bag of ice, rewrite the script to stern-daddy-disciplines-daughter, and Freddie could even skip the grease paint.

He carried her inside.

"Hola," he greeted the Mexican with the scarred face.

"Cola," Scarface replied, tipping his Pepsi. "Mr. Marsh is expecting you."

"*Mr.* Marsh?" Gemini said. "When did Freddie become respectable? Or did you mean it ironically, showing your defiance of the Yankee oppressors who stole your ancient lands?"

"I'm from Omaha," Scarface said, showing teeth. "So fuck a bunch of ancestors."

They laughed, Scarface unlocked the security door, and Gemini headed upstairs.

"I heard about your men," Freddie said, emerging from his office. "I'm very sorry."

"They knew the risks," Gemini said. "Where do you want the girl?"

"On the bed," Freddie said, nodding at the movie set.

Gemini put her down, arranged her hair.

"Well aren't you just the sweetest thing?" cooed Lindy Archer, Freddie's sister and principal director. She was an Amazon with a butt-length braid and stout-for-hell legs.

"Me, or her?"

Archer snorted.

"Story of my life," Gemini said. "She's asleep."

Archer spotted the bruises.

"What'd you tuck her in with, an anvil?" she said, kneeling to examine.

"You knocked her unconscious?" Freddie said sharply.

"She stood up while the cops were throwing bullets. I didn't want your property damaged, so I had to cool her out."

Freddie walked to the bed, rubbing his fingers like a safecracker. He poked and prodded. Touched and stroked. Sniffed, licked, and grunted. Turned her over, then back.

"She's marvelous, Karl," Freddie said, looking up. "And I already have a buyer. A certain member of Parliament who enjoys a little fat on his lamb chops—"

"Your business, not mine," Gemini interrupted. Chesters made him queasy.

"Coming from a blood-drenched sociopath like yourself," Freddie said, reading his mind, "that's saying something."

Gemini smiled. He and Freddie went back to junior high in New Orleans. They'd understood each other from the moment they'd sized each other up, and had enjoyed such hobbies as bum burning, microwaving cats, and beating up the retards from the workshop over on Loyola. After graduation, Gemini became a debt collector for the local mob. Freddie, more artistically inclined, went into "film." They stayed close, with Gemini doing his sister a few times but nothing romantic coming of it. When Hurricane Katrina wiped out their livelihoods, they hit the road, planting their flag in Chicago. Between drug-running for Maxx, child-snatching for Freddie, and the legitimate painting business, Gemini was on the road so much he used the shop as his legal address. Freddie got married, had three kids, and moved the family to Naperville for the schools. Lindy commuted from the city, where she tended bar and competed in roller derby as "Lindy Sin." The boys lived where the boys lived, showing up when he needed them.

"She everything I promised?" Gemini said.

Freddie nodded. "Too bad about the other girl. You know, sister acts. But I know what happened, and believe me, this one will fetch a pretty penny. Do you know her name?"

"Does it matter?"

"No," Freddie said.

He handed Gemini an envelope.

"Pleasure doing business," Gemini said, tipping his triangular head.

"There's sixty extra G's in there," Freddie said. "Bury the boys in style."

Lindy smiled as she watched them walk to the door. She'd suggested the burial bonus. Gemini was too cheap to care about niceties, but she did—the boys deserved it. Especially Virgo. He made her laugh every time they dropped off a girl. She liked his sense of humor even more than his smoking body. Well, almost . . .

She slipped a hit of Katrina under the girl's limp tongue.

Then picked up a camera and began the test shots.

* * *

"Come on, jagoff," Hawk muttered, staring at the cell. "Answer already."

"Mom," Tristen said. "Go to work."

Annie stiffened. Joshua was making coffee for the FBI agents monitoring the phones for ransom calls. Tristen had sat with them awhile, but wandered away to cry on Alexa's bed. Then crawled on the leather couch in the family room. Annie joined her, spreading a blanket across Tristen's tanned legs and bringing her hot tea with cinnamon and lemon. Now, her daughter was telling her to leave. She'd never felt so guilty in her life.

"I can't, honey," she said, stroking Tristen's arm. "I need to be here for you."

"But you're driving me crazy," Tristen said. "We're talking about everything but what happened."

Annie sighed. "All right, if that's what you want."

"Your heart's not in it," Tristen said. "You want to be out there hunting."

Annie froze, not knowing how to answer. She didn't want to leave. Yet, she did. What kind of mother . . .

Tristen pushed upright, tucked her right foot under her left thigh, and punched the blanket into the resulting hole. "That isn't a criticism, Mom," she said. "I want you out there hunting. You're the only one who can bring Alexa home."

"That's not true," Annie said, shaking her head. "Lots of cops—"

"They're not *you*." Tristen left the couch, stood next to the window. A wolf pack of cameras surged off the sidewalk. She shrank back, frightened. Annie sprang, yanked the curtains.

Tristen shivered in Annie's arms.

"She's out there, Mom," she said. "She's scared, but she

knows you'll save her. Just like I do, even though there are times I . . . well, I . . ."

"Hate me for doing what I do," Annie said. "Because you think I'm going to die and leave you all alone."

Tristen didn't look at her. But she nodded. "That doesn't matter anymore," she murmured. "Alexa's out there, and you have to find her. If that molester—"

"It's not a molester, honey," Annie interrupted. "It's probably a simple ransom. One of the knuckleheads I arrested way back when. We pay, she goes free."

Tristen's look was withering. "I'm not stupid, Mom," she snapped.

Then her voice cracked like eggs.

"If Alexa winds up dead," she said, "I'll never forgive my-self. Please, Mom, go find her."

Annie blew out her breath.

"You won't feel like I'm abandoning you?"

"No," Tristen said. "Though I'll probably say it anyway, to guilt you into stuff."

Annie loved her for the weak joke. Hugged her tight.

Walked into the kitchen.

"Heading for work," she told Joshua.

He motioned her down the hall, so the FBIs didn't hear.

"Are you out of your mind?" he said. "Tristen needs you here. She's so fragile—"

"It was her idea," Annie said.

Surprise washed his face.

"She just told me. It's something she desperately needs me to do. Not just wants, Joshua. Needs." She touched her husband's cheek. "But I won't go if you're not all right with it. There're a million cops. But only one us."

He thought about it.

Took her hands.

"Remember we said for better or for worse?"

"Yeah . . ."

"This is the worst. Make it better."

She kissed him.

Then picked up her combat bag and headed for the car.

If Virgo had gotten his way, Gemini recalled, they'd have called each other Billy, Jeffy, Dolly, and PJ, after the kids in The Family Circus. Virgo adored that newspaper cartoon as much as his Red Bulls with vodka. But everyone else detested the cloying little fucks, and told Virgo if he didn't quit yakking about their toilet-bowl heads and dog named Barfy, they'd shoot him. Ironic it had come to that in the end.

He turned east on One Hundred Eleventh Street, and anger replaced sorrow. Who did that bitch think she was, gunning down the boys like they were rabid? She'd laughed when she smoked Cancer. *Laughed,* lips stretched, teeth gleaming. Bitch needed to pay for that. Maybe he'd stick around, show her what pain was about. Freddie could find him a safe place to crash. Be easy enough to track her down, all the media attention this case would generate—

He threw up an arm as something smacked his windshield. Thought for a second it was a bullet. Realized he was next to a golf course. An errant ball had hit him.

Chuckling, he dug the phone from his pants pocket. Saw the message light flashing. In the rush to get the girl inside, he'd neglected to check it.

C U ON TV W/GIRL. WTF ? M

Maxximus.

He knew.

"Oh, man, he'll kill me," Gemini moaned, feeling sweat pop on his forehead. The man paid him top dollar to run drugs and straighten out suppliers. No side jobs. Especially no side jobs that smacked hammers into hornets' nests.

NO CHOICE, M, he texted back. NO LINK TO U. EXPLAIN WHEN I CAN. G

Send.

"Gotcha," Hawk said. His quarry was next to the Tamarack golf course. Not far from where he was now. He sped up, dialing Maxximus as he went.

"What?" a rough voice said.

"Put him on," Hawk said. The speech-changer software altered the pitch, timbre, and intonation of his voice. Last time, he was an Irish truck driver. Now, he was a forty-something female whose chipper-ness suggested she'd just gotten laid.

"The hell are you?"

"Tell him . . . Special K," Hawk said, improvising.

Disconnect.

Hawk called back.

"What?"

"Hang up on me again, I'll take my merchandise to the Columbians. Your boss will bite out the veins in your neck."

Silence.

"Wait."

Hawk did.

"I hear there's a sale on Special K."

Cash Maxximus.

"Got five boxes if you're interested," Hawk said.

"Who says I am?"

"Gemini and three dead zodiacs."

A low chuckle. "That was fast."

"What?"

"You contacting me for a deal. Thought it'd take a few days to work up your nerve. Figured you'd be all fainty with what you just pulled off."

"So you're interested."

"Did I say that?"

"No. But if you were, what might you pay?"

"I don't negotiate. Tell me what you're asking."

"Half million."

"Fair price," Maxximus said. "Here's my counter. Return what you stole from me, and I'll let you keep one of your tits. Your choice which one."

"Tough guy."

"You have no idea."

"Apparently I do," Hawk said. "Seeing I have my tits *and* your ass."

He imagined Maxximus fuming.

It was a pleasant thought.

"I'm not paying a half million for my own cereal."

"So you admit it's your cereal."

"Hell no. I'm just saying, whatever you're peddling, I ain't paying that much."

"Yes, you will," Hawk said. "Or my next call is to Mexico."

Maxximus looked at the phone. Juarez did not appreciate managers who misplaced inventory, and its discipline did not include counseling or suspensions. This woman, whoever she was, knew way too much about him. He had little choice but to cooperate, at least for now. Once things cooled, he'd find her and impose his own performance review. He smiled at the infinite possibilities.

"Suppose I play ball," he said. "How do I know you're not a cop?"

"I guess you'll have to trust me."

This chuckle was genuine.

"Sure, lady. I trust anyone calls me out of the blue and sings a pretty song."

Hawk shook his head, as if Maxx could see. "Don't believe me? Fine. I'll sell your cereal to the Chechens. You know how highly Juarez thinks of its competitors."

"Thought you said the Columbians."

"Tomato, tomahto."

"All right. When and where?"

"Noon. Today."

"Today?" Maxximus complained. "I can't get that much cash in four hours."

"World's smallest violin," Hawk said. "You have a mailbox at your house, right?"

Maxximus snorted. "Mailbox? Who you think I am, Joey the fuckin' mailman or something? I got staff for that."

"Fortunately for you, I know the answer. Yes, you have a mailbox. It's at the end of your driveway on Hobson Road. It's big enough to handle our transaction."

Maxximus drummed his chin. The woman's voice was oddly familiar. He didn't know where he'd heard it, but the answer would come in time. It always did. His memory for sounds was pitch-perfect, from music to television to conversation to traffic noise to birds singing in the pear trees in his backyard. It was one of the reasons he could create a rap so addictive the masses bought it like crack cocaine. "Keep talking, sweetheart."

"At five minutes of twelve, you'll wire-transfer five hundred thousand dollars to the following location."

"So I *don't* need to sell my plasma for cash," Maxximus said.

"Hey, good one," Hawk said, amused. He read the routing number of his bank in the Cayman Islands, which conveniently refused to honor American search warrants. "The moment I confirm the transfer, my courier will put all five boxes of cereal in your mailbox."

"That's it?" Maxximus said, surprised it was so uncomplicated. He'd envisioned 007-style cloak-and-dagger.

"That's it," Hawk said. "I go on with my life, you make another ten gazillion dollars singing that rap shit, and we don't speak again. Deal?"

"Deal," Maxximus said.

"My courier will spot surveillance," Hawk warned. "If he sees anyone in your driveway, or a car, van, truck, motorcycle, aircraft, or hitchhiker is a hair out of place, he'll bypass your mailbox and bring the cereal directly to the police. You'll never get it back."

"And if you don't deliver," Maxximus said, "I'll chain you to a toilet and cut off your eyelids, so you see everything that happens. I'll kidnap your children, your pets, and your maiden aunts, and fuck them with baseball bats. I'll soak them in kerosene and light them on fire. Then I'll start in on you."

Silence.

"Think what you'd do if I'd stolen ten pounds," Hawk said.

Maxximus smiled, impressed with her cool.

"Tell you what, Special K," he said, his mental voice-sorter still narrowing the possibilities. "This works out, we might find ourselves talking again. Man like me has fingers in a number of interesting pies. Might be a piece for you."

Hawk smiled. "I like pie better than kerosene."

"That mean you're interested?"

"It means see you at noon," Hawk said. "What comes after, who can say?"

Cops interviewed witnesses. The Camry engine cooled with now-and-again ticks. The bloating woman waited for the coroner to say, *Yep, you're dead*.

Emily took it all in, shaking her head.

She felt naked without her custom Glock. Cross had to book it into evidence. Standard procedure when cops shot robbers. Still, it frosted her. Cops without guns were . . .

Crossing guards.

She stuck her hands in her pockets, tried not to pout. She wanted to work this murder, but had no official assignment.

Hell with that.

She wandered through neighbor knots on sidewalks and front yards. They vibrated with excitement over the dramatic events, their chatter animated and loud. If she played this right, she might overhear something useful. Something that might provide a clue to this animal's identification. She corrected herself. The comparison was an insult to animals.

"Did you see how fast those two gals ran—"

"They blasted out of Sandy's yard, took the guy head on—"

"Sandy'll sue, she's nuts about those flowers—"

"She's nuts, all right—"

"Then he raised his gun and—"

"She was so brave, jumping on the other gal. I wouldn't have the guts—"

"Cammy got some great video—"

"So *she* says—"

"No, no, she got the whole fight. Start to finish. I told her to e-mail me a copy—"

"Excuse me," Emily interrupted.

Eyes turned, sized her up.

"If you're a reporter," one said, sticking out her jaw, "nobody here will comment. This is a nice neighborhood, not a freak show for your amusement."

"I'm not with the news," Emily said. "I'm Emily Thompson."

"It's *you*," Jaw said, face splitting.

"Guilty," Emily said.

Hands reached out. She shook them all.

"Thank you for killing those creeps," another said.

"I hated to, but they gave me no choice," Emily said.

"I'm glad," Jaw said, punching the air for emphasis. "Steal our children, you deserve shooting. We're glad you did."

So am I, Emily thought. But she couldn't say it. The social compact was that cops regretted any loss of life, even when they didn't.

"Are you all right?" a third asked, patting Emily's shoulder.

Emily flinched.

"Oh, sorry," she said, yanking her hand like she'd touched a hornet.

"No, no, it's fine," Emily said, rubbing the spot, which throbbed from . . . what? So much to choose from. "I hurt myself falling is all. Couple aspirin, I'm good as new."

Heads bobbed.

"We got coffee," one said.

"Cream?" Emily said hopefully.

Jaw produced half-and-half in a plastic thingy from a restaurant.

"Deal," Emily said.

Mrs. Coffee poured from a gold Thermos. Emily took a sip. Not bad. Macadamia, hazelnut, something like that. She preferred plain old coffee, but this was all right. Not something undrinkable like French vanilla. Which was funny. She was addicted to French vanilla ice cream, ate some every morning. But as coffee it tasted like soap.

"Someone said Cammy shot video?" Emily said, figuring she'd better get to the point.

"She thought it'd make good YouTube, so she stuck out her phone," Jaw said.

"Think she's home?" Emily said.

"Probably. She was here till a few minutes ago," the third neighbor said. "Then she had to go to the bathroom."

"She has that thing," Mrs. Coffee said. "Makes her go all the time?"

The others nodded.

"Thanks," Emily said, handing back the cup. "You've been a big help."

She started walking away.

"Uh, Emily?" Jaw said.

"Yes?"

"Could I have your autograph? Right here on my jacket?"

Emily was stunned. "Me?" she said, for lack of something better.

Jaw nodded. "You're a hero to a lot of us. With everything you've been through. Those serial killers? Losing your parents and your husband?"

"Poor Jack," another murmured.

"But every time you came back fighting," Jaw said. "I'd really like your autograph."

She was dead serious, Emily saw. It choked her up a little.

"I'd be honored," Emily said. "But not now, all right? If the reporters see me sign your coat, they'll call me a glory hound. Miss Hollywood, all that."

"Oh, sure, I understand," Jaw said, her voice small. A little embarrassed at the rejection.

"I'll come by later," Emily said, touching her arm. "Give me your cell—I'll let you know when I'm free. Maybe have a glass of wine . . ."

Jaw nodded eagerly, wrote it out.

"Let us know the minute she calls," she heard others say as she left. "We're coming over, and we're bringing our daughters."

Just when I thought they didn't care if we lived or died . . .

She approached Cammy's front door. It was bright red with a brass knocker.

"Detective?"

Emily turned to see Cross. She walked to the unmarked car.

"I was chatting with the neighbors," she said. "They said a woman named Cammy made a video of the entire sequence."

Cross raised an eyebrow. "This where she lives?" he said.

Emily nodded.

"So what are you waiting for?"

She cocked her head. "I thought I wasn't supposed to do field work."

"And yet," he said, "here you are."

"Um, yeah, I guess I am."

"Or perhaps," Cross said, "you needed to use the bathroom, and didn't think she'd mind."

Emily crossed her legs, made a wincey face.

"I knew you wouldn't detect without permission," Cross said. "Let's see what she's got."

"You're coming with?"

"I like movies," Cross said. "Oh, and you'll need this."

Emily turned back, saw a standard-issue Glock in his hand.

"What's that?" she said.

"My permission," Cross said.

She felt tears welling. This was against all procedure. Cross was supposed to keep her on a short leash till the state's attorney made his ruling. While she had no doubt Terrence Knox would call the shootings justified, the process could take a while.

"That's another thing," Cross said.

"What's that?"

"Sergeants don't cry. They make others cry."

A tear fell anyway. He smiled. Handed her his handkerchief.

She blew her nose.

"Feel free to keep that," he said, rolling his eyes.

Emily grinned, dabbed her cheeks dry.

Then filled her empty holster.

"Why?"

"Because I can," Cross said.

"And because you believe me. About why I didn't shoot him."

"I believe," Cross said, "there are two sides to every story, and occasionally they're both true. Let's see what Cammy has to offer."

They knocked on the door. It opened to a straw-haired woman wearing boat shoes, jeans, and a Chicago Cubs sweatshirt.

"Oh," Cammy said, clearly having expected a friend, not badges.

"Good morning. I'm Ken Cross, chief of the Naperville Police," he said. "This is Detective Emily Thompson. We hear you have video of this morning's incident."

"Best thing I've ever shot," Cammy said. "I'm just about to upload to YouTube."

Emily winced.

"I have a right to do that," Cammy said, eyes narrowing. "I'm a journalist. I'm covered by the First Amendment."

"No argument here," Cross said. "Who do you work for?"

"Well, I'm freelancing," Cammy said, sounding defensive. "For various blogs and websites. I'm trying to find a full-time position with a reputable news organization."

"I hope you do," Cross said. "We'd just like to see your footage."

Cammy's bleached eyebrows shot high as skyrockets.

"That's prior restraint," she said. "Censorship. You can't do that."

Emily stiffened, tiring of the attitude.

"We don't want to censor you," Cross said. "We want to watch your video. That man kidnapped a little girl, and we're trying to identify him." His voice dropped to a confidential semi-whisper. "You know, you might be the only one to have captured his face."

"Really?" Cammy said, eyes widening.

"The *only* one," Cross emphasized.

"Meaning you're sitting on an exclusive," Emily said, going along. "Producers pay big money for that. Why waste it on YouTube if you can get paid?"

Cammy mulled that over.

"If I officially confirm that your video is genuine, it will go viral," Cross said. "Putting your name and face in front of thousands of media people. Anyone who's hiring—"

"Please come in," Cammy said.

"Why are you here?" said Watch Commander Dan Reynolds.

"I'm back to work," Annie said. "Where's Ken?"

"Crime scene."

"Which one?"

"Camry."

Annie left.

Emily watched herself emerge from the mum garden. Annie was to her right, toting the silenced Uzi. She lost her footing, fell hard. The kidnapper raised his gun. Emily raised hers faster, touched the trigger. Alexa rose from the passenger seat. Emily jerked the barrel. The window blew apart. The kidnapper fired. Emily spun away, jumped on Annie. The kidnapper fled with Alexa.

"And lived to kill again," Emily muttered.

"What?" Cammy said.

"Just admiring your framing technique," Cross said. "Would you e-mail me a copy?" He gave the address. She hit ENTER. His BlackBerry beeped.

"Thanks, Cammy," Cross said, confirming it arrived safely. "You've been a huge help."

"I'm gonna give the producers your name," Cammy said. "As a reference."

"Deal," Cross said.

"Would you mind," Emily said, squeezing her legs for real, "if I used your bathroom?"

* * *

Hawk, driving as fast as he dared on the puddle-choked road, thumbed a return text.

ANSWER ME NOW. M.

He'd know in a minute if that was Gemini in front of him.

"God oh god oh god," the Jackson County deputy said as he pulled up next to the charred lump. It was so badly burned he couldn't tell he or she.

But the twisted badge screamed cop. So did the SIG-Sauer poking from the flood water.

"Dispatch, help, help," the deputy said into his radio.

The lead dispatcher heard the horror in his young voice.

"Hey, Garnet, it's Kaye," she said, chatty-like, talking him off the cliff he was dangling over. "What's going on?"

"It's it's it's it's it's—"

"Take it easy, son," Kaye said, clicking the feed into Sheriff Buehler's car so he could hear. "Tell me what's happening. Tell me where you are."

"Roasted," Garnet said. "Charred. I've never seen anything like . . . oh, I'm gonna—"

She heard the churning cascade.

"Come back on the radio, Garnet. Come and talk to me," Kaye said. The kid was new, but unflappable as a dairy cow. Whatever he was seeing must be awful. "Where are you? Just tell me that, and I'll send help. Y'all can sort things out together."

"Okay. Okay," Garnet said. "Okay."

He gave the location.

Kaye sent the four nearest cruisers.

"Need the, uhhhh, the coroner," Garnet said. "And a tow truck."

"Why?" Kaye said.

"A motor vehicle is residing in the ditch. A burned body is ensconced on the opposite side." He'd turned to cop-speak in order to function. Not good, but at least useful. "It appears the vehicle flipped at a high rate of speed and bottomed out on the steel culvert. It burned so completely I cannot tell what it is. Ditto for the body. There's . . ." He faltered.

"Tell me," Kaye said.

"There's a badge. It's one of ours, a county badge. And a gun. SIG-Sauer."

"Oh, dear," Kaye said. Deputy Kharise Lenell was long overdue, and units were looking. "Secure the scene, Garnet. Sheriff's on the way."

"You gonna make me look bad if I let you work?" Cross said.

"No worse than I usually do," Annie said.

She did seem clear-eyed and squared away. It was a risk having the mother of a victim in the hunting party. But what the hell. Annie was his best field commander, and with Branch out of town, he needed her out there. He'd deal with the fallout later. That there would be fallout wasn't a question—violence was rain, Naperville was Camelot, and he'd pay for it. But if he was going to get fired, it might as well be for doing things as he saw fit.

"Bring a gun?" he said.

"In my bag," she said.

"Gimme."

She handed him her .45-caliber Springfield Armory XDm.

He handed it to her, making it official.

"Welcome back, Deputy Chief," he said.

"Thanks," she said. "Where are we, and what do you need me to—"

Her face turned to flint.

* * *

Gemini read the text message. Thumbed that he was on the run and would contact Maxximus as soon as he could.
Send.

"Said the spider to the fly," Hawk murmured, slapping the Kojak flasher onto his roof.

"Deputy Chief," Emily said with a curt nod.
"Detective," Annie said, frost on all three syllables.
"Play nice," Cross warned. "Both of you."
"No problem here, Chief," Annie said.
"Not from me," Emily said.
"Make sure," Cross said.

"No, no, no," Gemini screamed, shocked, as a cop car zoomed up his ass. An arm snaked from its window and pointed to the curb.
Pull over.
Gemini was frantic. He'd do a thousand years, and only if he escaped the electric chair, which he wouldn't. He had to rid himself of any link to the kidnap and murders.
The phone. Get rid of the fucking phone.
But first, the cop.
He stood on his brakes, hunching his shoulders for the impact.

Hawk knew it was coming. Was counting on it.
He slammed into the back of Gemini's car. His air bags ignited. He slumped back in his seat, pretending unconsciousness.

Watched Gemini accelerate out of the bumper shot.

Watched the cell phone sail out the window.

"Don't come back," he said to the disappearing car.

"Hope you're dead," Gemini muttered as he sped away. He wasn't far from I-55, but the cop might have radioed their location. Time he got to the entry ramp, he might be walking into a blue buzz saw.

He needed new wheels. Now. Not enough traffic for a carjack, though.

He spotted a rental office.

Perfect.

He pulled the car behind a vacant store. Cops would find it, but not immediately, and that's all he needed. He pushed through the door of the rental office. A bell chimed.

"May I help you?" the counter bunny chirped.

Gemini gave her the bad-boy grin. "My car broke down, and a buddy dropped me here," he said. "You have a car I can take right away?"

"Sure I do," the bunny said. "And plenty are budget-friendly compacts."

"That'll work."

"But a man like you probably wants a big ride," the bunny said, leaning over, letting the tops peek out. Doing the hard sell soft. "Something with class and comfort. Am I right?"

Why not?

"Show me what you got," Gemini said.

He rode the bunny in the bathroom; then she put him in leather buckets.

Hawk retrieved the cell. Checked the call log. Found Maxximus's number, which he'd expected.

Found another, which he didn't.

He ran the number through the state's database of businesses.

Industrial Media Services, it said. *Frederic C. Marsh, owner.*

"Hmm," Hawk said. If Alexa had been in the car, Gemini would have tossed her out with the phone, knowing there wasn't a cop alive that wouldn't abandon a pursuit to save a child. He hadn't, so she wasn't. Meaning he'd already delivered her . . .

He needed firepower.

Now.

"Emily, continue interviewing neighbors," Cross said. "Annie, make sure the lab teams are doing their jobs. I don't want any slipups."

They headed for their assignments without looking at each other.

Cross's phone rang. He checked the display. Frowned. Hawk should be sleeping. Or at the hospital. He connected. "You better be with Sammy . . ." he warned.

His gray eyes lit up.

"Watch yourself," Cross said. "We'll be there soon."

He closed the phone, cupped his hands. "Emily. Annie. On the double."

They spun, started running.

"We may have found Alexa," he said.

Annie peeped.

"No guarantee, but it's promising," Cross said. "An informant called Hawk. Says he saw a man matching the description of our kidnapper carry a child-sized bundle into a building."

"Alexa," Emily breathed.

"Informant couldn't say. But if it's our kidnapper, it has to be Alexa," Cross said.

"What's the building?" Annie said.

"Industrial Media Services. In that new industrial park on Two Hundred Forty-eighth Avenue."

Emily glanced at Annie. "We did a stakeout there last winter, remember?"

"Those counterfeiters," Annie said, nodding.

"Hawk's there now," Cross said. "Annie, get your teams moving. Emily, head to the building, help Hawk with surveillance."

Annie looked overjoyed, raised her hand to high-five Emily. Pulled back when she realized.

"Let's go get your daughter," Cross said.

They ran for their cars.

"Good-bye, little lady," Freddie-Boy cooed to Precious. "I'll miss you."

"Am I going home?" Precious said, eyes lighting up.

"In a manner of speaking," Freddie said, nodding at Scarface.

Who seat-belted Precious into the unmarked delivery van and headed out. Next stop, county airport, for the private jet to Belarus.

"And now, my dear," Freddie said, turning to the klieg-lighted bed. "It's time to show us what you can do."

"I don't wanna," Alexa said, folding her arms over the Catholic school uniform Freddie dressed her in.

"Oh, sweetie, it's easy," Lindy Archer cooed, waving over the male star. She gave Alexa another peppermint patty. "Just lie back and have fun. He'll do all the work. Before you know it, you'll be going home too."

The stud approached.

"I don't like him," Alexa said, inching away.

"But I sure like you," the stud said.

"You . . . you do?" Alexa said as the Katrina hit her brain. "For real?"

"Sure I do, honey. To show you how much, we're going to play a game, you and me."

"Will I have fun?"

"I promise."

"Ohhhhhh," Alexa said, touching her hair. "Thass nice . . ."

Archer pressed *record*. The cameras didn't whirr.

"Take five," Lindy sighed, reaching for her tools.

"A van is exiting the premises," Hawk reported. "Heading south on Two Hundred Forty-eighth." He provided description and tags.

"I see it," Annie said. "Alpha team?"

"We have it in sight, Commander. Moving into position for felony stop."

"Commence when ready," Annie said.

"Understood."

"Sniper? Demolition?"

"Sniper."

"Demolition."

"We'll attack when the ram truck arrives."

"We're ready," Sniper said.

"Us also," Demolition said.

"Understood," Annie said. "Spotter?"

"I'm here," Emily said.

"What do you see?"

Emily looked around.

"Nothing," she said. "The parking lot's deserted, and nobody's walking around."

"Cameras?"

"None," Emily said. "I circled the building twice."

"Doesn't mean they don't exist," Annie said, more to herself than Emily.

"We'll save her, I promise," Emily said.

"Keep your mind on your assignment," Annie snapped.

"Roger that," Emily said, voice even.

Hawk looked at her. "I thought you guys settled your hash."

"I have," Emily said. "She hasn't."

"She'll be fine when we get her kid back," Hawk said.

"I shouldn't have to wait for that," Emily said. "I've earned the respect."

"I know," Hawk said. "But it's her kid. It's making her insane."

"Should we worry about that? I mean, is it clouding her judgment?"

Hawk shook his head.

"Even insane," he said, "I'd follow her into hell."

Scarface spotted the on-rushing SUVs. He slammed his brakes, shoved into reverse.

Saw laser dots dancing on his chest.

"Turn off the engine, step out of the vehicle," Alpha leader said.

It wasn't a request.

He thought about shooting his way out.

Saw more dots, and the machine guns to match.

Freddie doesn't pay me enough to take a bullet.

"All right, all right, I'm shutting down," Scarface said, pressing one hand on the windshield and turning the key with the other.

"Are we there?" Precious asked, clapping her hands.

The SWAT truck with the bumper of battleship armor picked up speed.

Smashed the door so hard half the wall disappeared.

"Go, go, go," Annie ordered.

Bravo and Charlie whirled into the dust. Emily, Annie, Hawk, and Cross followed.

"Ground floor clear," SWATs announced as they flushed each room.

"Where is she, where is she?" Emily said.

"Locked," Charlie leader reported, slapping the steel door to the second floor.

"Key," Annie barked.

Her demolition man slapped on charges, reeled out detonation wire as he retreated.

"Cover," Annie said.

Everybody grabbed a wall.

The door imploded.

SWATs rushed the stairs.

"Don't shoot!" Freddie-Boy screamed, running out of the office with his hands up.

"Girl on the bed," Charlie leader shouted as he spotted the wan form.

"Alexa!" Annie cried.

"Hi, Mommy," Alexa said, crawling unsteadily on the mattress. Her skin was oiled. Her hair was in pigtails. Her face was bruised, her grin, loopy. "Wasss hap'nin?"

"Oh my God," Annie said. "Honey, it's me, I've come to bring you home."

She froze when she saw Alexa's panties. The delicate pink cotton, a Christmas gift from great-grandma in Vermont, was monogrammed with the letter A. It hung from the belt of a woman whose hands were wrapped around a camera.

"What did you do to my daughter?" Annie screamed, smashing her forearm into Lindy Archer's face. Lindy staggered away, shrieking from a broken nose.

"Take Alexa and get outside," Cross ordered.

"I'm gonna sue!" Freddie-Boy shouted.

"She resisted," Cross said, whirling on him. "How about you?"

Freddie started to protest.

Saw Cross's expression.

Thought better of it.

"Did they touch you, baby?" Annie asked, hugging Alexa so close there was no light between them. "Did these people go anywhere they shouldn't?"

"No, Mommy," Alexa slurred. "But a nice man was going to, as soon as the camera got fixed. We were gonna play a game. He called it Hide the Salami. Did you hear of that game?"

Two SWATs pulled a naked man from under a desk. He was still Viagra-tumescent.

"There you are," Alexa sang. "Come on, let's play our game."

The SWATs dragged him to the stairs. Facedown. He screamed with every bounce.

"Arrest everybody in this hellhole," Cross said.

He turned to Hawk. "Your collar, Sergeant. You found 'em."

Hawk shook his head. "Thanks, but I should get back to Sammy. Give the glory to whoever's stuck with the paperwork."

"I'll do the paper," Emily said. "But you're getting the credit. If it wasn't for you, we would never have found her—"

"Chief. In here." The SWAT's tone was urgent. They rushed into Freddie-Boy's office. The SWAT pointed to a narrow door hidden by nature photographs but now forced open with a pry bar. They scrambled down a hallway, into another room.

Which was filled with girls.

Some no older than two.

All with Alexa's loopy grins.

Emily opened her mouth.

Closed it without speaking.

"Tear this place apart," Cross said, jaw flickering like heat lighting. "They've been drugged, and we need to know what it is."

Hawk blew out his breath.

"I already do," he said.

All eyes turned.

"It's Katrina, a new designer drug," Hawk said, looking extraordinarily unhappy. "A DEA buddy told me about it. One tab and you're hooked, down to the neural level. When you're on it, you're happier than you've been in your whole life. But when you're cut off . . ." He ran his hands through his hair. "Katrina's more addictive than meth. Than crack. Than heroin. Than anything. A few hours without, you're begging for a bullet."

"Which means . . ." Emily said.

"Yeah," Hawk said. "She's hooked."

"Omigod! Omigod! Omigod!" Tristen squealed, jumping like she was on fire.

"Your daughter says—"

"I heard," Annie said, laughing in delight.

"We'll come meet you," Joshua said. "Tell me where you are."

"Still at the scene," Annie said. "We're about to leave for Edward."

A sharp intake of breath. "Is she—"

"Not a scratch," Annie assured. "It's just a precaution." She was concerned about the singsong in Alexa's voice, but unwilling to quash her family's happiness by saying it. Not till Dr. Winslow could say for sure. "Alexa says the kidnappers didn't do . . . anything."

"Thank God," Joshua said, a catch in his voice. The phone shifted.

Tristen let out a little whimper-cry.

"She's safe; nobody hurt her," Annie said. "It's over."

"I love you, Mom."

"Me, too," Annie said. "See you at Edward."

She closed the cell. Kissed Alexa a dozen times. Got high-pitched squeals in return. She shook her head. Alexa never squealed like that. Ever.

She saw Emily striding her way, her face a mask. Annie knew that look.

"Tell me," she said, getting to her feet.

"Get Alexa to the hospital right now," Emily said.

"Why?" Annie said.

"She's been drugged," Emily said, and explained.

Annie's eyes became black ice. "I'll find the pervert who got her into this mess," she whispered, handing Alexa to a paramedic. "And I'll kill him."

"I'll help," Emily said.

Annie's lips twisted ugly.

"If you'd done that to start with," she said, "my daughter wouldn't be a junkie."

Emily reared back as if slapped.

"Fuck you," she said. "Deputy Chief."

Stalking away.

Annie heard the tremendous hurt in Emily's voice. Considered reaching out.

Climbed into the ambulance instead.

50

The deer was so exhausted his muscles twitched and burned. But he'd made it. He was home. Same as he'd left it several suns ago, searching for food.

Same trees.

Same bushes.

Same rocks.

Same hills.

Same grass.

Same water.

Except, it wasn't.

Something was different.

He twisted his ears back and forth.

Something was breathing.

Soft. Uneven.

He struggled to his feet, needing to see if it was a threat. Dragged himself over rocks and logs, stumbling several times. Sniffed deep.

Reared back, nostrils flaring.

Meat and sour.

The smell of the giants with the thunder-sticks.

The deer lowered his antlers. Peeked cautiously into the hole.

Two giants. Sprawled out, limbs crooked. He touched the closest with an antler tip. No movement. He touched the other.

Same.

The first was pale as a grub. Its eyes were open, but not seeing. It was missing a limb. It stunk of death.

The second was bigger and heavier. It wore the fur of the earlier giants, but had no thunder-stick. It breathed but did not speak. It smelled of meat and sour. It had . . .

The same bloody holes as the deer.

His tail twitched. Could the thunder-sticks have pierced this giant? How was that possible? Why would one giant pierce another?

There was no answer. Only their kinship of holes.

The deer shivered as the wind picked up. He needed to rest somewhere warm, protected.

He climbed down the slope.

Bent his legs into the nest of branches.

Snuggled up next to the breathing giant.

Whom he sensed would not hurt him.

And would not mind the warmth.

Marty strolled into the open-air latrine, toilet paper in hand.

Branch waited.

Waited some more.

"Bear!" he shouted at the top of his lungs.

Marty crashed out of the latrine, pants around his ankles, .44 in hand. Mud splashed, toilet paper flew. His feet tangled. He fell into a puddle.

"Where?" he shouted, looking at tent, table, Escalade, tent. "Where's the bear?"

"Don't you see it?" Branch said, falling to the ground laughing. "It's right there."

Marty followed the outstretched finger.

Which pointed at his shiny behind.

"You son of a bitch," Marty sputtered, clutching at his pants. "I'll get you for this."

"Bare!" Branch howled.

Spencer Abbott blinked.

Found himself in a pile of branches, drenched head to toe. Snuggled next to a snoring deer with a rack the size of Cleveland. At his feet, a bloated girl with shedding skin. In his head, the beat of a waltz . . . *Gèmini* is *Ca*jun is *Snake*-head is *Dett*mer . . .

That's `one crazy dream you're having, partner, Abbott decided.

Better sleep it off.

"I still got mud up my ass," Marty grumbled. "Oughta make you clean it out."

"Shhhh," Branch said, finger to his lips. "We're hunting wabbits."

Marty suppressed a laugh. Didn't want Branch to think he was funny.

Though the latrine bit *had* been pretty good.

They continued their exploration of the Lee River Valley. They'd set up camp east of Millston, in the remote southern portion of the Black River State Forest. The air was nippy, the sun inviting. Barn owls hooted in the distance. Red-tailed hawks swooped for breakfast. Dwarf milkweed bent to the puffing breeze, sunlight scattered off patches of sandstone. They'd watched a beaver dam give way to the relentless pounding of the river, opening the clogged channel and sucking the flood waters back into the main stream. Fish splashed here and there. Pine sap mingled with the mushroom dankness of wet earth. They felt civilization slipping away. They were cavemen in Gore-Tex, locked and loaded, minimizing their noise to the squish of boots in muck. Looking for bucks.

Branch spotted the first one, tapped Marty's shoulder.

Marty nodded, seeing the antlered deer. Compact body with a wide rump. Decent rack with several sharp tips. A keeper.

Branch eased to one knee and wrapped the sling around his arm, stabilizing the .30-06 for the shot. He welded the stock to his cheek, brought his eye to the 4x scope. He lasered the distance at one hundred ninety yards. He was zeroed for one hundred. He adjusted the scope to compensate. The Nosler Ballistic Tip would break the deer's shoulders and lungs, providing the instant kill all real hunters demanded. He took a deep breath, blew it out. Took another, held it. Put his finger on the polished steel trigger—

The roar made them flinch.

The buck dropped in its tracks.

"If it looks too good to be true," Branch muttered, putting the safety on.

"It usually is," Marty said.

Another pair of hunters emerged from the woods. They moved silently, their rifles on the deer in case it needed a mercy shot.

"Would have looked good on my wall," Branch said. "But they took it fair and square."

The hunters tied a rope to the deer's hind legs. Tossed the other end over a crooked tree branch. Hauled the trophy into the air and slit its throat with a sharp knife.

The ground accepted the blood sacrifice.

They began to skin the deer.

"Nice shot," Marty called.

The one who'd taken it grinned. "Were you lining up too?"

Branch nodded. "You were faster, though. Need any help with the field dressing?"

"Nah, we got it," the second hunter said as he separated meat from bone. "Thanks for offering, though."

"No problem. Keep or donate?" Marty said.

"Donate," the first hunter said.

"Good for you," Branch said. Wisconsin had a program that delivered fresh venison to food banks around the state. Hunters could bring their meat home or drop it off for the poor. Win-win. "See ya."

They continued their sojourn upriver.

The deer heard the thunder-sticks.

But they were distant, and he was tired.

He settled his head on the giant's arm, went back to sleep.

"How's your son?" Branch asked as they leaned against a sun-warmed rock.

"Good," Marty said, chewing a piece of elk jerky. "We've been e-mailing since his operation. He's still not ready to see me, but . . . well, it's good. The e-mailing, I mean."

Branch rubbed his hip.

"You all right?" Marty asked quickly.

"Scratching an itch," Branch said. "Quit worrying, Mom. I'm fine."

"Too bad," Marty said.

Branch smiled. "His new heart's working normally?"

"He says so," Marty said. Last year, he discovered his son needed a heart transplant. Problem was, the boy's mother—

Alice, Marty's high school sweetheart, who'd conceived on prom night in the backseat of Marty's car—left town with the boy a week after birth and refused all further contact. Marty was young and dumb enough to think that was a good idea. But he'd always wondered. Decades passed. When the heart problem surfaced, Alice called. His son, she explained, didn't have health insurance, and she couldn't raise enough money to pay the bill. Marty didn't have it, either. Emily found out about the boy—keeping his existence a secret had caused a painful rift between them—and confided one night to Barbara Winslow, one of her closest girlfriends. A few days later, Winslow called the hospital and put the operation on her American Express. Marty found out when Alice called to thank him. Astonished, he demanded that Winslow reverse the payment. Winslow said no. She had more money than God from shrewd investing and a CEO husband who made even more than she did, and it would be criminal not to use it for this good cause. It was the first time Marty cried since his wife died.

"He's running half marathons," Marty said. "Met a woman, thinks he might settle down. Got a job with health benefits that will cover his care. He's happy."

"So why won't he see you?" Branch asked.

Marty shrugged.

"Right," Branch said. The kid took the money quick enough, but gave his father the bum's rush on meeting face to face. That annoyed Branch no end—not being part of the kid's life was Alice's idea, not Marty's.

"Don't start," Marty said.

"Yeah, yeah," Branch said.

They ate their jerky in silence, enjoying the rush of the river.

"I'm beginning to think," Marty said slowly. "Maybe there wasn't any transplant."

Branch spit out the half-chewed meat. "Say *what*?"

Marty made a motorboat sound with his lips. "What if Alice made the whole thing up? What if she wanted five hundred thousand dollars and figured I was good for it? She knew I wouldn't give it to her. But I might give it to my son."

"She made up that stuff about your dying boy?"

"Like a Nigerian dictator," Marty said, shaking his head.

"That's colder than a serial killer," Branch said. "If it's true."

"Don't know that it is. Don't know that it isn't."

"Do we even know there's a son?"

"There was," Marty said. "I saw him with my own eyes. Kissed his little head. Did you know they smell like peanut butter? Baby heads? They do." He batted away a wasp taking too keen an interest in his moustache. "Alice and her parents took him away a week later, and I haven't seen him since. For all I know, he's dead."

"Or in cahoots with Alice, laughing his ass off at dear old dad."

"Or completely unaware of what his mother is doing."

"*If* she's even doing it," Branch said. "Alice didn't take Barbara's money. The hospital did."

"Maybe they're in cahoots."

"And maybe," Branch said, "you're getting paranoid in your declining years."

Marty smiled. "I considered that too."

"And?"

"I'm not declining."

Branch sighed. "No, you're not. What are we gonna do about this?"

"We?"

"You need me. You're much too dumb to fix this yourself."

"Why? Because I let Alice scam me?"

"'Cause you walk around with mud in your ass."

Marty snorted.

"So?" Branch said.

"I'm gonna think about it some more."

"Then?"

"We didn't go to detective school just to impress chicks."

"Good thing. We'd have flunked for sure."

"Ain't that the truth," Marty said.

They picked up their rifles and continued upriver.

Another pair of hunters checked their rifles.

Adjusted their scopes.

Headed downriver.

Looking for prey.

Twigs snapped.

Squirrels darted.

Disturbance in the forest.

The deer struggled to his feet.

"Wha . . ." Abbott mumbled, wondering how a fur blanket could possibly get up and walk.

"Two o'clock," Marty said, pointing with his Winchester. "Next to that bend in the river."

Branch lifted his binoculars.

"Wow," he said.

The buck was stunning. It stood as high as a small horse, with muscled flanks and a stout, meaty body. Its rack glittered in the dappled sunlight. Twenty-two separate points with perfectly sculpted tips. Trophy grade, and handsome enough for the cover of *Field & Stream*.

"You saw it first," Branch said.

Marty nodded. Went to one knee, steadied the .30-30 on a chunk of log. He loaded a shell with a *snick-snick* of the lever. Steeled himself against buck fever, because this was only the biggest, best animal he'd see in this lifetime . . .

"Hmm," he said, squinting into the scope.

"What?" Branch said.

"Something's not right. Look at the hide."

Branch raised his Zeiss lenses.

"Bullet holes," he said. "A dozen, easy."

"Yeah," Marty said. "And see how badly he's weaving? How tilted his head is? Somebody used that critter for target practice." He pulled the Winchester from his shoulder, disgusted. "I can't shoot him now. Not after he survived that."

"Pass up that kind of trophy? Are you crazy?" Branch sputtered. "Go ahead and shoot. Nobody's gonna know or care what happened before you killed him."

"I will."

Branch shook his head. "I can't believe I hang around with you."

"Said the pot to the kettle," Marty said, knowing Branch wouldn't shoot either.

The deer turned back to the hidey-hole, smelling but not seeing a predator.

Got dizzy.

Collapsed.

"Ah, shit," Branch said.

"We have to put him out of his misery," Marty agreed. "I hate to do it, but the damn coyotes will eat him alive if he can't defend himself."

They covered the distance quickly.

"Poor fella," Branch said, kneeling before the twitching animal. "Someone shot you all to hell. They're the ones ought to pay, not you."

* * *

The tallest of the hunters clicked in the range.
Raised his rifle.
Fired.

"Ahhhhhh," Branch screamed as a bullet smashed into his
hip.

Marty leapt for him as the gunshot echoed through the
forest. "I got you, man, I got you," he said, pulling a Quik-
Clot from the cargo pocket of his trousers. He stuffed it directly into the gaping wound, watched the chemical sponge
foam and bubble.

"Hurts," Branch gasped, turning white. "Burns."

"I know, but it's stopping the blood," Marty said, stuffing
another sponge over the first and pushing with both hands.
Branch howled. Marty kept up the brutal pressure. The flow
ceased as the battlefield coagulator formed a dam against the
arterial bleeding.

"We're sorry, we're sorry," he heard two men say as they
rushed up.

Marty snapped his head around.

"Are you stupid or what?" he growled.

"I saw the deer," the tall hunter bubbled. "I lined up my
shot, and just as it went off I saw your friend. Goddammit,
mister, I didn't mean to hit him, worse thing ever happened
to me."

Buck fever. It blinds you every time.

"You got a phone?" Marty said.

"Yeah, yeah, we do," the short hunter said.

"Call nine-one-one. You know where we are?"

"Not zackly . . ."

Marty spat map coordinates from memory. "Tell 'em to
send a helicopter. If they don't have one, send a truck or

boat." He tied off the mess with his sweaty bandanna. Didn't hear any dialing. "What are you waiting for?"

"You," Tall said.

Dangerous tone in his voice.

Marty turned.

Saw their rifles pointed at his head.

"Toss your guns this way," Short growled. "'Less you want yer head blowed clean off yer stem."

"What the—"

"We're robbin' you, dumb-ass. But first, toss me them rifles. Use one arm. I see you anywhere near them triggers, I'll kill you deader'n a roach motel."

Marty nodded.

Threw his Winchester.

Then Branch's .30-06.

Turned at the waist, trying to hide the .44.

Tall saw the movement.

"That a .44 magnum?" he said.

"Yeah," Marty said reluctantly.

"Always wanted one of those. Take it out, toss it over. Again, nice and slow."

Marty complied.

"Now, your buddy's sidearm."

Marty pulled the .45 from Branch's flap holster.

Hesitated tossing it.

Tall fired.

"All right, all right," Marty said, ears ringing, as the bullet plowed dirt just inches from Branch's feet.

"Then quit fuckin' with us," Short said. "And toss that sidearm."

Marty did, calculating the distance between them, the angles of attack, the odds of taking them out with a leaping burst of speed.

The math stunk.

"Can if I tie this bandage tighter?" Marty asked, noticing a thin drip. "I don't, he's gonna bleed to death."

"Go ahead, if you want," Tall said, shrugging. "But he's gonna bleed out anyway."

"Meaning?" Marty said, though he already knew. These two had the glassy stare that said they'd already made up their minds. He was stalling for time, trying to figure a way into his gun pocket. Hunched on the ground like this, his jacket was covering the opening. It'd take a few seconds to get in, pull the baby Glock, and fire. By which time they'd have unloaded both rifles into his sorry ass.

"We don't like witnesses," Tall said. "Where's your money?"

"Chest pocket of my coat," Marty said.

"Reach in with two fingers, wing it over."

Marty did. It landed at Tall's feet, flopped open. Emily's picture fell out.

"Purty gal," Short admired. "That your wife?"

"Keep her out of this," Marty said.

"Aw, and I asked so nice," Short said, lashing out with his boot.

"Uhn," Marty grunted as the toe slammed into his spine.

"It was a simple question," Tall said.

"Girlfriend," Marty coughed.

"Figures. Tits that creamy can't be no wife's." His grin showed perfect teeth. "You fuck her a lot?"

"Much as I can."

The hunters laughed.

"Maybe we'll fuck you," Tall said. "Like in that movie. The one with Burt Reynolds?"

"*Smokey and the Bandit*," Short said.

Tall gave him a withering look. "Not race cars. Bows and arrows."

"Oh, yeah," Short said. "*Deliverance?*"

"Yeah, that's it. *Deliverance*," Tall said.

Looked at Marty.

"G'wan, squeal like a pig."

Marty stared.

"You know, like this," Short said, puckering his lips and making the noise. "Go on now, squeal. 'Less you want me to put your friend out of his misery."

Marty raised his chin, hating them.

Squealed like a pig.

"Suuuu-weeee," Tall roared, clapping his hand on his thigh. "Mister, I gotta say, that was one great hog-call. But don't worry. We're not gonna fuck ya. We're not homos or nuthin'. That's an abomination against the Lord."

"We're just gonna kill ya and take your stuff," Short said.

"Yeah, the Lord likes that," Marty said.

"Ornery," Tall said. "Gotta respect that. You got a car?"

Marty felt something tug at his pants. Took it in peripherally, not moving his eyes.

It was Branch.

His hands blocked by Marty's bulk and coat.

Slitting the bottom of Marty's gun pocket with the knife from Marty's waistband.

Hope flared.

If I can stall them long enough . . .

"Well, I tell you what, boys. We don't have an automobile," Marty said, pumping air between each word. "A car's no good for traveling over this kind of terrain, with all the rocks and stumps. We do have a sport utility vehicle, though."

"That right?" Short said, interested. "What kind?"

"Big ol' Escalade," Marty said, shaking his head like he loved that thing to distraction. "It's brand-new. Shiny black. More muscle than a wrestling match. Made the way Cadillac used to, before the foreigners"—he pronounced it "ferr-ners"—"come along and messed things up."

Short's beady eyes went dreamy. "Always wanted me a Escalade. Drive down to the lake, attract a flock of girls, let 'em suck my Johnson."

"So let me take you to it," Marty said. "We're camped a couple miles from here—"

"Whaddaya think we are, idiots?" Tall sneered. "Only place you're going is in the river. You and your buddy."

The baby Glock fell from the bottom of the pocket. Marty felt Branch's hand spasm from the effort of cutting. He couldn't handle cotton candy right now, Marty knew, let alone a gun.

Up to me.

"You're . . . you're really going to kill me?" he said, larding his voice with panic.

"Well, duh," Short said.

"But I have money," Marty said. "Guns. Lots of guns. And drugs. I got a bunch I could give you." He forced tears out of his eyes. "I don't wanna die. Honest to Christ, I don't."

"Don't be taking His name in vain," Tall said, eyes narrowing.

"I'm not, I swear I'm not," Marty said. "Kill my friend, hey, he's half dead already. Just don't kill me." He began to rock, back and forth, screwing his face into abject terror, clapping his arms around himself. "I don't wanna die in a forest," he wailed. "Please, I'm begging you. I'll do anything to stay alive."

"Jesus, what a pussy," Tall said to Short, voice greasy with disgust. "Offering up his buddy to save his yellow ass."

"Man disgusts me," Short said.

Marty turned on the faucet.

"Please, no, please," he blubbered, clutching his belly, bending over like he was going to throw up. He forced up some half-digested jerky.

"Look at him, gettin' sick, the pus-chewin' jackoff . . ."

"I'm begging you," Marty wailed, rocking like a Texas

preacher, each bend bringing him closer to the Glock in the grass. "Let me live, please, let me live."

"Shut the hell up, you whiner!" Short screamed. "I'm gonna kick ya to death if you don't shut up and take your bullet like a man."

The screaming woke the deer.

Who looked at the giants.

Who held the thunder-sticks.

Who held the thunder-sticks . . .

He leapt off the ground.

The hunters flinched away.

Marty grabbed the Glock, rolled, came up in a combat stance.

Tall fired.

The deer screamed, the heavy copper bullet slashing a furrow across his flank.

Marty fired.

Greasing Short.

Tall took off running.

Blasting the rifle blind behind him.

Marty dove behind a rock. The bullets whanged off.

"Clear," Branch moaned.

Marty came around low, aimed at Tall's blaze-orange back.

Pulled the trigger.

"Ahhhh," Tall gassed as the hollowpoint buried itself.

Marty charged up the hill. Checked Short as he passed.

The deer was goring his eyeballs.

Marty ran as fast as he could, closing the gap with Tall, who ran surprisingly fast given the bullet in his back.

"Police! Freeze!" Marty commanded because sometimes it actually worked.

"You're a *cop*?" Tall hollered as he skidded to a halt.

"Detective," Marty said.

Tall turned. "Jesus, you don't know how happy I am to hear that," he said, grinning. "I'm unarmed and my hands are up. That means you can't shoot me. You gotta arrest me, read me those Mylanta rights. It's illegal to shoot an unarmed man who ain't attacking."

Marty kept the Glock on Tall's chest.

"You took an oath," Tall pressed. "Damn right you did."

"Yes," Marty said. "I did."

"So you know what you gotta do," Tall said. "Take me to the station and put me in your clink. The judge will hear my case. It's not as bad as it might look, you know."

"How's that?"

"My buddy made me do this. The one you aced back there. I'll testify that you had no choice, you hadda plug him. I'll make you the hero of this whole shebang, the man who saved your pal from my crazy friend."

"Saved my pal."

"Right. You'll get your picture in all the papers." He pronounced it "pitcher." "I didn't wanna do this robbery. But I was, you know, ah, what's the word?"

"Coerced."

Tall looked puzzled.

"Forced," Marty prompted. "Your buddy forced you—coerced you—to shoot my friend."

Tall's moony face lit up. "That's right, forced. I was scared he'd shoot me if I didn't . . ."

Marty nodded, lowered the Glock.

". . . but I aimed for your buddy's hip, so he'd only be wounded, maybe survive this thing. Like you said, I was coerced." Tall laughed. "Damn, that's a great word, coerced. I might even get out of jail time, I play this whole thing right. . . ."

Marty snapped the gun to eye level, twitched his finger twice.

Squirrels and birds scattered.

"You can't . . . do . . . that," Tall wheezed, incredulous, as he slumped to the ground. "You're the police. You can't shoot a man who's surrendered. You . . . just . . . can't. . . ."

Marty lined up on his head.

Shot him till brains splashed.

"I'm on vacation," he said.

He stuck the Glock in his uncut pocket, ran back to Branch. Inspected the hip wound. It wasn't dripping now.

He ruffled Short's pockets, found the cell. Dialed nine-one-one. No connection.

Branch's eyes opened.

"You're back," Marty said, joy flooding.

"Where'd he shoot me?" Branch groaned.

"Hip," Marty said.

Branch's face crumpled. "Ah, man," he said.

"I know," Marty said. "I gotta get you out of here."

No reply.

Marty looked around. Nothing looked easily turned into a stretcher.

"Guess I'm gonna carry you," he said.

Branch's eyes fluttered. "I heard you talking, you and the shooter," he said. "Is it true? Did he have his hands up?"

"Yeah," Marty said. Reluctantly. Branch was a stickler for the law.

"Was he unarmed?"

"Yeah."

"And you shot him anyway."

"Yeah."

Silence.

"Thank you. Really. I . . . thank you."

Marty nodded.

"Listen," Branch continued. "If I don't make it . . ."

"Stop that," Marty snapped. "You're going to be fine."

"But if I'm not," Branch said, taking Marty's hand, "you

gotta promise me something. I mean it, you have to promise."

Marty bent close. "What, Branch?" he said, squeezing the hand gently. "What do you want me to promise?"

Branch breathed out.

Breathed in.

Spoke as if a distant wind.

"If you do carry me, don't touch my wiener. It's un-American."

Marty shook his head. "Asshole. I should have let you bleed."

Branch laughed.

Came out a hacking, broken cough.

"Enough fun," Marty said, folding Branch across his shoulders in a fireman's carry. "We gotta scoot."

He turned upriver.

"Wait," Branch said, flailing.

"No more jokes," Marty said, already feeling the strain. He was strong, but Branch was big. "Gotta get you to a hospital."

"There's bodies," Branch said. "In that hole."

Marty looked.

Two bodies.

One in plastic.

One moving a little, muttering.

Both next to the struggling deer.

"Don't go away," Marty said, putting Branch on the ground and jumping into the hole. The deer snorted, but didn't try to defend himself. Marty spotted the badge, holster, and tattered uniform. He made a noise.

"What?" Branch said.

"One of them's a cop." He shook the man as hard as he dared. "Hey, I'm a policeman. I'm gonna take care of you. Can you hear me?"

"Gemini is Cajun is Snakehead is Dettmer," Abbott mumbled. "Gemini is Cajun is Snakehead is Dettmer."

"He's alive," Marty reported. "But talking gibberish."

"What about the other?"

Marty knew without checking her pulse. He told Branch, who shook his head.

"Gemini is Cajun is Snakehead is Dettmer . . . Gemini is Cajun is Snakehead is Dettmer . . ."

"Don't worry, pal," Marty said. "I'll get you out of here."

"How bad is he?" Branch said.

Marty looked at the bluish hue of the cop's skin. "Shot a bunch of times," he said. "And his skin's blue. Looks like he's been in the river."

"Leave me here, then," Branch said. "Carry him to Millston."

"And let you die alone?" Marty said. "Are you nuts? Your ugly ghost would haunt me the rest of my life. And, Lydia would kick my ass. I don't need that."

He moved the cop to a sitting position. No reaction.

"Stay with me," Marty said, slapping the cop's face. "Bad enough Branch wants to croak."

Abbott's eyelids snapped opened like a doll in a horror movie. "The subject's name is Dettmer," he said.

"Is that who shot you?" Marty said, carrying him over to Branch. "Dettmer?"

"Affirmative. Four subjects, male Caucasian, early twenties. Subject Dettmer is five-eleven, one-seventy, blond/green, DOB unknown, New Orleans accent, driver of a white cargo van bearing Illinois tag Adam Ocean Charlie . . ."

Marty recalled what he'd mumbled earlier. "Is Dettmer the Cajun?" he asked.

The cop stared.

"Gemini is Cajun," he said. "Is Snakehead is Dettmer."

His eyes fluttered. He passed out.

"He's a block of ice," Branch said, feeling the cop's wrist for a pulse.

"The hole was filled with river water," Marty said. "Till that dam collapse drained it."

Branch nodded. "That's what saved his life."

"The water?"

"The cold," Branch said. "Remember that little boy in Chicago? Jimmy something? From way back?"

"Rings a bell. Polish name, I think. Tomczak?"

"Tontlewicz," Branch said. "Jimmy the T. He fell through the ice, was underwater for nearly sixty minutes. Should have been dead in six."

Marty snapped his fingers. "The frigid water slowed his body functions. So he didn't drown. He was fine after they warmed him up."

"I think that's what happened to this cop," Branch said. "All those bullet holes, he should have bled out. But the water was so cold it stopped the bleeding. Saved his life."

"Well, he's gonna warm up now," Marty said. "So those holes could start leaking again. Need to get him out of here fast."

"Can you make a stretcher?" Branch asked.

"Yes," Marty said.

He went back into the hole. Picked up the girl. Carried her past Branch and the cop.

"Where you going?" Branch said.

"Away," Marty said. "She's a floater. Don't want to make you sicker than you already are."

He nestled her on a bed of pine needles. Flicked open his knife, cut away the clothesline belted around her middle. Took a firm grip on the leading edge of the plastic. Started unrolling. He groaned as the stench hit, but didn't stop. She rolled off the end, broke into several jellyfish-like pieces.

Marty broke into paroxysms of gagging.

"You all right?" Branch said.

"Never . . . better," Marty coughed, flapping the plastic like a dirty tablecloth.

Brought it back to Branch and the cop.

"Jesus, that stinks," Branch said.

"Then you're really going to like what comes next," Marty said. He doubled it over and moved the shot-up cop on board. "Gonna drag you two like a sled."

"Not to doubt your strength, Samson," Branch said. "But how you gonna haul four hundred pounds of dead weight?"

Marty shrugged. Placed Branch next to the cop. Made sure the bandage was tight. Folded the plastic over them, as if a sandwich wrap, then rolled the leading edge around a tree limb. Fastened it to the limb with the clothesline remnants, making a handle.

"Cut some breathing hatches," Branch said. "You'd feel bad if we suffocated."

"Or not," Marty said, slashing the holes.

He went back to the handle, started pulling. "How's the ride?" he said.

"Bumpy," Branch said with a groan. "But we're moving."

"No one's more surprised than me," Marty said.

"Girl," the cop cried. "Girl, girl, girl, girl."

"What's that, pal?" Branch asked him.

"Girl saved me. Can't leave her, can't, can't."

"I'll come back for her," Marty said. "I swear, I'll come back. We don't leave anyone, ever."

The cop's eyes went glassy.

Marty headed upriver, one step after the next.

"Get cop . . . talking," he huffed. "Want to hear . . . more . . . case he doesn't . . . make it . . ."

"I've been trying," Branch said. "He's not responding."

"Breathing, though?"

"Shallow but steady. A guy named Dettmer shot him?"

"Gemini is Cajun is Snakehead is Dettmer," Marty said,

muscling the sled over an anthill, his legs and lower back burning like napalm. "That's what he kept saying. Then his eyes popped open, like some kind of zombie."

"Like . . . zombie . . ." Branch said, deflating.

Marty stopped to check. Branch had passed out. But his pulse was steady, his breathing unlabored. Marty tightened the bandage, picked up the handle.

"Mush," he muttered.

A pack of coyotes stormed out of the trees, smelling fresh meat.

Marty bellowed. They slowed but didn't stop.

He grabbed the Winchester and shot the lead coyote. It yipped once, fell over.

The others fled.

"Warned . . . you fair . . . and square," he wheezed.

Two hours later, he was so blindingly exhausted he was sure he was hallucinating. Because there was no way a pickup truck would be bouncing his way. No way the driver would be waving from the window.

"Lotta venison on that sled," the driver said cheerfully. "Gonna keep, or donate?"

"Help . . . me," Marty gasped, stretching out an arm.

The passenger hopped out. "Don't you remember us from this morning?" he said, his bushy brows converging. "You offered to help us skin that deer?"

"Need . . . help . . ."

They looked at the sled.

Blanched.

"Holy Christ," the passenger whispered. "It's Spencer Abbott."

The driver unsnapped a large phone from his belt.

"Tried . . . cell," Marty panted. "No . . . signal."

"Satellite," the driver said, punching in a series of numbers. "Kaye? This is Linton. We found Abbott. . . . That's right: he's alive, repeat, alive. South bank of the Lee River, couple miles east of Millston. Two men are with him. One's walking, but the other's unconscious. Spencer's shot and blue, looks critical. Send everything you got, Code Three." He listened. "Chopper? Great. Here're the GPS coordinates. Should be enough open space to land if the pilot's any good. . . . Cabot's driving? You just made my day. Linton out."

"Who are you?" Marty asked.

"Firefighters," the driver said. "What the hell happened to you guys?"

"We're cops, shot by robbers," Marty said. "He's Spencer?"

Linton looked at the sled. "Yah. Spencer Abbott, a Jackson County sheriff's sergeant. Ten hours ago, he got in a firefight with a gang of assholes. Folks been looking for him since."

The truck backed up to the sled. The passenger, now driving, ran around back, started pitching deer meat into the grass.

"Aw, man," Marty said. "Your venison."

"Your ambulance," Linton said. "Chopper only holds one."

They heard the whopping in the distance.

"You sure there's enough clearance?" Marty asked.

"Guy that's driving," Linton said, "will cut his own hole if he has to."

The helicopter appeared over the trees. Marty and Linton dragged Branch and Abbott to the far stretches of the clearance. Cabot waggled the chopper to say he was good, then touched down, clipping only two tree branches with his main rotor.

"Hear you boys found Abbott!" Cabot yelled.

"These two did," Linton said. "Saved his life."

"You get the key to the city," Cabot said.

"Beer come with that key?" Marty said.

"Much as you could drink in a lifetime. Load him up."

They did, and the chopper lifted off.

"Let's roll," Linton said, lifting Branch into the truck bed then accompanying Marty into the cabin. "Ten minutes to Millston if I drive like a maniac. Twenty if I don't."

"Ten's better," Marty said.

The pickup threw twin roosters of dirt as it made the turn upriver.

"The guys who shot us are still there," Marty said as they slashed through low-hanging branches. "Deader 'n dirt. But there're two other casualties, and you gotta find them ASAP."

Linton picked up the phone.

"One's a deer," Marty said. "The other one's drowned."

Linton glanced at him.

"The dead one's a teenage girl," Marty explained. "She was floating with Abbott. Your man put up a fight at the thought of abandoning her. I promised I'd go back."

The driver gave Kaye the coordinates.

"And the deer?" he said.

"Saved our lives by attacking the shooters," Marty said. "He's shot bad—not by us, somebody else—but he's got that spark. Get him to a vet, he'll make it."

The driver added the information.

"And if it doesn't survive?" he said.

"Well, he's a championship buck," Marty said. "Boone and Crockett for sure. Finest trophy I'll ever see."

"So you want the head and antlers."

Marty shook his head.

"I want to make sure he keeps 'em. I'm gonna bury him with those antlers if I have to kill every man jack trying to saw 'em off."

Linton looked at him odd.

"Lemme get this straight," he said. "You're a hunter. You

kill deer. You have a buck just sitting there for the taking, one that'll get you in the record books. But you want to rush it to a vet and save it."

"About covers it."

Linton snorted.

"Cops," he said.

He emerged from the woods, thumping onto a gravel track. I-94 gleamed in the distance.

"Ambulance is waiting at the bridge," Linton said as he picked up speed. "They'll take your friend to the hospital in Black River Falls. Where do you want to go?"

"Where's your sheriff most likely to be?"

"Hospital," the driver said.

"Then that's where I need to be."

The driver nodded.

Stuck his flasher on the roof, lit the siren.

"Why you doing that now?" Marty said. "When you didn't do it before?"

Linton grinned.

"Couldn't impress girls before," he said. "Just rabbits and squirrels and shit."

"Firemen," Marty said.

51

Hawk's BlackBerry beeped.

TRANSFER RECEIVED, the message from his offshore bank read. FIVE HUNDRED THOUSAND DOLLARS AND ZERO CENTS, UNITED STATES CURRENCY.

He wired it to another offshore account, to cover his tracks, then transferred it to the account of Denton Schoolsby, the squishy-chinned man in hospital financial services.

TRANSACTION COMPLETE.

Hawk felt one huge weight disappear.

The other would go when Sammy was cured.

He started the truck, headed for Maxximus's mailbox. He hadn't bothered with a courier. Maxximus wouldn't cross him. This was business, and The Maxx was a businessman.

Especially when Door Number Two was the wrath of Juarez.

Hawk reflected on the bloodthirsty cartel. Even as a cop, he wouldn't want to cross it too openly. Its savagery made American gangsters seem like Girl Scouts.

Fortunately, his exposure would be over in four minutes.

52

Dr. Amanda Barrett slammed her bloody scrubs into the laundry cart.

"Schoolsby's an asshole," the nurse said.

"Tell me something I don't know," Barrett said, dialing Hawk's number.

53

Hawk spotted the mailbox.

Looked up and down, left and right.

Nobody, nowhere.

He glanced at the updated version of the Fuzz Buster that used to warn drivers of police radar. It analyzed passive, active, disturbance, infrared, laser, sound wave, and other stealth technology that might be aimed at his vehicle.

All quiet.

Let's finish this.

Sixty feet from the mailbox. Fifty. Forty.

He punched the gas.

Sailed past the rapper's mansion.

No gun-bearing narco-ninjas jumped into the street.

He made a U-turn, yanked down his ski mask, pulled up at the mailbox. Grabbed the handle with gloved hands, pulled it open.

His cell tootled the theme from Mighty Mouse. His special ring for Dr. Barrett.

"This is Hawk," he said.

"Good morning," Barrett said. "How's the weather out your way?"

Mist-dots pocked his windshield.

"Rain's coming," Hawk said, glancing at the iron-patch sky. "You're undoubtedly sunny."

"Yes, we're, ah, good in the weather department. . . ."

He knew tap-dancing when he heard it. "What's wrong?" he said.

She sighed.

"We have a problem," she said.

Hawk dropped the Katrina on the passenger seat.

"Tell me," he said.

"What the hell are you doing?" Maxximus grumbled, watching the proceedings on his monitor. He wasn't willing to risk physical spotters—he'd taken the woman's warning seriously—but there was no law against hidden cameras. "Dump the cereal, get out of here."

"What the hell are you doing?" Hawk screamed. "We have a deal. I expect you to honor it."

"I'm sorry," Barrett said. "But the price went up. There's a worldwide shortage of stem cells, and our supplier is putting the screws to us."

"You can't do this to Sammy," Hawk said, pounding the steering wheel.

"I don't want to," Barrett said. "But I have no choice. The price is four now, not three."

"Put me on with your boss," Hawk snapped. "Or that dough-faced bastard in patient services who shoved it up my ass the first time."

"They'll tell you the same thing," Barrett said. "Listen, I

offered to donate my services. The whole staff did. They said no. They don't care, Hawk. They're bean counters."

"I won't lose my girl when she's so close," Hawk whispered, feeling like she'd power-drilled his skull and poured in boiling water. "She'll be well enough to fly tomorrow—"

"What do you mean, 'well enough'?" Barrett interrupted.

"She had an attack last night," Hawk said. "Rabbo invaded her lungs. She was this close to dying, but Doc Winslow pulled a rabbit out of a hat."

"Oh, Hawk," Barrett said, flashing to the cement mixer surely parked on Sammy's sunken chest. "I'm so sorry."

"The people you work for are vampires."

"I'd do anything to change their minds. But I can't."

"How about you threaten to quit?" Hawk said. "High-powered doctor like you, they wouldn't dare take the risk."

Barrett laughed without humor. "Actually, I did," she said. "Want to know what Schoolsby told me?"

"What?"

"'Go ahead. We'll find someone else to make the doughnuts.'"

"He's not a vampire," Hawk said, outraged. "He's a fuckin' serial killer."

"He's typical. The guys running medicine aren't doctors. They're MBAs. Finance people. Their idea of triage is save the hedge funds first."

Hawk shook with anger, but knew further argument was fruitless. "Just be ready tomorrow," he said. "I'll be on your doorstep five hours after I send that million."

"You're going to raise a million dollars overnight?" Barrett said. "Is that reasonable?"

"Ain't nothing reasonable in any of this," Hawk said. "But yeah, I'll do it."

* * *

Alarms cascaded. Nurses sprinted. Winslow raced into ICU.

"Help, it's a monster!" Sammy cried as the fire roared inside her. She clawed at her belly button, her fingernails rending great, bloody rips in the flesh, trying to dig out the beast. "Daddy daddy daddy daddy daddy . . ."

Hawk put a pound of Katrina in the mailbox. Kept the rest.

Accelerated with a roar.

"Finally," Maxximus muttered as the car sped away.

He walked to the mailbox and removed the bag, his respect for the woman rising exponentially. She'd planned this with military precision, fooling not only himself, but Gemini, one of the brighter kids on the block. There was a place in his organization for that kind of talent. Way he figured, her smarts would bring in far more money than he'd lose buying back his own drugs. The balance sheet tilted in her favor. Which is why she'd live . . .

Maxximus screamed when he saw one pound instead of five. He spun for the house, punching the cell in short, powerful stabs.

"Yo, boss," Chief of Staff Artie Tatum said.

"Where you at?"

"Touching down in Minneapolis. I'll be at the supplier soon as traffic—"

"Turn that jet around, get back here fast as you can."

"Why?" Tatum said.

"We're going to war."

* * *

Hawk punched in the special number, trying to control the trembling in his hand.

"You thieving cunt," Maxximus snarled a moment later. "We have a deal."

"*Had* a deal," Hawk said. "Here's the new one—a million for the remaining four pounds."

"You think you're getting anything but pain?" Maxximus hissed. "I'll hunt you down and chop you into bitty pieces."

"If Juarez doesn't chop you first," Hawk said. "The only thing preventing that is one million dollars. You got thirty minutes to transfer the funds. Don't, and I call Mexico."

"Go ahead," Maxximus snarled. "Or stick a sombrero up your ass, I don't give a shit. I can't pay you now because I don't have it on hand. Believe it or not, I don't live like Scrooge Fucking McDuck. I gotta make some calls, move some things around. Some of the guys I deal with aren't available right now." It wasn't true, of course—he could snap his fingers and his bankers would climb off their girlfriends to get The Maxx his money. But he was tired of being pushed around. "You want a million, you'll wait till midnight. Deal?"

Silence.

"Fuck this up, I'll kill you," Hawk said.

"Suction," Winslow said, blood and pus spilling everywhere as she ripped the scalpel through Sammy's abdominal wall. "Clamp . . ."

54

Cancer.
Aquarius.
Virgo.

"Gotta do that bitch," Gemini muttered, the burn of humiliation and revenge swelling his belly like bad cheese. "Find her, snatch her, cut her up."

It was crazy, he knew. Against nearly impossible odds, he'd managed to escape. So why walk back into the lion's den? He was a businessman. Not a lunatic.

Cancer.
Aquarius.
Virgo.

"Where the hell is the U-turn?" he said, drumming the wheel of the rental.

55

The Maxx's eyes grew round.

It was *her*.

Rather, her voice . . .

"Naperville Police Detective Emily Thompson killed both kidnappers," a TV reporter was saying. "Just like she did two serial killers in the past. While we're tracking her down for comment, here're clips from her past interviews. . . ."

Television Emily: "As a police officer, I regret the taking of even a single life. But the suspect tried to murder me, and left me with no choice. . . ."

The voice on the phone: "The only thing preventing that is one million dollars. Do it, there're no more games, you get the remaining cereal. . . ."

"Gotcha," he said, amazed as always at how fast the voice detector between his ears worked.

So she was a cop. So what? The cartel had capped hundreds of police officers in Mexico and the United States. Couple of months ago, they left the severed head of a police chief in an ice bucket in his own station, as a message to knock off the raids. What was one more dead blue?

As for the missing Katrina, his bosses would accept his story of a rip-off by a greedy cop. They were used to it down there, the endless shakedowns from law enforcement. He'd tell them a corrupt police detective hacked into the secure phone system *they'd* provided to arrange the narcotics transfers and stole the Katrina, and The Maxx slaughtered her in retaliation, plus retrieved the drugs. The bastards would cream their serapes with happiness.

So, Emily Thompson would get got.

He went to his MacBook, to find a place to intercept.

56

Marty looked at the man with the snow-white moustache.

"Buehler," he said, voice flat. "Buehler . . . Buehler . . ."

"Yeah, that never gets old," the Jackson County sheriff said. "You must be Benedetti."

"How'd you know?"

"Ken said you think you're funny."

They shook hands.

"How do you know Cross?" Marty said.

Buehler dropped into a chair. "Homeland Security seminar. The G taught us how to protect ourselves if Eskimos invade."

"Your tax dollars at work."

"More federal pud-pulling, you ask me. But us rustics were grateful for the attention."

Marty snorted. Rubbed his legs.

"Hurting?"

"You have fire ants in Wisconsin?"

"No."

"Then they're hurting."

"Hauling a four-hundred-pound sled will do that." Buehler looked Marty top to bottom. "Add you, that's seven hundred. . . ."

"Hey," Marty said.

Buehler's moustache grinned with him.

"Sorry it took me so long to come by," he said. "All hell's broken loose, and I'm just now tearing away."

"Sergeant Abbott?"

"Among other things."

"Did the firemen give you my message?"

Buehler looked puzzled. "Nothing of importance . . ."

"Abbott said who attacked him."

The sheriff stiffened.

Marty told him about Dettmer a.k.a. Snakehead, Cajun, Gemini. Buehler listened, one finger tapping his lips. Then called someone named Kaye and told her to run it down.

"Fuckin' fire guys," Buehler said, settling back.

"Probably not their fault. Way my head was spinning in the truck, I might have thought I told them but didn't," Marty said. "Hope it's a good lead."

"It is, if Spencer wasn't hallucinating."

Marty's shrug said, *Maybe, maybe not.* "You have the proper facilities?"

"Hospital's top-drawer. But we're shipping him to Mayo Clinic. They've had more practice with this." Buehler glanced at the bed. "How's your friend?"

"Get shot, what can you say? Your doc says he'll be all right."

"Count on it, then. Doc's great when he's sober, and he hasn't had a drink since sunrise."

"I resemble that remark," the chief surgeon said from the doorway.

"How'm I gonna insult you proper," Buehler complained, "you keep sneaking around to hear me?"

The surgeon walked in. Buehler made introductions.

"And what am I, chopped liver?" Branch muttered from the bed.

Marty's face lit up.

"Thought you were sleeping," he said. "How long you been awake?"

"A few minutes. Haven't had the strength to talk."

"I'm not surprised," the surgeon said, checking the bandage. "Hell of a beating you took. Good news is I dug out the bullet, sewed you up right nicely."

"What's the bad?"

"Hip's cracked," the surgeon said. "Should heal all right. Then again, it may not."

"Doc's known for his decisiveness," Buehler said.

The surgeon snorted, turned to Branch. "If it doesn't, you'll need a new one."

"Group discount," Marty said.

"What?" Buehler said.

Branch explained he'd been shot before, got a new hip, it didn't take, got another.

"Third time's the charm, I hope," Buehler said.

"Me, too," Branch said. "Any instructions for me, Doctor?"

"No dancing," the surgeon said, wandering out.

"Rustic," Buehler said to his back.

"Vaughn, you mentioned Ken Cross," Marty said. "When did you talk to him?"

"Today. Several times."

"About?"

"What I came to see you about," Buehler said, crossing one dirt-streaked boot over the other. "Seems our cases are interconnected."

"Cases?" Branch said. "I got shot by a couple of punks, and here we are."

"Littl' more complicated, turns out," Buehler said. He

waved at a passing deputy. "Shorty, would you round up some coffee? The toothpicks in my eyelids need toothpicks."

"Hot caffeine, coming up," Shorty said. "You the guys who saved Abbott?"

"He did," Branch said, pointing at Marty.

Shorty pumped Marty's hand, eyes bright. "What you did with that sleigh ride . . . well, we can't ever repay you. But damn, we're gonna try. Anything you need, it's yours. Starting with my cabin in the woods whenever you feel like using it."

"It's on a lake with the sweetest view on God's green Earth," Buehler said. "I'd take him up on it if I were you."

"I'm not too proud to refuse a gift," Marty said. "But your guy saved himself, tough as he was. I just gave him a ride."

Shorty's grin said, *Bullshit.*

"Anything," he repeated.

Headed out for the coffee.

"Everyone admire Abbott that much?" Marty said.

"Even the guys who hate everyone," Buehler said. He took out a handkerchief, wiped sweat off his forehead. "Okay, here's what we know. Little after midnight, Abbott tells our head dispatcher, Kaye Barley, he's stopping on the Lee River Bridge in Millston. You familiar?"

They nodded.

"That's right, Ken says you've hunted up here. Anyway, Spencer sees four men with a flat tire. Stops to help. Doesn't clear the call."

"So you sent backups . . . ," Branch said.

"Intersections were flooded from the storm. Roads impassible. But we got there," Buehler said. "Abbott's cruiser is missing, the van's on fire, and nobody's around. The bridge deck's littered with spent shells."

Marty grimaced.

"Yeah," Buehler said. "They opened up on him. Abbott

fired back. We know because of the different shells. What we can tell, Abbott got off three magazines."

"Forty rounds," Marty said.

"More or less. Attackers fired three hundred," Buehler said. "From a machine gun."

Branch shivered.

"Yeah, I faced them in Desert Storm," Buehler said. "Don't care to repeat that experience. So, Abbott's fighting four guys with automatic weapons."

"Probably just one," Branch said. "Otherwise there'd be a thousand shells."

Buehler's nod said, Good point. "Automatic weapons suggest traffickers. They're the only ones around here with buzz guns."

"The guys shot Abbott are drug mules?" Marty said.

Buehler shook his head. "Mules get caught, they give up, do their bit. They don't open up with machine guns. I'm thinking cartel distribution team."

"Whaddaya got up here, Juarez?" Marty said.

"Among others. I-94's a big pipeline for them."

"Abbott carry artillery?"

"AR-15, six hundred rounds," Buehler said.

Branch raised an eyebrow at the huge amount of ammunition.

"Rural policing, you're lucky if backup arrives within the hour," Buehler said. "Bad weather, it takes forever. We pack appropriately." He cleared his throat. "We found Spencer's car keys under the bridge. They fell through the deck with pieces of his radio. So he couldn't open the trunk for his rifle. His radio was busted, and he was out of ammo."

"So he jumped in the river," Marty said.

"I would," Buehler said.

Shorty came in, passed out foam cups.

"Thanks," Buehler said. "Anything new?"

"Rillum and Bradshaw," Shorty said, "are the two guys who shot Marty and Branch."

"You know *already*?" Marty said.

Shorty grinned. "Local knuckleheads. Pinched a dozen times for drunk driving, stealing from unlocked cars, residential B and E. Guess they finally decided they were real gangsters."

"Taking on armed hunters?"

"Didn't say they were smart gangsters." He cracked his knuckles. "Whoever shot them did it most excellently."

"I hated to do it, as I mourn the loss of even a single life," Marty said.

"I'll note that, in the report," Shorty said.

"What about the girl?" Branch said. "And the deer?"

"Deer's at the vet. Girl's at the morgue," Shorty said. "A one-eyed wolf was pulling out her liver when the first cruiser rolled up. No more wolf."

Marty flashed a thumbs-up. "Abbott was unusually attached to that girl."

"Hey," Buehler said, eyes narrowing.

"Didn't mean it that way," Marty said. "Just that he appeared very protective of her. Like he knew she was a victim and it was his job to save her."

"Spencer has a soft spot for victims," Buehler said. "Helped a lot of them on his own time. So that'd fit. How'd you know?"

"When I put him in the sled, he started thrashing. Insisted we couldn't leave her behind," Marty said. "Says the girl saved his life. I promised to go back for her." He looked at Shorty. "Glad you were able to keep that promise for me."

Shorty nodded.

"If she was a shooter, Abbott would have let her rot," Buehler said. "So she was a victim. Bet those four killed her, wrapped her in that plastic."

"They stopped on the bridge and dumped her in the river," Branch picked up, voice mellowing as the pain pump whirred.

"Abbott comes along," Shorty said. "Assumes they're having car trouble. Gets out to help. They think he's wise, open fire."

"Abbott jumps, and the two float down the river," Marty said. "That's how we found them, together. 'Course, he'll tell you for sure when he's awake."

"Sure hope that's soon. It was a helluva sight, that girl," Shorty said, shaking his head. "She was just a kid, Sheriff. Not even eighteen and more holes than a Swiss cheese. What kinda sick bastards do that to a kid?"

"How's her ID coming along?" Buehler said, gently steering him back to business.

"Fine. We'll figure out who she is," Shorty said. "She's well-nourished, with a goodly amount of high-quality dental work. Coroner's making a full mouth impression, getting it out to dentists. We sent her fingerprints and DNA to Madison."

"Go national," Buehler said. "With Illinois plates on the van, she could be from anywhere."

"On it," Shorty said, disappearing.

Buehler blew steam off the top of his coffee. Explained how the killers got to Naperville.

"So that's how these things connect," Marty said.

"Uh-huh. The van was cruising a neighborhood near your downtown," Buehler said. "The kidnappers spotted two girls walking, swooped in. They're sisters, name of Bates—"

Marty and Branch flinched as if slapped.

"Yes," Buehler said. "Your SWAT commander's children. Good news is they're both safe. Annie was on her front porch with a friend when the kidnap occurred."

Marty stared.

"That's right," Buehler said, smiling. "That friend was

Emily. She chased down the kidnappers and killed two of them, then rescued Alexa from a child trafficker."

Marty's legs wobbled visibly.

"Gotta find a phone," he muttered.

Buehler's eyes followed him out. "Thought he'd be pleased," he said.

"He is. And he isn't," Branch said. "Three years ago, Emily was mauled by a serial killer. Last year, it happened again. A third is stalking her now." He explained the delivery of body parts and *Third time's the charm*. "Marty's worried she won't survive another attack."

"She's *that* Emily?" Buehler said. "Emily Thompson?"

"Yep."

"I know all about her," Buehler said, excited. "In fact, I have that photo of her in my office."

"The famous one?"

"Crouching in the mud like a wolf, teeth bared like she's gonna bite the cameraman."

Branch remembered it. She'd just crawled out of the Du-Page River after choking the first serial killer to death. The local *Naperville Sun* grabbed the shot, and it went viral, appearing on two million websites.

"Impressed the hell out of me, how she handled herself in that mess," Buehler said. "I keep the photo as a reminder that good cops can win."

"When everything says they shouldn't," Branch said.

57

Hawk sprang off the waiting room chair, eyes darting.

"She's all right, Hawk, she's fine," Winslow said, closing the door. "It was her appendix."

Hawk stared. "Her . . . *appendix*?"

"Sometimes a cigar is just a cigar," Winslow said.

Hawk wilted into the chairs.

"However," Winslow said.

He jumped back up.

"Sit," she said, worried he'd stroke out. "Did you get any sleep?"

"I was gonna," he said, starting to pace. "Got tangled up in that rescue."

"Alexa Bates?"

He nodded.

"That was terrific work," she said.

"Except for her getting hooked," he said.

"Not your fault. Now sit."

He did what she asked. "So, about Sammy . . ."

"Her appendix burst, plain and simple," Winslow said. "I took it out. Problem is, there's rhabdomyosarcomal in the abdominal chamber. Four separate spots, ripe for explosion."

"Oh, God," Hawk groaned.

"Next attack kills her, and I can't do anything about it. You have to get her to L.A.," Winslow said. "I'll set up the transfer."

"You can't," he said.

"Didn't I make myself clear?" Winslow said. "You have to go now. Sammy's in no shape to travel, but there's no choice anymore."

"L.A. won't take her," he said. "I don't have the money yet."

That confused her. "This morning you had all three million."

"Now the hospital wants four."

Winslow's eyes flared. "I'll straighten this out," she snapped, taking out her phone.

Hawk put a hand on her arm.

"Amanda already tried," he said. "I got no choice but to get the money."

Winslow did a mental check of her finances. Didn't have it. Most of their investments had cratered in the Great Recession.

"Thanks anyway," Hawk said.

"For what?"

"You'd put this on your own AmEx, but you don't have the money," he said, knowing what she'd done for Marty's son. "I know what that's like. If I hadn't moved the Sammy funds into bank CDs . . ."

Winslow sighed. "What are you going to do?"

Hawk looked at her.

"I already lined up a lender. I'll see him at midnight." He

feigned a look of embarrassment. "Keep that to yourself, okay? Chief wouldn't tolerate me borrowing from someone in the, uh, quick cash business. . . ."

Hawk's going to a loan shark.

That he had no other choice depressed her no end.

"I'll have the plane gassed and ready," she said.

Emily strode toward Alexa's room, holding a purple balloon. She ached to see her little "niece," but if Annie was there, she'd keep walking. . . .

Her cell chirped. The number was unfamiliar. "Hello?" she said warily.

"Please tell me you're all right."

"I'm all right," she said, relieved but surprised. She badly wanted to talk to Marty about what had happened, but he and Branch hunted old-school—no phones.

No phones.

"Wait a minute," she said. "If you're in the woods, how are you calling me?"

Marty mutter-sighed. "I'm at the hospital in Black River Falls. Branch got shot."

"*What?*" she said, backing against a wall as a gurney raced by. "Shot? How?"

"Two robbers posing as hunters. They shot Branch. They're dead now."

He said it was such finality she knew he'd done the killing.

"Are you all right?" she said, brutally repressing the dragon whispering in her ear.

"Not a scratch," Marty said. "Branch wasn't so lucky. Bastards got him in the hip."

"The . . . oh, no."

"Yeah. He'll be here awhile. Week at least. I'll drive back when he's released."

"What do you mean, drive back?" Emily said. "Aren't you staying?"

"I need to be with you," he said.

"Martin Benedetti," she said, flaring. "You're staying with Branch."

"He's a big boy, he'll be fine without me—"

"No," she said, stamping her foot. Winced at the pain. "He won't. Despite the tough-guy bologna he'll dish out, he'll be anxious without you there. I'm glad you want to be here for me, Marty. But Branch needs you more."

"Are you sure?"

"Hundred percent," she said. "Does Lydia know?"

"Haven't had time to call her."

"I'll go over," Emily said. "She shouldn't hear over the phone. Who else should I tell?"

"My boss," he said. "Cross and Annie. Anyone, actually. It's no secret."

"All right," she said. "Anything else you need to tell me?"

"Matter of fact. The four guys who shot a cop here are the ones who kidnapped Alexa."

"I know," she said, explaining about Cross and Buehler. "What we don't have are names. They didn't have IDs, and their prints aren't in the system."

"Not in AFIS? That's unusual for bad boys," Marty said. "I may have a lead you can chase. One of them is named Dettmer. Might also go by Cajun, Gemini, or Snakehead."

"Snakehead," she mused. "That could describe the guy who got away. His head's shaped like a triangle. Could look like a snake's head."

"Is he blond?"

"Blindingly."

"Height and weight?"

She estimated.

"Damn," he said. "That might be Dettmer. Did he speak with a New Orleans accent?"

"He was shooting, not talking," she said, scribbling madly in her notebook. "Why? Is he supposed to?"

"Abbott said so."

"We know anyone in New Orleans?" she wondered. "Who might know a scumbag killer off the top of his head? Be faster than messing with databases."

Marty thought.

Snapped his fingers.

"I met an NOPD dick at Quantico. He's familiar with every crook Louisiana ever spawned. Give him a ring, tell him I sent you."

"Will do," she said. "And Marty? This sounds terrible, but I'm glad it wasn't you."

"I'm glad it wasn't either," he said. "And Branch would say the same. Make your calls, let me know what happens."

"How do I contact you?"

"Um. Good question. I'm calling from a hospital land-line. I'll run to a drugstore, pick up a cell, e-mail you the number."

"All right. I love you. . . ."

She spotted Cross rounding a corner. Disconnected Marty, waved him over.

"Got a name," she said, explaining.

"I knew Marty was smarter than he looked," Cross said.

He noticed the purple balloon.

"Aw, you shouldn't have," he said.

Emily snorted. "It's for Alexa."

"I'll deliver it," he said, "and let Lydia know. You have work to do."

Tristen hugged her father.

"What's that for?" Joshua asked.

She held up her cell phone.

HAVEN'T HEARD FROM YOU. IS EVERYTHING ALL RIGHT?
LET ME KNOW.

He tousled her hair. "I forgot I sent you that."

"From the time stamp," she said, "it was right after the . . .
discussion we had in my bedroom. Thank you."

"Anything for you," Joshua said.

"Really? Can I get a tattoo?"

"Mommy's Little Angel?"

She wrinkled her nose. "Eeew. No."

"Then you have your answer."

Annie walked into the room.

"Dad said I could have a tattoo," Tristen said.

"Daddy's Little Girl?" Annie said.

Tristen rolled her eyes. "The two of you," she said.

Annie grinned, sipped her coffee. "Pretty balloon. Who's
it from?"

"Aunt Emily," Tristen said. "It was tied on the chair with
a note."

Annie looked. *Love you lots,* Emily's cursive said. *Get
better soon. Love, Auntie Em.*

Her smile turned glassy.

"What?" Tristen said.

"Nothing," Annie said, putting the note in her pocket. She
didn't want Emily around her children anymore, but she'd
deal with it later. "Any change in our patient?"

"Sleeping like a baby," Tristen said, letting out an enor-
mous yawn.

"Go home, get some sleep," Annie suggested. "I'll call
when Alexa wakes up."

Tristen nodded. "Good idea, Mom. I'm tireder than shit."

"Language," Annie said sharply.

"I thought I could get away with anything now."

"You thought wrong."

Joshua laughed. "Come on, potty mouth. Let's get you
home and napping."

"Oh, wait," Tristen said. "Is Mr. Hawkins around? I want to thank him."

"He'll appreciate that," Annie said. "But do it later. You need sleep."

They left, and she scooted as close as the bed would allow.

Took her daughter's hand.

Wondered when it grew so big.

Or maybe I just feel so small. . . .

"Lullaby . . . and good night . . ." she sang to the beeps of the monitors. It was Alexa's favorite bedtime song till she got old enough to insist she didn't like it anymore. But Annie still heard her sing it to herself at night, when she thought nobody was listening.

Her cell beeped. She checked it. Incoming video from Cross. She hit play, wondering why he hadn't attached a message.

Blurry imagery as the camera whipped frantically from a window to a yard. A moment later, a street appeared. Trees. Houses.

Her.

Charging across a lawn with an Uzi, next to Emily and her Glock.

"The attack," she whispered.

The view widened. A car moved into the frame. A man with electric blond hair jumped from the driver's side. Annie's feet went out from under her. Emily was rock steady, touching the trigger. . . .

A little body popped up in the foreground, directly behind the shooter. Annie knew that chubbiness like the back of her own hands.

Her heart roared in her ears.

Emily's muzzle jerked. The Camry's back window shattered.

Annie flinched, as if slapped.

Electric Blond fired. Screams erupted from neighbors outside the frame. Emily dove backwards, covering Annie. Electric Blond jumped in the car. Swung an elbow. Alexa went down. Electric Blond drove away. Emily struggled to her feet, ran a few steps.

Collapsed, writhing.

"I was wrong," Annie whispered. "Dear God, I was wrong."

Monitor beeps turned rapid, dissonant. Annie leapt from her chair, yanked off the blanket.

Alexa's fingers crawled like spiders. Her chest heaved. Her head rocked. Her limbs jerked.

"I need help in here!" Annie shouted into the hallway.

Alexa's eyes fluttered open, pupils dilated to marbles. "I don't feel so good. . . ."

Projectile vomit blew out of her mouth.

"Now!" Annie screamed as the monitors went full orchestra.

The Code Blue team crashed into the room, followed by Winslow. Annie clung to Alexa. Winslow shoved between them, peeled back Alexa's eyelids. "She's crashing," Winslow said, rapid-firing commands. Nurses dumped chemicals into the IV tube, inserted a second line.

The convulsions increased.

"Do something," Annie said as Alexa flopped like she'd been Tasered.

"Get Mom out of here," Winslow ordered.

"What are you going to do?" Annie shouted as Hulk-sized orderlies pushed her into the hall. "Tell me what you're going to do."

"Put her in a coma," Winslow said.

* * *

"Well, now, darlin'," the detective said, chuckling with a New Orleans smokiness Emily could practically smell over the phone line. "I haven't heard that name in years."

"You know him?"

"Sure do. He's Karl-with-a-K Dettmer," he said. "Debt collector for the local mob. A nasty little booger, our Karl, used a can opener to make his point."

"Ouch," Emily said.

"What his victims said. Given the age and description, we have to be talking about the same guy. Not too many criminals with moonbeam hair."

"You can't miss it, that's for sure," she said. "I wonder why he didn't dye it?"

"It's his trademark. The peckerwood version of 'Bam!'"

Emily laughed.

"Karl hasn't been on our radar since Katrina," the detective continued. "He and half our criminal population relocated to other parts of the United States."

"Thanks," Emily said drily.

"Consider it our full-employment program for the rest of y'all."

She flipped to a fresh page in her notebook. "Three others were with him," she said. "Any chance they're New Orleans too?"

"Karl was tight with three guys," the detective said. "Could be them. Got pictures?"

She dumped Cammy's video into his in-box, along with the Naperville and Wisconsin crime-scene photos.

"Harris, Blaine, Dunwoody," the detective said. "Dettmer was their fuehrer. Always a bright one, Karl was. Mighta gone legit but for his old man, who was a good argument for coat-hanger abortions."

"He was an abuser?" Emily said, taking note after note.

"Beat that kid every which way but loose," the detective said. "Till Karl turned fourteen. That's when dear old dad got broke with a steel pipe and filleted with a can opener. Took four hundred stitches to close his wounds."

"How tragic," Emily said.

"What I said. Old man didn't file charges, though. Probably too embarrassed to admit his own boy done him."

"Maybe afraid."

"Whatever, it worked," he said. "Old man left Karl alone after that."

"Whereupon he became a mobster."

"Started as a leg-breaker," the detective said. "Did well, was moving up. Then Katrina hit. All the work disappeared, criminal and legit. So he moved on. Took his three amigos and a brother-sister act rumored to have been involved in child porn."

"We shut down a kiddy factory this morning," Emily said. "Owners aren't talking."

"Names?"

"He's Frederic C. Marsh. She's Lindy Archer."

"Neither ring a bell," he said. "But names are easy to change."

A narcotics cop plopped fresh coffee on Emily's desk.

"Any photos you can share?" she said, blowing the narc a kiss.

"Anything we had was washed away in the flood," he said. "Thing you need to know is Karl loved to hurt people. He wasn't compelled by voices or demons or moon pies. He just didn't give a shit." He laughed. "Do me a favor when you see that psychopath?"

"Name it."

"Tell him New Orleans's Finest is looking forward to the many times he'll be violated in prison."

"I will. Thanks for all your help, Detective."

"It's Harrison. And it's my pleasure, darlin'."

She disconnected and called Marty. Left a message.

Called Cross.

"The fourth kidnapper is Karl Dettmer," she said. "Born and raised in New Orleans, washed up here after the hurricane."

"Good work," Cross said. "Send the particulars to our guys and Buehler. Then give it to the feds. I want every cop in the country hunting his ass."

He stared at his computer screen, horrified.

BOLO Karl Jonas Dettmer, the FBI alert said. *Wanted for child kidnapping and attempted murder of a police officer. All field offices, be advised. . . .*

"They know who he is," Hawk mumbled. "They'll trace him back to me."

Which would condemn his daughter.

Which he wouldn't allow to happen.

No matter what filthy thing he had to do to prevent it.

His cell burped. PRIVATE CALLER.

He had no time for this, and his patience was rubbed to onionskin. He answered anyway.

"I'm coming home," Bonnie said.

"You . . . you are?" Hawk said.

Overjoyed.

Overwhelmed.

If the million wasn't delivered . . .

If storms delayed the takeoff . . .

If the rabbo patches exploded . . .

If Sammy wasn't cured completely . . .

Bonnie would flee forever.

"Aren't you happy? I thought you'd be happy," she said, sounding a little hurt.

"I am," he said, wiping sweat from his eyes. "It's just that, uh, you took me by surprise, that's all."

"Are you sure, Hawk?" she said. "Are you having second thoughts?"

"About what?"

"Me. Coming back."

Reads me like a map . . .

"None," he said.

"Then I'm leaving my sister's now," Bonnie said, happy and relieved. "I can't wait to see you, Hawk. You and Sammy. It's time we're family again."

Hawk did the math. Nine hours' drive from Memphis to Naperville.

Putting her here before midnight.

They could fly to L.A. together. Be a family.

If he could just keep the plates spinning.

Third time's the charm.

Third time's the charm.

Third time's the charm.

The thought of what he had to do now made him physically ill.

But he no choice.

"Just come home," he said, pulling the tool kit from his closet. "I'll take care of the rest."

58

Two more pounds, Christina Tsigaras huffed. *Till I fit in that stupid dress.*

That dreadful floor-length abomination of pumpkin, puce, and flounces that her best friend L'Adore insisted—*insisted*—the maid of honor wear at her Wedding of the Universe next Saturday. The gown was so garish it made Christina look like a gift-wrapped sumo.

"I'll get you for this," she vowed, shaking her fist at the pregnant sky as she picked up speed. "I'll dress you like a box of crayons at my wedding."

Her vow echoed off the trees flanking the limestone paths. She was at Herrick Lake because she was a sausage-and-pasta kinda gal, and running was the only way she'd lose those final pounds.

She churned north.

* * *

Hacksaw snuggled in the underbrush. The forest preserve across from Emily's apartment was virtually deserted. That was good, and bad. Bad, because pickings were slim.

Good, because when he did decide, there'd be no witnesses.

A bicycle flashed by. The rider looked like a NASCAR driver with all the logos on his shirt.

Next.

Christina fingered her pepper spray, rolled her eyes at herself. She knew it was paranoid, running with tear gas. Naperville was statistically the safest large city in the United States. There was virtually no violent crime, and the street gangs that plagued surrounding towns hadn't gotten a foothold 'cause the cops kicked their ass. There were drugs, oh Lord yes, there were drugs. Domestic violence. Auto theft. Burglary. The usual ills of modern society. But it stayed indoors, so she could walk the streets twenty-four-seven and not feel that hair-on-the-back-of-the-neck itch she got in other places.

But paranoid didn't mean someone wasn't out to get you. She was a criminal defense attorney, and clients she failed to save from jail made threats. So she kept the spray handy.

Maybe I could practice on L'Adore.

The thought brought a grin to her flushed face, which made her think again of the dress, which segued to those two stupid pounds. . . .

Hacksaw judged the approaching woman. Medium tall with a fine bearing. Straight brown hair, long and lively. Shiny white teeth. Wide, curious eyes. Great legs.

Perfect.

She flashed past, shoes clapping water from the overnight storms.

He rolled from the shrubbery and onto the limestone path.

Pulled the trigger.

Christina's brain coughed, "What the—" before it scrambled into eggs.

She flopped to the ground, unable to move, frightened beyond speaking, a pair of torches burning holes in her back.

For some reason she thought of the villagers hunting Frankenstein. . . .

God bless Tasers, every one, Hacksaw thought as he dashed to his prey. She'd taken the full boat of electricity, turning her to human Jell-O. Exactly what he needed.

Her attacker wore a Nixon mask, the lawyer part of her brain noted.

She tried to cry out.

Couldn't.

Nixon came close.

She thrust out the tear gas and pushed the spray nozzle.

Nothing. The synapses between brain and muscles were fried.

"Wuuuuhh . . ." her throat secreted.

"Shhhhhh," Nixon said back, gloved finger to lips.

Then he kicked her in the skull.

Hacksaw/Nixon slung the dead weight over his shoulder, high-stepped into the woods, where he'd set up his tool kit:

Pliers.

Knives.

Hacksaw.

Bucket.

Rope.

Mallet.

Nails.

Lumber.

And a palm-sized, high-def videocam.

Spit of rain.

Hacksaw glowered at the sky. He didn't have the time or patience for rain.

Realized it was tears, from the woman's unfocused eyes.

He snickered at himself, pulled down her lids.

Water bubbled through the lashes.

He shrugged.

First, tie her down. . . .

The rope was Wal-Mart's best, three-eighths of an inch with a breaking strength of one thousand three hundred fifty pounds. This woman weighed one-twenty-five, tops.

No contest.

He took off her clothes. Admired her panther beauty. He was, after all, human.

Pried apart her legs.

Lashed the two-foot piece of lumber to one ankle, then lashed it to the other, forming a triangle with her crotch. He looped the rope back and tied it in the middle of the lumber.

Whistling tonelessly.

He tossed the other end of the rope over the limb of an oak tree and pulled it taut.

Then hauled the woman into the air.

Her body formed an L as her legs went up, then turned

into an I as she hung straight, her head eighteen inches off the grass, swinging with shifts in the wind.

Her breasts were large for a runner's, he thought. Runners were normally the size of oranges. Sometimes grapefruit. He wondered if hers had always been this big, or if they'd shrunk because of the running. . . .

Thoughts for another time, he decided.

Blood rushed to Christina's head, jolting her out of the fog.

Her eyelids fluttered open. She saw trees. A table. Nixon's feet in gray cross-trainers.

All upside-down.

She felt herself turning, as if on a spit.

She started to scream.

Felt something sharp pull across her neck.

Felt wind slide into her throat.

Hacksaw jumped back to avoid the spurt.

"Damn, you're a good bleeder," he told the woman a few minutes later.

She didn't answer.

The steaming red blood pattered off the bottom of the galvanized bucket. The neck wound gurgled from time to time. Hacksaw shooed the flies homed in on the musty scent.

Ready for skinning, she was.

He inserted the knife into the hollow space above her collarbone. Sawed through skin and fat and muscle. When he reached her pubic bone, he turned the blade sideways, cut over to one hip, then to the other. Inserted his gloved hands and pulled the flap-doors open, exposing heart, stomach, liver, and other organs.

He sliced and diced and trimmed and tore, alternating

blade and gutting hook, clearing the cavity, piling the organs on the table to let the meat chill in the cold November air.

Stood back, admired his work.

Then inserted the knife into the slash in her throat.

Cut all the way around, freeing the head from the neck.

Picked up the hacksaw, splintered through the spinal bones.

The head popped free.

Bounced off the ground.

Tears still leaking from the lifeless eyes.

Using her ears as jug handles, he picked up her head. Placed it in the middle of the organ recital, eyes above mouth, where they belonged. Flies were everywhere. He ignored them.

He took the knife and zippered the skin of her leg, hip to ankle.

Then the other, then the arms.

Peeled back the skin like he would a chicken leg's, but left it hanging, ribbons on a gift.

Took an ergonomically correct stretch break . . .

Picked up hammer and nail.

Read the note he'd typed on the Underwood, then tacked it to the woman's forehead, swinging the hammer to drive through the stubborn bone.

Moved back to take in the scene.

Weeping Jesus, that's good.

He recorded seven minutes on the digital video camera, mixing wide shots with close-ups and scene-setters. He lingered on the woman's face, making sure to capture the tears. Panned over the typed note, then the newspaper clippings.

Satisfied, he pulled out his cell and clicked on the Web address he'd pre-loaded. The cell was an untraceable throwaway bought in another city. He plugged in the camera and uploaded the movie.

Send.

He double-checked he hadn't left clues. Everything was clean. He peeled off Nixon, the body suit, and the gloves, and stuffed them into a backpack. Pulled on fresh clothes. Jogged out of the forest and to his car, which he'd left, cleverly he thought, in Emily's parking lot.

The wind flapped the note he'd left nailed to the grinning skull.

Third time's the charm, it read.

59

Barbara Winslow put her hand on Sammy's forehead. No fever. The monitors told her to a tenth of a degree, but she still liked to do it by touch. It made patients feel like somebody gave a damn about *them*, not just their disease. Soothed the healer, too.

"How do you feel?" Winslow said.

"I can't feel anything," Sammy said, running her fingers over the gauze. "I'm all numby."

"It's the medicine I gave you," Winslow explained. "During your surgery."

Sammy's eyes went wide.

"I had an operation?" she said.

"You don't remember?"

"Uh-uh," she said.

The rhabdomyosarcoma!, Winslow knew. It shorted out Sammy's short-term memory.

"Your tummy was hurting pretty bad," she said, taking

Sammy's hand. "So I took a look inside. Your appendix was sick."

"Did it whoops?" Sammy said. "I do when I'm sick."

Winslow grinned. "Do you know what an appendix is?"

"Sure," Sammy said, nodding eagerly. "We learned about it in school."

"That's nice," Winslow said. "Anyway, it was sick, so I took it out. The medicine is helping you heal."

"Thank you, Miss Barbara," Sammy said. "I'm glad you're my friend."

Winslow's throat tightened.

She really wanted this child to be well.

"Are you afraid of going to Los Angeles?" Winslow asked.

"Oh, no," Sammy said, shaking her head. "Daddy said everything would be perfect. So I'm not afraid. Do you think Mommy's in Los Angeles waiting for me?"

"Maybe," Winslow said, not wanting to lie, but not wanting to raise the girl's hopes. "Would you like that?"

Another eager nod. "She can play games with me. I love games, don't you?"

Winslow nodded. "Would you like play one with me?"

"Sure!" Sammy said, face lighting up.

"How about cards? Do you like Go Fish?"

"It's all right, I guess," Sammy said doubtfully. "What I really like is Hearts."

"Well, that's funny."

"What?"

Winslow put her finger on Sammy's chest. "Hearts is my all-time favorite."

"Yay!" Sammy said, clapping.

Winslow fished out the deck she used when her trauma-clotted head needed a break.

Sammy dealt.

Rabbo faded to aces wild.

60

"Got a minute?"

Emily turned to see Annie Bates in the door of her cubicle. Her face was starched. Not from anger. More from holding back a tidal wave.

"Sure," Emily said warily.

They exited detectives, headed for interrogation.

"Hey, Chief," a patrol cop hailed. "Got a minute?"

"Not right now," Annie said, voice tight. "I'll find you."

"No problem," the cop said. "And hey, congrats on the promotion. . . ."

They entered the room, closed the door. Emily sat. Annie faced her.

"You saved Alexa's life," Annie said.

"Yes, I did," Emily said. "But why do you believe it now?"

"Ken sent me the video. . . ."

She began to cry. Emily sprang to her feet.

"I'm so sorry," Annie said, hugging her with the stiffness

of someone trying desperately not to break down. "You did the right thing, and all I did was shit on you."

"Actually, it was spit," Emily said, recalling Hawk's observation that parents go insane over their children's safety. "But it's all right. It's your daughter. I get it."

Annie broke the hug, stalked the room. "I hate it when I cry," she muttered.

"I know."

"The way I treated you is inexcusable."

"I never argue with deputy chiefs," Emily said.

A wan grin peeked out. "Forgive me?"

Emily nodded, then sat. Annie took the other chair, looked at her with red eyes.

"Your balloon deflated," Annie said.

"The store was out of the good ones," Emily said, used to Annie's head-snapping segues. "All they had were those cheap latex."

"Still, it was pretty."

"Purple's still Alexa's color, isn't it?"

"This week," Annie said. She pulled a handkerchief, blew her nose. "She's in a coma, Em."

Emily stiffened, shocked. "Coma? What *happened*?"

Annie's face pinched. "Katrina withdrawal," she said. "I've never seen anything like it. One minute she's peaceful. The next, she's in full spasm, her body wild with pain. She was screaming so loud Barbara put her in a medically induced coma." More tears. She wiped them angrily. "She'll stay that way till withdrawal's complete."

Emily rubbed her suddenly chilled arms. "How long will that take?"

Annie's shrug said volumes. "Katrina's so new there's not much experience," she said. "Barbara's consulting with Mayo and Johns Hopkins."

Emily tried to recall what Hawk said about the designer drug. Couldn't. Way too much happening today. "She'll get through this," she said. "Alexa's a fighter. I mean, look what she did to that kidnapper."

Annie brightened. "She bit him like a bulldog, didn't she?"

"A story you'll tell at her wedding someday," Emily said.

They savored the possibility.

"Good to have you back, Thelma," Emily said.

"Ditto, Louise," Annie said. "Let's get out of here before the boys call us girly."

They exited interrogation, headed back to detectives. Emily remembered that her iPhone had been ringing when Annie appeared. She pressed the button for messages. Saw she had a video. Switched over, hit *play* . . .

Staggered into the wall.

Annie rushed to her side. "What's wrong?"

Emily held up the cell with a trembling hand.

"Good . . . God," she heard Annie say.

Over the flames roasting her body.

Over the ignition of her extremities.

Over the cackling of the dragon.

"Go . . . away . . ." Emily gritted as she slid to the floor. "You . . . bastard . . ."

Annie got on her knees. "Is it the dragon?"

Emily nodded, once, hard, her neck so stiff she couldn't add another.

Annie put her mouth to Emily's ear. "Leave her alone or I'll tear your lungs out," she whispered. "Breathe fire without them and it'll blow out your ass like a bad taco."

Emily stared.

Started laughing.

So did Annie.

The dragon fled.

"I know exactly where that video was taken," Emily said. "I've passed it a million times."

Annie grabbed her radio.

"Chief?" she said. "We have a problem."

61

"Well damn," Marty murmured.

"What?"

"That's hugely tasty," he said, holding the blue-black beer to the light. "What is it?"

"Stout. The sheriff makes it," Cabot said.

"What, in his bathtub?"

The chopper pilot laughed. "Naw. He owns a micro-brewery down by the river. A couple of guys do the heavy lifting, but he's brewmaster, makes all the recipes."

"Cool hobby," Marty said. "Care to join us?"

Cabot shook his head. "Abbott's stable enough to trans-fer, so I'm flying the medevac."

"And your point is?"

Cabot laughed. "Old days I would have. Now, I have to deal with those three little words."

"'I love you?'" Marty said.

"'Random drug test.'"

Marty shook his head. "The old days are gone and buried."

"I hear ya, brother. Good news is Mayo called, they'll see him right away."

"Thought they had a waiting list."

"They made an exception when they heard the story."

"I'm sure it's not for the good publicity," Branch said.

"Absolutely not," Cabot said.

Marty raised his glass.

"Happy tailwinds," he said. "Or whatever you fly-guys consider luck."

"Thanks," the pilot said. "It's only a hundred miles, so I'll be back in a few hours. We'll have us a serious drink."

"Works for me," Branch said.

"You," Marty said, "are gonna be dry as Carrie Nation for the next three weeks."

Branch growled.

"Down, boy," Marty said, settling back in his chair.

Cabot laughed, waved, and walked out.

Marty suddenly felt uneasy.

"Nickel for your thoughts," Branch said.

"Thought it was a penny."

"Inflation," Branch said.

"I'm troubled about Abbott," Marty said. "Don't know why. Probably gas."

"All that jerky you ate today," Branch said. "What time you got?"

Marty glanced at his watch, told him.

"Two more hours," Branch said, "my baby walks through that door."

Marty smiled. "Looking forward to seeing your wife, are you?"

"Uh-huh."

"And Mr. Excitement?"

"Not so much." Branch's brother-in-law was a blowhard investment banker who knew everything about everything. But he'd volunteered for the trip so Lydia wasn't driving alone, so Branch planned to eat his annoyance.

They fell silent.

"You were walking so damn perfect, too," Marty said.

"Yeah," Branch said, glum. "It's gonna be hard this time, man. Hip rehab's worse than root canal, and I don't know if I'm up for it."

"Beats the alternative," Marty said.

Branch sighed. Nodded.

"Did I ever thank you, by the way?" he said. "For beating my alternative?"

Marty waved it off. "No thanks necessary. I'm just glad you're feeling—"

"Yoooou . . . light up my liiiiiife . . ." Branch sang.

"Jesus Christ," Marty muttered.

"Somebody castrate a moose?" Buehler said, walking through the door.

Branch snorted. "Jealous. Both of ya."

Marty lifted his glass. "Only thing I'm jealous of is this beer, Vaughn. What do you call it?"

Buehler hung his coat on the back of the door. "Buehler's Folly when the yeast doesn't rise," he said. "Otherwise, Blue River Stout."

"As in, you're a blue and you work by a river?" Branch said.

Buehler looked at Marty. "I told you he's not as ignorant as he looks."

"That's right, beat up on the cripple," Branch said. "Care to join us in a drink?"

"I'm on duty," Buehler said.

"But you're the sheriff. The man. The cheese."

Buehler accepted the bottle from Marty.

"And so I am," he said. "Shame you can't join us, Branch."

"What he gets for not making the bullet bounce off," Marty said.

"Go easy on me, goddammit," Branch said. "I'm fragile. The doctor says so."

"The doctor," Buehler said, "is a pinhead."

"I heard that," the chief surgeon said, poking his head in the room.

"Be no fun saying it," Buehler said, "if you didn't. Pull up a chair and have a cold one."

He did.

"Anything new on our cases, Vaughn?" Marty said.

Buehler stroked his white moustache. "Three felons are in toe tags," he said. "And the big heat's on for Dettmer, who's lamming it like a wildcat on a sissy."

"Cop talk," Branch said. "It never gets tiresome."

"Are we exhausting every lead and leaving no stone unturned?" Marty said.

"Ten-four," Buehler said. "Sergeant Abbott's vitals are strong, thanks to the doc. So he's winging off to Mayo. We're getting return calls from dentists on the mystery girl, maybe put that to bed the next few hours. And your deer underwent five hours of surgery from the finest vet in metropolitan Black River."

"You have a metropolitan?" Marty said.

"Yeah," Buehler said. "But it's mostly deer shit. Don't tell the Chamber."

Marty raised his glass. "What's the verdict from your vet?"

"Too soon to know," Buehler said. "Deer was hit with a flight of 9-millimeters. They match the ones in Abbott."

Branch's eyebrows shot up. "They did a deer first, then Abbott?"

"Appears so," Buehler said.

"I hope they get dick cancer," Marty said.

They toasted to that.

"Hate to say it, but we're doing all right," Buehler said. "What am I missing?"

Everyone thought.

"Your case is wrapped up," Marty said. "Alexa and Tristen are safe. The child traffickers are in jail, and their little victims are in state services." He took another sip. "Much as I hate to agree with a rustic . . ."

His cell rang.

"Home," he said, looking at the number. He clicked in. "Hey, sweetie, how's it going?" He listened to her long answer. The tectonic plates in his face locked into position.

Branch shot a worried glance at Buehler.

"Time to get Abbott in the air," the surgeon said. "If you'll excuse me . . ."

Marty disconnected, scowling.

"What?" Branch and Buehler said.

Marty punched up the video, handed over the phone.

"Hacksaw just hit Naperville," he said. "And it's on the air."

62

"Christina Tsigaras," Annie read from the driver's license as a phalanx of cops pushed yellow tape. The Hacksaw serial killer had uploaded the slaughter video to YouTube. Site monitors yanked it in less than sixty seconds, but it had already gone viral. Reporters from around the country were headed their way, wearing war paint. "She's a defense lawyer. I faced her a few times in court. She was good."

Emily nodded wordlessly. Whatever Christina was once, she now was a side of beef.

With a head that looked at them with unblinking curiosity.

It reminded Emily of her nightmare, when her own severed head bounced across her burning bedroom floor. She shuddered.

A CSI handed Cross a sheaf of yellowed newsprint. "Found this in the torso," he said. "Bout where the liver would be."

Thunder coughed to the west. A light rain began. *Pat-pat . . . pat . . . pat-pat-pat . . .*

The CSI gave the sky the finger.

The articles were the coverage of the first and second serial sprees—news stories and features, profiles and commentaries. Even sports, noting that Emily had played softball when she was a kid. They were stapled to the photo of Emily snarling like a rabid wolf.

Rabid wolf . . .

"This is deer camp," Emily said.

Annie raised an eyebrow.

"When hunters take a deer, they field-dress them so the meat won't spoil," Emily explained, recalling what her father had taught her in Wisconsin's north woods. "They hang them upside-down and slit the throat to drain the blood. Then they split the carcass and remove the hide, preserving the head so game wardens can verify the sex." She looked around the woods, back at Christina. "This is deer camp. Christina's the deer."

"There's her rack," a forest preserve cop snickered, staring at Christina's chest.

"Shut the fuck up," Cross snarled.

The cop raised his hands. "Hey, I'm just saying . . ."

"Get him out of here."

Four Naperville cops hustled him out of sight.

"Tell me about the doer, Detective," Cross said.

Emily appreciated his "busy hands are happy hands" philosophy. It kept her from thinking about the serial's real target. "We know he's strong," she said. "Handling and butchering this much dead weight takes a lot of strength. He planned the kill with precision, so he's intelligent. That reinforces what we knew from the body-part deliveries. He's not heavy"—she pointed to the shallow shoe prints in the crushed limestone—"and he's not overly tall."

"Explain that," Cross said.

Emily pointed at what had been Christina's belly. "He'd position her so his knife hand is dead center of her body. Makes his job easier. That provides a decent estimate of his height."

Annie did the calculation. "So, five-eight, five-nine?"

"Something like that."

Cross agreed. "And the crime scene? What does it tell us?"

Emily stuck her hands in her pockets, so her trembling didn't show. "That it's really about me," she said. "Christina's a runner, so am I. He butchered her in the woods where I run every day, in full view of my apartment. The clippings. The snarling-wolf photograph."

"And the note," Annie said. "Hacksaw's bragging that he'll kill Emily where the first two serials couldn't. That's the real meaning of *Third time's the charm*: that he's better than the others, and he's going to win."

"And how he butchered Christina?" Cross said, looking at Emily. "What does that say?"

Emily blew out her breath.

"That he's really, really going to enjoy killing me."

Cross nodded unhappily. "We'll put you in a hotel under an assumed name. I wish it were a safe house."

"But you need me around to attract him," Emily said. "I'm his prey."

"Is that all right with you?"

"I would have suggested it if you hadn't, Chief," she said. "This guy's a maniac, the worst yet. We have to get him or there'll be more Christinas."

"Unfortunately, yes," Cross said. "You'll stick with Annie when you're not locked in your room. I assume that's no longer a problem, working together?"

"Correct," Annie said.

"Then let's get cracking—"

The keening wail was that of a broken animal.

Thirty cops turned.

A man in a gray flannel suit staggered toward the yellow tape.

"Christina," he said, voice glassy with shock. "I saw you. I saw your face. It looks . . . like . . . oh my sweet Jesus, Christina, it's Daddy, I've come to take you home. . . ."

Two cops gently hooked his arms.

The man spotted Emily, began to thrash. "This is your fault," he howled as reinforcements jumped in. "If it wasn't for you my Christina would be alive. Why didn't that animal butcher *you*, goddammit? Why my baby and not you?"

Emily had no answer.

63

"If Emily gets killed by that maniac, you're gonna pout and whine," Branch said. "You'll write flowery haikus and make me listen. You'll try to hug me while you cry. Well, forget that. I've got all the pain I need." He slapped his bandage, winced theatrically.

"So basically, you want me gone," Marty said.

"My wife's gonna jump my bones 'cause of my bravery, and three's a crowd."

Marty turned to Buehler.

"Can you believe this shit?" he complained.

Buehler looked at him. "The man'll have beer and a purty gal. So the bigger question is, why *aren't* you going home to protect your sweetie?"

Marty thought about what Emily had said about Branch secretly wanting him to stick around, even though he'd camouflage it in bluster and testosterone.

Ah, what does she know, anyway?

"Call your state troopers?" Marty said, looking at Buehler. "Warn them I'm coming?"

"Sure thing," Buehler said. "You got lights and siren in that Escalade?"

Branch shook his head.

Buehler looked at Marty.

"Raise your right hand," he said.

"Why?"

"'Cause I'm the cheese, that's why."

Marty rolled his eyes. Raised his head.

"Do you solemnly swear to uphold the office of deputy sheriff?" Buehler said. "And all that other good shit?"

"Play ball," Marty said.

Buehler removed a key from his ring.

"It's my personal cruiser, and it's new," he said, tossing it. "You break it, you bought it."

Marty nodded slowly.

"You're all right," he said. "For a rustic."

Buehler laughed.

"Break that bastard in two," he said.

64

The doorbell rang.

Emily touched the Glock on her hip, the hideout gun in her pocket, and the assault rifle next to the bed. She checked the entryway monitor. Grinned. Went to open the door.

Shavon Little's omnipresent toothpick moved up and down, waving hello.

"I'd love to go racing, Trooper," Emily said. "But someone dinged up my Charger."

"So I heard," Shavon said. "Bring it down to the hunting lodge. We'll fix it up nice."

"Deal. Come on in."

Shavon shook his head. "Places to be, Nancy Drew," he said, entry light gleaming off his freshly shaved skull. "Just wanted to stop by a minute, see how you're doing."

"Never better," Emily said.

The toothpick twitched.

"Yeah, I am full of it," Emily admitted.

Shavon laughed, then turned on his heel. She didn't recognize the car he was driving. His latest acquisition, no doubt. Shavon swapped cars like others traded Beanie Babies.

"It's good to have friends," she murmured as he drove away.

65

"Everyone ready?" Cabot yelled over the thunder of the main rotor.

The two critical-care nurses checked Abbott one more time. They had thousands of hours in the Bell 222 air ambulance, and liked what they saw in their patient—rosy skin, steady pulse, good vitals. Still unconscious, but that was all right—with the storms between here and Rochester, better he should sleep through the turbulence.

The lead nurse gave a thumbs-up.

"Next stop, Mayo," the pilot said, lifting the blue-and-white chopper from the helipad.

The chief surgeon saluted Cabot as he disappeared in the blackening sky.

66

Hacksaw splashed across the Riverwalk pavers, the tool kit heavy on his shoulder, the rain sheeting so hard even ducks were taking cover.

He climbed the concrete steps of the Naperville Millennium Carillon, peered through its heavy glass doors. The stone tower held seventy-two chromatically tuned bells, from hand-size to six-ton, and stood nine feet higher than the Statue of Liberty. A winding staircase let hardy souls see Chicago, thirty-two miles to the east.

He unlocked the door and went inside.

He slipped the first explosive out of his kit. Pushed it into the base of the tower, then inserted a detonator, a tiny radio transceiver that generated an electrical pulse when a remote button was pushed. He repeated every three feet, enrobing the tower in C-4. Unlike the movies, it didn't have a red flashing countdown. Real C-4 looked like Silly-Putty with a rectal thermometer.

He closed the kit, hustled to a nearby tree. Pulled out a

knife with a note looped around the handle. *Third time's the charm*, it read. He stabbed it into the tree, then headed for his truck, which he'd parked on the other side of the river that bisected downtown.

Once he got there, he'd push the button. The radio signal would fly through the air, unaffected by the rain, then hit the transceiver.

Igniting the C-4.

Bringing down the tower in a thunderous roar.

Creating the distraction he needed to keep the police off his trail for just a few hours more.

He hurried away.

67

The doorbell rang.

"More traffic than rush hour," Emily grumbled. She looked at the monitor. Ken Cross.

"Hi, Chief," she said, opening the door. "I was just heading out."

Cross dangled a set of keys.

"What's that?" she said.

"Your ride," he said.

"The Charger still works," she objected.

"He knows that," Cross said.

She thought about it.

"Oh," she said.

"Uh-huh," he said. "So I brought you an unmarked. Does the word 'GT' mean anything to you?"

"The new Mustang?" she said, eyes lighting. "Four-point-six V-eight?"

"That's the one."

"I take back every bad thing I ever said about you," she said.

He handed her the keys. They weren't from a Mustang.

"What's this?" she said, eyes narrowing.

"I asked if GT rang a bell," Cross said. "I didn't say that's what you're driving."

"So . . ."

Cross smiled. She didn't like what that implied. She grabbed her suitcase and followed him into the parking lot.

"Oh. My. God," she said, her heart sinking. "It's . . . it's . . ."

The bathtub-beige Dodge Caravan winked at her.

She realized she'd crushed the key fob, and the wink was the headlights flashing.

"It's a . . . *mom van*," she sputtered.

"None but the finest for my hard-working detectives," Cross said.

A passing golden retriever sniffed the rear wheel.

Lifted his leg.

"Good dog," Emily said. "Chief, I'd rather die than drive a minivan."

"Hacksaw knows that too."

She hated to admit he had a point.

"Can I take your silence for agreement?"

"Maybe," she said.

"Good enough," he said, handing her a hotel key card. "There're two bodyguards in your room. Play Parcheesi or something till Annie picks you up." He tapped her arm in warning. "I'm serious about this, Emily—stay out of sight till I put you out for bait. Hacksaw's a serious whack job, and I don't want to lose you."

"All right," she said. "Need a lift somewhere?"

"I'll take the Charger," he said. "I'll put it in the impound garage, where he can't get to it."

She realized what Cross was saying. If the serial knew where she lived, he knew what she drove, and he could cut her brake line. Or plant a bomb.

"Thank you," she said.

"For?"

"Everything."

She meant it. Her chief had seen something in her, something that said she'd make a good officer, and detective, and sergeant. He'd nurtured that something. Made it sing.

She handed him the key, told him where she parked.

"Oh, and Chief?" she said as he walked away. "If your offer's still good, I'd like to take it."

Cross turned back. He was smiling. "Outstanding. You'll be one of the greats."

"If I live that long," she said.

Cross shook his head. "Get yourself killed, I'll look like a weenie. I can't afford to look like a weenie. Now let's go catch a killer—"

The southern sky erupted.

Emily yelped like her ears were boxed. Cross called dispatch.

"Carillon just blew up," he said.

"I didn't hate it *that* much," she murmured, recalling her and Annie's conversation about it just eleven hours ago. Louder: "It's Hacksaw."

"Hacksaw," Cross said, running for the Charger.

She scrambled into the mom van. He squealed onto Washington Street, heading toward downtown and the burning carillon. She started to follow. A brown car cut her off. She called the unseen driver an idiot, waited for a gap in the stream of southbound traffic.

Hit the gas.

68

"When Vaughn said 'cruiser,'" Marty murmured, "who knew he meant race car?"

The big-hog engine of the Crown Victoria let him do one-forty, cutting the trip home to a measly two hours. Traffic was light because of the rain. His roof lights and grille flashers pulsed authority every quarter second. The Vic ran smooth as glass.

Marty kicked it to one-sixty.

Pushed the voice dialer on his cell, not daring to take his eyes off the road. At this speed in this weather, one false move would be his last.

"Who do you want me to call?" the synthesized voice said.

"Call Emily," he said.

The voice tried.

No connection.

"Call Naperville Police," he said.

No connection.

"Call Black River Hospital," he said.

No connection.

"Call bite me," he said.

No connection.

Undoubtedly it was because of the storm, which was cracking the air above and around.

He shrugged.

Settled in, enjoying the purr of the valves.

69

"Deputy chief is rolling from Modaff Road," Annie reported over the scream of her siren. "Responding Code Three to downtown carillon."

70

"Got you, bitch," Arthur Tatum murmured, easing his brown car close to the Charger's backside, the machine gun on the passenger seat cocked and ready.

71

"Got you, bitch," Karl Dettmer sneered at the Charger as he swung the rental onto southbound Washington, the .45 under his leg cocked and ready.

72

The helicopter jinked and shuddered.

"Sorry about the ride," Cabot yelled as he wrestled the controls. "Freak cell came out of nowhere. I'll break free."

The nurses nodded, too busy with the rapidly waking Abbott to speak.

Cabot spotted a hole in the whirling black. Shoved the chopper into it, rode the elevator to the top. Popped into calm air, clear sky, twinkling stars. "Yarrrrr!" he exulted as the nurses cheered. "Haven't made the storm that could best ol' Richie Cab—"

He never saw the bolt that set them ablaze.

"The girl . . . where's the girl . . . ?" Abbott croaked.

"Mayday, mayday, mayday," Cabot spat as his ship spiraled toward the ground. "Medical Flight Charlie Alpha Niner requests fire and rescue at GPS coordinates—"

The farmer told police he thought the fireball was lightning.

73

Cross busted the red at Ogden Avenue. So did the two cars following him. Emily had traffic, so she slowed. Changed her mind, punched the gas, drawing a flurry of horns and fingers.

"Remind me to write myself a ticket," she said, gassing it to catch up.

Hacksaw admired the miniature mushroom cloud. Wouldn't be many flames because the tower was stone and steel, but the terror effect was everything he'd hoped for. . . .

Things to do. Let's go.

He headed for Edward Hospital.

Emily sailed under the railroad viaduct, passed the children's museum. Pulled over as Engine Three thundered by, lights and sirens screaming.

"Get 'em, boys," she said, envious. If she wasn't a cop, she'd be a firefighter.

Or a cowboy. Or a ballerina.

She laughed. Pulled back onto Washington.

Saw Cross do the same.

Along with the two cars.

"That's kinda weird," she muttered.

Karl Dettmer moved in close.

Arthur Tatum punched the accelerator.

Ambush, Emily's lizard brain bleated.

"Get out of there, Chief!" she screamed, pulling her iPhone.

"Who the fuck are you?" Dettmer screamed at the brown car.

"Fuck you, you fucking fuck!" Tatum screamed at the rental.

Emily spotted electric blond hair. Her body caught fire.

"Naperville nine-one-one," the dispatcher said. "Where is—"

"Mayday, mayday, it's Karl Dettmer!" Emily screamed as the panic dragon tore into her. "He's trying to kill Chief Cross. Officers need help, Washington and Spring . . ."

Cruisers roared, sirens screamed, every cop, condition red.

*   *   *

Annie passed the hospital, passed the cemetery, passed the Burger King. Passed Hillside and Chicago and Jackson and Jefferson and Benton. Snapped her machine gun into her chest harness, ready for Dettmer, ready for anything. "Deputy chief thirty seconds out," she radioed. "Vector units to the following intersections . . ."

Dettmer yanked the wheel.

Pushed the Charger over the curb.

It sailed across the broad lawn of Washington Junior High and smashed into the statue of Officer Friendly. Ripped the head off the bronze cop and flattened the two bronze school kids. Spun out of control, sparks cascading, ramming a tree, air bags blowing.

Dettmer leapt out of his car.

Sprinted to the Charger.

Unloaded his gun into the passenger compartment, flashes lighting the gloom.

Emily bared her teeth as Cross flopped and jerked from bullet strikes.

She cut her wheel to the right, keeping the gas at max.

Jumped the curb, engine roaring.

Dettmer turned, yellow hair glowing in her headlights, panic rippling across his triangular snake-face, gun turreting her way, slash mouth a big mawing O.

She felt the meaty thump in her bones.

Dettmer bounced off the mom van, spinning high, spraying blood and teeth.

Came down on Officer Friendly's torn-away neck.

Impaling him.

The brown car peeled away, tires squealing.

Emily screamed the update into the phone.

"I see it. Executing felony stop," Annie said as she raced for the brown car.

Emily leapt from the mom van. Tried opening the door of the smoldering Charger. It wouldn't budge. She grabbed the gun Cross gave her, shot the lock, shattering it. Yanked the door open.

His shirt was bleeding.

His pants were bleeding.

His hair was bleeding.

His left eye wasn't.

But the rest of him was gone.

Annie skidded into a roadblock maneuver as squads rolled in for the takedown. She bailed out of the car, brought her Heckler & Koch MP-5 machine gun into combat lock.

The brown car fishtailed, trying to avoid the phalanx of cops and guns.

Slammed into a row of parked cars.

The driver tumbled out, raising a weapon.

"Gun!" Annie warned, opening up with the rest.

Sixty-two hollowpoints mowed him like dandelions.

Annie ran up, kicked his weapon away.

"Anyone hurt?" she yelled.

"No," the rest of the cops said.

"Secure the gun, get this place locked down."

Grabbed the radio.

"Deputy chief to watch commander," she said.

"This is Dan," Reynolds said.

"I took out the brown car," she said. "Send paramedics and crime scene. Get a sergeant to the carillon to take command, then call FBI, Homeland, and ATF. Notify the state's attorney there's been a shooting."

"Roger that," Dan said.

"How's the other situation?" she said.

"Chief's down," Dan said, grim.

"On my way," Annie said, forcing all emotion from her head.

"How's my little girl?" Hawk said.

"I'm fine," Sammy said, reaching for a hug.

"Of course you are," Winslow said. "You beat me ten hands straight."

Sammy smiled, jingling the nickels she'd won.

Hawk walked across the ICU room, snuggled her in his arms.

"I love you, Daddy," she said.

"I love you more."

"You more."

"You win," Hawk said. "Ready to fly to L.A.?"

"Yes," Sammy said. "Are we going now?"

"Soon, Ladybug," he said, tousling her hair.

Looked at Winslow.

"Medi-jet's at the airport," she said. "They'll leave the moment you get there."

"Good," Hawk said, eyes darting. "That's really good."

Winslow studied him. Hawk's face was sunken. His normally raked-up hair was matted. He was jumpy, his exhaustion gone supernova. He was a walking derailment.

"See you got some sleep," she said under her breath.

Hawk caught it. Half laughed.

"I have a few things to do before we leave," he said. To Sammy: "Stay with Miss Barbara. I'll be back soon. Then we'll drive to the airport."

"Can I sit by a window?" Sammy said.

"You can fly the plane if you want," Hawk said.

Winslow walked him out.

"She looks good," Hawk said.

"Better than you."

"Don't start," he said.

"Lead a horse to water, et cetera," Winslow said. "Sammy's pulse is strong. Her vitals are good, her pain controlled. She'll be all right, assuming the rabbo-dabbo doesn't reassert itself. Normally, the plane carries two critical-care nurses."

"Normally?" he said.

"I swapped one for a pediatric trauma surgeon," she said. "Not that he'll be needed, but . . ."

Hawk's jaw quivered with emotion. "Thanks, Barbara. For everything. I'd . . . we'd . . . be lost without you."

"Come home soon," she said, meaning it. "And get some sleep, will you?"

"On the plane, I swear," he said, grinning like Hawk of old. He reached out, caressed her cheek. She didn't move away. He started to say how much he—

Their pagers went off.

Both looked.

Winslow's jaw sagged.

Hawk reared like he'd been punched.

"No," she whispered. "Oh dear sweet God, no."

Hawk broke into a run.

74

"No," Emily said over the finger-pops of thunder. "I'm not all right."

Went back to her thousand-yard stare.

Squeezing her chief's bloody hand.

Annie sighed. Witnesses said Emily lifted Cross from the burning Charger, carried him fifty yards, and propped him against this tree. Then sat next to him, Glock in lap, lacing her fingers inside his, not saying anything, just watching, rocking a little, keeping guard.

"You did it," she tried, nodding at the killer impaled upside-down on Officer Friendly. Blood dripped from his hair and mouth. His pockets hung inside-out, white flags against blood-crusted denim. A rusty can opener, DRINK BLATZ BEER stamped on its steel handle, glittered next to Officer Friendly's bronze shoe. "You got Karl Dettmer."

"Yeah," Emily said, nodding slowly. "I ran him over and watched him die. Know what?"

"What?"

"It doesn't make it hurt less."

Annie nodded, knowing that all too well.

"He was taking my car to the station," Emily said. "I was going to the hotel. Then the carillon exploded. We headed here. Both cars went after him, and he crashed into the statue, then the tree."

"That's when Dettmer started shooting?" Annie said.

"Yes. I rammed him five seconds too late." Her bitterness leaked like sulfur. "If I hadn't stopped for that light, if I'd read the ambush faster . . ."

Annie squeezed her arm. "You didn't do anything wrong."

"I know," Emily said. "But Chief is dead because he was in my car, so it's . . . it's . . ."

"Hey," said the man walking their way.

Annie stiffened.

"Sir, you need to leave," she said. "Civilians aren't—"

"He's a state trooper," Emily said. "A friend."

"Shavon Little," he said, pulling his badge from his pocket and pinning it to his belt. "Elgin District." He put out his hand.

"Sorry, I didn't recognize you," Annie said, shaking it. "Annie Bates, chief of police."

The words hit Emily hard.

"I'm off-duty," Shavon said. "Heard the bulletins, came to see if I could help." He looked at Cross, whose eyes were filmy with death. "Sorry about Ken. He was a good man."

"I appreciate it . . . uh, Shavon, is it?"

"Shavon Little, right," he confirmed.

"Thanks for the offer, Shavon," Annie said. "But we've got this under control—" Her cell rang. She held up a finger, took the call. "This is Bates. Uh-huh. Uh-huh . . . what? Are you sure? Damn. Hustle a team to the mansion; I'll meet you there."

She closed the cell.

"Arthur Tatum," she said wondrously, "was the assassin driving the brown car."

"That's Cash Maxximus's leg-breaker," Shavon said, eyes widening. "Does the dirty work so The Maxx can sing his hate music."

"Why would a rap star order a hit on the Chief?" Emily said.

"He's the Juarez cartel's man in the Midwest," Shavon said.

"Same question," Emily said.

"I'll ask him," Annie said, getting up.

"I'm going with," Emily said.

"Absolutely not," Annie said.

"But Chief—"

"Don't 'but' me," Annie said. "You're in no shape to work. Go to the hotel. That's an order."

"I can't, I have to—"

"Annie's right, Em," Shavon said. "You're pretty messed up. Take a ride with me. My car needs testing, and you can drive. It'll clear your head; then you can come back."

Emily blew out her breath, considering. "All right with you, boss?" she said.

Annie nodded. "Moving targets are harder to hit. Let me know where you wind up."

Emily looked at Cross.

Then at Annie.

Who nodded gently.

Time to let go.

She sighed.

Released his hand.

Walked away.

Summoning every ounce of willpower to not look back.

* * *

Hawk screamed down Hobson Road. He had one chance at the million before The Maxx was hauled away for questioning. If he blew this, Sammy was dead.

"I already told you," Maxximus spat into the phone. "No cereal till midnight—"

"Cops are heading to your house," Hawk interrupted.

Maxximus sprang to his feet. "What the hell you talking about?"

"Your boy Artie Tatum just tried to kill Ken Cross. Every cop in Naperville assumes you put out the hit. They're rolling your way, making your life expectancy, oh, six minutes."

"Cross? The chief of police?" Maxximus sputtered, so deeply shocked his head spun in ten directions. "Why would Artie hit a chief of police? He was supposed to hit you."

"Me?" Hawk said.

"Yeah, you, Detective Emily Thompson," Maxximus sneered. "You think I wouldn't figure out who you are? You're on TV more than Oprah. Shoulda taken some time to disguise your voice when you called me."

The voice synthesizer, Hawk realized with a shock. *Jesus, it does sound like Emily. . . .*

"We don't have time to debate this," Hawk said. "I'm in front of your house."

"Good. I'll come out and shoot you."

"What you're going to do," Hawk snapped, "is transfer one million dollars to my bank account. When it's complete you get all the Special K. Send out a flunky to pick it up."

"I'd rather kill you."

"I know. But as soon as you get your cereal back I got nothing to hold over you. So be smart and make this happen."

Maxx nus thought about it. Made sense.

"What about your cop buddies?" he said.

"Tatum was operating on his own," Hawk said, thinking furiously as the sirens grew louder. "You didn't know anything about it, and you're furious. Capping a police chief brings heat and bad publicity, and that's the last thing you need. As for rumors that you're Juarez's man in the Midwest, those are strictly rumors, right?"

"Nobody in this house knows nuthin' about no narcotics," Maxximus said. "Anyone says otherwise, it's slander and libel. Besides, drugs are federal, and those guys can't find their ass with a map and flashlight."

"No, they can't," Hawk agreed. "And now you got four minutes."

Maxximus barked at an aide, who ran for the mailbox.

"I see him," Hawk said, ready to hit the accelerator if the man so much as sneezed. "Make the transfer or I'll swear on a Bible you gave me this Katrina."

"On its way," Maxximus said, hitting SEND.

"Waiting for it . . ." Hawk said, sweat pouring off his face as the maddening little "working" symbol spun round and round. "Come on, make the transfer, make it, make it . . ."

ONE MILLION DOLLARS AND NO CENTS, UNITED STATES CURRENCY.

"Got it," Hawk said.

"Got it," the aide radioed.

"Got it," Maxximus said.

"Get that cereal out of the house," Hawk warned, squealing away from the mailbox. "Cops have a search warrant. They catch you with a single gram . . ."

"Go, go, get that shit out of here!" Maxximus screamed at the aide. "Get over to the safe house and wait for my call."

The man took off running.

"We done, Emily?" Maxximus said.

"Forever, Maxx," Hawk said.

Both disconnected. Hawk pointed the car back at Edward. Thumbed instructions as he drove, sending the million directly to Los Angeles.

TRANSFER COMPLETE. YOUR ACCOUNT BALANCE IS FOUR MILLION DOLLARS AND THIRTY ONE CENTS, UNITED STATES CURRENCY.

"Eat that, accountant man," Hawk said.

Maxximus straightened his shirt.

Flicked invisible dust from his slacks.

Opened his front door, walked onto the Tuscany-inspired front porch.

A dozen Naperville black-and-whites screeched to a halt.

"Hello, officers," he greeted a tiny blonde with a honking big machine gun strapped to her chest. "What can I do for you this fine November night?"

75

Spencer Abbott blinked his eyes clear. Looked around. Still had no clue.

"Help?" he said.

A man ran his way.

"Mister, mister, you all right?" the man cried.

"I . . . I don't know," Abbott said, dazed. "Where am I?"

"Viola, Minnesota," the man said.

"What am I doing in Viola, Minnesota?" Abbott said, confused.

The man pointed to the jumble of metal and glass.

"You were on that chopper," he said. "It crashed a few minutes ago. We thought it was lightning. Decided to take a look, and found you."

Abbott shook his head in disbelief. The helicopter was a smoking wreck. Its rotor blade stuck out of the ground like corn stalk. Three bodies were next to it, limbs akimbo.

Abbott bit his lip.

"We found them too," the man said, whispering like Sunday church. "You bounced clear when you hit. They weren't so lucky."

"Who . . . are they?"

"A man and two women. Burned up when the gas tank blew. Lucky you bounced out."

"Lucky," Abbott murmured.

"That's right," the man said. "Do you know your name?"

"Abbott. Spencer Abbott."

"Any idea where you were headed, Mr. Abbott?"

"Sergeant," Abbott said.

"You're a policeman?" the man said.

"I don't know," Abbott said. "But I think so. Is there anything near here I might have been flying to?"

"Mayo Clinic. It's a big hospital fifteen miles from here, in Rochester."

"Doesn't ring a bell . . ."

The ambulance shriek made Abbott look over the man's shoulder.

"That for me?" he said.

"You're hurt bad, judging from all these bandages," the man said. "I called the volunteers. That's them." He hesitated. "Coroner's on his way too."

Abbott hissed out his breath. "I wish I knew who they were."

"Sheriff'll sort that out, don't you worry."

A stretcher crew ran their way.

"Thanks, mister, for helping me," Abbott said. "What's your name?"

"Ham," the man said. "Leonard Ham. This is my farm. My wife and kids are looking around for any other . . . ah, passengers."

Abbott reached for Ham's callused hand. The farmer bent to take it. Abbott saw his cap.

Started laughing.

"What's so funny?" Ham said.

"That," Abbott said, pointing to the cap. It was bright green, short-billed, and embroidered with the gold outline of a running animal.

"What's wrong with my hat?" Ham said.

"Nothing," Abbott said. "Who's it from?"

"John Deere," Ham said. "They make tractors. Mowers. Earthmovers. That kinda stuff."

"And the embroidery? What's that about?"

"Just a decoration," Ham said, shrugging. "It means, 'Nothing runs like a Deere.' Why you laughing so much about it?"

"Because if the deer's still running," Abbott said, "that means I survived."

"Survived what?"

"No idea," Abbott said, cracking up again.

The ambulance crew tucked him into the gurney.

"Watch out for his head, fellas," Ham warned them. "Man's talking gibberish. Might have cracked his skull bouncing out of the chopper."

Abbott shrieked with laughter.

76

Winslow grabbed her doctor's bag.

Hawk looked at her, surprised. "You're coming to L.A.?"

"I'd love to. Beaches are nice this time of year. But the airport's as far as I go."

An attendant rolled in a wheelchair. It was festooned with balloons.

"Are those for me?" Sammy said.

"From all the nurses," Winslow said. "And me. We'll miss you here."

Sammy jumped off the bed, ran to Winslow.

"I love you, Miss Barbara," she said, muffled by Winslow's white coat.

"I love you too," Winslow said, throat tightening.

"How about you, Daddy?" Sammy said. "Do you love Miss Barbara?"

Hawk held his index finger and thumb an inch apart.

"Hmph," Winslow said.

Hawk spread his arms like he was hugging a whale.

"Better," Winslow said.

Sammy hopped into the wheelchair. Hawk gripped the handles.

"Off we go," Winslow said. "Into the wild blue yonder."

They headed for the ambulance.

77

Annie worked in her own office, unwilling to move into Cross's. The wounds were too fresh.

The phone rang.

"Chief Bates," she said, not recognizing the number. "Who's this?"

"Special Agent Judy Fair, FBI," the caller announced. "I'm calling about your money."

"What money?" Annie said.

"The twenty thousand found in the van driven by your kidnap team?" Fair said, sounding perplexed Annie wouldn't know.

"Right. Sorry," Annie said, annoyed it had slipped her mind. "It's pretty insane here."

Fair made sympathetic noises. "I'm a forensic accountant at the Chicago field office. Ken Cross asked my SAC to trace the bills, and he tasked it to me."

"And?" Annie said, all ears.

"They were unremarkable," Fair said.

"Not traceable," Annie said, disappointed.

"Oh, no, I did trace them," Fair said. "They're unremarkable. They're from different parts of the United States, in different denominations, with different issue dates."

"I hope there's a 'but' in there."

"One," Fair said. "A group of hundreds with sequential serial numbers. I traced them to something called Save Our Samantha, which is a fundraising website—"

"I know," Annie interrupted, feeling her mouth go dry. "It's run by one of our police sergeants, Robert Hawkins. He's raising money to cure his daughter of cancer."

"Oh, I hope it's working," Fair said. "I have two children myself, a boy and a girl."

"Two daughters for me," Annie said.

"That's right," Fair said, apologetic. "I'm sorry I didn't make that connection, Chief. How is your baby doing?"

Who knows? Nobody seems able to tell me. But she said, "Better. Thank you for asking."

They exchanged more daughter talk; then Annie pushed back to business.

"The hundreds were withdrawn from the Save Our Samantha charitable trust registered to Robert and Bonnie Hawkins of Naperville," Fair said. "GoBank of Naperville, which manages the trust, confirmed an hour ago. . . ."

The money in Dettmer's van was supplied by Hawk.

Which connects Hawk to Dettmer.

And the Katrina.

And Alexa's kidnapping. And Ken's murder. And Abbott's shooting . . .

An ice ball formed in Annie's belly.

"When did Sergeant Hawkins make the withdrawal?" she said.

"Yesterday. Does this information help?"

"Unfortunately, yes," Annie said.

She hung up, punched up Edward. "Goddamn you, Hawk," she whispered.

The operator picked up. Annie recited Sammy's room number.

"I'm sorry, that patient has checked out," the operator said.

Annie dialed Hawk's house.

"We can't come to the phone right now . . . ," Bonnie's voice said.

Annie tried Hawk's cell.

"This is Hawk. Leave a message. . . ."

She called Edward Security.

"We heard," the director said. "Our sympathies, Annie. Ken was a great guy."

"Yes, he was. Thank you for saying so."

"But that's not why you're calling."

"No," Annie said. "I need to find a patient of yours. Samantha Hawkins."

"Hawk's kid."

Everyone knows the Hawkster. "I heard she checked out," Annie said.

"Let me see. . . ."

Annie scrolled Homeland Security bulletins as she waited.

"Yep, they just left," the director said.

"'They'?"

"Sammy, Hawk, and Dr. Winslow. You know her, right?"

Annie drummed her desk. "Yes. Did Barbara say where she was going?"

"I'll transfer you to Emergency. Doc keeps her team apprised of comings and goings."

A couple of clicks.

"Emergency department."

"This is Chief Bates at NPD."

"Hey, Annie, it's . . ."

Annie bit her tongue at the line dance of remorse and thanks. She appreciated it, but didn't have time. "Do you know where Dr. Winslow went?" she interrupted.

"Uh, I can check."

A minute later: "She's on her way to the airport. Accompanying a patient who's flying to Los Angeles."

"Sammy Hawkins?"

"That's right."

"Which airport?" Annie said. "O'Hare? Midway?"

"County," the woman said. "Their runways can handle small jets, so the air ambulance crews base there. If she calls in, should I say you're looking?"

"No," Annie said. Hawk was savvy enough to read the minutest change in someone's expression. If Winslow learned he was tied to Karl Dettmer . . . "I'll call back."

"Night, then."

Annie thought about her options.

Each sucked.

She sighed, then grabbed her battle gear. Rounded up troops as she pulled her assault truck out of the police station parking lot. Called the airport tower, then turned up her radio so she could hear what was happening at her various crime scenes.

Her cell rang. She picked up. "It's Dan," her watch commander said, his voice higher than normal. "You have to see this video." A moment later, the imagery was unfolding.

"What am I looking?" she said.

"Kids keep vandalizing a guy's backyard," Reynolds explained. "He sets up a video cam."

"So?"

"Yard backs up to the Riverwalk. He captured the carillon blast."

The video was blurry from the sheeting rain, but she could make out the multistory tower. Glancing between cell and highway, she watched a black-clad figure enter the tower, then exit without the tool bag he'd carried in. He hurried to a tree on the riverbank, stabbed something into the trunk, hurried away. A few minutes later the video flashed white. The explosion.

"What did he put on the tree?" she said.

"A note," Reynolds said. "*Third time's the charm.*"

It took a second for that to sink in.

"Oh, shit."

"Yeah, the bomber is also our serial killer," Reynolds said. "Problem is, the video doesn't show his face. No way to figure out who he is."

Annie rewound, watched it again. Dan was right: the bomber's face never showed. But there was something familiar in the way he ran. The way his head hitched to the right when he reached full speed . . .

She nearly swerved off the road.

"Mother of God, it's Hawk," she gasped. "Hawk's our bomber, and Hawk is Hacksaw." The head hitch sealed it—she'd seen him do that a million times in SWAT training. She filled Reynolds in on the connections to Dettmer and the rest.

"Hawk a serial killer? I wouldn't have guessed that in a million years," Reynolds said.

"Me neither," she said, badly shaken. She'd trusted that man with her life, and more than once. Trusted him with her whole damn team. . . .

"Want me to put out an APB?"

Annie shook her head. "No. I don't want to tip him. I know exactly where he is."

She pushed the pedal to the floorboard.

The assault truck jumped.

78

The engine coughed like bronchitis.

"Dammit," Marty groaned, easing the Crown Vic to the shoulder of the interstate.

He popped the hood, did some jiggling. Got back in the cruiser, lit 'er up.

Clank, sputter, moan.

Recalled that Shavon Little lived a mile from here, just off the Peace Road exit. He'd never been to the house, always meeting Shavon at the hunting lodge.

Luckily, he remembered the address. As a cop, Shavon was unlisted.

He nursed the cruiser up to thirty.

Aimed for Peace.

79

"What's the holdup?" Hawk asked irritably.

"Tower hold," the pilot grunted, pointing to the mildew green sky. "Probably the storm."

"Sick little girl here," Hawk said. "We need to leave."

"We all hate it, Mr. Hawkins," the critical-care nurse assured. "But these holds happen all the time. We'll be wheels-up soon."

Winslow popped her head through the cabin door.

"Weather hold," Hawk explained.

She rolled her eyes.

Behind her, he spotted dozens of cop cars turning into the airport. Their roof lights painted the darkness red and yellow, blue and white.

He sagged.

Winslow rushed into the cabin, thinking his exhaustion had finally overwhelmed.

"So close," Hawk muttered. "I'm so damn close. . . ."

Dozens of sirens kicked in.

"Wow," Winslow said, turning to look. "What's that about?"

Hawk stared. He had nowhere to run. No more moves to make. Sammy's hourglass had finally run out.

Unless . . .

"They're coming for me, Barbara," he said.

"You?" Winslow said. "Why?"

Hawk ran his hand through his limp hair.

"That extra million dollars? I stole it from a drug dealer," Hawk said.

Winslow stared.

"Don't give me that," he snapped. "I sold my *entire existence* to raise that cancer money, and it wasn't enough. So yes, I tricked a drug courier into delivering a load to me. I sold the drugs back to his boss, and I sent the money to L.A. I'd do it again. "

"So would I," Winslow said, recovering from his uppercut. "It's narcotics money. Why shouldn't it save a little girl's life?"

The look on his face said it was so much worse.

"Tell me everything," Winslow said. "I'll help if I can."

The cruisers rolled onto the runway.

"The courier was Karl Dettmer," Hawk said. "He works for Cash Maxximus, head of the Juarez cartel in Naperville. I conned Dettmer into giving me the Katrina; then I sold it back to Maxximus. Then Dettmer went on to kidnap Alexa, get her hooked, and sell her to a pervert." His face was drained of color. "Dettmer shot that cop in Wisconsin. Murdered Ken Cross."

Winslow moaned. "How could you get involved in—"

"I didn't know any of that," Hawk said, sweat pouring off in long, liquid sheets. "I had a simple plan, Barbara—steal Maxx's drugs, then sell them back. Nobody gets hurt."

"But something went wrong."

His face burned. "I had no idea Dettmer was a child

freak. Or that Maxximus would put out a hit on Cross. This is . . . horrible."

She sensed he was still holding back. "I said everything, dammit," she said. "Or I'll—"

"I'm also the Hacksaw killer," he said.

She stared, speechless.

"But only in name, I promise," he added hurriedly. "I had to throw my colleagues off my trail till I got Sammy to L.A. Hacksaw was the distraction I chose."

Winslow remembered the revolting YouTube video. It didn't track with the man standing in front of her. "You didn't butcher that woman in the woods," she said, hardly able to breathe. "There's no way in hell you could do that."

Hawk smiled without humor. "Thank you for that. You're right; it wasn't me. I have no idea who killed Christina—the real Hacksaw, I suppose, whoever he is. I only put his name on a tree, so Annie would abandon the Katrina investigation." He shook his head, anguished. "I didn't butcher that poor woman, and I didn't send Emily those bones."

Winslow stared, unsure if she could trust him. "Swear it," she demanded. "Swear on your daughter's life that you're not the Hacksaw killer."

Hawk placed his hand on his sleeping daughter's head. The seven-year-old rustled, but didn't wake. "I swear on her life that I'm not the real Hacksaw," he said. "I haven't murdered anyone, and I never will."

"Never?" she challenged. "Even if murder keeps her alive?"

Hawk took a deep breath, blew it out. "That's impossible to answer, Barbara. If it truly came down to someone else or her, I don't know what I'd do. I just don't. Fortunately, we never got to that point. All I can say is that I've murdered no one."

"But that explosion . . ."

"Sticks and stones, nobody hurt," Hawk said. "Soon as

my 'Third time's the charm' note hit the Internet, all the cops would rush to the Hacksaw manhunt, and I'd have the window I needed to get her to Los Angeles." He stalked the cabin in a tight circle. "That's all it was, I swear to God."

Winslow rubbed her temples. "I believe you, Hawk. But you set this chain in motion, and you have to answer for it. You'll probably go to prison."

"I know. I'm going to surrender," he said, dropping his hands. "But you have to do something for me in return."

"What?"

"Get Sammy to L.A. Bonnie won't get here in time."

The lead vehicle screeched to a halt. Annie jumped out.

"Bonnie?" Winslow said, incredulous. She'd assumed the mother was still out of the picture. "She's coming here?"

"Yes. She called me; she's coming home. To make us a family again." He shook his head. "She's driving in from Memphis, arriving at nine. But I got the money early." He looked around the jet, at his daughter. "Without me, Ladybug will be so frightened. . . ."

"I'll do it," Winslow said. "I'll take care of your little girl."

"Hawk," Annie shouted, marching toward the stairs to the cabin. "It's over."

"I know, Chief," Hawk said, pulling out the special cell. "I'll be right out."

Back to Winslow.

"Ken dead. Alexa hooked. Tristen scarred." He shuddered like a junkie off his fix. "I'll pay for my sins. But don't let them take it out on my family."

Winslow took his hand. It was ice cold. "I'll get Sammy to L.A. and bring her home again. I'll make sure Bonnie gets where she needs to be, and I'll look after them while you're in prison. I promise. Then you'll get out, and pick up where you left off. Not as a cop, but as a husband and father. And that'll be all right."

"Come out of the plane, Hawk," Annie said. "Now."

"You'll take care of my family no matter what, Barbara?" Hawk said.

"No matter what," Winslow said.

Hawk nodded.

"Love you," he said.

"Love you more," Winslow said, remembering the game he played with his daughter.

"You win," he said.

Climbed down the stairs.

"Your gun," Annie said, holding out her hand. "Nice and slow."

He removed his service pistol with two fingers, handed it over butt-first.

"And your backup."

He pulled the revolver from his pocket.

"Knives?"

"None. I'd only cut myself."

She smiled faintly.

"Why'd you bomb the carillon, Hawk?" she asked. "For laughs? Or to cover the fact you're the Hacksaw serial killer?"

He flushed. "I'm not Hacksaw."

"Bull," Annie snapped. "I saw the note you left on that tree."

"You were supposed to," Hawk said. "But that doesn't make me the guy."

"Jury'll say so."

"Jury'd convict a sandwich with the right prosecutor," Hawk said. "How'd you know about the carillon, anyway? There were no witnesses. I made sure of that."

She explained about the movie.

"Ah, you can't figure everything," he said.

"No," she said, staring lasers. "You can't."

Hawk sighed. "I'm sorry," he said. "I never meant to dishonor the department, or you. But maybe this'll make up." He tossed her the cell. She caught it, raised an eyebrow.

"I recorded every conversation we had since this began," he said. "Me, Dettmer, and Maxximus, every word. You can put him away forever. 'Course, Juarez will have him whacked before he sees the inside of a courtroom, but . . ."

Annie called for an evidence bag, slipped it inside. "It'll help." she said. "Now tell me what you did, from the top."

Hawk laid out the Katrina ruse, the money laundering through the Sammy fund, his relationship with Dettmer and Maxximus, and the explosion. "But I'm not Hacksaw," he insisted. "I only borrowed his name. I'd never hurt Emily, and you know it."

"I don't know anything anymore," Annie said. "Except that you did this for Sammy."

"Everything I did was for her," Hawk said. "To keep her alive. I'd do it again."

So would I. But she couldn't tell him that.

"I know what's it's like to almost lose a child," she said, thinking of Alexa lying comatose in a lonely ICU room. "How far you'd go to save her. You'd do anything. Even serial killing."

"Not that," Hawk said. "But a lot. Things you can't forgive."

Annie knew what he meant. "You'd never deliberately hurt my girls, I know you wouldn't," she said. "Dettmer did that. But you had a hand in it."

"Yes," he said. "I did."

"So why don't you admit you're Hacksaw?"

"Because I'm not."

"Come on, Hawk, get it off your chest. It's not like we won't find the proof now that we know what we're looking for—"

"I'm *not*."

He said it so fire-eyed she almost believed him. Then again, he'd lied about so much. . . .

"I'll tell Terrence you cooperated fully," she said, referring to the state's attorney. "Even though you didn't. Maybe it'll keep you off death row."

"Doesn't matter."

"It does to me," Annie said. "I don't want you to die."

Hawk smiled. "It won't be your fault."

"What won't be?"

"Me dying . . ."

He yanked the baby Glock hidden in his waistband.

"Gun!" an airport cop screamed, raising his Smith & Wesson.

"Red light, hold fire, don't shoot!" Annie screamed, waving her arms.

Hawk shoved the muzzle at Annie's face, put his finger on the trigger.

The airport cop opened up.

Hawk made a noise between a sob and a moan as six copper slugs blossomed in his chest.

"No!" Winslow cried.

Annie whirled on the airport cop. "Are you fucking deaf?" she raged as Winslow scrabbled to save Hawk's life. "I told you not to fire."

The cop shrank back, despite being a foot taller. "He was going to shoot you, Chief—"

"He would never have pulled that trigger," Annie said. "He wanted you to kill him—it's suicide by cop. Son of a fucking *bitch*."

She turned on her heel and knelt to Hawk. Blood bubbled from both sides of his smile. Winslow shook her head. Annie pursed her lips, blew out her breath.

"Who carries three guns?" she said gently.

"Lousy . . . shot," he gurgled. "Still . . . alive."

She glanced at the airport cop. "Get an ambulance."

He jammed a radio to his mouth, barked orders.

"Why'd you do this, Hawk?" she said, turning back. "We could have worked things out."

"Disgraced . . . family," he coughed. "Mine. Ours."

"So you screwed up," Annie said. "So what? I blamed Emily for not saving my daughter from Dettmer. That was a screw-up, too. I would have forgiven you, Hawk, I swear."

"Couldn't . . . forgive myself," Hawk said. "Did wrong. . . . Had to cleanse . . . my little girl's name. Make sure she . . . understands . . . someday . . ."

"Quit talking," Winslow said as the surgeon and flight nurse raced over with medical kits. "Save your strength."

"Get . . . daughter . . . to L.A. . . . I sent the money. . . . It's all paid for. . . ."

"I swear on my life, I'll get Sammy well," Winslow said, weaving her fingers into his.

Hawk smiled a little more.

Died.

Winslow's sob was oceanic.

Then she got hold of herself.

"You heard the man," she said brusquely to the pilot, who'd stuck his head out the window to watch. "Let's roll." He disappeared into the cockpit. The surgeon and nurse ran up the stairs. Winslow got to her feet, turned for the jet.

Annie put her hand on her arm.

"That money," she said, "comes from narcotics. By law I have to confiscate it."

"You can't," Winslow said, not believing what she was hearing. "It's in the hospital account, so you can't touch it."

"FBI's got a Los Angeles office. They can be at the hospital in ten minutes."

"Are you insane?" Winslow said. "You know what it means if you make that call."

"I've got a job to do. Just like Hawk did protecting Sammy."

They fell silent.

Winslow looked at the jet.

"Isn't what happened," she said, "federal jurisdiction?"

Annie thought about it. "Ken's murder is local. Blowing up the carillon is joint, us and the feds. But bank money transfers tied to multistate narcotics shipping, telephone fraud, Internet sites, and money laundering? Who the hell knows? You could make the argument it's federal, I guess."

"So why don't you?"

"Why don't I what?"

"Make the argument," Winslow said. "To the feds. Say, next week. After you've had the fullness of time to untangle all Hawk's crimes."

Annie saw where this was going. "The FBI would seize the assets from Hawk's illegal drug money transfer," she murmured. "Sometime *after* Sammy's procedure."

"Mm-hm."

"But the work would already be complete," Annie argued. "The hospital would be forced to eat the three million. It's an innocent bystander, so that's not right."

Winslow kept looking at the plane. "Hawk got a call this morning," she said. "From the hospital. They informed him the price of treating Sammy was now four million dollars."

"I thought it was three and they had it already."

"They wanted more."

Annie's face hardened to diamond plate.

"They used Hawk's dying kid as leverage. For more *money.*"

Winslow nodded. "That's why one could appreciate the irony of a hospital's pockets being picked by an FBI forfeiture order. If only one had the power to make that happen."

Annie thought about that.

Got on the cell to the airport tower.

"Lift the hold," she said.

Disconnected.

"Get her to L.A., Barbara," she said. "Before somebody figures out I'm full of shit."

Winslow smiled.

Looked at Hawk.

"Sleep well, child warrior," she murmured.

Headed up the stairs.

"Miss Barbara?" Sammy called sleepily. "What's all that noise?"

"Um, a police escort," Winslow said. "Your father's friends came to say good-bye."

Sammy waved at the windows opposite her hospital bed.

"I told you everyone loves my daddy," she said.

"That's right," Winslow said, tearing up for the dead man on the tarmac. For everyone torn apart by this dreadful affair. "They do."

The jet whined into takeoff power.

"Where's Daddy?" Sammy said, alarmed, head darting. "He's coming with us, isn't he?"

Winslow wiped her eyes, took the girl's hands.

"He can't. He asked me to fly with you, make sure you're all right."

"How come he's not here?" she said, face twisting in confusion. An old rabbo scar twisted with it.

"Well, it was supposed to be a surprise, but I guess I can tell you now," Winslow said. "Your mommy's coming to be with you."

Sammy sucked in her breath. "Really?" she whispered.

"Really," Winslow said, praying Hawk was right about Bonnie. "But her flight from overseas was delayed, and she wasn't going to get here in time. Your daddy decided to wait for her. They're flying to L.A. together."

"Mommy's coming!" Sammy sang. "Mommy's coming!"

"When you wake up from your treatment, she's the first person you'll see," Winslow said.

The plane thundered down the 7,600-foot runway.

"What do you want to do while we're in the air?" Winslow said. "Read? Watch videos?"

"Hearts," Sammy said.

"Okay," Winslow said, reaching for her purse as the plane fought through the storm clouds. Wondered how she was going to explain when Hawk didn't show up.

She looked out the window.

Watched the lightning flashes below.

They were leaving a storm, heading into sunshine.

Winslow shook her head.

Ripped out the first shuffle.

Hell with explaining, she decided. *Tomorrow is another day.*

Annie froze mid-step.

"What, Chief?" the Bravo team commander said.

"I *do* believe him."

"Who? Hawk?"

"Yeah. If he was the real Hacksaw, he would have taken his daughter hostage the moment he saw our lights. Or put that bullet in my brain and died laughing. But he didn't. He doesn't have what it takes to be a psychopathic serial killer."

"He cares too much," Bravo said.

"Yeah. And that gives me a bigger problem."

"What's that?"

"If Hawk isn't Hacksaw, and Dettmer isn't Hacksaw, and Maxximus isn't Hacksaw, then who the hell is?"

They looked at each other.

"Oh, no," Bravo said.

"Hacksaw's still out there hunting," Annie said, the ice

ball reforming in her belly. "We need to find Emily and get her into a safe house ASAP. Last I heard she was driving around with Shavon Little. I hope he's good with a gun. . . ."

They sprinted for their cars.

80

"Shavon? You home, amigo?" Marty said, easing through the front door.

No reply.

He'd already found the go-fast in the garage. He'd counted on that, as Shavon without a race car was like . . . well, it couldn't be imagined. He wrote a note apologizing for picking the front-door lock, then looked for the car keys. Nothing in the living room. Nothing in the bathroom. Nothing in the hall closet or back bedroom.

Hmm . . .

He rummaged the master bedroom. It made him uncomfortable, poking through another man's intimacies, but he needed to get moving. Telephone, alarm clock, boxer shorts, flashlight, magazines, big-screen TV, and a box of Trojans, extra-large, ribbed, in grape. *Gettin' some, good for you,* Marty thought with a grin.

Still no luck.

"Where would I be, if I were a key?" he said aloud as he

wandered into the kitchen. Looked around, found nothing.
Considered the basement door. Maybe a rec room? He retrieved the key he'd spotted in Shavon's bed table. Put it in
the Medeco lock, wondered why Shavon would put a vault-
grade security lock on a basement. Kinda squirrely . . .

Click.

He trundled down the creaky stairs. Fumbled around for
the switch. Found and flipped it, flooding the cedar-paneled
room with bluish fluorescent light.

He staggered back as if punched.

The walls were a collage of *Field & Stream*-like hunting
photos. But the trophies were human. Men. Women. Young,
mostly, but several were middle-aged. One in her seventies,
judging from the blue-rinsed hair. White, black, yellow,
brown. Shavon grinned over them, smoke curling from the
barrel of his silenced Uzi, hunting boot on their lifeless
backs, showing them off like downed moose or elk or deer.
One of the photos was bigger than the rest. It was Emily as
the she-wolf, covered in mud, teeth bared, emerging from the
river.

Her eyes were ripped out.

Marty's heart pounded.

There was a blond coffee table in the center of the room.
It held an Underwood manual typewriter, black enamel with
gold trim. A box of Crayolas, the sixty-four pack with built-
in sharpener, and only one color used, orange. Silver paint
and a small paint brush. A pair of scissors and a pile of
newspapers with missing letters. The letters were glued to
small rectangles of card stock, and they all bore the same
message.

Third time's the charm.
Third time's the charm.
Third time's the charm.

"It's you," he breathed.

He tore apart a cabinet and a chest of drawers, looking for

evidence of what Shavon had done with the people he'd slaughtered. Found nothing. He started to walk away, then reconsidered. The sides of one drawer were discolored, where the others weren't. Someone had removed it from its tracks enough to leave permanent finger smudges.

Marty dumped out its contents, kicked the junk around. Nothing indictable. He checked the bottom and sides, then flipped it back-side-up.

A brass key peeked through the packing tape.

Marty pulled his knife and cut the key free. Hidden like this, it had to fit something significant. He looked around.

A Medeco on a utility room door?

Marty walked over, inserted the key.

Yes.

Inside was a forced-air furnace and an air-conditioning condenser. A forty-gallon water heater. A utility sink of molded plastic, a sump pump with battery backup, a hundred-amp circuit breaker. Three bottles of bleach. All normal for a utility room.

What wasn't was the industrial-grade table in the middle. It was handmade, eight feet long and four feet wide, crafted from marine-grade plywood—waterproof—with steel posts for legs. It held a block of knives, butcher to fillet to paring. The knife handles were stained. So was the table top. Marty bent, examined the stains. Rubbed lightly with a knuckle.

Blood.

A hardwood box the size of a casket was bolted to the foundation wall, opposite the circuit breaker. A motor was attached to the side. It was whirring. Marty put his hand on the hinged door. It was warm, and smelled like hickory smoke.

It's Shavon's jerky maker.

Marty had made jerky himself, knew how the process worked. You took lean meat—deer, elk, pork, beef, what have you—and washed off the blood. You cut the cleaned meat into bacon-sized strips and soaked them in saltwater with spices. Salt was a preservative; spices added flavor. Then you hung the strips inside the jerky maker. The meat dehydrated—that's what the motor was for, to speed the process by injecting hot wood smoke—into jerky, a tough, leathery food that required no refrigeration. Marty recalled how much he'd enjoyed Shavon's elk jerky up in Black River. Beefy, smoky, with a hint of sweetness . . .

He opened the door.

Rattling back at him were bones—leg, arm, hand, foot, spine, clavicle. A torso stripped of organs. A nose and a pair of testicles. A small breast with a brown nipple. Three heads with no eyes, each as leathery as a catcher's mitt.

They were human.

Strips of meat hung from thin wires. They were bacon-sized, and in various stages of jerking—raw; caramelized from the marbled fat weeping from its pores; leather; and black 'n' cracked. They smelled beefy, smoky, with a hint of sweetness.

That wasn't elk jerky. . . .

It was human jerky.

Marty staggered backwards and vomited into the sump. The mechanism whirred, kicked it into Shavon's yard.

He vomited again.

Again.

Again.

Glimpsed the hacksaws dangling from the underside of the table, their steel teeth clogged with gristle and bone and hair.

Dry-heaved awhile . . .

He pulled himself upstairs and picked up the phone, cursing Shavon's name. They'd hunted together, fished together, gone racing together. Got so stinking drunk in the bender

Marty went on after his wife died that sometimes they couldn't remember where they'd been. How could he *not know* one of his closest friends was a serial killer?

"Illinois State Police," a familiar voice said.

"Hey, Boyce," he said to the captain who ran Shavon's district. "It's Marty."

"Thought you were in Wisconsin."

"Was, till an hour ago. You know that Hacksaw killer sending Emily body parts?"

"Yeah . . ."

"It's Shavon."

Silence.

"Shavon Little? *My* Shavon Little?"

"He fooled us all," Marty said. "Any idea where he is?"

"Last I heard, he was driving around with your gal. She killed Karl Dettmer right after he murdered Cross, and Shavon offered to—"

"Ken Cross is *dead*?"

"You didn't know?"

"No, no, I didn't," Marty said, dizzying. "And Emily shot Dettmer?"

"Ran him over, actually. She saw Dettmer shoot Ken, so she flattened him with a van and impaled him on a stake. I heard he looked like a blond fuckin' vampire."

"Jesus, Boyce . . . who's in charge now? Annie Bates?"

"Right."

Marty ached to hear more about Emily, but seconds were critical now. "Where's Shavon right now? Do you know?"

"Uh-uh," Boyce said. "It's his day off. I had to change the duty schedule and needed to let him know, though. I called around, wound up talking to Annie. She said Emily took off with Shavon a while ago. She was pretty fucked up from killing Dettmer, Annie says."

"I can imagine."

"She done good. But it gets up on you, killin', even a

germ like Dettmer. Shavon offered to take her for a ride, let her clear her head. Maybe he's going back to the house?"

"Maybe," Marty said, but he didn't believe it. Shavon didn't hang around DeKalb much, preferring the lodge. . . .

The hunting lodge.

"Boyce, can you send over some people you trust?" Marty said. "There's bodies here, lots of 'em, inside a jerky maker."

"What?"

Marty explained. "Use people who won't tip Shavon, that we know."

"Guys I send'll keep their yaps shut," Boyce said. "They'll lock the place down tight, but hide themselves, case he comes back. He does, they'll, uh, detain him."

Marty knew what that meant. "Good," he said. "I'll call when I know anything else."

"Good luck, man."

"Gonna need it," Marty said, disconnecting.

"Jesus, Marty, I'm glad you called, you have no idea—"

"I already heard. Did Emily go driving with Shavon Little?"

"Uh, yes," Annie said, muting her siren so she could hear. "Why?"

"Shavon's our serial killer. He's the Hacksaw, and I can prove it."

Annie broke into a sweat. "I knew it wasn't Hawk."

"What?"

"Forget it," she said, deeply shaken she'd sent her best friend off with a whack job who wanted to kill her. "Tell me everything. . . ."

Marty explained the wall photos, utility room, smoke box, human heads.

"Jerky?" Annie said, incredulous. "He fed you *human jerky*?"

His stomach gurgled anew at the thought. "I don't care right now."

"Got to rescue Emily," Annie said. "Any idea where they might be?"

"Shavon's got a hunting lodge in Lorenzo," Marty said. "I'll bet my pension he's there. He loves that place, works on all his dreams there."

"Cars and killing," Annie said.

"'Bout covers it," Marty said. "His backyard is six hundred acres of hills and ravines. Heavily wooded. He walks out the door and starts hunting."

"Lots of guns there, too. Great." She typed a flash message to Alpha, Bravo, and Charlie: *Got location, we'll roll in five.* "Where exactly is this lodge?"

"Thirty-five miles south of Naperville, not far from I-55."

She called it up on Google Earth, studied the terrain and buildings. "I've got a thirty-mile head start, so I'll arrive first. Want me to go in?"

"I know Shavon pretty well," Marty said. "Maybe I can talk him out of whatever he has in mind. Wait for me if you can."

"No promises. I hear screams or shots, I'm gonna smoke his little rat ass," Annie said.

"Deal."

"And call your boss on the way. I don't want a turf war."

He blew out his breath.

"We'll save her, Marty," she said. "We will."

He prayed that was true. But wasn't at all convinced.

"I'll hurry," he said.

He ran to the garage, hot-wired the Ferrari, peeled rubber to the interstate.

* * *

"I got no problem Annie being here," the county sheriff said on the phone.

"She didn't want to intrude on your authority."

"Never stopped her before. She just didn't want the turf war, her being a chief now."

"My version's prettier."

The sheriff snorted. "And that's why you're my trusted consigliere, my friend. But like I said, we're cool. Our guys are busy rolling up the Juarez drug cartel anyway."

"What's that about?" Marty said.

The sheriff explained.

"Yow. You've been busy in my absence," Marty marveled.

"Didn't miss you a bit."

"Yeah, you did."

The sheriff laughed, a rich baritone. "Well, maybe a little."

"Good enough. Which feds are you working with on this, DEA?"

"The whole can of alphabet soup, actually. Everyone wants credit for fucking Juarez."

"But your dick is the biggest."

"No contest," the sheriff said.

"Vaughn just told me," Branch said. He sounded hollow. "I can't believe Ken's dead."

"You don't know the half of it," Marty said, filling him in.

"Shavon Little's a serial killer," Branch breathed. "Who would have ever thought?"

Marty's speedometer bumped one-ninety. Road signs whipped hurry-blurry. "I just hope he doesn't find out we know. He does, she's dead."

"Any way Shavon would ever think you'd ever find his play room?"

"None," Marty said. "I've never been to his house, never

expected to, don't have a key. We hang at the hunting lodge. Or the auto tracks. Never at his place."

"Then you'll probably keep the element of surprise."

"Only silver lining in this mess," Marty said. "Unless you've got some."

Silence.

"All right, tell me."

"Chopper went down in a storm," Branch said. "Abbott survived; Cabot didn't. He burned up in the fireball, along with two flight nurses. . . ."

"Aw," Marty said, slamming the steering wheel with a knotted fist. "Aw, aw, aw . . ."

"I know, man," Branch said. "But Abbott's all right. Fire crew hustled him to Mayo Clinic, and they're fixing him up."

Marty blew out his breath.

"Seems like forever ago," he said. "That we ate cheese curds."

"And beat up an asshole for breakfast," Branch said.

81

"Thanks for letting me drive," Emily said, leaning deep into the engine compartment of a seventy-seven Thunderbird. The pine-paneled hunting lodge never failed to charm, with its mounted game heads—moose, deer, buffalo, grizzly—silently overlooking Shavon's classic cars, racing vehicles, and automotive restoration tools. "It really cleared my head."

"Good ride'll do that," Shavon said. "See if you can tighten those bolts, would you? Under the engine? My hands are a little big for that space. . . ."

82

"Jesus. I hear her," the dispatcher said, bolting upright.

"You hear Jesus?" the second dispatcher said, confused.

The dispatcher shook his head. "Not Jesus. Emily. I hear Emily. She didn't hang up from before. She's talking to some guy about engine bolts. . . ."

83

"AT&T's tracing her signal," Annie said, shutting off her engine.

"What signal?" Marty said.

"Emily called nine-one-one when the attack started on Ken. She apparently put the phone in her pocket without disconnecting. We're hearing her and Shavon in real time, and her iPhone's transmitting her GPS coordinates. We'll know in a few minutes where she is."

Marty sagged with relief, knowing she was still alive. "They at the lodge?"

"Sounds like," Annie said. "We set up a half mile away. Easy hike, and we're separated by a blanket of trees. Shavon won't see us. Where are you?"

"I-55, passing Arsenal Road."

"Nine minutes away?" she said, incredulous. "What are you driving, a fighter jet?"

"Ferrari Spider," Marty said. "How's Alexa?"

"Still fighting Katrina withdrawal, so Barbara's keeping her under."

"I'm really sorry to hear that," Marty said.

"Me too. See you in nine."

Annie disconnected and swung out of the assault truck, hauling her guns.

84

"Hand me that torque wrench, would you?" Emily said, voice muffled by the T-bird's infrastructure. "Might as well do this right."

No reply.

"Shavon? Did you hear me? I need the torque wrench."

"Get it yourself, Nancy Drew," Shavon said.

She turned awkwardly, wondering what the problem was. Froze.

"Shavon," she said, shocked. "Why are you pointing an Uzi at me?"

"Shavon's got an Uzi," Annie told her SWATs. "Get to your assault positions."

They took off into the woods.

* * *

"Because it's opening day," Shavon said. "And you're the deer."

"Shavon, please," Emily said, having no idea what he meant. "Tell me what this is about—"

He put a burst into a stack of Goodyears.

Annie heard the sewing-machine stutter of the silenced machine gun. "Audio, tell me what's happening," she radioed, breaking into a trot. "Are they still talking?"

Emily's hand smacked empty belt. She remembered that her Glock lay on a workbench thirty feet away. She'd taken it off to avoid scratching the T-bird's finish.

"Next one's in your spine," Shavon said. "You don't do what I say."

She opened her mouth to protest, closed it without a word.

"Good girl. Now put your backup gun on the floor."

"I don't carry a—"

His eyes narrowed dangerously. "It's the bulge in your right pocket," he said. "Take it out with two fingers and slide it this way."

She complied, sweat beading, panic dragon starting to roar.

"Now your knives."

She kicked one over.

He put his laser dot on her chest.

She pulled out the second knife and kicked it.

"Two guns," he said, putting the hardware in a drawer. "And two knives. Bit over the top for a suburban cop."

"You never know when you'll run into a serial killer," Emily said.

Shavon raised an eyebrow, then pointed at himself, as if to say, *Moi?*

She nodded.

"Oh, that. Yes. I'm Hacksaw. Now take off your clothes."

Marty powered into the Gardner Road off-ramp, tires squealing.

"Why do you want me to undress?" Emily asked, surprised she was functioning so well with the dragon gobbling her insides. But she was, and used her peripheral vision to scout weapons. The lodge was lousy with them—sheet metal, spark plugs, hammers, screws, antlers, knives, guns. A million-and-one things she could use.

But none was faster than an Uzi.

"'Cause trophies don't wear clothes," he said. "Drop 'em, Detective. Or I'll drop you."

She flushed as she unbuttoned her top, then her jeans.

"Damn. I knew you'd be hot undressed," Shavon said, running his unblinking eyes over her tawny skin. "Good thing for you I'm a psycho."

"Meaning?" Emily said as the jeans puddled around her feet.

"I don't care enough to rape you." His giggle was high-pitched for such a big man. "Are you surprised I know I'm a psychopath?"

"A little," she admitted.

"Been one as long as I remember," he said. "Liked it that long, too. Now kick away those clothes, don't want you using them as a weapon." He smiled. "I saw you looking around. . . ."

* * *

"The phone moved," the Audio cop said. "I can barely hear them."

"Keep your ears peeled. If we hear them breathing," Annie said, "that's enough."

"Happy?" Emily said, goose bumps rising from the chill of the room.

"Delighted," Shavon said. "Now take off the rest."

She hesitated.

He moved the laser dot to her forehead.

She closed her eyes. Unsnapped her bra and slid down her thong. Knelt to untie her running shoes.

"Leave those," he said. "You'll need them."

"A thoughtful psycho," she challenged. "Whoda thunk?"

He laughed, genuinely amused. "Nothing's more fun than an animal with a sharp horn. Now come here."

She hesitated.

Bullets whanged off the polished concrete floor, sand-blasting her legs with chips. "Comply or die," he said. "Last warning."

"Gunfire," Alpha leader radioed as he cleared the tree line and ran onto the deep lawn surrounding the lodge. "Recommend we go in, boss."

"Negative," Annie said. "Do not attack. They're still talking."

"Roger, staying on red light . . ."

Emily walked slowly toward the grinning Shavon, judging angles and distances. She looked at the mounted grizzly. It stared back with glassy, lifeless eyes. She knew he was lying about not raping her—the look on his face when her

nipples stiffened from the cold spoke volumes. So the hell
with the machine gun. The moment he touched her she'd go
for his eyes. . . .

He surprised her by moving toward the back door overlooking the woods.

"He's moving faster than we can get into position," Annie
said. "Make the call."

"Dialing," Marty said as the Ferrari bumped into the staging area.

"If it's for me," Emily said sarcastically, "take a message."

Shavon looked at the display. Black River Falls area code.

"Probably your boyfriend," he said, thrusting the Uzi at
her. "One word and I'll gut you."

She drew a zipper across her lips.

"Duuuude," he said lazily.

"Hey, Shavon," Marty said, bailing from the Ferrari with
his .30-30. The lodge glowed faintly through the trees.
"What's happenin'?"

"Same shit, different day," Shavon said. "Surprised to
hear from you. Thought you didn't phone while hunting."

"It's raining so hard we can't keep the cook fire going,"
Marty said. "So we came into town to grab some dinner."

"That's what the jerky's for."

"Hell, man, I finished that on the way here," Marty said.
"Your best ever, by the way."

"Thanks," the serial killer said, amused. "Thought you'd
like it."

"I did. Do. Anyway, here I am. Seafood place, right on the
Black River."

"Let me guess—you ordered walleye."

"Pan-fried with cornmeal coating," Marty said, smacking

his lips. "We just ordered, so I thought I'd call Emily, say hey. I tried the apartment and her cell, no answer."

"Maybe she's at Annie's."

"Tried there, too; no answer."

"Could she have gotten called into work? Some case broke or something?"

"If she did, she's busy, and I don't want to bother her," Marty said, keeping his voice perfectly casual because Shavon would smell a rat given the slightest off-note. "I was hoping she's with you, taking apart carburetors."

"I wish; that'd be fun," Shavon said. "But it's just me and the cars." He paused. "What's up with the Wisconsin area code? Your cell always displays the Naperville number."

The question caught him off-guard. "Ahhh, the battery died. Nobody in this little town sells the right replacement, so I had to buy a throwaway." He faked a sneeze. "Sorry. Probably catching a cold this damn rain. So whatcha doing tonight? Anything fun?"

"Boning up," Shavon said.

Emily rolled her eyes.

Shavon grinned, pleased at his little joke. "I'm racing this weekend."

"The classic in Knoxville?"

"Yup. So I'm prepping the T-bird. In fact, I should get back to that—lots of bolts to torque. How's opening day been for you guys?"

"Poor. Rain made the critters scarce. We went out twice today. Spotted a couple deer, but they weren't worth taking."

"So Bambi *is* gonna kick your butt again."

"Still got a few days," Marty said, forcing himself to chuckle. "Let's get a beer when I'm back, and I'll tell you about it."

"Cool, fool," Shavon said. "Trooper Little out."

* * *

"You could sell ice to an Eskimo," Annie said.

Marty snorted. "Think he bought it?"

"I would have," Annie said. "Nice tap dance on the Wisconsin area code."

"Did I stall him long enough?"

"Almost," Annie said. "'Nother five minutes we're set."

"Good. I'm heading your direction from the staging area. Don't shoot me. . . ."

"Enjoy the middle finger I sent you?" Shavon said. "I thought it was fun."

"You would," Emily said, trying not to think about the hacked-off digit he'd placed in this morning's home delivery. Get him on another topic. . . .

"So what's all this about 'You're the deer,'" she said, crossing her arms over her breasts.

Shavon smiled.

Told her.

Her legs went numb.

Alpha reached the front of the lodge. Bravo crept to one side, Charlie to the other. Everyone kept away from the back of the building. A line of windows looked onto the woods, and if Shavon spotted even one SWAT, he'd buzz-gun Emily into pink marmalade.

Emily was in no hurry to start this macabre run for her life. Shavon was every bit as good a hunter as Marty or Branch, and had the additional advantage of not caring she was a human being, not an elk.

"Tell me about the bones," she tried. "Weren't you afraid we'd track you through DNA?"

"No. I boiled them in bleach," Shavon said. "That destroys DNA. Even if it didn't, I'd have been fine—I sawed them out of whores. Addicts. Bums. People who don't matter, who've been discarded by society. Nobody was going to call nine-one-one when they disappeared."

She ground her teeth, knowing he was right.

"You kidnapped your victims from around the Midwest," she said, recalling the various postmarks on the boxes. "Brought them here and . . . then what?"

Shavon scratched his gleaming head. "I made them strip, told them to start running," he said. "I promised if they reached the other end of the woods, I'd take them home. If they didn't, bang, they were jerky. It gave them an incentive to do well." His grin showed perfect teeth. "No one got more than two hundred yards before I shot them."

She shivered. "And then what did you . . ."

"Stuffed them in my trunk, brought them to DeKalb, took their picture for my rec room, and turned them into jerky."

"Including the bag you gave Marty?" she said, the connection dawning.

"That was Levon," Shavon said fondly. "Thirteen years old, blew the streets of Detroit for nickels and dimes. I showed him a twenty, got him into my car. Tasered him."

"Like you did Christina Tsigaras," Emily said, recalling the twin burns on the butchered woman's back.

"Same Taser," Shavon confirmed. "Anyway, Levon ran one hundred seven yards before I put a bullet in his brain. His young flesh made an especially sweet jerky, as you yourself can attest. Marty said you ate a piece. . . ."

She managed to keep the vomit down.

"Why did you become a cop?" she said. "And make friends with me and Marty? That's exceptionally risky, even for a psycho."

"Dear girl, that's why I did it," Shavon said, nodding.

"The risk. I knew if I made even the tiniest little slip, you'd catch on and hunt me like I hunted my victims." He smiled. "You have no idea how satisfying it is, killing people under the nose of law enforcement."

Marty circled through the woods behind the lodge, keeping a line of trees between him and the row of windows.

The Audio cop groaned, flipped switches.

"What?" Annie said.

"Phone signal's gone. I can't hear anything they're saying."

"Get it back, goddammit," Annie said.

The cop flipped more switches, cursing.

Thunder rattled the roof. Rain poured down a faucet. Lightning strobed the pitch-black forest. Shavon opened the door. "Two-minute head start," he said. "And the same promise—reach the other side of the woods, you go home."

Emily crossed her arms defiantly.

"Sorry, Shavon, I'm not playing," she said. "I'm staying right here."

He put his finger on the trigger.

"Go ahead," she said. "I'd rather die than be your deer."

Shavon's look was respectful. "Actually, I expected this. You're tougher than those pretty green eyes admit. You clearly need more motivation than my other prey."

"What's higher than my life?" she said.

"Marty's," he said.

She felt a chill, and not from the storm.

"The call proves he doesn't have a clue about me," the

trooper said. "So he'll walk in here all dumb and happy from his fucking walleye, ready to drink beer with ol' buddy Shavon."

"Unless he made it all up and he's outside with a bunch of SWATs, ready to put a thousand bullets in your face," Emily countered, hoping to rattle him.

"He's not that smart," Shavon said, waving in dismissal. "No, our boy will stroll in without a clue, and I'll cut him down." He looked at the trophy heads, stroking his chin. "I'll jerk that big ol' body, but save his head for the wall. Put him next to the grizzly bear, I think. They'd get along well, Marty and the bear. They both shit in the woods. . . ."

She shuddered, and Shavon knew he had her.

"Run like a good little deer, and I promise I'll leave Marty alone," he said. "I'll even nurse him through his inevitable breakdown when they find your decomposed body in a forest preserve. I was there for him when his wife died, and I can do it again, no problem."

"You think I believe your promises?" she scoffed. "Do I look that brain-dead?"

Shavon's expression darkened. "Believe, don't believe, I don't give a shit," he snapped, pointing the Uzi. "Start running or I'll kill you, then wait for Marty. I'll cut off his arm and jerk it, then his leg and jerk that. I'll keep him alive for weeks, and the only thing he'll get to eat is . . . you." His smile was cruel. "So, Detective, what's it going to be? You or him?"

She stared.

Then dashed out the door, breasts flying.

"Tallyho!" she heard the psycho cry.

The foxhunt was on.

"Emily's running out the back, repeat, Emily's escaping," Charlie leader reported.

"Green light, green light," Annie shouted. "Take the psycho."

The demo man blew the front entrance. Alpha, Bravo, and Charlie swirled in.

Shavon heard the shouts, knew instantly who was there. He'd been fooled, and badly. But he knew these woods like the back of his hand. He'd track and shoot Emily, then run to the four-by-four he'd stashed on the other side of the ridge for just this eventuality.

They'd never catch him.

Marty glimpsed Shavon's disappearing back, swung up the deer gun, pulled the trigger.

The shot plowed into a tree.

He worked the lever and lined up again, but Shavon was gone.

He checked the topographical map in his head, plunged in after him.

"Where are you, where are you?" Annie shouted into her cell, racing through the forest as green thunderheads unleashed full electrical fury.

"Heading for the ridgeback, top of the ridge," Marty shouted back, call breaking up from the lightning blasts. "Emily knows I hunt the high ground. She'll go there, look for me."

"Why would she?" Annie said, spotting Shavon. She skidded a little on the sopping ground, snapped up her rifle. Nope. An animal of some sort, quaking by a juniper bush. She resumed running. "How would even she know you're here?"

"She knows, she knows I'm here, she'll know. . . ."

* * *

Left-right-left-right-left-right . . .

Emily sprinted till her lungs spasmed, then eased off a
fraction.

Heard Shavon crashing through the woods, not far
enough behind.

Marty's here. She didn't know why she knew, but she did.
She'd heard the SWAT commands, knew he'd never let her
die like this, and so he was here, hunting. She wasn't armed,
so she'd have to let Superman's cape stretch over them both.
Okay, where would you be if you were Marty . . . ?

She spotted the ridge in the distance. Marty had told her
about the ridge, as part of his Shavon stories: it was high,
rugged, and steep, denuded of growth because it was made
of acidic strip mine tailings, a cancer scar bisecting the lush
forest. Yes, that's where Marty would go, the ridge. He always took the high ground. . . .

The machine gun sang behind her. Dismembered a tree
limb just to her right.

She darted sideways, swearing she could feel the laser dot
on her spine.

"Next one's you," Shavon howled.

Marty's lungs burned like match heads as he legged up
the bank of tailings. Annie was a hundred yards back, shouting encouragement through the cell. He reached the military
crest—that spot just below the actual ridge where a tank or
soldier would hide from enemies on the other side—then
said hell with hiding and crested the real top. He heard shots,
dove to the crumbly surface. No bullets pinged. He lifted his
head and got his bearings, water pouring off his head, down
his back. Oaks, maples, evergreens, left, right, front. A couple of trails and a tiny lake, a watering hole really, kidney-
shaped with cattail banks. Several deer and dozens of game

birds lay mute at the edge line of the cattails, in various stages of decomposition. This was a private hunting reserve, meaning Shavon could use it whenever he wanted, in season or out, and so he did, leaving the smaller trophies to rot 'cause they'd attract more animals and he could shoot them too.

He searched frantically for Emily. If he'd judged her direction correctly and accounted for stumbles and falls, she should emerge from the woods in ten seconds . . . nine . . . eight . . .

No way she'd make the top of the ridge without Shavon dumping a load in her back. She had to trust that Marty would know where she'd be, and that'd he'd be ready.

Lightning freeze-framed the woods into a series of still photos. Thunder shook the trees, churned the pond. The rain roared like end times. Her heart beat out of her chest. The panic dragon out-screamed all of it. She ran for the closest photo, hoping to lose her pursuer.

The Uzi stuttered.

She heard it and dove into a pond. The bullets missed, but she felt their fire they were so close. She rolled through the wormy mud, dead leaves and needles sticking to her naked flesh, then scrambled to her feet and resumed her pursuit of the ridge and Marty.

The Uzi stuttered again. . . .

Marty caught the flashes in the tree line, knew they weren't lightning.

Shavon's burp gun . . .

Saw Emily burst into the clearing at the foot of the ridge, naked but for gym shoes. Fast as she was running, Shavon had to be only moments behind.

He jammed the Winchester into his shoulder. Judged the distance at two hundred fifty yards. Long, but doable. Pulled back the hammer till it clicked, knowing the trigger needed only four pounds of pressure to launch the killing payload. Blew rain off his moustache, wiped it from his trigger finger. Shavon flashed into the clearing, shaved head gleam-gleam-gleaming from multiple lightning strikes. Marty fired just as a Z-for-Zorro exploded blue, startling him. The shot roared off target.

Emily jerked, then fell.

"No!" Marty screamed. "No. No. No . . ."

Shavon heard the rifle blast, scrambled back into the woods.

The bullet struck the heel of Emily's right shoe, shredding rubber, nylon, and heel meat. She yelped, more from surprise than the wound, which her lizard brain said was minor, and lost her footing, tumbling full-face into something soft. The something-soft stunk like death and tasted gelatinous, like pork a month from the fridge.

The decomposed deer didn't care.

She didn't either, not anymore. It was a place to hide. Breathing through her mouth, she wormed under the fly-blown creature. It clung to her like a soggy bed sheet, and its weeping flesh washed her in stink-juice. But it concealed her pretty well.

Now what?

No more gunfire. Maybe the shooter was hit by the lightning.

Shavon crept cautiously to the tree line, painting everything with the Uzi, knowing Emily was close by, 'cause he'd seen her tumble too.

* * *

The deer's jaw plopped to the ground as the hammer-rain battered wedges into the flesh. The blowflies buzzed away in a cloud, then noticed Emily, came over to play.

"Get away from me, you freaks," she groaned, shooing them from her mouth and eyes.

Then she put them out of her mind. Bigger fish to fry. Namely, what was she going to do? Wait Shavon out and hope he overlooked her? Or take the fight to him?

Door number two, she decided.

But attack with what, exactly? Her winning smile? Shavon had confiscated her weapons.

Another plop. The deer's moldy snout. She'd be out of cover soon.

Weapon. I need a weapon. . . .

"Sit-rep," Annie demanded as she dove onto the ridge.

"I shot her," Marty grunted.

"Do you know for sure?" Annie challenged.

"I fired. She jerked, then went down."

"Can you see her?" Annie said.

"Not since she fell."

"Then we'll think positive. Where's Shavon?" she said, tenting her hands over her eyes so she could see better in the fire hose rain.

"Ran back in the woods when he heard my shot," Marty said.

"There's two of us now. Let's go dig him out," Annie said.

Marty nodded grimly.

They skidded down the front slope, rifles up and hunting.

Shavon saw two forms sliding down the ridge. Annie and Marty. Son of a bitch, they were better than he'd ever given them credit for. But it didn't matter, they were still hundreds of yards away. Plenty of time to do Emily and hightail it for the truck.

He ran out of the tree line, gun up and hunting.

The rack. The rack. The rack . . .

Emily snaked out her hand and patted around the buck's sagging skull. Felt the base of an antler. Pulled. It didn't move. She wiggled to a position with more leverage, tried again.

.It came out of the meat with a sucking *Ffffft*.

She ran her hands over it, unable to see much in the dim, greenish light. The antler was short because the buck had been young. But its main tip was sharp, and its shaft was studded with still-forming tips, each shaped like a fishhook. She patted around for the other antler, but couldn't find it. Forget it. No more time to waste.

She rolled away from the decaying beast and into the tree line, her antler up and hunting.

Shavon saw movement near the tree line. Pulled the trigger.

The giant raccoon pitched over, his burglar's mask sheeting with blood.

Marty shoved Annie to the ground when he heard the shots, spread himself over her.

No bullet strikes.

"Not us," Annie said, rolling out from under. "He wants Emily."

*   *   *

Shavon's seen me, shooting at me, he's shooting, out of time, get him, get him now . . .

Emily charged out of the trees, brandishing the paper-white antler. Shavon heard the noise, started to turn. She wasn't yet close enough to stab him, she saw, so whipped the antler overhand, as if a throwing star. It plunged into his belly. He staggered, groaning. The Uzi slid from his fingers. She slammed herself into him, screaming incoherently.

"That's Em. She's still alive," Marty said, scrambling to his feet.

"I see them, that way. Go that way," Annie said, pointing.

"Take too long, we'll shoot him from here," Marty said, snapping up the Winchester.

Emily sunk her teeth into Shavon's neck as lightning hit the tree right over them. "Eat this, you son of a bitch," she screamed as bark rained, thrusting the antler, thrusting, thrusting.

He punched her in the side of the head. She stumbled away, gasping. He scrambled for the Uzi, found it, swung it on her. She batted away the barrel as he pulled the trigger, sending the burst in a harmless direction, and smashed her forearm into his Adam's apple. He made gagging sounds but recovered, clawing for her eyes and missing, tearing her cheeks instead.

Spitting blood, she moved in close and rammed her knee into his crotch. He turned just enough that she struck his inner thigh instead. He staggered, and she cardio-kickboxed his thigh and calf and hip. He howled and bent double, clutching his knees in agony. She cocked her leg for the kill kick to his temple.

But he was faking to draw her in, and sank his fist into her belly.

"Don't fire, don't fire. . . . Too close, they're . . . too close together," Marty warned as Shavon and Emily dipped and swayed as if ballroom dancing.

"Can't see them, no shot; I don't have the shot," Annie said, searching frantically through the sniper scope. "You got it, you got it?"

"Got it, got it, still too close together," he said. "One second's all I need, just a one-second opening. C'mon, Em, get away, push free. . . ."

Emily bleated as her stomach convulsed. Shavon cackled and pulled back his knee, aiming for her face, letting loose, connecting. Her head whammed back, and she felt front teeth shatter. She dove back into the killer, ripping open his antler wounds with her fists and fingers. He fought back, frenzied, blood spraying everywhere. She kept her hand on the antler as they wheeled and swung, widening the wound, increasing the damage. He wedged his hands between them and shoved. She stumbled back, the antler coming with, tearing from his body with a blood-covered *sluuuuck*. He roared in agony, but instead of retreating he lunged, clamping her in a stranglehold.

Lightning struck one tree then the next. The explosions rained squirrels, branches, bark.

Shavon squeezed till Emily saw stars. Her hand sagged. Shavon wrenched the antler free. She watched the bloody tip reverse itself and plunge toward her eyes. Desperate, she thrust her head backwards. . . .

Marty's and Annie's rifles barked as if one. . . .

Emily felt a hammer blow on the crown of her head. A moment later she heard herself scream. The pain was literally blinding; she couldn't see anything but a fast-collapsing tunnel. Snot ran from her nose, blood from her ears. She'd been shot, by Marty or Annie, she didn't know which; it didn't matter. Her brain was shutting down from the titanic impact, and the tunnel was a pinpoint, and the dragon clapped and cackled and laughed, and she screamed for it to go away because she was dead and dragons couldn't hurt her anymore, and surprisingly it obeyed, and she prayed for quick merciful unconsciousness because she couldn't live knowing the people she loved had accidentally killed her. . . .

Weeping Jesus weeping wept . . .

She faded to black.

85

"Here's another good reason to live in Naperville," Marty said.

"What?" Emily said.

"No earthquakes," Marty said, snapping the *USA Today* with a fingernail. "There was a sizeable one yesterday in Los Angeles."

"Mmm," Emily said, wiggling her new front incisors. Implants were amazing—they did feel like real teeth. "Anybody killed?"

"Only one," Marty said. "Guy named Denton Schoolsby. Apparently, a sinkhole opened in a sidewalk and ate him like an Oreo."

"Poor sap," Emily said.

"Yeah."

They considered the growing pink of dawn.

"Vaughn was right," Marty said, refilling his cup from the coffee they'd brought onto the lakeside deck. "This cabin has the sweetest little view." Emily noticed his flicker of sadness. "I wish I could have met Cabot," she said, touching his arm.

Marty nodded. "You would have liked him. He was pretty cool for a chopper pilot."

"Yeah, he was," Vaughn Buehler said, stepping onto the deck.

"Give me a heart attack," Marty complained, shaking his head. "Sneaking up like that."

"Rustic traditions," Buehler said. "When did you shave your moustache?"

Marty fingered his denuded lip. "Couple months ago," he said, glancing at Emily. "Figured it was time she saw all of me."

"Poor woman, making her suffer like that," Buehler said, turning to her.

"I bear it well," Emily said, rising from her Adirondack chair.

"It's great to finally meet you," Buehler said, shaking her hand in a double clasp. "I've got your photo on my wall, you know. Between the mayor and my beer distributor."

"Didn't Marty tell you I hate that picture?" she said, recalling how inane she looked baring her teeth like some stupid wolf. 'Course, with the implants she'd have looked better. . . .

"He might have," Buehler said. "But I never pay attention when he talks."

"You should, Sheriff," Emily said, playfully hitting Buehler's arm. "Marty says so many good things about you."

"I do not," Marty said.

Emily leaned back, smacked his shoulder.

"Ow. Police brutality," Marty said, flopping his arm like it was broken.

"That's not possible," Buehler said. "Police sergeants are all about peace and love."

Emily snickered.

"Congratulations, by the way," Buehler said.

"I got your card," she said. "It was beautiful, what you wrote. Poetic, even."

"God forbid," Buehler said, waving his hands, slightly embarrassed. "I'm just glad you liked it. Sorry I couldn't make the ceremony. State legislature hauled me in to testify about the Karl Dettmer affair and what it means to Our Rural Way of Life."

"As if you had the slightest clue," Marty said.

"No kidding. I sure looked good on TV, though," Buehler said. "That's what counts." He looked at Emily. "Feel weird, them calling you Sarge?"

She nodded. "But not unpleasant."

"It's a nice reminder that you survived Shavon Little."

"A reminder I had luck," she said. "That limb should have killed me."

Buehler nodded soberly.

Lightning bolts had blown apart a line of trees, crashing a thirty-pound branch onto the top of Emily's head, splitting her skull. SWAT medics kept her alive long enough for surgeons to drill her skull and relieve the massive swelling. She spent two months in the hospital and another in rehab, but recovered unremarkably. Marty was at her side around the clock, one of the few good things to have come from this rotten affair. . . .

She sipped her coffee. "What wasn't luck was Marty putting that bullet between Shavon's eyes. If he'd gotten that Uzi up in time, this would have ended a lot differently. Wasn't luck saved me; it was Marty. . . ."

"Lucky shot," Marty coughed, uncomfortable with all the praise. "Gonna stay for breakfast, Vaughn?"

"You cooking?"

"No. Emily is."

"Then sure, I'll stay," the sheriff said, pulling over a chair.

Emily poured him a cup of coffee. They sat silently, admiring the lake.

"Opening day," Buehler said, shaking his head. "I still can't believe it happened."

"I still can't believe Ken's gone," Marty said. "At least he had a great sendoff. Five hundred squad cars and couple thousand cops, from across the country. The feds sent a bunch of guys, ATF to FBI. Annie even got the Army to send a tank."

Buehler's eyebrows shot up.

"It was sweet, that tank," Marty said, grinning. "Ten bagpipe bands. Twenty-one-gun salute, Navy color guard, the whole *sturm unt angst*." He realized he'd butchered the German, shrugged. "Well, you know what I mean. The kind of funeral every cop wants, even if we won't admit it." He drank more coffee, ran a tongue over his teeth to dislodge an errant ground. "You lost a lot of good people that day. Richie Cabot. His nurses."

"My deputy, Kharise Lenell," Buehler said. "She drove hard to save her sergeant, but in the end the culvert got her."

Emily winced. She was deathly afraid of burning to death. She'd rather be shot again. "The vending-machine repairman," she said. "That old couple who went to the bridge."

"Walter and Doris Meesely," Buehler said, steam curls dancing around his oversized nose. "Walt got shot by Karl Dettmer, and Doris slashed her wrist."

"She couldn't live without him," Emily said, squeezing Marty's hand. "Then there's the girl in the plastic wrap. Jacy, right?"

"Jacy Bedweller of Minneapolis," Buehler confirmed. "Typical teen drama—she had a fight with her parents and decided to run away, teach them a lesson. Way these things go, she would have been back the next day."

"But she ran into a buzz saw named Dettmer," Marty said.

"At least her family was able to bury her," Buehler said. "Thanks to Abbott protecting the girl, and you insisting we retrieve her 'fore the coyotes picked her apart." He freshened Emily's cup. She nodded thanks. "Then there're the losses in Naperville," he said.

"Thirteen people turned to jerky," Marty said. "Christina Tsigaras butchered. The carillon blown apart." He took a breath. "Which brings us to . . ."

"Sergeant Robert Hawkins," Emily said. "Dead and buried without an honor guard, even though his goal was the most honorable of all."

"Poor damn Hawk," Buehler said. "That wasn't a loss as much as a fuckin' tragedy. Glad your medical examiner ruled it homicide, not suicide."

They nodded. Suicide gave the insurance a way out. Homicide, they had to pay.

"How's Sammy doing?" Buehler said.

Emily smiled. "It's like she was never sick, Vaughn— Amanda Barrett's a genius. The cancer is gone."

Buehler's eyes twinkled. "And the hospital?"

"FBI confiscated all four million. Hospital had to eat it," Marty said.

"Score one for the good guys," Buehler chuckled, check-marking the air.

"Sammy and her mom are back in Naperville," Emily said. "Got a new place, and Sammy's back in school. Bonnie's making it work."

Marty splashed cream in Emily's cup. "I had serious doubts, given she skipped on her daughter when it counted most," he said. "But she really is trying. Maybe that's enough."

"Aunt Barbara will make sure it is," Emily said.

"Hell of a woman, your trauma doc," Buehler said, raising his cup.

"Christ, don't tell her that," Marty said. "She lords it over me enough as it is."

"Speaking of lords, I got a letter from Branch," Buehler said. "He's worked himself up to a cane. Course, you knew that."

Marty nodded. "He's healing way faster than the first two times, thanks to your surgeon. The work was so meticulous that Branch's orthopedic guy made him a job offer. Won't take it 'cause he likes this little town, but it says volumes about how good your man is."

Buehler mimed a zipper over his lips. "Keep that between us, too. He'd never let me hear the end of it. How's Branch like being chief?"

Follow the bouncing segue. "We don't know for sure because Branch never says if he likes or dislikes anything," Emily said. "Sure does suit him, though—he's a great chief." It had been long enough she could say it without choking up. "And Annie loves being deputy chief. She thinks five steps ahead of everybody else, has the street cred to win over anyone who thinks that being a girl makes you girly."

"Machine guns and toenail polish," Buehler reflected. "Works for me. Maybe I'll hire her, seeing as how you tried to poach our doc."

"You do," Marty warned, "I'll gut you like a fish."

Buehler laughed. "So, you're coming to the bridge dedication, right?" Kaye Barley, his lead dispatcher, arranged the ceremony at the Lee River Bridge. It was being renamed for Richie Cabot, Kharise Lenell, and flight nurses Susanne Bishop and Erica Lillifeld.

"Cumbersome new name, all those hyphens," Marty said. "But memorable."

"As will be the beer," Buehler said. "I made a special

batch for the party we're throwing after the ceremony. I call it Spencer's .38 Special."

Marty grinned. "I think he'll like that."

"Yeah, he will," an unfamiliar voice said from the back of the deck.

They turned.

Sheriff's Sergeant Spencer Abbott limped aboard, a four-footed cane in each hand.

"Jesus, Spence," Buehler said, jumping to his feet. "You should have told me you were coming. I would have picked you up."

"I'm not supposed to be here," Abbott said in a froggy voice. "Doc insisted I sleep in today, build up my strength for the ceremony. But I figured hell, I should meet the man who drug my ass through a forest. You know, before we get drunk and say mushy shit we don't mean."

Marty laughed, put out his hand. Abbott took it.

"I've got something of yours, I think," Marty said, pulling a scraped and battered object from his pocket. "Thought it was time you got it back."

A huge grin broke across Abbott's face.

"I thought it was gone forever," he said, accepting the Strider folding knife that had seen him through his storm. "Where did you find it?"

"At the river, where we found you," Marty said. "It was clipped in your pocket like it was supposed to be there. I took it for safekeeping, figured I'd return it when we met. . . ." They drifted to a corner chattering, Abbott shaking Marty's hand again and again.

"Speaking of Annie," Buehler said, "how are the girls?"

"Tristen still has nightmares of the zodiacs grabbing her," Emily said. "But they're fading. I'm helping her get through it."

Buehler raised an eyebrow.

"I started getting flashbacks to the first two serial killings after Shavon started sending those body parts," she explained, having decided to go public with it. "Accompanied by nightmares so intense I still remember every detail."

"And now?"

"It's funny," Emily said, getting up and stretching. "They're gone. Completely. They went away when I thought I'd died, and they've never returned."

"Maybe dying convinced you that life is more than bad memories," Buehler said, flicking the tips of his snowy moustache. "Had some myself, after 'Nam. Not mean like yours, but persistent. I'm glad they're not plaguing you anymore."

"Doesn't mean they can't come back," Emily said. "But I can handle him now."

"Him?" Buehler said.

She crinkled her eyes at the dragon in the wayback of her mind. It snorted, looking annoyed in its cage and leash. "Long story for another time," she said.

Buehler nodded. "What about Alexa? She's recovered fully?"

Marty turned his head. "Two weeks in the coma, another three to detox completely," he said. "She's fine now, proud she saved her big sister. It's all over her face, that pride. Best thing in the world for her confidence. But you'll see that for yourself."

"They're coming up?" Buehler said, surprised.

"Annie, Tristen, Alexa, and Joshua. They want to meet you, see what the fuss is about. There's plenty of room in the cabin, so they'll stay with us."

Buehler grinned. "Can't wait to meet them too. So what happened to Cash Maxximus, the source of all this mess?"

"Like every good musician, he's singing like a bird," Marty said. "Feds are dropping the charges and putting him in federal witness protection, but that's the price we pay for obliterating a multination drug cartel. Hawk's tape recordings of those calls and text messages nailed ol' Cash to the cross, and he was smart enough to see it."

"He's a businessman," Emily said. "Knows how to read a profit statement."

"The Juarez gang is history," Marty said. "American and Mexican police rolled up every damn one of 'em. In the end, Hawk came through like the cop he was."

"Here's to Hawk, then," Buehler said, raising his cup. "The mace that smashed a thousand drips. . . ."

Emily wandered off. Looked at the forest across the lake. Winter was disappearing fast, and the broadleaves were starting to bud. Birdsong floated across the water, lilting and bright. Squirrels scampered the deck cap, chattering in a language only they understood. The smell of pine sap, sharp as gin, rose in the shifting breeze, which ruffled whitecaps on the bejeweled lake. It reminded of her own forest preserve, the one Shavon Little despoiled but Nature had made right again. It felt like she was home—

She stared.

Watched a magnificent horse-sized animal move into the clearing.

It was a deer.

The deer. Marty's and Branch's and Abbott's. It had to be, with the shape of the body, the royal tilt of his head, the stone-melting beauty of his thunderous crown of antlers . . .

The scarred discoloration of multiple bullet holes.

She opened her mouth to call the men. Closed it without a word. Like a soap bubble, the moment would pop with the slightest disturbance.

She recorded it instead, in her mind, like a movie, so she could tell them later, every scene and take and detail, when stories of Cabot and Abbott flowed with his namesake beer. She knew exactly what she'd call her movie, too. *Third*

Time's the Charm. No other name made sense. Because after three serial killers, she'd finally taken her life back.

"Here's looking at you, kid," she said, tipping her cup.

The deer sniffed the giants across the water. Startled. Began to run.

Stopped. Sniffed again.

They were familiar, these giants. He flared his nostrils, trying to remember where he'd smelled them before, and why he wasn't fleeing at the memory of their thunder-sticks.

Remembering . . .

Remembering . . .

Yes. He knew.

And he was no longer afraid.

He moved completely into the open. Thrust his chest out and his head high, antlers gleaming amber in the bright sun. Shook them at the female giant with the colorful fur and shaggy brown hair. The giant raised her cup of steam into the air.

The deer dipped his antlers to the pine-needled floor.

Snapped them high.

Whinnied.

Then melted back into the forest.

Picking up the river.

Heading for home.

Where he belonged.

AUTHOR'S NOTE

My first shout-out goes to my editor extraordinaire, Michaela Hamilton of Kensington Publishing Corp. Her keen eye and unflagging enthusiasm kept my thoughts on track and my prose from blushing (too) purple. You're the best. Seriously.

My second goes to Bill Contardi, my longtime agent at Brandt & Hochman, for his wise counsel and knowledge of All Things Publishing. Thanks, Bill.

To Chief David Dial and the men and women of the Naperville Police Department. While my cops are total figments of my heavily caffeinated imagination, they're powered by your commitment to the ideals of "serve and protect." Thanks to all of you. I particularly salute Sergeant Betsy Brantner Smith. Like Ginger Rogers to Fred Astaire, Betsy does everything guy cops do, but backwards and in high heels. I couldn't have been blessed with a better dance partner in the world of female cops, and my work is smarter and richer because of your advice. Emily and Annie consider you a friend, and so do I.

To the people of Naperville, Illinois, the Chicago suburb that gets "blowed up real good" every time I put fingers to keyboard. Thanks for suffering for my art, and, uh, sorry about the carillon. I know you liked it. . . . Likewise the citizens of Black River Falls and Millston, Wisconsin, who let me move their waterways around to accommodate my fictional cops and robbers. Speaking of Wisconsin, the Mars Cheese Castle is real, and sells the cheeses, meat sticks, jerky (though not human!), and gifts I describe here. It sits along I-94, just like in my novel, but in Kenosha, not in the Wisconsin Dells where I placed it. Do stop at Mars if you find yourself near Kenosha. It's a slice of Wisconsin you shouldn't miss. Pun intended.

Samantha Hawkins's rhabdomyosarcomal is a real cancer, though I made up the nickname to reflect how a seven-year-old girl might think of it. A friend of mine died from the adult version of "rabbo-dabbo," so I'm glad to be able to "save" someone else from this dread, stubborn serial killer.

To my manuscript whisperers, who provide the valuable insights that make fiction readers say, "Wow, this happened for real!" They are Jason L. Fleener and Paul Sandgren of the Wisconsin Department of Natural Resources; Roy Huntington, veteran cop and publisher of *American Cop, Guns,* and *American Handgunner* magazines; muscle car enthusiasts David and Lee Taylor, who swore Emily would love driving a Dodge Charger, and they were right; Hunter Taylor, who taught me how a bad guy could text-message without leaving digital fingerprints; and Bill and Jan Page and Dennis and Susan Siy, who volunteered to see if my story made sense from a reader's point of view. Also to a pro's pro, P.J. Nunn of Breakthrough Promotions, my publicist, for introducing me to more readers and reviewers than I could manage in a lifetime with a Rolodex; and my website manager, Steve Bennett of AuthorBytes, for the glam new site he delivered when I asked for "something better than I have now." Check out **www.ShaneGericke.com** to see what I mean.

To my wife of thirty-one years, Jerrle. My appreciation of your support and encouragement when I decided to quit a perfectly good newspaper job to become a Famus Riter Guy cannot sufficiently be put into words. To my parents, Lee and

Almarimor Gericke, who've encouraged me to write since I was little. To big sis Marianne Taylor and her family, David, Lee, and Hunter; lil' sis Diana Varvel and her family, Gary Caswell and Christina Varvel; in-laws Marshall and Gwendolyn Miller; and our legion of friends and relatives. Love you all.

To my friends and colleagues at International Thriller Writers, an extraordinary convocation of storytellers with whom I'm proud to be associated. Your help and advice has been invaluable, and I thank you profusely. Particular thanks to Kathleen Antrim for making me chairman of ThrillerFest. It's quite the honor.

To my readers, whose unflagging encouragement—and occasional pointed reminders to quit using so many exclamation points!!!!!—are an ever-growing source of joy and satisfaction.

And finally, as a reward to those who persevered to the very last sentence of this novel, a contest just for you. Find the chapter that most closely resembles the darkly poetic writing of my dear friend Irish crime writer Ken Bruen and you could win something fun. Go to my website—**www.ShaneGericke.com**—and click the contest link for details. Good luck!